The Angel on the Roof

The Angel on the Roof

THE STORIES OF

Russell Banks

HarperCollins*Publishers*

Some of the previously uncollected stories in this volume were published in the following periodicals: Esquire ("Plains of Abraham," "Djinn," "Lobster Night"); The Village Voice Literary Supplement ("The Visit"); The Boston Globe Magazine ("Xmas"); Conjunctions ("The Moor"); GQ ("Cow-Cow"); Ploughshares ("Quality Time").

Grateful acknowledgment is made to the University of Illinois Press for permission to reprint "Indisposed," "The Caul," and "The Rise of the Middle Class." From The New World. Copyright © 1978 by Russell Banks. Used with permission of the University of Illinois Press.

The previously collected stories were originally published in the following volumes: Searching for Survivors (New York: Fiction Collective/Braziller, 1975); Trailerpark (New York: HarperCollins, 1981); Success Stories (New York: HarperCollins, 1986).

HarperCollins books may be purchased for educational, business, or sales promotional use. For information please write: Special Markets Department, HarperCollins Publishers Inc., 10 East 53rd Street, New York, NY 10022.

FIRST EDITION

Designed by Joe Rutt

Printed on acid- free paper

Library of Congress Cataloging-in-Publication Data
 Banks, Russell, 1940–
  The angel on the roof : the stories of Russell Banks.— 1st ed.
   p. cm.
  ISBN 0-06-017396-3
  I.Title.
 PS3552.A49 A85 2000
 813'.54—dc21   99-057738

00 01 02 03 04 ❖/RRD 10 9 8 7 6 5 4 3 2 1

To C.T., the beloved,
and in memory of Arturo Patten (d. 1999) and Alex McIntyre (d. 1999)

Contents

By Way of an Introduction

Every angel is terrifying.
—RILKE, *The Duino Elegies*

For years, my mother told me stories about her past, and I didn't believe them, I interpreted them. She told me that in 1933 she had the female lead in the Waltham High School senior play and Sonny Tufts had the male lead. She claimed that he asked her to the cast party, but by then she was in love with my father, a stagehand for the play, so she turned down the boy who became a famous movie actor and went to the cast party instead on the arm of the boy who became a New Hampshire plumber.

She also told me that she knew the principals in Grace Metalious's novel, *Peyton Place*. The same night the girl in the book murdered her father, she went afterwards to a Christmas party given by my mother and father at their house in Barnstead, New Hampshire. "The girl acted strange," my mother said. "Kind of like she was on drugs or something, you know? And the boy she was with, one of the Goldens, he got very drunk and depressed, and they left. The next day we heard about the police finding the girl's father in the manure pile."

"Manure pile?"

"She buried him there. And your father told me to keep quiet, not to tell a soul they were at our party on Christmas Eve. That's why our party isn't in the book. Or the movie they made of it, either," she added.

She also insists, in the face of my repeated denials, that she once saw me being interviewed on television by Dan Rather.

I remembered these three stories in a cluster one day when, pawing through a pile of old newspaper clippings, I came upon the obituary of Sonny Tufts. Since my adolescence I have read two and sometimes three newspapers a day, frequently clipping an article that for obscure and soon forgotten reasons attracts me. I usually toss the clippings into a desk drawer, and later, often years later, I'll find myself reading through the clippings, throwing most of them out. It fills me with a strange sadness, a kind of grief for my lost self, as if I were reading and throwing out old diaries.

I'd kept the obituary because I'd liked the rough justice implied by my mother's story of having forsaken the now largely forgotten 1940s film actor, Sonny Tufts, for my father. She grew up poor and beautiful in a New England mill town, Waltham, Massachusetts, the youngest of the five children of a clockmaker whose wife died ("choked to death on a pork chop bone"—another of her stories) when my mother was nineteen. She was invited the same year, 1933, to the Chicago World's Fair to compete in a beauty pageant, but didn't accept the invitation, although she claims my father went to the fair and played his clarinet in a National Guard marching band. Her father, she said, made her stay in Waltham that summer, selling dresses for Grover Cronin's department store on Moody Street. If her mother had not died that year, she would have been able to go to the fair. "And who knows," she joked, "you might've ended up the son of Miss Chicago World's Fair of 1933." That's the reason I liked my mother's stories, and why I wanted to believe them: she let me think they were about me.

The truth is, I don't know much about her life before 1940, the year

I was born and started gathering material for my own stories. Like most people, I have paid too little attention to the tales I've been told about the lives and events in my family that precede the remarkable event of my own birth. It's the same with my children. I watch their eyes glaze over, their attention drift on to secret plans for the evening and weekend, as I point out the second-floor tenement on Perley Street in Concord, New Hampshire, where I spent an especially painful chunk of my childhood. Soon it will be too late, I want to say. Soon all you'll have of me will be your diluted memories of my stories about my life before you were born.

The death of a parent is a terrible thing, but because our parents usually have not been a part of our daily lives for years, most of us do not really miss them when they die. When my father died, though I had been visiting him at his house on Sunday mornings once every six or eight weeks, I did not miss him. For a decade, he had not been a part of my day-to-day life. Yet his death, unexpectedly, was for me a terrible thing and goes on being one now, twenty years later. This is why, I think: my father, a depressed, cynical alcoholic from an early age, did not tell stories. Sadly, if he had told them—about his childhood in Nova Scotia, about stepping on Sonny Tufts in the courtship of my mother, about playing the clarinet at the Chicago World's Fair—I would not have listened. No doubt, in his cynicism and despair of ever being loved by me or anyone else, he knew that. The only story my father told me that I listened to closely, visualized, and have remembered, he told me a few months before he died. It was the story of how he came to name me Russell. Naturally, as a child I had asked, and he had simply shrugged and said he happened to like the name. My mother corroborated the shrug. But one Sunday morning, the winter before he died, three years before he planned to retire and move to a trailer in Florida, I was sitting across from my father in his kitchen, watching him drink tumblers of

Canadian Club and ginger ale, and he wagged a finger in my face and told me that I did not know who I was named after.

"I thought no one."

"No. When I was a kid," he said, "my parents tried to get rid of me in the summers. They used to send me to stay with my uncle Russell up on Cape Breton. He was a bachelor and kind of a hermit, and he stayed drunk most of the time. But he played the fiddle, the violin. And he loved me, Russell. Yes, indeed, he loved me. And he was quite a character. But after I was about twelve and old enough to spend my summers working, my parents kept me down in Halifax. And I never saw Uncle Russell again."

He paused and sipped at his drink. He was wearing his striped pajamas and maroon bathrobe and carpet slippers and was chain-smoking Parliaments. His wife (his fourth—my mother, his first, had divorced him when I was thirteen, because of his drinking and what went with it) had gone to the market as soon as I arrived, as if afraid to leave him without someone else in the house. "He died a few years later," my father said. "Fell into a snowbank. Passed out. Sonofabitch froze to death."

I listened to the story and have remembered it all these years after, because I thought it was about *me*, my name, Russell. My father told it, of course, because for a few moments that cold February morning he dared to hope that he could get his eldest son to love him for it. His story was a prayer, like all good stories, but it went unanswered. The one to whom he prayed—not me, but an angel on the roof—was not listening. At this moment, as I write this, I do love him for the story, but it's too late for the saying to make either of us happy.

After my father died, I asked his sister Edna about poor old Uncle Russell, the fiddler hermit from Cape Breton who froze to death in a snowbank. She said she never heard of the man. The unofficial family archivist and only a few years younger than my father, Aunt Edna surely would have known of him, would have remembered how my father spent his early summers, would have heard of the man he loved enough to name his firstborn son after.

The story simply was not true. My father had made it up.

Just as my mother's story about Sonny Tufts was not true. When I came upon the obituary for Sonny Tufts from *The Boston Globe*, dated June 8, 1970, and written by George Frazier, a journalist with a weakness for the lives and deaths of Social Registrants, I remembered her story freshly and knew why I'd clipped the article years earlier, read it quickly, and kept it for a later look. The title was "Death of a Bonesman," which meant, of course, that Tufts had gone to Yale and had been tapped for Skull and Bones. Unusual, I thought, for a man in that era to have graduated from Waltham High School and gone to Yale and become a Bonesman. Rather than toss it back in the drawer for another decade or into the wastebasket, I read it through this time to the end, as if searching for a reference to my mother's having brushed him off after the senior play. Instead, I learned that Bowen Charlton Tufts III, scion of an old Boston banking family, had prepped for Yale not at Waltham High, but at Phillips Exeter. His closest connection to the daughter of a Waltham clockmaker, and to me, was probably through his father's bank's ownership of the building where the clockmaker had his shop.

I had never believed the entire story anyhow, but now I had certain proof that she had made up the whole of it. Just as the fact that I have never been interviewed by Dan Rather is proof that my mother, in her apartment in San Diego, never saw me on television being interviewed by Dan Rather. As for Grace Metalious's characters from *Peyton Place* showing up at a Christmas party in my parents' house in Barnstead, I never quite believed that one, either. *Peyton Place* was indeed based upon a true story about a young woman's murder of her father in Gilmanton, New Hampshire, a village some twenty-five miles from

Barnstead, but in the middle 1940s people did not drive twenty-five miles over snow-covered back roads on a winter night to go to a party given by strangers.

I said that to my mother. She had just finished telling me that someday, thanks to my experiences as a child and adult living in New Hampshire, Massachusetts, Florida, the Caribbean, and upstate New York, and my travels to South America, Europe, and Africa, I should be able to write another *Peyton Place*. This conversation took place some years ago, and I was visiting her in San Diego, an extension of a business trip to Los Angeles. I was seated rather uncomfortably in her one-room apartment. She is a tiny chickadee of a woman with few possessions, most of which seem miniaturized to fit her small body and the close confines of her lodgings, so that whenever I visit her I feel huge and oafish and lower my voice and move with great care.

She was ironing her sheets, while I sat on the unmade sofa bed, unmade because I had just turned the mattress for her, a chore she saved for when I or my younger brother, the only large-sized people in her life then, visited her from the East. "But we *weren't* strangers to them," my mother chirped. "Your father knew the Golden boy somehow. Probably one of his drinking friends," she said. "Anyhow, that's why, after the story came out in the newspapers about the murder and the incest and all, your father wouldn't let me tell anyone."

"*Incest?* What incest?"

"You know, the father who got killed, he got killed and buried in the manure pile by his daughter because he'd been committing incest with her. Didn't you read the book, Russell?"

"No."

"Well, your father, he was afraid we'd get involved somehow, so I couldn't tell anyone about it, not until after the book got famous as a novel. You know, whenever I tell people here in California that back in New Hampshire in the nineteen-forties I knew the girl who killed her father in *Peyton Place*, they're amazed! Well, not exactly *knew* her, but you know . . ."

There's always someone famous in her stories, said I to myself—Dan Rather, Sonny Tufts, Grace Metalious. She wants her stories, although false and about her, to seem true and about her listeners, and she's figured out that having characters who are famous helps. When people think a story isn't true, when they believe it's only a fiction and not about them, they don't listen to it, they interpret it—as I was doing that morning in my mother's room, treating her story as a clue to her psychology, which would let me compare my own psychology and, noting the differences, sigh with relief. (My stories don't have famous people in them.) I had done the same thing with my father's drunken fiddler, Uncle Russell. Once I learned that he didn't exist and the story, therefore, was about my father and not me and, worse, was made up, I rejected it by using it as a clue to help me unravel the puzzle of my father's dreadful psychology, hoping, no doubt, to unravel the puzzle of my own and safely distance it from his.

One of the most difficult things to say to another person is, I *hope that you will love me for no good reason.* But it is what we all want and rarely dare to say to one another—to our children, to our parents and mates, to our friends, and to strangers. Especially to strangers, who have neither good nor bad reasons to love us. And it's why we tell each other stories that we pray will be transformed in the telling by that angel on the roof, made believable and about us all, no matter who we are to one another and who we are not. It's certainly why my mother tells her stories to anyone who'll listen, and why my father told me how I got my name. And though it's too late for me now to give him what, one snowy Sunday morning long ago, he risked asking me for, by remembering his story and recounting it here, I have understood a little more usefully the telling of my own stories. And by remembering, as if writing my memoirs, what the stories of others have reminded me of, what they have literally *brought to mind*, I have learned how my own function in the world—regardless of whether I'm telling them to my mother, my wife, my children, my friends, or, especially, to strangers. And, to complete the circle, I have learned a little more usefully how to read and listen to the stories of others.

As I was leaving my mother that morning to drive back to Los Angeles and then fly home to New Hampshire, where my brother and sister and all my mother's grandchildren were then living and where all but the last few years of my mother's past had been lived, she told me a new story. We stood in the shade of clicking palm trees in the parking lot outside her glass-and-metal building for a few minutes, and she said to me in a concerned way, "You know that restaurant, the Pancake House, where you took me for breakfast this morning?"

I said yes and checked the time and flipped my suitcase into the backseat of the rented car.

"Well, I always eat breakfast there on Wednesdays, it's on the way to where I baby-sit on Wednesdays, and this week something funny happened there. I sat alone way in the back, where they have that long, curving booth, and I didn't notice until I was halfway through my breakfast that, at the far end of the booth, a man was sitting there. He was maybe your age, a youngish man, but dirty and shabby. Especially dirty, and so I just looked away and went on eating my eggs and toast.

"But then I noticed that he was looking at me, as if he knew me and didn't quite dare talk to me. I smiled, because maybe I did know him, I know just about everybody in the neighborhood now. But he was a stranger. And dirty. And I could see that he had been drinking for days.

"So I smiled and said to him, 'You want help, mister, don't you?' He needed a shave, and his clothes were filthy and all ripped, and his hair was a mess. His eyes, though, something pathetic about his eyes made me want to talk to him. But honestly, Russell, I couldn't. I just couldn't. He was so . . . I guess dirty and all.

"Anyhow, when I spoke to him, just that little bit, he sort of came out of his daze and sat up straight for a second, like he was afraid I was going to complain to the manager and have him thrown out of the restaurant. 'What? What did you say to me?' he asked. His voice was weak, but he was trying to make it sound strong, so it came out kind of loud and broken. 'Nothing,' I said, 'nothing.' And I turned away from him and quickly finished my breakfast and left the restaurant.

"That same afternoon, when I was walking home from my baby-sitting job, I went to the restaurant to see if he was there. But he wasn't there. And the next morning, Thursday, I walked all the way over there to check again, even though I never eat breakfast at the Pancake House on Thursdays. But he was gone then, too. And yesterday, Friday, I went back a third time. But he was gone." She lapsed into a thoughtful silence and looked at her hands.

"Was he there this morning?" I asked, thinking that a mild coincidence was perhaps the point of her story.

"No," she said. "But I didn't expect him to be there this morning. I'd stopped looking for him by yesterday."

"Oh. Why did you tell me the story, then? What's it about?"

"About? I don't know. Nothing, I guess. I just felt sorry for the man. And because I was afraid, I shut up and left him alone. And then he was gone." She was still studying her tiny hands.

"What were you afraid of?"

"You know, sounding dumb and naive. And making him mad at me."

"That's only natural," I said and put my arms around her. "Everyone's afraid that way."

She turned her face into my shoulder. "I know, Russell, I know. But still . . ."

The Angel on the Roof

Djinn

Some years ago, before I married and took a position with a company whose entire operation was domestic—before I came home, as it were—I was employed by a Hopewell, New Jersey, company owned by a multinational consortium based in Amsterdam. We manufactured and sold women's and children's high-style rubberized sandals, and our assembly plant was located in Gbandeh, the second largest city in the Democratic Republic of Katonga, then a recently de-Socialized West African nation. With an area the size of Vermont and a population just under that of Spain, Katonga in those Cold War years was a capitalist pawn on the African chessboard and was thus the recipient of vast sums of U.S. foreign aid, which, as usual, financed a thuggish oligarchy of connected families who sent their children to private schools abroad and drove about the country in fleets of Mercedes-Benzes and Land Rovers. Thanks to American military engineers and civilian contractors, roads were paved, electric and gas utilities were reliable, and the Gbandeh airport could handle the air traffic of a city the size of Toronto or, if necessary, launch a fleet of B-52s against targets from Libya to the Seychelles. Also, there was the inevitable undisciplined but well-armed police force that kept order over an impoverished population of displaced rural peasants eager to assemble Western goods for a few dollars a week.

I don't apologize for these conditions, nor do I judge them. Simply, they were, for me, working conditions, just as they were for our Katongan assemblers and managers. History created the conditions, and I, like my African cohorts, saw myself as merely an ordinary man with a small job to do, a job that could have no effect on history one way or the other.

As the newly hired head of the company's research-and-development division, I was obliged early in my tenure to visit our assembly plant in Gbandeh and make the acquaintance of the company representatives and local managers, ostensibly to facilitate future communication between the New Jersey home office and its African outpost, but mainly to evaluate the Katongans' ability to adapt to the fast-changing demands of our sales force. The design and materials for our product were subject to the shifting whims of American and European women and children with disposable incomes and self-images easily manipulated by advertising. We were working, therefore, in a very competitive field. Our people, all our people, from manufacturing and assembly to advertising and sales, had to be extremely adaptable: we had to be both creative and reactive in equal measures. In Africa, I stood at the crossroads of the two.

From the day I arrived, I was fascinated by the nature of my assignment, which was essentially to be a translator, not of languages—the national language of Katonga was English, after all—but of economic customs and procedures. My goal was to replace inefficiency, corruption, and indolence with competence, honesty, and service. To that end, I had to find ways for the Africans to adapt to us and ways for us to adapt to them. Both parties had to change. For years my predecessor had ignored this difficult task, but, luckily, I found the work at once wonderfully engaging and even began to wish the job were a permanent one. I had no desire to return home to New Jersey anytime soon.

Then, early one evening, when I had been in Gbandeh for nearly three weeks, I took my now customary stroll around the sadly neglected Binga Park, named for the assassinated national hero, Henry Binga, and things unexpectedly changed. Bordered by stately royal palms, the rectangular park was faced by the five most important buildings in town: the modernist, black-glass, local branch of Citibank; the slat-windowed police bunker; the crumbling, neoclassical manse that served as a municipal office building; the Masonic temple, a forbidding, yellow brick ziggurat; and my neobaroque hotel, the Gbandeh Grande. At the end of the day, when the sun drooped behind the western hills, and the cooling shadows of the buildings and royal palms began to lengthen, it was pleasant to walk the square, nodding to the guards, doormen, peddlers, and lounging taxi drivers whose faces I had come to recognize, and end my stroll at a quiet café located in a narrow cul-de-sac off the square a short block from my hotel. There my habit was to sit alone at an outdoor table and drink two chilled bottles of Rhino, the national beer, and over dinner enjoy the sight of the locals trickling into the square from the nearby tenements, rooming houses, and crowded worker-hotels. At such times, even after only three weeks, I felt almost at home in Africa.

Since my arrival, most of my days had been spent out at the assembly plant, a dozen kilometers from downtown Gbandeh. Our plant was one of three low, cinder-block cubes in the optimistically named Gbandeh Industrial Park, which was less a park than a permanent construction site, a huge, windblown plain burned and bulldozed out of the equatorial rain forest a decade ago. There were small camps of squatters growing like dingy coral along the far edges of the park—clusters of corrugated tin huts, cast-off shipping containers, and abandoned cars, trucks, and buses. Some of our workers came from these camps; the rest lived in Gbandeh in conditions not much better. All had once been subsistence farmers who had abandoned their rural land holdings for wage-earning jobs in the city.

Inside the factory, which was not air-conditioned, everyone sweltered, management and assemblers alike, and red dust from the eroded plain blew without letup through the open windows, covering materials, tools, packaging, and people, whether on the assembly line or behind a desk in the manager's office, with a powdery skin of ferrous oxide. I had a driver and car at my disposal and consequently at every opportunity slipped back to Gbandeh to my air-conditioned hotel room, where I showered, changed into clean clothes, wrote my reports for the home office, and, before heading out for my afternoon stroll, briefly recovered in the familiar comfort of solitude from the dissonant, invasive company of the Katongans.

Not that I disliked the natives. In general, they were decorous and intelligent people, friendly to foreigners, especially Americans. I liked them. But they possessed a puzzling type of ethnic and national pride. It flew in the face of their social and political realities, which were hardly the realities that inspire and justify a true pride, the things, for instance, that make Americans proud: independence, the work ethic, cultural and economic achievement, and so on. Perhaps it was only false pride that made the Katongans seem querulous and loud and self-admiring—a defensiveness fueled by generations of colonial and post-colonial dependency, deracination, poverty. Nonetheless, I found it irritating. They blew their own horns, as it were, continuously, especially to strangers, and loudly sang the praises of the most trivial expression of their national character and culture—their affection for the roasted flesh of chimpanzees, for instance—as if it were something to be universally admired and imitated.

Katongans generally, and Gbandehans especially, socialized outdoors and at night, when it was finally cool enough to eat a large, lingering meal of rice and beans, hot peppers, and bits of what they called bush meat, and drink cheap liquor distilled from palm wine, talk politics and religion, and later dance and make love. Every evening, the

Gbandehans, rich and poor and young and old alike, shed their work clothes, washed their red-ocher skins, and dressed up—the men, sockless in American running shoes, wearing dark, sharply creased slacks and starched, white guayabera shirts; the women in high heels and provocative, colorful rayon dresses, their oiled black hair elaborately plaited and pinned into thick, uplifted wings and blades—and headed for the cafés, bars, and restaurants that crowded the alleys and side streets off Binga Park.

I was halfway through my first Rhino, waiting for the local people to start appearing, when I glanced up and noticed in the distance a strangely contorted figure pass along the square, his shape silhouetted sharply against the yellow glare of fading sunlight off the park. Dressed in a few scraps of dark cloth, barefoot, filthy, and hunched over like an ape, he lurched more than walked, and then suddenly he glanced in my direction, straightened, and, stiff-legged, lumbering like Dr. Frankenstein's monster, turned off the square and entered the cul-de-sac, where, at the far end, at what had become my usual table, I sat staring.

The street was narrow, a cobbled walkway barely wide enough for a single car to enter. The attached, three- and four-story, unpainted, wood-frame buildings that lined the street dated from early in the colonial era. On opposite sides of the street, tilted balustrades and balconies loosely attached to shuttered French windows nearly met each other overhead. The buildings once housed the waiting rooms and offices of the home country's clerks and administrators. Now these dusty, unlit, high-ceilinged rooms were used mainly for the permanent storage of empty file cabinets, rotting rolltop desks, glass-fronted bookcases, and countless cartons of moldering, mouse-eaten colonial records. The only commercial action on the street nowadays took place at ground level, where the numerous small repair shops, grocers, barbers, and other native businesses had drawn down their slatted metal shutters for the day. My café was the only business open for business, and at the moment I was its sole customer. The barman and a waitress were lounging inside, flirting with each other and smoking American cigarettes in the shadows.

When I first sat down, I had felt sociable, a citizen of the town, practically. But now, with this strange creature bearing down on me, I suddenly felt alone and cut off and, for the first time since entering the country, vulnerable. Even at a distance, I could see that he was just another madman, a dust-covered, ill-coordinated, mumbling man of indeterminate age. Such a figure was not an unusual sight in the cities and towns of Katonga, where there were no insane asylums, no mental health services of any kind, for that matter, and where a large segment of the adult population still suffered from the horrors of the 1960s revolution and the civil war a decade later. The thousands of young men and women who had been maddened by the savagery of the wars and had survived into middle and old age were generally homeless and either alcoholic or drug-addicted. But nonviolent. One did not have to fear them. They seemed to have a place, a niche, in the community, as in a family, and were gently tolerated and even cared for by the people.

This madman, although much taller and more muscular than others I had seen, was typical. His hair and beard were matted into thick, unkempt locks, and, except for a torn undershirt and a single filthy rag that partially covered his private parts, he was naked. What was unusual was the light that appeared in his face when he first saw me and that increased steadily in brightness as he neared my table. His heavy brow was lifted, and his large eyes glowed like coals. His nostrils flared with expectation, and his lips were drawn back from his teeth in a happy grimace. I had never anywhere encountered a look like that before. His expression was that of a man who, after years of seeking wisdom, had been surprised by it mere seconds ago; and the simple, overwhelming pleasure of at last having obtained wisdom was temporarily keeping him from applying it.

He seemed to be looking straight at me—understandably, I suppose, since I was the only person in his line of sight—but his gaze made me uncomfortable in the extreme, as if he thought somehow that I had made him mad and not the wars. As he neared my table and locked, not just his face on to mine, but his eyes on to my eyes as well, my discomfort grew worse. I tried to look away, but could not. I reached into my pocket for coins—an old reflex when approached by mad people and beggars, whether I mean to give money or not—but he shook his massive head, swirling his heavy locks like boas, and indicated with a scolding forefinger that he did not want money. Strangely familiar was his face and expression, as if we were old friends much altered, meeting unexpectedly after many years, or lost childhood cousins suddenly reunited as adults—yet he was, of course, an utter stranger to me. He couldn't have been more a stranger to me, this African man who had endured what I could not even begin to imagine: years of hallucinatory butchery, immeasurable loss, grief, and pain, and, for the rest of his life, poverty and woe, helplessness and ridicule, charity and invisibility. Yet I knew him somehow. And he knew me.

He finally lurched to a stop before my table and stood there, his ecstatic expression unchanged. He towered over me unsteadily, as if he were about to fall upon my neck and embrace me or else give me a terrible beating. And still I couldn't break his gaze. I was afraid to look away, to seek out the barman, for instance, and signal him somehow to come and help me, free me from this man's rapt attention, distract him, scold him, send him on his way. It was as if the madman had cast a spell upon me, or as if I were dreaming and struggling vainly to wake myself.

Finally, I managed to address him, my voice quavery and fearful. "What do you want?" I asked. "What do you want from me?"

At that, the man's face seemed to break its hold on mine, or my face broke its hold on his. His brow slipped lower, and the light behind his eyes slowly dimmed and went out. His mouth loosened. He licked his cracked lips with a large, pink tongue, and he put his fists to his ears like a baby about to cry. In a high, thin voice, an embarrassed tenor's voice, he said, "I know you, mistah! I know you longtime. You back this time to stay wit' us, mistah?" he asked, and cackled derisively.

Suddenly, he reverted to his earlier ape-walk and bolted away from my table. He grabbed a ceramic Cinzano ashtray from the adjacent table and placed it on his head like a sailor's cap, until, finally, the barman, whose name was Andrew, noticed his presence and came running from inside the café. Andrew was a slender, fawn-colored young man with a pencil mustache and gold-rimmed spectacles, and he managed the café as well as ran the bar. "Hey, Djinn!" he said, laughing. "Gimme that!" He held out his hand for the ashtray.

The madman removed the ashtray from his head and slowly passed it over to Andrew, who gave him a twenty-pence coin, as if in payment.

"G'wan, now," Andrew said. "Don't bother the gentleman." He placed a hand on Djinn's shoulder and turned him back the way he had come. Slowly, with unaccountable sadness, the madman, still hunched over and lurching side to side, walked away. I watched him, as unable to remove my gaze from his bent form as when earlier he had captured me with his enraptured face. Who was he, really? And how had he gained such power over me, even if only for those few seconds?

When at last he rounded the corner at the end of the street and disappeared, I flagged the barman and asked for my check.

"You don't want your second Rhino, sir?" he asked. "And then to eat dinner, same as every night? We got a special native meat 'n' vegetable pie tonight, sir, something English peoples like more'n anybody else." He feared he was losing a regular customer. He assured me that Djinn was just a harmless madman and rarely came here this time of day anyhow and would probably not come tomorrow or any other day for as long as I stayed in Gbandeh. He, Andrew, would guarantee it personally.

I said no, the madman hadn't bothered me. I had a difficult week, I explained, and was rather tired and would be eating in my hotel this evening. "Don't worry, friend," I said to him. "I'll be back again."

The truth is, for the remainder of my stay in Gbandeh, I did not return to that café. Nor to any other. Nor did I take my daily stroll around the square. Instead, I kept to myself and took my meals in my room or in the hotel dining room and drank my Rhinos at the hotel bar, where the only other patrons were a half dozen European tourists and four or five American and Asian businesspeople. I made friends with none of them. Also, my contacts with Africans from then on were pretty much limited to my driver and our employees out at the assembly plant, people whose private lives I pointedly did not try to imagine. Even the Gbandehans I passed in the street now seemed faceless and nearly invisible to me. I checked daily at the hotel desk for the call from the home office to return to New Jersey, until finally, at the end of my fourth week in Gbandeh, it arrived. The next morning, I fled the country.

In April of the following year, nearly fifteen months after my anxious departure from Katonga, I returned, sent over this time to open and bring into full production a second assembly plant at the Gbandeh Industrial Park. The Dutch consortium that owned our company had recently purchased from a bank in Frankfurt a failed Japanese furniture maker's defaulted mortgage on one of the two buildings out there by ours on the eroded red plain. Of all our American employees, I was thought to be the most capable of dealing efficiently with the Africans and thus had recently been promoted to manager of foreign operations. My assignment this time was to purchase the machinery and hire and train the workers so that by summer the second plant would be running smoothly alongside the first. This would double our sandal production and bring it into line with our projected sales figures for the upcoming fall and winter.

It was near the end of the rainy season, and while the air had been cleared of the ubiquitous red dust of my previous visit, now the ground, streets, alleys, and courtyards, even the floors of locked interiors, were carpeted with thick, red mud. Other people, entering the room after you had departed, picked up your mud on their shoes, clothing, and hands and carried it to new places. Cars, donkey carts, bicyclists, and pedestrians splashed it over your shoes and trousers, and you carried the mud from the streets onto tiles, rugs, and polished mahogany floors, accidentally rubbing it against drapes, chairs, and sofas. If you touched your face or hair or your clean white shirt, you left behind a red stain resembling an unhealed wound.

This weather and its unpleasant consequences were sufficiently different from those of my previous tour that Katonga seemed an altogether different country from the one I had left fifteen months earlier. In addition, I had pretty much forgotten by then my unsettling encounter with the madman, Djinn, and the subtly alienating shifts in attitude and consciousness that I underwent afterwards. I remembered only my early enthusiasm for the place and the people, my first impressions, as it were, and my still unsatisfied curiosity about their lives, along with the self-examination occasioned by my passing irritation with one or another of their, to me, incomprehensible native ways. I remembered, in other words, having been a good traveler, little else.

Then one evening a few weeks into my stay, at last the rain let up for a few hours, signaling the approach of the close of the rainy season, and for the first time I went out from my hotel without an umbrella and, as in the old days, circumambulated Binga Park. Inadvertently, at the end of my walk, I found myself at the same cul-de-sac close by the hotel and strolled into the café at the end of it, the place where I had met the madman. The barman, Andrew, was still there and remembered me at once and, surprisingly, was even able to hail me by name and, without my asking, brought me an opened bottle of Rhino beer, nicely chilled.

"You arrive in Katonga at the perfect time, sir!" he said in a loud voice. "The rain is over, and the heat not yet begun. That's the reason we call this time the season of in-between! The whole city, sir, the entire country, gets washed clean like a newborn baby! We get rid of the mud and get ready for the dust," he proudly declared, as if announcing an elaborate rite of spring practiced only here in Katonga. "Will you be ordering your dinner with us, sir? We got excellent grilled fish. Fresh-netted fish floated by the rains down to us from the mountains."

The café was filling with newcomers, local folks who, like me, were out for the evening to socialize for the first time in weeks. I decided to stay awhile, to order dinner and watch the natives take their pleasure. The idea of eating a scavenged fish rain-washed from a stream onto the muddy floodplain did not especially appeal to me, however, so I asked Andrew if he still offered the meat and vegetable pie that the English were said to be so fond of.

He was very happy to say that, yes, indeed, he had that pie ready to be placed into the oven this very minute, a pie for me and me alone, he said, made with all the native vegetables and various meats from the countryside. Which included chimpanzee, I assumed, but, on reflection, decided not to verify one way or the other and hoped instead for wild pig, or at least something with a texture and taste that would let me pretend I was eating wild pig.

I had finished my second Rhino and was about to order a third, when the waitress delivered my pie, steaming hot and smelling for all the world like a delicious roasted pork loin. I asked for a glass of South African red wine, usually quite reliable, and proceeded to eat. It was pig, I was sure of it. And yams, groundnuts, bitter greens of some sort, peppers, and onions. And the wine was more than adequate. Very good, I signaled to Andrew, and he smiled broadly.

The café was nearly filled by now with neighborhood men and women of various ages, most of them in groups of four or five, happily drinking and intensely exchanging political news and sexual gossip—

the two were often the same here. The women flirted with the men, who competed with one another for the attention of the women: all the old erotic and social moves of the species on display again, now that the rain had ceased. My attention wandered from one table to the next, finding some more amusing and interesting than others, conducting the sort of private, anthropological research that had always engaged me, regardless of where I found myself, even at home, in Hopewell, New Jersey.

Then, from the corner of my eye, I noticed off to my right a figure turn into the cul-de-sac from the square, a large, dark person hunched over in a familiar way and lurching erratically from side to side as he made his way down the narrow street toward the café. It was Djinn, and instantly the same fascination and fear I'd experienced before fell across my shoulders like a heavy woolen cloak. No one else in the café seemed to notice him; everyone continued to talk, drink, and eat normally. I, however, at once put my fork down and stared at the man. He looked about the same as he had the first time—large and muscular, nearly naked, with long, matted locks and beard. But now he was covered with caked red mud, instead of dust. It was a coating rather than a skin, as if he'd been basted with it over a fire, and it made his body seem somehow more fierce than it had before, more potentially violent. He wore on his face the same strange expression of near-ecstatic clarity of feeling as before, an almost transcendent look, one we associate with the god-intoxicated.

I looked around me. Did no one else see what I saw? It seemed somehow grandiose to ask, but was I the only one here open to the meaning of this man's expression? When he drew near, one or two people glanced up, then quickly resumed their previous activity, as if the madman were no more diverting than a stray dog wandering into the café. Everyone else simply treated him as if he weren't there at all or, if there, as if his presence weren't worthy of comment. This time, Djinn did not come to my table, nor did he lock eyes with me. Instead, he ignored me altogether, and, to my surprise, I found myself disappointed by it and, in a childlike way, saddened. What was *wrong* with me? I wondered, and simultaneously wondered how I might regain his attention. I could wave my hand, perhaps, or call out to him, notions I dropped at once, for it would have looked absurd to the others, a foreigner inviting contact with the madman, Djinn.

He passed within a few feet of my table—smelling of wet hay and overripe fruit, like a horse or other large domestic animal—but didn't acknowledge me. Or anyone else, for that matter. He seemed on a mission, focused and directed, as he moved clumsily between the tables to the far side of the café, where suddenly he reached up and with one hand grabbed onto the support of a second-story balcony and pulled himself up to the first railing and climbed over it. Now he had everyone's attention, no longer just mine. An odd silence came over the café, as everyone turned and stared at the madman, who was climbing up a rainspout from the second story to the third. He swung himself from the pipe out along a narrow ledge, then stood on the ledge and inched his way along it to a place from which he could reach a wrought-iron window balcony. Turning his broad back to the crowd below, in the process casually exposing his buttocks to us, he grabbed the balcony and pulled himself up to the shuttered window, turned, and faced us like a pope.

At the edge of my awareness, while the madman was climbing the side of the building, I had half-observed a bulky man with a handlebar mustache get up from his crowded table and step alone to the spot where Djinn had begun his climb. The man wore the dark blue guayabera shirt that I had learned to associate with members of the plainclothes police force, and when he slipped his right hand under his shirt, I knew that he was reaching for a gun. In a second, he had it out and aimed at Djinn, who was almost directly overhead, three stories up.

Now everyone's attention was on the policeman's nickel-plated gun, not the man at whom it was aimed.

"All right, Djinn," the policeman said in a harsh, but utterly relaxed voice. "Come down now. You know the rules."

I looked for Djinn's reaction, hoping against hope that he would immediately descend. I nearly called out to him myself. But I couldn't. His face was still lit by a knowledge or emotion or memory that was more powerful and clarifying than anything we here below had ever experienced. He looked like a man to whom everything had at last been elucidated. There was something new there, however, something that he seemed to have obtained only in the last few moments, or possibly obtained only from his perspective on high.

This must be the true face of *love*, I thought, and in that instant felt myself transformed, not into a beloved object—which, when viewed by a lover, would more normally be the case—but into a beloved *subject*. Which is dramatically, even metaphysically, different. Djinn's large brown eyes gazed down on all of us with a compassion and humor that could not help but make us feel truly beloved—most of us for the first time in our lives. I know that I was not alone in this. Many of the people around me had left their chairs just as I had and were staring up at Djinn, wide-eyed and slack-mouthed, struck dumb with awe and inexplicable gratitude.

"Come on down now, Djinn, or I'll have to shoot you! Last chance!"

Djinn climbed to the top rail of the balcony and balanced there momentarily, then nonchalantly reached above his head and grabbed onto the clay tiles of the roof with both hands. He swung free of the balcony, caught the top ledge of the French window with his toes, and hefted himself toward the roof, when the policeman fired, once, then a second time, the bullets jarring Djinn as they hit him in the middle of his back. For a second he clung there, unmoving, as if he might have actually absorbed the bullets into his body and rendered them harmless. But, no, he let go of the roof tiles, his toes slipped off the window ledge, and he tumbled backwards, off the building, down to the cobblestone street, where his body slammed against the stones with bone-breaking force. We heard the bones break and the flesh rip and tear like rotted cloth. All of us. Not just me. And yet not one of us, not even me, acted as though anything untoward had happened. The policeman walked slowly back to his table, and the others returned to their seats, and everyone seemed to pick up eating, drinking, and talking where he had left off.

Andrew, looking sour and impatient, hurried from his kitchen with two teenage helpers in tow, dishwashers or busboys, and the three of them swiftly lifted the body of the madman and dragged it up the street, disappearing with it around the corner at the square. I watched, aghast, bewildered, astonished. What had happened? When, a few moments later, the barman returned, he stopped next to my table and untied his bloodstained apron with evident irritation. He started to move on, and I grabbed his arm. "Where did you take him?" I asked.

"Who?"

"The madman! Djinn!"

"Oh. To the police station," he said, and headed toward the bar, where customers were awaiting his return. Over his shoulder, as an afterthought, he called to me, "The police will take care of the body, sir. Don't you worry yourself."

I sat a long time, stunned and very confused by what I had seen. Finally, I paid and left the café, hoping that I had at least partially imagined what I had seen tonight. Or maybe I had imagined *all* of it. That would be even better.

I wanted to be alone and to sleep. I very much wanted to sleep.

The following day, I arrived early at the Industrial Park, distracted and cross. From the start of the day to its end, I couldn't seem to cope with the usual difficulties of training the natives. I could not accept those difficulties as being natural and legitimate. This was not like me. I was trying to teach them to operate the German-made lathes that turned the heels of our sandals out of mahogany that we imported at great expense from the Cambodian highlands, milled in Goa, and trans-shipped here to Katonga. For hundreds of thousands of years, these people, our Katongan employees, had been equatorial rain-forest hunters and subsistence farmers, and I probably should not have expected them to adapt as quickly as nineteenth-century New England-ers to working with industrial machinery, day in and day out, year in and year out, on assembly lines manufacturing products that they themselves would never use or even see used by others. Ordinarily, I understood the obstacles they faced and, without prejudice, scaled my expectations accordingly. But today, for some reason, I was baffled by their ineptitude and inattention and consequently found myself screaming at them for the slightest offense or oversight. By midafter-noon, whenever I approached the line, the workers looked down or away, and when I retreated to the office, the clerks and managers started shuffling through their files as if searching for a lost letter. Finally, I gave it up and called for my driver and returned to town.

I asked to be let off at Binga Park, and walked straightaway to the café at the end of the cul-de-sac near my hotel. When I reached the cor-ner of the narrow street, and from the square peered down its length to the deserted café and bar at the end, where Andrew calmly washed yes-terday's mud and Djinn's blood off the cobblestones of the courtyard that surrounded his tables, something turned me away—a *felt*, rather than heard or seen, warning was issued to me. This place is terribly cold, I thought. Quickly, I walked on and went directly to my hotel room, where I poured myself a tumbler of whiskey and sat by the win-dow, looked out on the park, and waited for dark.

Several drinks later, night had arrived. From my window, I saw the lights of the town come up—strings and chains of lights brightening rooms and lobbies and public spaces and along streets and alleys, illuminating in strips and spots the lives of the people who lived with one another in the cramped tenements and worker-hotels, the boarding-houses and restaurants and outdoor cafés of Gbandeh. My gloom lifted somewhat then, and, for the first time since the previous night, solitude and difference eased their grip on my sense of myself. I left my hotel for the street, and made for the café.

At the crowded bar, I signaled to Andrew, who broke off his conversation with an attractive young woman, Japanese or Korean, in jeans and T-shirt and, without being asked, he brought me an opened Rhino and glass. "Welcome back, sir," he said.

"Andrew, I have to ask you something. About Djinn."

"No problem, sir. What about him?"

I said that I had been shocked by what had happened to him. And shocked even more that no one had objected or even seemed to care when he was shot and killed. "Killed for what? For climbing the wall of a building? For refusing to come down when the policeman ordered him to? Andrew, that hardly deserves shooting," I said.

"He broke the rules, sir. He never should have climbed the wall."

"But he's a madman! That could have been you!" I said. "Or me! Any one of us could be mad. Maybe we are mad, and he's the sane one. Who can say for sure?"

"Doesn't matter, sir. It's the rules that matter, and he broke them."

"But they were small rules that he broke. He was killed for it!"

Andrew shrugged, then abruptly asked me how I had enjoyed my meat and vegetable pie.

"What? Well, fine," I said. "I mean, it was actually delicious."

Did I wonder about the meat? he wanted to know. He no longer looked at me, but seemed to be trying to catch the eye of the Asian woman at the far side of the bar.

"What has this to do with Djinn, may I ask? And by the way, Andrew, I don't want this beer, I want a whiskey. Neat."

He smiled graciously and poured from the best bottle in the place, and when he set the glass before me, he said, "I hope you're not upset there was no bush meat for it, sir. No chimp."

"Upset?" I laughed. "Certainly not!"

"Green monkey can taste just as fine, you know, if you cook it right. But you probably noticed the difference, since you are a smart man mighty familiar with our nation. So my apologies, sir, for having to replace the bush meat with the green monkey."

I backed away, staring at him in disbelief. He kept a thin smile on his face and poured my untouched beer into the sink, wiped the counter, and returned to his pretty Asian customer.

I didn't feel it, but I must have been drunk, because I have difficulty otherwise explaining my actions then. At the time, though, everything I did made great good sense and had a strict purpose. It was only afterwards that it made no sense and seemed purposeless. By then, however, it was too late. By then, my actions had filled me with feelings that would not leave me, just as a dream will, and those feelings I would eventually be forced to act upon, for they had already begun to act deeply upon me.

I walked through the crowded café directly to the place where Djinn had started his fatal climb the night before. Reaching up, I grabbed onto the wooden support of the balcony and swung myself up onto the balcony itself, and from there, just as Djinn had, shinnied up a rainspout and inched my way along a secondary drain to a further balcony on the left and just above me. By now, the café and bar customers had spotted me and were watching from their tables, giving me the same rapt attention they had given Djinn the night before. I quickly scanned the crowd for the policeman, but didn't see him. With one hand, I grasped the bottom rail of the balcony overhead, and, with the other, clung to an adjacent ledge, and in that way managed to swing myself from the drainpipe up and onto the balcony. I was three stories high now, over forty feet from the cobblestoned street. I was sweating, but it was more from excitement than exertion, and breathing in rapid gulps, like a tiny, trapped animal, and my heart drummed loudly against my ribs. This was the strangest, most unpredictable thing I had ever done in my life, and while it thrilled me to be doing it, it also terrified me. I had no *reason* for doing it, only a compulsion.

I climbed atop the upper rail of the balcony, as Djinn had, and, balancing there, turned and looked down upon the people, many of whom had left their tables and had gathered excitedly below me, staring up with the same awestruck, slack-jawed gaze they had given the madman, as if they saw in me tonight what we had seen in him the night before, as if I were transforming them into beloved subjects.

Now I saw the policeman—not the same man as last night: this was a taller, darker man with a nearly bald head. He wore the same blue shirt and retrieved his pistol from under it. Slowly, almost casually, he aimed the gun at me and called out, "Sir, you must come down now! You cannot climb these walls!" I laughed in response, a laugh of sheer hilarity, of great good humor. I felt nothing but warmth and affection toward this man with his gun, and for that reason alone the absurdity of his command delighted me.

I was three stories from the ground now, with only the tile roof above and, beyond that, the African night sky. I turned away from the crowd and, exposing my back to them, reached up and grabbed hold of the lip of the roof, swung both feet onto a narrow wall molding, where I managed a toehold, and drew myself slowly into the air, moving my body inch by inch toward the roof. I was dangling from the edge of the roof, with my shoulders and head above it, but just barely, and most of my weight still suspended out there in the air. I heard the policeman call to me, "You must come down, or I'll have to shoot you!" Then he said, "Come down, Djinn, or I'll shoot." I know he said it; I know he called me that. It meant many things, but at that moment, it meant to me only that, if he could kill me, he would.

It was impossible now to turn back. If I groped blindly in the air behind me with my feet, trying to find the railing of the balcony below, in seconds I'd surely lose my grip on the roof tiles and fall, as good as shot. It was taking all my strength just to hold on to the tiles, just to stay where I was. Somehow, though, I found enough strength in my hands and arms to draw my body slowly, agonizingly, up and over the lip of the roof—first my chest, then belly, pelvis, and thighs, and finally one knee—when I heard the crack of a gunshot. The bullet ricocheted off the tile closest to my face, stinging my cheek with bits of clay, and I made one final lunge to safety, over the edge entirely and onto the sloped roof, out of the shooter's line of sight.

I scrambled to the high ridge of the roof and over, turned, and made my way along the far side of it, out of sight for the length of the roof to the gable at the end, where I finally stopped and sat, hunched like a large bird with my legs crossed beneath me and my arms wrapping my shoulders like feathered wings. In the distance, I could see from my perch the crowd at the café, still milling about, peering up at the place where I had disappeared from sight. In the other direction, I overlooked the park. Palm trees clattered dryly in the night breeze. A strange weightlessness and euphoria had come over me. I checked again at the café and saw the policeman put away his gun, and he and the others returned to their tables and to the bar and resumed their normal evening activities. Andrew, with feigned delight, was serving an Asian man who had joined the Asian woman at the bar. A great thing had been inflicted upon me, but it was clear, nothing had happened to anyone else.

Soon, the red dust would return: this was, indeed, the season of in-between. I leaned back and looked away from Gbandeh, away from

Katonga, away from the continent and the planet itself. The clouds had parted, and the dark blue sky billowed overhead like a bedouin's tent. The equator, cut from north to south by the prime meridian, crossed the sky from east to west, and beyond the lines of empire, the stars, like endless grains of desert sands, flowed in vast, uncharted waves across the universe. All night long, I perched on the roof of the old colonial warehouse, staring away from myself until dawn, and when at last I climbed down to the ground, the sky had turned milky white. The stars were gone from sight, as invisible as the equator and the time line now, and the streets and sidewalks of Gbandeh were deserted. I was alone.

Defenseman

For my father, the idea of loneliness was early on separated from the idea of solitude, a condition imposed on him by geography. Or it may be something he picked up from his father. Regardless, it's a distinction that served him well. It enabled him to be literally fearless in the face of constant loneliness, and later on, when the pressure of geography had been removed, it explained to him his continuing solitude.

He played hockey, of course. Like almost all Canadian boys, even solitaries. A tough defenseman with great maneuverability, but not too much speed, he had the will, size, and ability, but especially the will, to break up a three-on-one rush for the goal by rapping one kid with his stick (up under the jaw, usually), taking out the second with a hard check to the kidneys, and the third by hurling his entire body across the oncoming skater's path, slapping wildly with his stick at the skittering puck, his back, slammed against the third boy's rush, blocking any view of the puck, the goal, and the kid's own feet, bringing the kid finally crashing down to the ice as, at the same time, his own stick discovered the puck and punched it back to one of his grinning, slightly embarrassed, slightly envious teammates.

Hockey, especially as played by Canadian schoolboys, is a violent game. But the violence usually lies dormant until the game is played by older, heavier, more motivated, and darkly competitive adolescents. Until then, a boy's violence is ordinarily a clumsy, harmless imitation of what a man-sized player can do gracefully with harm. Hundred-pound kids skating like the wind, barking and yelling at each other in French or Nova Scotia English, growling through red, contorted faces, bumping theatrically against one another, they only rarely, and then almost always by accident, enact violence upon one another. For them, the game, insofar as it is violent, is pure theater, with themselves, their opponents, their own friends, and their opponents' friends as audience.

Whether for my father it was merely an extreme version of this theater, I couldn't say, but I do know that for others his violence was real enough (I've been told by those who knew him then) and that consequently, before he was twelve, he had earned a reputation as a hatchet man on the ponds and public rinks of Halifax, which is very unusual. Also, until one is old enough to play in the tough, even brutal, Junior League, such a reputation is useless, is possibly even a liability.

To understand him, I try to recall how it was for me at that age, because as a skater I had about the same ability and lack of it that he had—maneuverable, with quick hands and feet, large for my age, but not very fast and with a weak slap shot no amount of solitary, early morning practice could improve. I could never combine the hard charge for the net with the sudden shot from fifteen feet out that sent the puck like a rifle slug about eight inches off the ice all the way without once touching down past the goalie's dropping glove and lifting stick and into the net with a neat, quick, kissing thud.

Like my father, I was a defenseman, and to increase my value as a defenseman, I, too, relied on the will to extremity that I knew the other players neither possessed nor expected to encounter in anyone else. Though we expected each other to imitate the older players, it was merely to mimic their threats and gestures, the textures of their violence. Consequently, anyone willing at that age to go all the way, unhesitatingly checking, tripping, body-blocking, rapping hands, heads, and legs with his hockey stick, anyone willing actually to *be* violent, had the considerable advantage of surprise going for him.

Though I'm not sure why I should happen to seize onto how as a child my father, or for that matter I myself, played hockey, it is certain that, for a child raised in the northeastern United States and southern Canadian provinces, hockey and ice skating in general are of surprising emotional significance, combining as they do, so early and for so long, social and private experience. Also, they provide an arena in which other people and an intense physical environment are positioned precisely to confront one's young and relatively untested, unknown body. As evidence of the staying power the experience holds, this past winter I've walked down to the pond in the meadow in front of my house perhaps as many as eight or nine times, where, lacing on my skates, pushing off, gliding in slow, rhythmic ovals around the pond, alone and out of sight of the house, my mind backtracks in time, until, before I am aware of it, my physical responses (*to the glassy smoothness of the ice, a slight pinch of the toe in the left skate, ears, nose, and chin crystallizing in the breeze caused by my body's swift movement through still, cold air . . .*) and the loose flow of my fantasies (*of suddenly breaking free of a tie-up at the boards, he's got the puck, he's going all the way in, the goaltender's ready for him . . . and, whap! a slapper, and the goaltender goes down to his right for the puck, too late, and HE SCORES! glides humbly, suddenly relaxed, past the net, shakes loose clumps of ice shavings from his skate blades, moves like a gentle bear down the ice toward his own goal and his jubilant teammates . . .*), at times like that, when I'm skating alone, my physical responses and my fantasies are coming straight out of childhood.

I've noticed in men from the Midwest a certain glazed, timeless look drift over their faces when they're bouncing and heaving a basketball around and through a hoop tacked to the side of their own or a neighbor's garage. For Southerners, at least the ones I have known, it happens around hound dogs, shotguns, and rolling, tangled, half-cleared farmland in fall and early winter. I suspect at these times they're making the same restful, return trip that I make when skating on the pond down in front of my house. Besides being a connection to one's childhood, a brief slip backwards into the subjectivity of one's ordinarily objectified past, it's a connection with other men, as well. Including my father, I suppose.

It's never been clear to me whether for my father the realities of ice and dreamlike motion across its surface evoked images of family and origin, as they do for me. I don't think my grandfather even knew how to skate, and I always assumed that my father had to learn to skate on his own, with boys from the neighborhood. But because when I was a child we lived far from anything even vaguely resembling a neighborhood, I was allowed to learn to skate with my father on Saturday and Sunday afternoons the winter I turned six. It was an event, formally announced as such. One Friday night in November, my father simply said, "This winter I'm going to put that boy up on skates."

My mother chuckled that I wasn't old enough. They were in the kitchen, after supper. My mother was sitting at the table over the clutter of dishes, resting a few moments before moving to the sink to clean up her kitchen and utensils one more time. She was smoking a cigarette and drinking coffee. My father was restless that night, pacing, stopping occasionally to peer out the window into the frosty darkness. My brother and I were playing on the floor like small dogs, nipping and yipping, imagining tails. At the sound of my name, I stopped playing and sat attentively, a human again. My brother, two years younger, went on barking and growling.

The fire in the stove crackled softly, the kitchen was close and warm, dimly lit by kerosene lanterns that filled the room with a fluid, golden light darting and disintegrating into flat planes of light and shadow, as my father, huge in the low-ceilinged room, moved from window to door to woodbox to black cookstove and back to the window again, talking throughout in a low, rumbling voice of his work, how it had gone this week, the men he worked with and for: his inestimable value to the larger world. The air was filled with the odors of hardwood chunks slowly burning and food, Friday night supper, fish, though we were not Catholic.

"I bet it hits zero tonight," my father announced.

My mother observed that at least there'd been no snow yet. She stubbed out her cigarette in the wet saucer.

"I haven't had my skates on in years," he said. "They're still up in the attic, aren't they? I remember hanging them on a nail up there two summers ago, when we unpacked."

"No one's touched them, so they must be where you put them," she said.

He left the kitchen and in a few seconds could be heard clumping around overhead in the attic, looking for his skates.

In the morning, after breakfast, my father said to me, "C'mere, we're going to get you some ice skates and teach you how to use 'em." And with his, to me, enormous, blocky, leather-and-steel skates tied together by their thick laces and slung over his shoulder, he headed out the door to the barn to start the car.

Recalling her own freezing discomfort from some night years ago, the abject misery of the nonskater who must stand at the edge of the ice stamping heavy, numbed feet or else must skid in small, choppy circles on rubber soles, waiting like a cripple while the others glide gracefully past in long arcs that sweep them into the darkness at the far side of the pond, my mother tried to buffer me against the force of her remembered misery by wrapping me in heavy layers of wool and rubber clothing, until I stood in the kitchen stiff and immobile as a chair, red-faced and sweating. My father had backed the car out of the barn, idling, then racing the motor. He rapped impatiently on the horn. My mother swung the door open for me, and I entered the cold morning air, moving like a penguin.

The air was crystalline, almost absent. The fields lay like aged plates of bone—dry, scoured by the cold until barren of possibility, incapable even of decomposition. Clumps of trees, mostly pine and spruce in roadside woodlots, stood in the windless cold like bears crossly aching to sleep.

When we got to Maxfield's store in Pittsfield, my father peeled off several layers of the clothing my mother had laced onto me at the house, and I was able to move my arms somewhat and bend my legs at the knees. My new skates were beautiful. Just like my father's, but about one-quarter scale. They were stiff outside, as if carved from blocks of wood, yet when laced onto my feet they felt like a gentle pair of hands. Brown and black, hockey-style skates, the shoe was cut fairly low, except for the tendon guard at the back, and the blades, the lovely steel strands that were going to lift me off the ice and free me from the yank of gravity, were toughly snubbed at the toe and heel. And sharp.

"Hollow-ground," the salesman assured my father, who tied the two skates together by their thick, yellow laces and draped them over my shoulder. I felt the sudden, surprising, downward tug of their weight.

Returning to the car, we got in and drove the half mile or so to the east end of town, to White's Pond, a small, shallow, man-made pond used in summer months as the municipal swimming pool, in winter as a public skating rink. A log touching the shore, frozen where it had floated months ago, was the obvious place to sit and exchange shoes for skates. A dozen pairs of various-sized and -shaped shoes lay in the vicinity of the log, and out on the ice a couple of men and a crowd of boys were slapping a puck erratically back and forth in furious, structureless sport. It was early, and they had been on the ice only a short time and were merely testing themselves, each other, and their equipment before choosing sides for a game.

My father pulled my shoes off and replaced them with the new skates and laced them up for me, asking me, when he had finished, if from now on I thought I could do it for myself, telling me that I must remember to lace them each time all the way from the toe. "And *tight*, as tight as you can get them. That is lesson number one," he said seriously.

Then he put on his own skates and stepped gingerly from the bank to the ice. As if he had suddenly taken flight, he was gone.

I stood, and my weight wobbled on the short, thin lines that the blades had become, and then my ankles gave way, and I tipped and fell on the ground behind the log, wondering what had happened. I could not see my father anywhere.

Deciding that ice would make the difference and that, once on it, I, too, would fly off with incredible, weightless grace, I dragged my body like a bundle of sticks and cloth down to the log, over it, and out onto the surface of the pond. Once again, I stood. Then I waited for it to happen, for the beautiful speed to come.

But in seconds my body, seeking balance from some point in space high above the blades, overcompensated and tipped, pitching me to the ice, where I remained for some time, utterly bewildered, my ears reddening with shame. My vision was rapidly narrowing, closing in on me, and now I was afraid that I *would* see my father, would see him watching me with scorn in his eyes.

Again and again, I struggled with my body and lifted it to a position that roughly approximated a standing position, and before I had a chance to locate it relative to the bank and log behind me and the vast expanse of ice in front of me, it was lying facedown again, arms and legs splayed, as if thrown to the ice from a great height.

Eventually, knees and elbows aching, the base of my spine a star of pain, I was able to hold my body in a standing position for what seemed like hours. Slowly, carefully, I raised my eyes from my feet, trusting them finally not to betray me, and saw that I had traveled halfway across the pond. The shore looked like a horizon. Not twenty feet away, a crowd of large boys and larger men slashed viciously at the ice with hockey sticks. They surged back and forth, like a dogfight in water, skate blades like ravening teeth against the ice.

Then, suddenly, they were gone, racing away in raucous pursuit of the tiny, black, fleeing puck. Their legs and shoulders seemed to move only from side to side. It was as if the skaters were casually bouncing off the opposite banks of a narrow stream in the middle of a large, flat field—and yet they flowed smoothly away from me. Attempting to imitate that powerful side-to-side motion, I pushed off my right skate and toppled over like a stack of bricks.

This went on for a long time, until I discovered that I could move—slowly, clumsily, and with great pain—in a forward direction. The cold, from my having lain on the ice so often and for so long, had crept through my coat, sweater, and flannel shirt, and I was shivering. The small of my back and my neck had contracted into icy knots that were spreading quickly through the rest of my body. I ached everywhere, and my ankles felt like thick drums of gum rubber.

I headed painfully back toward the bank, sliding-single-step by sliding-single-step. I imagined that I was pushing off my skate blades from one side to the other and was cruising across the surface of the pond at an incredible speed, when suddenly my father swept out of nowhere, like a moving waterfall, sliced hugely across in front of me, careened powerfully over to my other side. Where he changed direction! Skated *backwards*! And I saw then that I was plodding, step by step, at about one-eighth my normal walking rate.

My father grinned and nodded and said, "Good, good. You're doing fine. *Real* fine."

The ride home, about seven miles, seemed to take mere seconds. My father and I talked almost not at all, which, normal for us, seemed espe-

cially so that day. My mind was filled with a new sense of my body, a
sense that, while it may well have been made of some kind of malleable
substance, it nonetheless possessed a shrewd, persistently willful, and
possibly cruel mind of its own.

I did not see the trees and fields as we passed, did not even notice
that we were home, until my father, having shut off the motor and
opened his door, said, "You coming in or going to sit there till dark?" I
jumped, but then saw that he was smiling.

As soon as we were inside the house, my mother rushed to me, and
I quickly showed her my skates and said that I had learned how to ice-
skate. My father did not contradict me. Taking off our coats, he and I
stood together near the stove for a few minutes, warming our hands
and feet, and when I asked him if we could go skating again soon, he
said, "Sure. Tomorrow, if you want."

I said that I wanted to, right after breakfast, and he grinned at me
with appreciation and then at my mother in triumph.

Trying to remember if I've ever seen any pictures, snapshots, of my
father and me that show us skating together, I realized that none of the
pictures that have come down to me from those years shows us, any of
us, in the winter. The wintertime snapshots inevitably are of the house
banked in with head-high snowdrifts, the dates and descriptive comments always written on the back by my mother.

Jan. 12th, 1943! Wow! The big one! Taken to impress our cousins living
in regions to the south of us, a way for us to brag of our hardiness.

Our house, March 21st, 1946! First day of spring! Ha-ha! Just the house,
or maybe nothing more than the fluff-crowned roof and tops of the
windows barely visible above the snow. There are never any people to
be seen. My mother and my brother and I must be inside the house,
looking out of one of those dark, small-pane windows at my father, who
stands out by the road, snow up to his waist. Holding the box camera

squarely in front of his belt buckle, he squints down into the viewfinder, finds the view sufficiently desolate, and snaps the picture.

Probably the cameras most people owned in those days were not very effective in the dim, gray light of winter. But even so, it is odd that fully one-half of our yearly existence then is represented by fewer than a dozen pictures of our house and automobile, when the other half of the year seems to have been photographed endlessly.

Another curious aspect is that, even though my memories of those years are almost completely of summertime, it was the winter that dominated our activities, filling our talk and views of the rest of the world, so that we could not even speak of a place without first mentioning that it enjoyed a kinder climate than ours. Of events that took place in summer, however, I recall only the general condition and have obtained my formal knowledge of the events themselves solely as data. It's as if they could as easily have occurred in someone else's life.

The context of an event, the textures, physically, emotionally, spiritually, these remain uniquely our own; the particulars of an event, what we use to name it for strangers, are no more ours alone than our dates of birth. Perhaps this is why so much of the act of remembering is an act of the body, and why, sitting in my living room late at night, I can recall none of the particular, isolate experiences that, inevitably, come to me in a solid, complete block when, at the end of a November day, I grab my ice skates off the nail in the barn, walk across the road, and cross through the gray butts of winter grass to the pond. The sky is like a peach-colored sheet drawn taut at the horizon, a high rim miles away that circles the center of the pond. The air is still, thin, and cold. In a week, there will be a thick pelt of snow over everything that today stands before me like gray, brown, and lavender bone, cleaned and scoured by cold alone, neither dead nor dormant, but fixed, held in time the way a snapshot freezes a gesture at its completion or its start.

And as long as the fading daylight holds, the pond, black and smooth as a gigantic lens, is the precise center of the sphere of space into which I have placed myself. I cannot see the house or the road from here, can see no way out.

I sit on the steep, rock-hard eastern bank and take off my boots and put on my skates, and when I stand up, I am on the ice, moving across the black surface of the pond like a man running slowly through a dream, on a level plane, but also inside a matrix, as if underwater, free of gravity's grating tug, and free as well to ply the weight of my body gracefully against it, like a dancer sliding against the felt measures of time.

The Caul

You are in Richmond, Virginia, and you can't remember your mother. She was an actress, she was beautiful, they say. No one remembers your father. Of him they say nothing, and so, you believe, it is "natural" that you do not remember him. But your mother carried you here to the city of Richmond—in her arms, in her arms. She languished through the sweltering months of summer. The play moved on to Charleston without her. Her pain increased daily. The coughing from the attic room, the groans, the sudden shrieks. The women muffled your ears against them. You were bad, a bad boy, bad little boy. She died. You can't remember her face, her touch, her smell, her voice, all of which were beautiful, they say. They tell you this even today, the few who knew her those last months. Women, young women then, old women now. You remind them of her. If only *they* could remind *you* of her. You are Edgar Poe the poet, author of "The Raven." In a few moments, you will recite that beloved, that "magnificent and profound" poem to the literary citizens of Richmond, Virginia. Afterwards, in the Reverend Doctor Woolsey's parlor, you will describe how you actually composed the poem, the rational procedures by which you constructed it, and they will be amazed. You, too, will be amazed at this new account of your ingenuity and self-sufficiency, your mastery of the intricacies and logic of language and emotion. And your mother would be amazed, had she lived to see it, hear it, watch you mystify them by means of demystification, enchant them by means of disenchantment, bewilder them with your clarity. They will feel privileged and released, for you will have demonstrated how any one of them could have written your beloved poem himself, had he merely been willing to apply himself to the task. But you, of course, have been the only one willing to apply himself to the task, and that is the reason the poem is yours, the reason you are its author, Edgar Poe the poet. Anyone could be Edgar Poe the poet, anyone, were he merely willing to apply himself to the task. You believe that, and when you politely excuse yourself and depart from the company of these literary ladies and gentlemen of Richmond, Virginia, they will believe it, too. It will give them a certain relief. How wonderful, they will each separately think, to know that one could be Edgar Poe the poet if one merely applied oneself to the task. And how wonderful, they will each separately think, to be free not to apply oneself to the task! They will each accept one more glass of sherry, and, in your absence, will admire your elegant yet forceful presence upon the stage, your charm and lucidity in private conversation, your erudition, your "profound and tender" eyes, your "musical" voice, all quite as if each person in the room were separately admiring his own presence upon the stage, his own charm, lucidity, erudition, eyes, voice. They will each separately admire your irresistibly beautiful mind. Your fame. Your position among men. Your role with women. Your exotic past. Your dead mother.

You have been seated on a straight-backed chair in the center of the stage. A few feet in front of you, the Reverend Doctor Woolsey reads at the lectern from his prepared introductory speech. You watch his broad back, his speckled hands, his rising fluff of white hair. The thick tube of fat at the base of his skull contracts and hardens, and the Reverend Doctor lifts his gaze to the heavens so as more adequately to praise the poet,

Edgar Poe, author of "The Raven." You. Who cannot remember your mother. In your dreams she appears with her back to you, her arms outstretched before her. She ignores your call of, *Mother! Mother! It is I, Edgar Poe the poet!* But she does not flee or otherwise remove herself from you. She stands there in a white dress, as if at a lectern, with her arms outstretched, her gaze lifted heavenward, as if more adequately to praise her son, or as if to pray for permission for him to join her. For, without permission, you cannot join her, you may not move your feet, you may not take a single step toward her. It is as if you are bad, a bad boy, bad little boy. That is how she appears in your dreams of her and how you also appear there. A moribund tableau vivant, a frieze cut in a wall of darkness. Not a conscious memory, though. When awake, you try to remember your mother, as you do now, and you remember nothing, and since no mind can picture nothing, you remember Mr. Allan and the tobacco warehouses, the canal alongside the James River, your cousin Virginia and her mother. You recall your room at the college in Charlottesville, the parade ground at West Point, and then your half-empty bottle of Madeira on the spindly table offstage right. You remember your white handkerchief, slightly spotted with the wine wiped from your chin, now tucked neatly into your breast pocket to hide the purple stains from view of the audience, who can see you clearly up here stage center. Someone in that audience is coughing, nervous, repeated coughs coming from her throat, habitual and not the consequence or sign of illness. It will have a slight, negative effect on your recitation, for, unless you can pick up the rhythm, the pattern of her coughing, and can arrange always to be speaking at the same time, she will succeed in coughing while you are silent between stanzas or when you pause momentarily for dramatic effect, and it may have the effect of silencing you completely. You listen closely for the pattern of her coughs, and, surreptitiously, you hope, slip your watch from your vest pocket and study its face, while the Reverend Doctor Woolsey continues his lengthy introduction of the poet Edgar Poe and the unseen woman coughs, then coughs again, and, after thirty-two seconds, yet again. You calculate that if you commence reciting the poem seventeen seconds after a given cough, she will cough again in the middle of the third line and after that at the middle of every twelfth line (the fifteenth, twenty-seventh, thirty-ninth, et cetera) and at the end of every twelfth line from the beginning (the twelfth, twenty-fourth, thirty-sixth, et cetera). This particular spacing will minimize the effect of her coughing, will make it only slightly negative. But negative just the same, for it means that you will have to run each of those twelfth end-stopped lines rapidly into the following line, which will blur your every sixth rhyme and somewhat diminish the dramatic structure of the poem. As for its effect on the raven's harsh refrain, you can only hope that the audience is sufficiently familiar with the poem to hear with its collective ear the croak of *Nevermore* in the very coughing of the woman, as it were, as if you Edgar Poe the poet said nothing, as if you merely mouthed the words, for the raven, for the unseen woman in the audience coughing, for the woman in your dream, for your mother dying in an attic room in Richmond, Virginia, your mother, whose consumptive cough and groans and finally her shrieks are muffled into silence by the women in the kitchen wrapping your head with a scarf so that you cannot hear your mother dying, will not remember this awful time in your life, and will not remember your mother.

You return to the hotel, sober and alone, exchange greetings and complaints about the midsummer heat with the desk clerk, and climb the carpeted stairs to your room on the second floor. The recitation went well. You overcame the woman's coughing interruptions just as you'd planned, and at the end the audience rose and applauded with gratitude. A few women near the front, when they rose from their seats to thank you for reciting your "magnificent and profound" poem, could be seen with tears washing their cheeks. Afterwards, when you departed the stage, you discovered that someone, a janitor probably, had removed your half-emptied bottle as a blessing and a sign, and later, at the Reverend Doctor Woolsey's gathering for the literary ladies and gentlemen of Richmond, Virginia, you declined the sherry and asked for water, a glass of cool, clear water with a bruised leaf of mint dropped into it. And so now you arrive at your hotel room sober. But late, past midnight, for, because tonight you were sober, you spoke to the ladies and gentlemen with a lucidity driven by logic that astonished them and made them beg you to stay and continue to mystify, enchant, and bewilder them. One is always amazed by what is most rational, you muse as you enter your darkened room. The irrational, even though it makes one feel helpless, out of control, childlike, seems more "natural" to one. You light the lamp, sit on the bed, and slowly remove your shoes. You think: And one is *right* to believe in the "naturalness" of unreason. And right to be amazed by what is most rational, to be simultaneously shocked and relieved by a person who presents himself as demystification, disenchantment, and clarity personified. Both right and *good*—for those are the modern vices we set against the ancient virtues of faith, hope, and charity!

You hold your head in your cool palms. Oh my! Oh my! To aspire to purge one's mind and all its manifestations of every taint of unreason—such an aspiration must be *blasphemy*! To be pure reason, to be self-generating, to be unable to remember your mother—is to be a *god*! Is that why you can't remember your mother's face, her smell, her touch, her voice? Is this painful absence the necessary consequence of your o'ervaunting ambition? Evil. You say the word aloud, over and over. *Evil. Evil.* You draw off your socks and your trousers, your jacket, vest, shirt, and necktie, your underclothes, all the while murmuring, *Evil, evil, evil.*

Until at last you are naked, the poet Edgar Poe, author of "The Raven," naked in the dim light of a hotel room in Richmond, Virginia. You peer down at your toes, bent and battered, each toe topped with a thin wad of black hairs. Your knees, knobbed, the skin gray and crackled, and your gaunt thighs, your genitals, dry, puckered, and soft, half-covered with a smoky patch of hair. You look at your drooping belly and your navel, that primeval scar, and your breasts, like two empty pouches. You study your hands, twin nests of spiders, and your thin arms, the moles, freckles, discolorations, fissures, hairs, and blemishes, and your gray, slack skin.

You try to look at your face—but you cannot. There is a dresser mirror across from you to your right a few paces, but that will not do. You want to look upon your face directly. And you cannot. You know that if you look directly at your own face, you will be able to remember your mother's face. And then her touch, her smell, her voice. You touch your face with your fingertips, rubbing them across nose, lips, eyes, ears, and cheeks. You can get the facts of your face, but you cannot look upon it directly. Just as you can get the facts of your mother's life, from the memories of the women, those young women now old, but you cannot remember her directly yourself. Is that why you have for so many years aspired to what is evil? Because it was easier for you than to become a "natural" human being, easier than remembering your mother? Easier to be evil than good? You are weeping silently. Which is it? Are you unable to remember your mother because you are evil and persist in blasphemy, or are you evil and persist in blasphemy because you cannot remember your mother? Which? For one must be a cause, the other the effect. Which the cause? Which the effect? Why are you weeping? Why are you naked? Why are you the poet Edgar Poe author of "The Raven"? Why are you not a particular, remembered, and memorialized mother's son?

In the graveyard beside the church on the hill is your mother's grave. You will depart this city in an hour by train for Baltimore. You have eaten breakfast alone in the hotel dining room and have arranged for a driver to carry you first to the church on the hill, then back into the city to the railroad station. You pay your bill, lift your satchel, and leave the hotel for the carriage waiting outside. You stop a moment on the veranda and admire the soft morning sunlight on the brick buildings and sidewalks, the elm and live oak trees that line the streets, the white dome of the capital building a few blocks east, and beyond that, with the river between, the white spire of the church next to where your mother's body was buried nearly four decades ago. This will not be the first time you have visited your mother's grave, to stand before it with your mind mutely churning, and then, after a few moments of vertigo, to leave. You have made this pilgrimage hundreds of times, as a young boy, as an adolescent, and as a man, even in military uniform, even while drunk. And it has always been the same. From the very first, when Mrs. Allan took you outside the church after the service one Sunday morning and walked to the graveyard and stood hand in hand with you above the freshly cut plaque laid in the ground and told you that your mother's body was buried here, precisely here, at this spot, from that very first time until this, it has been the same for you. Silence in your ears, no noise from without, no words from within, and a feeling, painful and frightening, of falling, as if down a well that reaches to the center of the earth. Yet, despite that feeling, you have returned to this spot compulsively, like an animal driven by an instinct. You have no sense of there being a reason for it. It is as if you are drawn there by a force that originates there, at the grave, not here inside your own head, among your sensations, memories, and ideas of the sanctified and holy. No, the power lies in that graveyard, in that one, all but unmarked grave. And now, as a middle-aged man in the middle of an illustrious career, as the poet Edgar Poe author of "The Raven," you find yourself standing once again in that cool, tree-shaded cemetery beside the old Episcopal church on the hill, and once again you descend into a well of silence. Your mind has gone mute, and you no longer hear the wind in the leaves overhead, the wagon and carriage traffic on the cobbled street behind you, the morning twitter of birds and the coo of the doves from the niches of the steeple. You look down at the grassy plot of ground before you, the tarnished plaque at your feet, and you feel yourself begin the descent. But this time, for no cause you can name, now or later, at the point of its beginning, before you have become terrified, you resist. You pull away and step back a few paces as if from a slap, and you bring the entire grave into your gaze and sharply into focus, the rich green grass, the switching patterns of shadow and sunlight on the grass, the square plaque sinking into the ground at the head of the grave. You can see each individual blade of grass, even those bent and crushed beneath the feet of some passing cleric or attendant this very morning. You are still wrapped in silence, as if in a caul. You can hear nothing, nothing. And you have no thought. You watch the shadows cast on the grave by the fluttering leaves of the live oak overhead, and slowly they organize into an image, one that you yourself are surely creating as you watch, but an image which nonetheless exists in the world outside you, a configuration of shade against sunlight on the grassy plot of your mother's grave. The shades separate, move together, slowly swirl, separate, and come together again, until you begin to see the shape of a single eye, large, wide open, an extraordinary eye, a wholly familiar eye, yet one that you have never seen before. It resembles an eye you have seen in daguerreotypes. And in mirrors. It is the eye of a close blood relation, it is your mother's eye, it is your own eye. You stare peacefully into it, and feel it stare peacefully back. Then, gradually, the image fades, the shadows move apart, and the eye is gone from your sight. But you can remember it. You instantly recall it to your mind, as if to test the reality of the experience, and it appears there, as tender and filled with love for you as when it first appeared out of the shadows. You turn and slowly leave the cemetery. As you climb into the waiting carriage, you try once again to remember your mother, and you see her beautiful dark eye, her loving gaze on you, her only son, her beloved child.

The Fisherman

In the northcountry, if you have an abstract turn of mind, you tend to measure the approach of winter by the sun, how in late October it starts slipping toward the southern horizon, spending less and less time each day in the sky and, because of that, seems to move across the sky at an accelerated rate, as if in a hurry to depart from this chilled part of the globe and move on to the Southern Hemisphere, there to languish slowly through the long, hot afternoon of the pampas, the outback, and the transveldt. Or, on the other hand, you might measure the approach of winter by the ice, which seems a more direct, less abstract and mathematical way of going about it. You wake up one morning toward the end of October, and when you glance out your window at the lake, you see off to your left, where a low headland protects a shallow cove from the wind, a thin, crackled, pink skin of ice that spreads as far as the point and then suddenly stops. There is no ice yet in the swamp, where the trickling movement of inlets to the lake and the pressure of tree stumps, brush, and weeds forbid freezing this early, though by tomorrow morning or the next it will be covered there, too; and there is no ice where the lake empties across the flat stones of the old Indian fishing weirs to form the Catamount River, though it, too, will gradually freeze solidly over; and there is no ice along the western shore, for here the

43

ground drops down quickly from the tree-covered hills, and the water is deep and black.

The man named Merle Ring, the old man whose trailer was the last one in the park and faced one end toward the weirs and the other toward the swamp, was what you might call an iceman. When the ground froze, his walk took on a springing, almost sprightly look, as if he were happy to find the earth rock-hard, impenetrable, and utterly unyielding. Every October, the morning he saw the first ice on Skitter Lake, he pulled on his mackinaw and trotted down to the shore as if to greet an old friend. He examined the ice, reading its depth, clarity, hardness, and extension the way you'd examine a calendar, calculating how many days and weeks he'd have to wait before the entire lake was covered with ten or more inches of white ice, cracking and booming through subzero nights as new ice below expanded against the old ice above, and he could set up his bob-house, chisel into the ice a half dozen holes, and commence his wintertime nights and days of fishing for pickerel, black bass, bluegills, and perch.

For over a half century Merle had been an ice fisherman. Where most people in this region endure winter to get to summer, Merle endured summer to get to winter. Ice fishing is not what you would ordinarily think of as a sport. You don't move around much, and you don't do it with anyone else. It's an ancient activity, though, and after thousands of years it's still done in basically the same way. You drop a line with a hook and piece of bait attached into the water, and you wait for an edible fish to take the bait and get hooked, and then you haul the thrashing fish through the hole and stash it with the others while you rebait your hook. If you are a serious ice fisherman, and Merle was serious, you build a shanty, and you drag it onto the lake, bank it around with snow, and let it freeze into the ice. The shanty, or bob-house, as it's called, has trapdoors in the floor, and that's where you cut the holes in the ice, usually with a harpoonlike, steel-tipped chisel called a spud or with a long-handled, steel auger. At some of the holes, depending on what kind of fish you are seeking and what kind of bait or lure you are using, you set traplines, or tip-ups, and at others you drop handlines. With live bait, minnows and such, you can use the traps, but if you're jigging with a spoon or using ice flies, you need to keep your hand on the line.

The bob-house is only as large as need be, six feet by four feet is enough, and six feet high for a normal-sized person. At one end is a door with a high step-over sill to keep out the wind, and at the other a homemade woodstove. Along one of the long walls is a narrow bench that serves as a seat and also a bed when you want to nap or sleep over the night. Your traps and lines are set up along the opposite wall. There is a small window opening, but it remains covered by a hinged, wooden panel, keeping the bob-house in total darkness. When no light enters the bob-house, you can sit inside and peer through the holes in the ice and see clearly the world below. You see what the fish see, and you see them, too. But they cannot see you. You see the muddy lake bottom, undulating weeds, and decaying leaves, and, in a cold, green light, you see small schools of bluegills drift over the weed beds in search of food and oxygen, and coming along behind them three or four pickerel glide into view, looking for stragglers. Here and there a batch of yellow perch cruise past, and slowly, sleepily, a black bass. The light filtered through the ice is still, hard, and cold, like an algebraic equation, and you can watch the world pass through it with a clarity, objectivity, and love that is usually thought to be the exclusive prerogative of gods.

Until one winter a few years ago, Merle Ring was not taken very seriously by the other residents of the trailerpark. He was viewed as peculiar and slightly troublesome, mainly because, while he had opinions on everything and about everyone, when he expressed those opinions, which he did frequently, he didn't make much sense to people and seemed almost to be making fun of them. For instance, he told Doreen

Tiede, who was having difficulties with her ex-husband, Buck, that the only way to make him cease behaving the way he had behaved back when he was her husband, that is, as a drunken, brutal crybaby, was to get herself a new husband. "Who?" she asked him. They were in the car, and she was giving Merle a lift into town on her way to work at the tannery. Her daughter, Maureen, headed to the baby-sitter for the day, was in the back, where she was unaccustomed to sitting. Doreen laughed lightly and said it again, "Really, Merle, who should I marry?"

"It don't matter. Just get yourself a new husband. That way you'll get rid of Buck. Because he won't believe you're not his wife until you're someone else's." He looked out the window at the birches alongside the road, leafless and gold-tinted in the morning sun. "That's how I always did it," he said.

"What?" She was clasping and unclasping the steering wheel as if her fingers were stiff and cold. This business with her ex-husband really bothered her, and it was hurting Maureen.

"Whenever I wanted to get rid of a wife, I married another. Once you're over a certain age and have got yourself married, you stay married the rest of your life, unless the one you happened to be married to ups and dies. Then you can be single again."

"Maybe Buck'll up and die on me, then," she said with a quick grimace.

"Mommy!" the child said and stuck her thumb in her mouth.

"I was only joking, sweets." Doreen looked into the rearview mirror. "And stop sucking your thumb. You're too old for that." Then, to Merle: "Is that how you got to be single, after all those wives? How many, six, seven?"

"Numerous. Yup, the last one died. Just in time, too, because I was all set to get married again."

"To who?"

"Oh, I don't know. I didn't have anybody in particular in mind at the time. But I sure was eager to get that last one off my back."

"Jesus, Merle, isn't anything sacred to you?"

"Sure."

"For instance."

"Marriage, for instance. But not husbands or wives," he quickly added.

"I can't take you seriously, Merle," she said, and they drove on in silence.

That was the form most of his conversations took. It didn't matter whom he was talking to, Merle's observations and opinions left you feeling puzzled, a little hurt and irritated. To avoid those feelings most people told themselves and each other that Merle "wasn't all there," that he didn't really understand how complicated life was, and that he really didn't like anyone, anyhow. But because he was orderly and quiet and, like most small, neat, symmetrical men, physically attractive, and because his financial life was under control, he was accepted into the community. Also, he didn't seem to care one way or the other if you took him seriously or if you followed his advice, and, as a result, Merle was never an agitated man, which, naturally, made him an attractive neighbor. No one thought him a particularly useful neighbor, however.

Until he won the state lottery, that is. That same October morning, the morning he saw the first ice on the lake and a little later had the brief conversation with Doreen Tiede concerning her ex-husband, Buck, he purchased, as he did every month, a one-dollar lottery ticket. It was a habit for Merle, ever since the state first introduced the lottery back in the 1960s, to go into town the day after his social security check arrived in the mail, cash his check at the bank, and on the way home stop at the state liquor store and buy a fifth of Canadian Club and a single lottery ticket. There were several types available, but Merle preferred the Daily Numbers Game, in which you play a four-digit number for the day. The winning number would be printed the next morning in the Manchester *Union Leader*. For your one-dollar bet, the payoff on four digits in the exact order was $4,500. At that point, your number went into another lottery, the Grand Prize Drawing, made later in the year, for $50,000. Merle won $4,500, and here's how he did it. He bet his exact age, 7789—on October 30, 1978, he was seventy-seven years, eight months, nine days old. He had always bet his age, which of course meant that the number he played varied slightly, but systematically, from one month to the next. He claimed it was on principle, for he did not believe, on the one hand, in wholly giving over to chance or impulse or, on the other, in relying absolutely on a fixed number. It was a compromise, a realistic compromise, in Merle's mind, between randomness and control, two extremes that, he felt, led to the same place—superstition. There were, of course, three months a year when, because he was limited to selecting four single-digit numbers, he could not play his exact age, and in those months, December, January, and February, he did not buy a ticket. But those were the months he spent ice-fishing, and it seemed somehow wrong to him, to gamble on numbers when you were ice-fishing. At least, that's how he explained it.

Merle took his $4,500, paid the tax on it, and spent about $250 refurbishing his bob-house. It needed a new floor and roof and a paint job, and many interior fixtures had fallen into disrepair. The rest of the money he gave away, as loans, of course, but Merle once said that he never loaned money he couldn't afford to give away, and as a result of this attitude, no one felt especially obliged to pay him back. Throughout November, Merle hammered and sawed away at his bob-house, while people from the trailerpark came and went, congratulating him on his good luck, explaining their great, sudden need for $300 or $400 or $500, then, while he counted out the bills, thanking him profusely for the loan. He kept his prize money inside a cigar box in his toolbox, a huge, locked wooden crate far too heavy for fewer than four men to carry and located just inside the door to his trailer.

Meanwhile, the ice on the lake gradually thickened and spread out from the coves and shallows, creeping over the dark water like a pale shadow. Merle's bob-house was a handsome, carefully fitted structure. The bottom sills had been cut to serve as runners, so that Merle could push the building out onto the ice alone. The interior was like a ship's cabin, with hinged shelves and lockers, hooks and drawers, a small woodstove made from a twenty-five-gallon metal drum, a padded bunk that folded against the wall when not in use, and so on. The interior wood, white pine, had been left raw and over the years had darkened from woodsmoke and moisture to the color of old briar. The exterior, of lapstrake construction to stave off the wind, Merle covered with a deep red stain. The pitched roof was of new, unstained, cedar shingles the color of golden palomino that would silver out by spring.

Clearly, the structure deserved admiration, and got it, especially from the denizens of the trailerpark, for the contrast between Merle's bob-house and the cubes they all lived in was notable. As November wore on and Merle completed refurbishing the bob-house, people from the park daily came by and stood and studied it for a while, saying things and probably feelings things they had not said or felt before. Until Merle won the lottery, the people had more or less ignored the old man and his bob-house, but when they started coming around to congratulate him and ask for loans, they noticed the tiny, reddish cabin sitting on its runners a few feet off the lake, noticed it in a way they never had before, for they usually found him working there, and their attention got drawn to his work, and also they were curious as to how he was spending his money, so as to determine whether there would be any left for them. And when they saw the bob-house, really took a close look at its precision and logic and the utter usefulness of every detail, they were often moved in strange ways. It was as if they were deserted on an island together and suddenly had come upon a man among them who was building a seaworthy boat, and it was a boat that could carry no more than a single person off the island. They were moved by the

sight of Merle's bob-house, moved to hate the sight of their own rust-
ing, tin-and-plastic trailers, the cheap, manufactured clutter of their
shelters, and this unexpectedly disturbed them. The disturbance
moved them, unfortunately, to envy Merle's bob-house.

"How come you making it so fancy?" Terry Constant sneered.

Merle looked up from the floor where he was screwing down the
new two-by-eight-inch plank flooring and saw the black man silhouetted darkly against a milk-white sky so that his features couldn't be seen.
He wore an orange parka and Navy watch cap and was chewing a toothpick. Merle said nothing and went back to work.

"You win the numbers, like they said?"

"Yup."

"That's how come you're making it so fancy, then."

" . . . "

"Luxury!"

" . . . "

"Who's gonna see it, a little fish house? I coulda slapped this thing
together in half the time for half the cost outa plywood."

" . . . "

"This thing'll last longer'n you will. You realize that? You'll be dead
a hundred years, and this thing'll still be sitting here by the lake."

Merle picked up a new plank and with a stubby plane shaved
blond, sweet-smelling curls off the wood. He lay the board against the
first, cast his gaze down its length, retrieved it, and gave it another half
dozen smooth strokes of the plane, until finally the plank fit snugly,
perfectly, into place.

"Well, it *looks* good, anyhow," Terry said. He shifted his toothpick
and, placing one foot onto the high sill, dropped his right forearm onto
his thigh and leaned forward and into the close, dim, resin-smelling
interior of the bob-house. "Say, Merle, I was wondering, see, I'm outa
work. Marcelle's all done winterizing the park, so she don't need me

anymore until spring or unless the pipes burst or something, and there ain't no work in this damn town in winter, especially for a black man. So I was wondering if you could help me out a little, till I could get some more work."

"Sure."

"I was thinking of maybe heading south this winter, getting some work in Florida. I got a cousin in Tampa, but it'll take some bucks to do it. You know, for bus fare and after I get there, till I get a job."

"What about your sister?" Merle asked without looking up. "She'd be pretty much alone here without you. Being colored and all. Come spring, you could get work again, maybe for the highway department or something. You don't want to leave her all alone up here."

"Well, yeah. . . ." Terry let his glance fall across the oak framing of the structure, noticing for the first time how it had been notched and fitted together with pegs. "But I can't take any more handouts from her. Maybe you could loan me enough to get me through the next three or four months," he said. "I got problems, man."

"How much?"

"Five, six hundred, maybe?"

"Sure."

"Seven would be better."

"Sure."

"I'll pay you back." He stood up straight again and stepped away from the door as Merle got slowly to his feet and came out to the yard.

"Sure," he said. "Money's in the house."

"Okay," Terry said almost in a whisper, and the two men crossed the yard to the trailer.

There were other loans: Bruce Severance, the long-haired kid in number 3 who sold dope, needed $300 fast, to get a very heavy dude off his back, he said; Noni Hubner, the college girl in number 7, was recuperating from her first nervous breakdown and wanted to do what her mother had so far refused to do, buy a proper gravestone for her father's grave, which, since his death two years ago, had gone unmarked; and Leon LaRoche, the bank teller in number 2, said he needed money to help pay his sick mother's hospital bills, but it came out (only as a rumor, however) that his mother was not ill and that he was spending money recklessly to support a young man supposedly going to college in Boston and whom Leon visited almost every weekend; and Claudel Bing, who was no longer living at the trailerpark but still had friends there, and after having lost his job at the Public Service Company, said he needed money to pay for his divorce from Ginnie, who was living with Howie Leeke; Tom Smith was dead by then, but his son, Buddy, somehow heard about Merle's good luck and wrote from Albany asking Merle for $500 so he could pay off the debts he claimed his father's burial had left him with, and Merle mailed the money to him the next day; Nancy Hubner, Noni's mother, insisting that she did not want the money for herself, explained that she had got herself into an embarrassing situation by pledging $1,000 to the Clamshell Alliance antinuclear people and had only been able to raise $750; Captain Dewey Knox, in trailer number 6, who certainly seemed affluent enough not to need any of Merle's money, suddenly turned out to owe three years' back taxes on the last bit of land his father had owned in Catamount, a rocky, hundred-acre plot on the northern edge of what had been the elder Knox's dairy farm, and to keep the Captain from losing that last connection to his sanctified past, Merle loaned him $638.44; and then, finally, there was Marcelle Chagnon, the manager of the trailerpark, living in number 1, and needing money to protect her job, because the Granite State Realty Development Corporation was billing her personally for the cost of replacing all the frozen pipes in trailer number 11, then vacant, which Marcelle had neglected to drain last August when the previous tenants, a pair of plasterers from Massachusetts working on a new motel over in Epsom, had left. And then, well—then all the money was gone.

*   *   *

By mid-November, the sun was setting early and rising late, and the daily temperatures rarely got above freezing, the nights often falling to zero and below. Except for where the water rushed across the weirs, the lake was frozen over entirely. The bob-house was ready, and Merle's tip-ups, lines, jigs, and chisels were repaired, cleaned, oiled, and packed neatly into the bob-house. First thing every morning, Merle pulled on his cap and mackinaw and trotted from his trailer down to the shore to read the ice. It was going to be a good winter for ice—no snow so far, very little wind, and lots of steady, unbroken cold. A Canadian high had moved southeast in late October and hunkered over northern New England for two weeks straight, so that, with clear nighttime skies, the ice had formed, spread, and thickened several weeks ahead of schedule.

So far as fishing went, winter or summer, Skitter Lake was Merle's. Three sides of the lake adjoined the Skitter Lake State Forest, which made it fairly inaccessible from the road, except through the trailer-park, and people, strangers especially, were reluctant to drive through the trailerpark and stop their cars before the short, sandy beach at the end of the peninsula, get out their gear, launch their boats, canoes, or bob-houses, and commence fishing. It was a little too public, and also a little too private, as if the trailerpark were actually a boardinghouse with all the tenants watching you cross their shared front yard to get to their shared fishing place. The same went for ice skating and swimming. The residents of the trailerpark skated and swam Skitter Lake, but other people went elsewhere, which wasn't much of an inconvenience, since in town there was the mill pond, and throughout the surrounding countryside there were dozens of small, accessible ponds and lakes where the fishing was as good as, if not better than, the fishing at Skitter Lake.

As a result, when Merle decided at the end of the first week in December that the ice was thick enough to support the weight of his bob-house, he made the decision alone. He couldn't wait until someone less cautious or patient than he had dragged his bob-house safely out to the middle of the lake. He couldn't wait until schoolboys from town, eager to play hockey, had crossed and crisscrossed the lake a dozen times the way they did down at the millpond, whacking the ice with hockey sticks and listening to the cracks and fault lines race away from the blow, rather than down, revealing in that way that the ice was now thick enough to support the weight of large human beings.

Merle took his long-handled chisel in hand and, tapping lightly in front of him as he walked, moved like a blind man carefully onto the ice. He walked twenty or so feet from the shore and parallel to the shore toward the marshy area west of the park, where the hermit they called the Guinea Pig Lady had built her shack. Here, he knew, the water was late to freeze, because of the several trickling inlets and the marsh grass and bushes, and here, too, the water was not very deep, so that if, indeed, it was not safe and he fell through, he would not be in any danger. It was late in the day, and the sky was peach-colored near the horizon and blue-gray where thin clouds had scudded in from the northeast. Merle, in his dark green mackinaw and plaid trooper's cap with the fur earflaps tied down, tapped his way away from the trailer-park toward the swamp, then past the swamp and out along the point, crossing the cove, and then beyond the point, until he was over deep water. Below him, the lake was a hundred feet deep, and the ice was black and smooth, like polished obsidian. This first solitary walk on the ice is almost like flying. You leave the safe and solid earth and move over what you know and can see is an ether, supported by a membrane that you can feel, but cannot quite see, as if the difference between the ice below and the air above were merely a difference in atmospheric pressures. Later, your mind will accept the information coming from your body, and then there will be no difference between ice with a hundred feet of water below it and the frozen ground itself, so that when you cut a hole in the ice, and it fills with water, you will be surprised, but no more frightened than if you had dug a hole in sand at the beach and watched it fill with water.

Confident now that he could safely put his bob-house onto the ice, Merle spent the following day picking through the brushy, overgrown fields out by Old Road, collecting galls from dried stalks of goldenrod. Inside each gall slept a small, white grub, excellent bait for bluegills, and it wasn't long before Merle had collected in his mackinaw pockets half a hundred of the woody containers. On returning to the trailer-park, he was hailed on the roadway just opposite Marcelle Chagnon's trailer by Bruce Severance. Bruce drove his black Chevy van with the Rocky Mountain sunsets on the sides up behind the old man—it was midafternoon, but almost dark, and he probably hadn't seen Merle until he was almost upon him. He stopped a few feet away, raced his motor until Merle turned, then waved him over to the driver's side and cranked down the window.

"Hey, man, what's happening?" The sweet smell of marijuana exhaled from the vehicle, and the kid took a last hit, knocked the lit end off the roach, and popped it into his mouth.

"Temperature's dropping," Merle said with a slight smile. He peered up at the boy, and his blue, crinkly-lidded eyes filled and glistened in the wind.

"Yeah. Wow. Temperature's dropping. That's what's happening, all right." Bruce swallowed the roach.

"Yep." Merle turned to walk on.

"I've been meaning to ask you, man, I saw you this morning, when I came in from Boston, you were in those old fields out by the road. Then later I came back out, and you were still there. And now here you are again, this time coming in from the fields. What's going on out there, man?"

"Nothing. Temperature's dropping there, too. That's all."

"No, man. I'm curious. I *know* you know things, about herbs and things, I mean."

Merle said, "You want to know what I was out there for? Is that what you're wondering, boy?"

"Yeah."

The old man reached into his mackinaw pocket and drew out one of the goldenrod galls. "These."

"What's that?"

"Goldenrod gall."

"What's it for, man?"

"I'll show you. But you'll have to spend a while first, helping me move my bob-house out on the ice tonight."

"Tonight? In the dark?"

"Yep. Got to bait the camp with chum tonight, so's I can start to fish tomorrow."

With a slow and maybe reluctant nod, the kid agreed to help him. Merle walked around and climbed into the van, and the two drove through the park to Merle's trailer.

When an old man and a young man work together, it can make an ugly sight or a pretty one, depending on who's in charge. If the young man's in charge or won't let the old man take over, the young man's brute strength becomes destructive and inefficient, and the old man's intelligence, out of frustration, grows cruel and inefficient. Sometimes the old man forgets that he is old and tries to compete with the young man's strength, and then it's a sad sight. Or the young man forgets that he is young and argues with the old man about how to do the work, and that's a sad sight, too.

In this case, however, the young man and the old man worked well together. Merle told Bruce where to place his pole so he could lift the front of the bob-house, while Merle slid a second pole underneath. The same at the back, until, practically on its own, the bob-house started to roll down the slope toward the ice. As each roller emerged from the back, Merle told Bruce to grab it and run around to the front and lay it down, which the young man did, quickly and without stumbling, until, in a few moments, the structure was sliding onto the ice, and then it was free of the ground altogether. It slid a few feet from the bank, and the momentum left it, and it stopped, silent, solid, dark in the wind off the lake.

"Incredible!" the kid said.

"Everything's in the bob-house except firewood," Merle said. "Put them poles inside, we'll cut them up out on the lake."

The kid did as he was told.

Merle walked around to the front of the bob-house, away from the land, and took up a length of rope tied to a quarter-inch-thick U-bolt. "I'll steer, you push," he called to the kid.

"Don't you have a flashlight?" Bruce yelled nervously. The wind was building and shoved noisily against the bob-house.

"Nothing out there but ice, and it's flat all the way across."

"How'll I get back?"

"There's lights on here at the park. You just aim for them. You don't need a light to see light. You need dark. Stop gabbing and start pushing," he said.

The kid leaned against the bob-house, grunted, and the building started to move. It slid easily over the ice on its waxed runners, at times seeming to carry itself forward on its own, even though against the wind. As if he were leading a large, dumb animal, Merle steered the bob-house straight out from the shore for about a quarter mile, then abruptly turned to the right, and headed east, until he was a few hundred yards from the weirs, where the lake narrowed and where, Merle knew, there were in one place a gathering current, thirty to forty feet of water, and a weedy, fertile bottom. It was a good spot, and he spun the bob-house slowly over it until the side with the door faced away from the prevailing wind.

"Let it sit," he said to the kid. "Its weight'll burn the ice and keep it from moving." He went inside and soon returned with a small bucksaw and his long chisel. "You cut the wood into stove lengths, and I'll dig us in," he said, handing the saw to the kid.

"This is really fucking incredible," Bruce said.

Merle looked at him silently for a second, then went quickly to work chipping the ice around the runners and stamping the chips back with his feet, moving swiftly up one side and down the other, until the sills of the house were packed in ice. By then Bruce had cut two of the four poles into firewood. "Finish up, and I'll get us a fire going," Merle told him, and the kid went energetically back to work.

In a short time, a fire was crackling inside the round belly of the stove, the kerosene lantern was lit, and the bob-house was warmed sufficiently for Merle to pull off his mackinaw and gloves and hang them on pegs behind the bunk. Bruce laid in the wood carefully below the bunk, then looked up at Merle as if for approval, but Merle ignored him.

"Now," the kid said, shaking off his blue parka and, following Merle's example, placing it on a peg, "show me what you got there, those whachacallits from the fields." He sat down next to Merle and rolled a joint. "Smoke?" he said, holding out the cigarette.

"No, thanks, I got whiskey."

"You oughta smoke grass instead," the kid said, lighting up.

"You oughta drink whiskey. 'Course, you got to be smarter to handle whiskey than you do that stuff. " He was silent and watched Bruce sucking on the joint.

The kid started to argue with the old man. Grass never did to you what whiskey surely did, made you depressed and angry, ruined your liver, destroyed your brain cells, and so on.

"What does grass do to you?" Merle asked.

"Gets you high, man." He grinned.

Merle grunted and stood up. "If it can't hurt you, I don't see how it can get you high." He opened the trapdoors in the floor, exposing the white ice below, and with his chisel went to work cutting holes. With the lip of the steel, he flaked ice neatly away, making a circle eight or nine inches across, then dug deeper, until suddenly the hole filled with water. Moving efficiently and quickly, he soon had a half dozen holes cut, their tops and bottoms carefully beveled so as not to cut the line, and with a small strainer he scooped the floating ice chips away, until there was only clear, pale blue water in the holes.

On a lapboard he proceeded to chop hunks of flesh off several hand-sized minnows he'd plucked from a bait pail. This done, he placed the chum into a tin cone with a line attached to the top through a lever that released the hinged bottom of the cone when the line was jerked. He let the cone slowly down the center hole, slightly larger than the others and, hand over hand, let out about thirty feet of line, until he felt the cone touch bottom. He jerked the line once, retrieved it, and brought the cone back into the bob-house, dripping and empty.

Bruce watched with obvious admiration as the old man moved about the confines of the bob-house, adjusting the draft of the stove, taking out, using, and wiping dry and putting back his tools and equipment, drawing his bottle of Canadian Club from under the bunk, loosening his boots, when suddenly the old man leaned down and blew out the lantern, and the bob-house went black.

"What? What'd you do *that* for?" Bruce's voice was high and thin.

"Don't need it now." From the darkness came the sound of Merle unscrewing the cap of the whiskey bottle. Then silence.

"How long you plan to stay out here tonight?" The kid sounded a little frightened.

"Till morning," came the answer. "Then for as long as the fishing's any good and the ice holds."

"Days and nights both?"

"Sure. I only have to come in when I run outa whiskey. There's plenty wood along the banks, I'll have to step out now and then for that, and, of course, you got to piss and shit once in a while. Otherwise. . . ."

They sat in darkness and silence awhile longer, when finally the kid stood up and groped behind him for his coat. "I . . . I gotta go back in."

"Suit yourself."

He took a step toward the door, and Merle said to him, "Those goldenrod galls you was asking about?"

"Oh, yeah," the kid said.

Merle struck a match, and suddenly his face was visible, red in the glow of the match as he sucked the flame into the barrel of his pipe, his bearded face lurching ominously in and out of the light when the flame brightened and dimmed. When he had his pipe lit, he snuffed out the match, and all the kid could see was the red glow of the smoldering tobacco. "Bait."

"Bait?"

"Yep. Old Indian trick."

The kid was silent for a few seconds. "Bait. You mean, that's how you got me to push this thing way the hell out here tonight?"

"Old Indian trick."

"Yeah," Bruce said coldly. He drew open the door and stepped quickly out to the ice and wind, looked into the darkness for the lights of the trailerpark, found them way off and dimly in the west, and started the walk back.

No one brought Merle any Christmas gifts or invited him to any of the several small parties at the park. The reasons may have been complicated and may have had to do with the "loans" they all had received from him, but more likely the residents of the trailerpark, as usual, simply forgot about him. Once in a while, someone mentioned having seen him walk through the park on his way to town and return later carrying a bag of groceries and a state liquor store bag, but otherwise it was almost as if the old man had moved away, had gone west to Albany like Buddy Smith or south to Florida like Captain Knox's mother and father or into town to the Hawthorne House like Claudel Bing.

The week before Christmas, there was a snowstorm that left a foot and a half of snow on the ground and on the lake, followed by a day and a night of high, cold winds that scraped the snow into shoulder-high drifts along the shore, and that further isolated Merle from the community. Now it was almost as if he had died, and when in the morning you happened to look out at the lake and saw way out there in the brilliant white plain a red cube with a string of woodsmoke unraveling from the stovepipe chimney on top, you studied it the way you would the distant gravestone of a stranger reddening in the light of the rising sun.

A week later, just after Christmas and before the turn of the year, Noni Hubner's mother was reading the Manchester *Union Leader* at breakfast, when she started up excitedly, grabbed the paper off the table, and hurried back through the trailer to her daughter's bedroom.

"Noni! Noni, wake up!" She shook the girl roughly by the shoulder.

Slowly Noni came to. She lay in the bed on her back, blinking like a seal on a rock. "What?"

"The Grand Prize Drawing! They're going to have the Grand Prize Drawing, dear! Think of it! What if he won! Wouldn't that be wonderful for him? The poor old man."

"Who? What the hell are you talking about?"

"Don't curse, dear. Merle Ring, the old fellow out on the lake. He won the lottery back in October, remember? And now, on January fifteenth, they're going to hold the Grand Prize Drawing. Apparently, they put all the winning numbers for the year into a basket or something, and the governor or somebody draws out one number, and whoever holds that number wins fifty thousand dollars! Wouldn't that be wonderful?"

"Yeah," the girl said, and rolled over, yanking the covers over her head.

"No, you can't go back to sleep! You've got to go out there and tell him! He hasn't been out of that cabin of his for days, or even weeks, so he can't know yet. You can ski out there with the news! Won't that be *fun*, dear?"

"Let someone else do it," Noni mumbled from under the covers. "It's too cold."

"You're the only who has skis, dear," the mother said.

"Most of the snow is off the ice."

"Then you can skate out!"

"Oh, God," Noni groaned. "Can't you leave people alone?"

"He's such a sweet old man, and he's been *very* generous. It's the least we can do."

"He's a grumpy pain in the ass, if you ask me. And he's weird, not generous." She got out of bed and looked at her reflection in the mirror.

"Well, no one asked you. You just do as I say. You have to involve yourself more in the fates of others, dear. You can't always be thinking only of yourself."

It took Noni an hour to prepare for the journey—first breakfast and then, as she ate and dressed herself in three layers of clothing, bickering with her mother about the necessity for the trip in the first place—and another hour for the trip itself. It was a white world out there, white sky, white earth beneath, and a thin, gray horizon all around, the whole of it centered on the red cubicle where the old man fished through the ice.

At the bob-house, sweating from the work of skating against the wind and, having come to rest, suddenly chilled, Noni leaned for a few seconds against the leeward wall, knocked at the door, and, without waiting for an answer, entered. The door closed behind her, and instantly she was enveloped by darkness and warmth, as if she had been swallowed whole by an enormous mammal.

"Oh!" she cried. "I can't see!"

"Seat's to your right," came the old man's gravelly voice. The interior space was so small that you couldn't tell where in the darkness the voice was coming from, whether from the farthest corner of the bob-house or right up next to your ear.

Noni groped to her right, found the bench, and sat down. A moment of silence passed. Gradually, her eyes grew accustomed to the darkness, and she was able at last to see the six holes in the ice, and in the green light that rose from the holes she saw the hooked shape of the old man seated at the other end of the bunk next to the stove. He held a drop line in one hand and jiggled it with the other, and he seemed to be staring into the space directly in front of him, as if he were a blind man.

"Why is it so dark in here?" she asked timidly.

"Window's shut."

"No, I mean how come?"

"So I can see the fish and they can't see me," he said slowly.

More silence passed. Finally, in a low voice, Noni spoke. "How strange you are."

Merle didn't respond.

"I have some news for you, Mr. Ring."

Still nothing.

"You know the lottery you won back in October?"

Merle jiggled his handline and continued staring straight ahead. It was almost as if he'd entered a state of suspended animation, as if his systems had been banked down to their minimal operating capacity, with his heart and lungs, all his vital organs, working at one-fourth their normal rate, so that he could survive and even thrive in the deprivation caused by the cold and the ice and the darkness.

"It seems ridiculous," the girl said, almost to herself. "You don't care about things like lotteries and Grand Prize Drawings and all."

A few seconds passed. Merle said, "I bought the ticket. I cared."

"Of course. I'm sorry," Noni said. "I just meant . . . well, no matter. My mother saw in the paper this morning that they're holding the Grand Prize Drawing in Concord on January fifteenth at noon, and you ought to be there. In case you win."

Merle said nothing.

"It's a lot of money. Fifty thousand dollars. You have a good chance to win it, you know." He didn't respond, so she went on, chattering nervously now. "Think of what that would mean. Fifty thousand dollars! You could have a wonderful old age. I mean, retirement. You could go to Florida in the winter months. You could go deep-sea fishing in Florida. Maybe buy one of those condominiums, play shuffleboard, have lots of friends. . . ." She trailed off. "God, I sound like my mother." She stood up and moved toward the door. Tenderly, she said, "I'm sorry I bothered you, Mr. Ring. My mother . . . she wanted you to know about the drawing, that's why I came out here. She thought you'd be . . . excited, I guess."

"I haven't won yet."

"But you have a good chance of winning."

"Good chance of dying, too. Better."

"Not by January fifteenth, Mr. Ring."

"About the same. I'm old. Not much left to do but think, and then, in the middle of a thought, die."

"Oh, no," she said heartily. "There's *lots* for you to do."

"Like what?"

"Well . . . fishing, for instance. And spending all that lottery money you're going to win."

"Yes," he said. "Yes, there's that." Then he lapsed back into silence again.

The girl opened the door and slipped out, and the bob-house filled again with darkness and solitude.

The door to the bob-house was flung open, and a blinding light entered, bringing with it a blast of cold air and the hulking shape of a man in a hooded parka. The man splashed the light from his flashlight around the chamber, located Merle stretched out in his blanket roll on the bunk, and let the beam droop deferentially to the floor. The man closed the door behind him.

"Mr. Ring?"

"Yep."

"I'm . . . I'm Leon LaRoche. You know, from the trailerpark?"

Merle swung his body into a sitting position. "You can shut out that light."

Leon apologized and snapped off the flashlight. "May I sit down and get warm? It's mighty cold out there tonight." He chuckled. "Yes, sir, mighty cold."

"Suit yourself."

They were silent for a moment. Merle opened the stove front, throwing shadows and sheets of dancing red and yellow light into the room; he tossed a chunk of wood onto the crimson coals and closed the fire door again.

The young man nervously cleared his throat. "Well, Mr. Ring, how's the fishing?"

"Slow."

"I've been hearing a lot about you lately, from folks at the park, I mean . . . how you stay out here night and day, only coming in now and then for supplies . . ."

"Whiskey," Merle said, and he went under the bench with one hand and drew out his bottle. "Drink?"

"No. No, thank you."

Merle took a slow pull from the bottle.

"Anyhow, it's all very interesting to me. Yes, maybe I will have a drink," he said, and Merle fetched the bottle again and passed it over. "So tell me, Mr. Ring, what do you eat out here? How do you cook and all?"

"Fish, mostly. A man can live a long time in this climate on fish and whiskey."

"Very interesting. And you use lake water for washing, I suppose?" Merle grunted.

"How long do you plan on staying out here, Mr. Ring?" Leon took another drink from the bottle and passed it back.

Merle said nothing.

As if his question had been answered, Leon went on. "And do you do this every winter, Mr. Ring? I mean, stay out on the ice, isolated like this, living off fish and whiskey and solitude?" He chuckled again. "I'm relatively new to the park," he explained.

"I know."

"Yes, of course. Well." He wrestled himself free of his parka and flexed his shoulders and hands. "Say, it's really comfortable in here, isn't it? Smells a bit of whiskey and fried fish, though," he said with a light laugh. "You wouldn't mind if I had another sip of that, would you? What is it, by the way? It's quite good! Really warms a man's insides, doesn't it?"

Merle handed him the bottle. "Canadian Club."

Leon unscrewed the cap and took a long swallow, then slowly screwed the cap back on. "Yes. So, yes, I was saying, do you do this every year?"

"Man and boy."

"But *why*?"

"It makes the rest of the year more interesting," Merle said wearily.

Leon was silent for a moment. "I wonder. Yes, I'll bet it does. I couldn't stand it, though. The isolation. And the cold, and the darkness."

"It's a good idea to get used to the idea. Like I said, it makes the rest of the year more interesting."

Leon's voice was tight and frightened. "Are you talking about dying?"

"I'm talking about living."

"Speaking of living," Leon said, suddenly hearty again, "you are probably wondering why I came all the way out here this evening."

"Not particularly."

"Yes. Well, anyhow, it has to do with the Grand Prize Drawing next week. You know, the state lottery?"

"Yep."

"Folks in the park have been wondering, Mr. Ring, if you plan on attending that drawing over in Concord, and if not—assuming you win, for you just might win, you know—folks are wondering how you plan to pick up the prize money. You have to be there in person to pick up the prize money, you see . . .," he trailed off, as if waiting to be interrupted.

Merle said nothing.

"Well. It occurred to some of us that you might not care to take the time off from your fishing to go all the way in to Concord and deal with those state officials and the reporters and so forth, seeing as how you enjoy your privacy and like to spend your winters alone out here on the lake, and we thought you might be able to empower someone else to do that chore for you. So I did a little checking around at the bank, which is where I'm employed, and, sure enough, you *can* empower someone else to pick up your prize money for you!" He waited a few seconds, but nothing more than the crackle and spit of the fire came out of the darkness, so he went on. "Anticipating your reluctance to leave your fishing at this time of year, I went ahead and took the liberty of having the necessary document drawn up by the bank attorney." He went into his shirt pocket and brought forth a crisp, white envelope. "This document empowers me to act as your agent, should you win the Grand Prize Drawing," he said, handing the envelope to Merle.

The old man took out the paper folded inside, and, at the sound, Leon snapped on his flashlight. "Where do I sign it?" Merle asked. His voice was strangely woeful and riddled with fatigue.

Leon directed him to a line at the bottom of the paper and handed him a pen.

Slowly, the old man placed the paper against his knee and scrawled his name on it. "There," he said, and he handed the paper, envelope, and pen back to the bank clerk, who doused the light. "It's your problem, now," the old man said.

"No problem at all, Mr. Ring. None at all," he said, as he stood and pulled his parka on. "I assume," he went on, "that, if you win, you'll want your check deposited in a savings account down at the bank."

"No."

"No?"

"Bring the money here."

"Here?"

"In cash."

"Cash?"

"Cash. No point letting some bank make money off my money. The government owns all the money anyhow. They just let us use it for a while. It's the banks that foul everything up by getting in the middle. You bring me anything I win in hundred-dollar bills. You might use one of them to buy me a case of Canadian Club. I've always wanted a case of Canadian Club," he said wistfully.

Leon seemed to have been struck dumb. He moved toward the door in the darkness, groping for the latch, and finally found it. Then he let himself out.

From here on out, it was as if everyone who knew Merle knew that he was going to win the lottery. Consequently, his solitude rarely went a day without being broken by a visit from someone who wanted to congratulate him and talk about the money. Also, the weather broke into what's called the January Thaw, and people found the half-mile walk over ice and log floes of crusted snow less formidable than before. The wind died, the skies cleared to a deep blue, and daytime temperatures nudged the freezing mark, so at one time or another during the week following the visit from the bank clerk, practically everyone else in the park found an occasion to visit the old man. Even Claudel Bing (though he had not lived at the trailerpark for several years, he was still paying for a trailer there and, in his fashion, was courting Doreen Tiede, and as a result had kept up his links with the park) came out to Merle's bob-house early one sunny afternoon.

He was already drunk when he arrived, a not uncommon occurrence that year, and, therefore, he wanted to talk about luck. In particular, his own bad luck. As compared to Merle's good luck. Luck was Claudel's obsession that year. It was the only way he could understand or even think about his life.

"You, you sonofabitch, you got *all* the luck," he told Merle, who silently arranged his lines in the tip-ups and scooped ice chips away from the holes. "And that means there's none left over for people like me! That's the trouble with this goddamn country." Claudel had brought his own bottle of whiskey, which he held between his legs and every now and then swigged at. "Now you take them fucking Commie bastards, like that Castro and them Chinese, their idea is to get rid of luck completely, so *nobody* gets any. That's as bad as what we got here. Worse, actually. What I'd like to see is a system that lets everybody have a little luck. That's what this country needs. Nobody gets a lot, and nobody gets none. Everybody gets a little."

"How about bad luck?" Merle asked him. "Everybody going to get a little of that, too?" His beard and face and hands were pale green in the light from the holes, and as he moved slowly, smoothly over his traps and lines, checking bait and making sure the lines were laid precisely in the spools, he resembled a ghost.

"Sure! Why the hell not? When you got a little good luck, you can handle a little bad luck. It won't break you. If I had money, for instance, it wouldn't bother me that Ginnie run off with that goddamn sonofabitchin' Howie Leeke," he said earnestly. "But you wouldn't understand. Not with your kind of luck. Shit," he said and took a long drink from his bottle. "You ever lose a woman you loved, Merle?" he asked suddenly. "No, of course not. You've had all them wives, got wives and kids scattered all over the country, but none of them ever left *you*. No, you left *them*. Right? Am I right?"

"Can't say exactly that I intended to leave them, though," Merle said. "I guess I just willed it. You can will what you actually do, but what you intend is all you accomplish in the end."

"You preaching to me, Merle, goddamnit?"

"Nope. Just thinking out loud. Not used to company."

"Hey, that's all right, I understand. Shit, it must get awful lonely out here. I'd go nuts. It's good for thinking, though. Probably. Is that the kinda stuff you think about out here, Merle, all that shit about will and intending?"

"Yep." A red flag on one of the tip-ups suddenly sprung free, and in a single, swift motion Merle was off the bench and huddled over the line, watching it run off the spool and then stop. He jerked it, set the hook, and started retrieving the fish. "Black bass," he said to no one in particular. It was a small one, not two pounds. Merle drew it through the hole, removed the hook from its lip, and deposited the fish in the bucket of ice chips scooped from the holes.

"If I was you, I'd be thinking all the time about how I was going to spend all that money," Claudel went on. "You talk about will and intentions!" he laughed. "How do you intend to spend the money, Merle? Fifty thousand bucks! Jesus H. Christ."

"Can't say." He rebaited the hook and wound the line back onto the spool.

"You mean, you don't know?"

"What d'you think my intentions toward that much money ought to be? Can't spend it, not the way I live. 'Course, I haven't got it yet, so it ain't like we're talking about reality."

"No, we're talking about money!" Claudel said, leering.

"All I know is death and taxes. That's reality. I intend to pay my taxes, and I intend to die."

"Merle, you are fucking crazy," Claudel said. "Crazy. But smart. You're smart, all right. You coulda been a lot of things if you'd wanted to. Big. A businessman."

"I always did what I wanted to," Merle said gloomily. Then, as if writing a letter, he said, "I was a carpenter, and I was married, and I fathered some children. Then I got old. Everyone gets old, though, whether he intends to or not."

They were silent in the darkness for a moment.

"Yeah," Claudel said, "but you got lucky. You won the lottery!"

"It don't matter."

"Of course, it matters, you *asshole!*"

"Not to me."

"Well, it matters to me, goddamnit!"

Merle remained silent this time, and, after a while, Claudel's bottle was empty. Without leaving his seat, he reached over, opened the door, and pitched the bottle out. "It'll sink in spring," he mumbled. Then slowly, awkwardly, he pulled his coat on and stumbled out the door, not bothering even to say good-bye.

Daily, with and without ceremony, they came out to the bob-house. The younger ones, Terry Constant, Noni Hubner, Bruce Severance, Leon LaRoche, Doreen Tiede, and poor Claudel Bing, could pretend they just happened to be in the neighborhood, ice-skating, skiing, walking, or, as in Claudel's case, bored and lonely and thought to drop in for a visit. The older ones, however, found it difficult to be casual about their visits. As Merle had said, you expect the actions of adults to have intention behind them and therefore meaning. The adults tend to expect it of themselves, too. Carol, Terry Constant's older sister, claimed she walked all the way out to the middle of the lake against a cold wind because she had never seen anyone ice-fishing before and wanted to learn how it was done. While there, the only question she asked Merle directly was how would he spend the money, if he won on the fifteenth. He said he didn't know. Nancy Hubner baked Merle a minced meat pie (she said it was his favorite) and insisted on carrying it to him herself. While he ate a piece of the pie, she told him how excited she was at the prospect of his becoming a wealthy, carefree man, something she said *everyone* deserved. He agreed. Captain Dewey Knox appeared one morning at the bob-house to confirm Leon LaRoche's claim that Merle had signed a document authorizing Leon to act as his agent at the Grand Prize Drawing. Merle said yes, he had signed such a document. "Without coercion?" the Captain asked. Merle said he couldn't be sure, because he didn't know how a person went about coercing someone to sign something. "But you understood fully the meaning and consequences of your act?" the Captain asked. Merle said he wasn't drunk or crazy at the time. "And is it true," the Captain went on, "that you requested young LaRoche to bring your winnings out here in cash? Hundred-dollar bills?" Merle said it was true. The Captain thought that extremely foolish and told Merle, at great length, why. Merle went about his business of fishing and said nothing. After a while, when the Captain had finished telling Merle why he should have Leon LaRoche deposit the money in a savings account at the bank where he was employed, he departed from the bob-house. The last person from the trailerpark to visit Merle's bob-house came out the day of the drawing, January fifteenth. It was Marcelle Chagnon, and, as the manager of the trailerpark, she felt it was as much her duty as her privilege to announce to Merle that on that day at twelve o'clock noon he had won the $50,000 Grand Prize Drawing.

The winter continued to bear down, quite as if Merle had not won the lottery. There were snowstorms and cruel northeast winds out of Nova Scotia and days and nights, whole weeks, of subzero temperatures. Merle's money, the five hundred one-hundred-dollar bills delivered by Leon LaRoche, remained untouched in Merle's cigar box under the bunk in the bob-house. The brand-new bills, banded into thousand-dollar packets, filled the cigar box exactly, and the box, with an elastic band around it, sat in the darkness of the bob-house and the well-lit minds of everyone who lived in the trailerpark. Everyone carried the image of that box around in his or her head all day and night. Some even dreamed about it. Leon LaRoche told Captain Knox that when he delivered the money, the old man in stony silence, as if angry at being interrupted, took the money from the bank pouch, and, without counting it, stacked it neatly into the cigar box and tossed, literally tossed, the box under his bunk. The Captain, as if disgusted, told Marcelle Chagnon, who, worriedly, told Doreen Tiede, who told Claudel Bing that night after making mild, dispassionate love, and Claudel, stirred to anger, told Carol Constant the next morning when, on her way to work, she gave him a lift into town because he hadn't got out of bed in time to go in with Doreen and her daughter. That evening, Carol told her brother, Terry, because she thought Merle would listen to Terry, but Terry knew better. "That man listens to no one," he said to Bruce after telling him about the cigar box that contained $50,000, and Bruce, full of wonder and admiration, agreed with Terry and tried to explain the pure wisdom of the act to Noni Hubner, but she didn't quite understand how it could be wise, so she asked her mother, Nancy, who thought it was senile, not wise.

In that way, within twenty-four hours of Leon's having delivered the money to the bob-house, everyone in the trailerpark shared an obsession with the image of the cigar box full of hundred-dollar bills. They could think of little else. Merle's earlier winnings had not achieved anything like this status, but their experience with that considerably lesser amount had gone a long way toward determining how they looked at this new money. The October lottery had dropped $4,500 into Merle's lap, and the residents of the trailerpark each went to him and asked for some of it and directly received what he or she asked for. This new amount, however, was so incomprehensibly large that no one could apply it to his or her individual needs. Consequently, they applied it to what they saw as the needs of the community as a whole. It was not Merle who had won the $50,000; the trailerpark had won it. Merle had merely represented them in that magical cosmos where anything, absolutely anything, can happen. Of course, it's probably true that if, on the other hand, what happened to Merle through no effort on his part had been as colossally, abstractly *bad* as the $50,000 was *good*, the residents of the trailerpark would not feel that it had happened to the community as a whole. If, for example, Merle were shot in the head by an errant bullet from the gun of a careless deer hunter out of sight in the tamaracks on the far side of the lake, the people in the park would blame Merle for having been out there wandering around on the ice during hunting season in the first place. They would mourn for him, naturally, but his death would be seen forever after as a warning, an admonition. Anyone can be a cause of his or her own destruction, but no one can claim individual responsibility for having created a great good. At least, that's how the people in the trailerpark felt. Which is why they believed that Merle's winnings belonged, not to Merle alone, but to the community of which he was a part. And, of course, there was their earlier experience with the $4,500. That sort of proved the rightness of their feeling, gave them something like a logic.

The days went by, and Merle showed no sign of recognizing that something extraordinary had occurred in his life and the lives of everyone else at the park, as well. Every morning they peered out their windows and saw again the red bob-house in the distance, a horizontal strip of smoke trailing from the stovepipe chimney if the wind was blowing, a vertical stick of smoke if the wind had let up. In the after-noon, as it grew dark, they looked toward the lake again and saw that nothing had changed. Because Merle refused to act any differently than he had in the weeks before he won the lottery, no one else could act any differently, either, and it almost came to seem that they had imagined it, which is one reason why they were eager, whenever possi-ble, to talk about the money with one another. It *was* true, wasn't it? I didn't just *dream* that Merle Ring won the lottery, did I? And then, as time passed, with the continuous discussions having satisfactorily proved that Merle did in fact win the Grand Prize Drawing, they began to take and present to one another their respective positions on what Merle ought to do with the money he had won.

"The man's obviously incapable of behaving responsibly toward money," Captain Knox explained to Leon LaRoche. "Money demands to be taken care of in a responsible manner. You can't treat it like some sort of waif, you have to take *care* of it," he said.

Leon agreed. Wholeheartedly. They were sitting in the living room of the Captain's trailer, Leon on the sofa, the Captain slumped back into his red leather easy chair. Behind him on the wall hung a map of the world. In the center of each of a large number of countries, mostly cen-tral European and southeast Asian countries, the Captain had pinned a small red flag with the Communist hammer and sickle on it. Earlier in the evening, having delivered to Leon a lengthy oration on the subject of the insidious workings of what he called Castroism in the very cor-ridors of the United States State Department, he had ceremoniously pinned a red flag to Panama. That led him to a discussion of the respon-sibilities that go with power, which in turn had led him naturally to a discussion of the responsibilities that go with wealth, and that was how they had come around to talking about Merle again.

And now that people were taking positions on what should be done—with Merle, with the money, or, in certain cases, with Merle and the money—they had begun quarreling with one another. For while the Captain and Leon, for example, believed that one had a moral obligation to take care of money in a responsible manner, they were not in anything like clear agreement as to what, in the case of Merle's lottery winnings, constituted a responsible manner. Nor did either of them agree with what Carol or Marcelle or Claudel or anyone else thought ought to be done with Merle and the $50,000 that, through no particular effort or even intent of his own, he had so recently come to possess. And since everyone had a stake in what was done with the money, the feelings ran pretty high, and it didn't take long for the residents of the trailerpark to think that everyone else in the trailerpark was stupid or greedy, or stupid *and* greedy, while he himself, or she herself, was neither. Here, then, are the ways the people in the park thought the situation should be handled.

DOREEN TIEDE: There are some of us here who have children to support, who work for a living, who don't get any help from ex-husbands or dead husbands or big government pensions. I think we know who we're talking about. There are some of us here who won't take welfare, who don't have fancy jobs in fancy doctors' offices, who don't stay home and collect other people's rent while other people are out working their asses off at the tannery. There are some of us who would like a normal American life. And who deserve it, too. I think we know who we are.

TERRY CONSTANT: We could form a corporation and buy out the trailerpark, develop the beach, fill in the swamp, and put up a restaurant and bar. We have to think for ourselves and take over control of our destinies. Enough of this business of making somebody else rich while we get poorer for it. Make a summer resort out of this place. Swimming, fishing, water skiing. Or maybe a summer camp for city kids. Nature walks, arts and crafts, sports. Put up cabins for the kids, while the rest of us live in the trailers. I'd get number 9, where that guy who shot himself lived with his kid. We could run the place in winter as a lodge for snowmobilers. Maybe, if you promoted it right, ice fishing would catch on. The point is, we'd all be working together for the common good. You don't just spend the money, you use the money, because it doesn't matter how hard you work, it takes money to make money. Not work. Not time. Money. Leon could be treasurer, old Captain Knox could be chairman of the board. I could be the executive director. We'd make Merle president of the corporation or something honorary like that. I'd get a good salary. Marcelle could run the restaurant. Carol the infirmary.

BRUCE SEVERANCE: When you've got money, unless you're stupid, the first thing you do is eliminate the middleman. That way you control the entire operation, like Henry Ford did. What do you think pissed off the Arabs? All those American oil companies, man, they controlled the entire operation. I got connections in Jamaica like Shell had in Saudi Arabia, man. You could bring a plane in here in winter and land it on the lake. Simple. Easy Street. How the hell do you think the Kennedy family got started? Running booze from Canada during Prohibition, man. It's not like we're Mafia or something. I mean, *everybody* smokes grass!

NONI HUBNER: It's important to be fair. That's what I believe in. Fairness. Right?

LEON LAROCHE: In an interest-paying savings account at the Catamount Trust, Merle's money will earn enough for him to live without financial anxiety for the rest of his natural life. The stock market goes up and down, government and municipal bonds, though they offer a distinct tax advantage, are a young man's game, and there's no need to speculate on the risky commodities market. After all, Merle only wants to live in a modest way, free of worry or risk, that's obvious and natural, and with his social security, plus interest on his lottery winnings, he certainly ought to be able to do so. What kind of selfishness would prompt a person to deny him that opportunity? The bank would be happy to take care of Merle's funds for him. He'd be our single largest depositor, and I myself would handle his account for him. I'd probably become an officer of the bank, maybe eventually a vice president. It's not every teller can bring in a fifty-thousand-dollar savings account. The publicity would be good for the bank, too. We could have a picture-taking session, Merle signing the deposit slip, me taking the cigar box out of his hands. We'd need an extra guard. I don't care what the Captain says, I know money.

CAROL CONSTANT: With that much money, he could do something useful for a change. He could help others. The whole thing makes me sick. He sits out there on top of fifty thousand dollars, while back here people are struggling to survive. If he doesn't want the damn money, let him give it to the town, so it can help the poor, for Christ's sake. I see people from this town every day so poor and sick they die before they're supposed to, people whose houses burn down, people who've been out of work for years. I see kids with nutritional diseases, birth defects, kids who need glasses to read but can't afford them so they do lousy at school. While that old man, that senile jerk, sits out there fishing through a hole in the ice. It makes me sick. I'm sure he's senile. Those are always the ones who end up with money to burn, the ones who are too feeble-minded to know what to do with it. He doesn't even know how to use it for himself. I wouldn't mind so much if he just took off for Florida and spent it on some old lady and a condominium on the Gulf. I hope someone steals it off him. I just hope it's not Terry. Though, God knows, Terry could make better use of it than that old man is. Terry might at least pay me back a little of what I've spent taking care of him these last few years.

CLAUDEL BING: You hear all the time about an old geezer dying and they find a million bucks or something stashed under his mattress. All those years the sonofabitch has been cashing welfare checks and living like a fucking rat in a hole, and meanwhile he's sitting on top of a fucking million bucks or something. Then the government goes and takes it all for taxes or something. I think we oughta just go on out there, get the bastard drunk, and take that goddamn cigar box off his hands. He'd never know the difference anyway. Sonof-abitch. If I do it, no one's gonna know about it. I'll be long gone from here. California. No reason why his dumb luck can't be my good luck. Nothing wrong with that. I earned it, for Christ's sake.

BUDDY SMITH: You probably remember the tragic death of my father by his own hand. He was very fond of you, Mr. Ring, and often spoke highly of you to me, telling me himself what a kind and generous man you are. I will soon be returning to N.H. on business of a personal nature and was thinking of dropping by the trailerpark, where I have so many fond but also sad memories of my childhood. I thought, if you had the room, because my father was so very fond of you, I could perhaps visit with you a few days and we could talk about the old times. I'm a young man, alone in the cold world now, and without the kind of wise counsel that an older man like yourself can provide. . . .

NANCY HUBNER: The man is obviously depressed. You people amaze me. He's depressed. It happens often to elderly people who live alone and don't feel needed anymore. We simply have to take better care of our senior citizens. The man needs company, he needs to feel wanted, and especially he needs to feel needed. We ought to make up an excuse to have a party, a Valentine's Day party, say, and march out there and say to him, "Merle, if you won't come to our party, then we'll bring the party to *you!*" We'll all have a lovely time.

We've got to bring him back into our circle, a man like that should not be allowed to be alone in life. The money has nothing to do with it. Really, nothing.

DEWEY KNOX: The man's obviously incapable of taking care of himself, so it shouldn't be difficult to have him declared incompetent to handle his own affairs. The money can then go into a blind trust, which clever and aggressive management ought to be able to double in a matter of a few years. Imagine, if you'd bought gold five years ago, as I did, when it was going for $112 an ounce, you'd now have nice little nest egg. I myself, if pressed to it, would certainly be willing to put together a management team to handle the trust. Other than asking for a nominal fee for services provided, the capital accrued would, of course, go directly into the trust and ultimately to Merle Ring's heirs. It could be arranged so that Merle himself received a modest monthly stipend. People like Merle need looking after. Not vice versa, the way some of you would have it.

MARCELLE CHAGNON: Am I crazy, or is everybody trying to figure out how to get Merle's money for themselves? It's his money, and I don't care what in hell he does with it. He can wipe his butt with it, for all I care, if you'll excuse my English. So what if he's got lots of money he don't need and you don't have enough. So what else is new? That's life. Do I expect my sons, all grown up and making good money, to send me money just because they got lots of it now and I don't have enough? No, I do not. That's life, is all I got to say. All I care now is that Merle does *something* with that money, spends or gives it away or loses it, something, anything, just so life can return to normal around here. I wish to hell he'd never got it in the first place. Thinking about it, all this talk and argument about it, gives me a goddamned headache. I hate thinking about money, and here I've been doing it all my life. I get the same damned headache every time one of my sons writes and tells me he just bought a new dishwasher for his wife or a big screen TV or just got back from Bermuda or someplace. What do I care what he just bought or where the hell he went on vacation? What the hell do I care about money? There's lots more important things in life than money. I just want to forget it exists.

It's hard to know more about a person's life than what that person wants you to know, and few people know even that much. Beyond what you can see and are told (both of which are controlled pretty easily by the person seen and told about), what you come to believe is true of who a person is, was, and will be, comes straight from your imaginings. For instance, you know that a man like Merle Ring had a mother and a father, probably brothers and sisters, too, and that for most of his life he was a working man and that he was married and had children. He has said as much himself, and besides, these things are true of almost any man you might choose to read about or speak of. That he was married numerous times (you might imagine four or five or even more, but "numerous" was all he ever said) and fathered numerous children explains only why in his old age he was as alone in the wide world as a man who had never married at all and had fathered no one. Whether he meant to, Merle had avoided the middle ground and in that way had located himself alone in the center of his life, sharing it with no one. In fact, you could say the same of everyone at the trailerpark. It's true of trailerparks that the people who live there are generally alone at the center of their lives. They are widows and widowers, divorcées and bachelors and retired Army officers, a black man in a white society, a black woman there, too, a drug dealer, a solitary child of a broken home, a drunk, a homosexual in a heterosexual society—all of them, man and woman, adult and child, basically alone in the world. When you share the center of your life with someone else, you create a third person who is neither you nor the person you have cleaved to. No such third person resided at the Granite State Trailerpark.

In any event, though you knew all these things about Merle's inner and outer lives, you could know little more about them than that, unless he himself were to provide you with more information than he had already provided, more actions and reactions, more words. And, unfortunately, as the winter wore on, he seemed less and less inclined to say or do anything new. People's imaginings, therefore, as to who he really was, came to dominate their impressions of him.

This, of course, was especially true after he won the money. By then most of the people at the park were frightened of him. The money gave him power, and the longer he neither acted on nor reacted to the presence of that money, the greater grew his power. For the most part, though they argued among themselves as to how Merle should exercise his immense power, no one dared approach him on the subject. They spoke of it, naturally, and made plans and commitments to send one or another of the group or several in a delegation out onto the plain of ice to ask Merle what he was going to do with the money, but by morning the plans and commitments got broken, ignored, or forgotten altogether—until the next time a group of them got to bickering, accusing one another of selfishness and greed and downright stupidity, when a new agreement would be made as to who should make the trip. The trouble was, they no longer trusted anyone or any group from among their number to return with accurate information as to Merle's behavior, and for that reason they could not be relieved of their imaginings. Finally someone, possibly Marcelle Chagnon and probably as a bitter joke, suggested they send a child, the only true child who lived at the trailerpark, Doreen Tiede's five-year-old daughter, Maureen.

Her mother dressed the child warmly in a dark blue, hooded snowsuit, mittens, and overshoes. It was an overcast Sunday afternoon, the low sky promising snow, when the residents of the trailerpark walked Maureen down to where the land ended and the ice began. Smiling and talking cheerfully together for the first time in weeks, they called advice to their tiny emissary:

"Don't forget, ask him about his fishing first! *Then* ask him about the money."

"Just say we all miss him here and wonder when he's coming back in!"

"No, no, just ask if we can *do* anything for him! Can we bring him any supplies, wood for his fire, tools—anything!"

The child looked about in bewilderment, and when she got to the edge of the ice, she stopped and faced the crowd.

"All right, honey," her mother said. "Go ahead. Go on and visit Uncle Merle, honey. He's out there waiting for you."

They could trust the child. Merle, they knew, would tell her the truth, and she in turn would tell them the truth.

"Go on, sweets," Doreen coaxed.

The little girl looked up at the adults.

"Merle's probably lonely," Nancy Hubner said. "He'll love you for visiting with him."

"It's not very far, you'll have fun walking on the ice," Terry assured her.

"She doesn't want to go, man," Bruce said to Terry in a low voice.

"For Christ's sake, make the kid go!" Claudel told Doreen. "I'm getting cold standing out here in my shirtsleeves."

"Shut up, Claudel, she's just a little nervous."

Marcelle snorted. "First time I've seen her nervous about playing on the ice. Usually you can't get her to come in off it."

"Go on," Doreen said, waving good-bye.

The child took a backward step and stopped.

"G'wan, honey, Uncle Merle's waiting for you," Carol said with obvious impatience. "Whose idea *was* this anyway?"

"You're the child's mother," Captain Knox reminded Doreen. "You tell her what to do, and if she doesn't do it, punish her. It's her choice." He turned and stepped from the group, as if all this fuss had nothing to do with him.

"If you don't march out there and visit Merle Ring right now, young lady, I'll . . . I'll . . . take away TV for a month!"

The little girl looked angrily at her mother. "No," she said.

"I will too! Now get out there! He's *expecting* you, dammit!"

"You come, too," Maureen said to her mother.

"I can't . . . I . . . have to do the laundry."

"He only likes kids," Terry said. "Grown-ups like us just bug him. You'll see. He'll be real glad to see you come all the way out there to visit him."

"He might have some candy for you," Bruce said.

The child turned and started waddling away.

"Don't forget about the money!" Noni Hubner called.

The child turned back. "What?"

"The *money!*" several of them bellowed at once, and the child, as if frightened, whirled away.

The adults stood for a moment, watching the blue-hooded figure get smaller and smaller in the distance. The ice was white and smooth and, because of the constant wind, scraped free of snow, so that the blue figure of the child and the red bob-house way beyond stood out sharply. The sky, the color of a dirty sheet, stretched over the lake, and lumpy gray hills lay like a rumpled blanket between the ice and sky. Slowly, the people drifted back to their trailers, until only the child's mother and her friend Marcelle remained at the shore. Once, the child stopped and turned back, and the mother waved, and the little girl resumed trudging toward the bob-house. Then the mother and her friend Marcelle walked to the mother's trailer together.

"Kid's got a mind of her own," Marcelle said, lighting a cigarette off Doreen's gas stove. "Just like my kids used to be."

"Why do you think I let her go all the way out there alone?" Doreen asked.

"You can only protect them so much."

"I know," Doreen said, sighing. "Otherwise you got 'em clinging to you the rest of your life."

"Yeah."

The child, Maureen Tiede, pushed the door of the bob-house open an inch and peeked inside. The wind had come up sharply, and snow was beginning to fall in hard, dry flecks. Maureen's face was red and wet from tears. Outside, a rag of smoke trailed from the chimney, but inside the bob-house it was as dark as a hole in the ground and, except for the howl of the wind, silent. The little girl let the door close again and backed away from it. For a few moments she stood outside, looking first across the ice to the trailer-park, then at the closed door of the bob-house. At the trailerpark, the frozen beach was deserted. The trailers, their pastel colors washed to shades of gray in the dim light, sat like two parallel rows of matchboxes. Finally, Maureen moved toward the door and pushed it open once again, wider this time, so that a swatch of light fell into the bob-house and revealed the hooked shape of the old man seated at the end of the bunk. He was squinting out of his darkness at the open door and the child beyond.

"Come inside," Merle said.

The girl stepped carefully over the high threshold and, on closing the door behind her, realized that, while she could no longer make out the old man, the place was not entirely dark, for an eerie green light drifting from circles cut in the ice was bright enough to cast shadows against the ceiling and walls. Immediately, Maureen backed to the bunk, and holding to it with both hands stared down at the holes in the ice, looked through the ice, and saw the fluid, moving world there—tall, slender weeds and broadleaf plants drifting languorously back and forth, schools of minnows and bluegills gathering, swirling skittishly away from one another, then, as if at a prearranged signal, quickly regathering. The little girl was mesmerized by the sight, possibly even reassured or comforted by it, for she seemed to relax. She pulled off her mittens and stuffed them into the pockets of her snowsuit, then untied and pushed back her hood, all the while keeping her gaze fixed on the world beneath the ice, the world that moved beneath the cold, granitic, windblown world here above.

"All by yourself today?" Merle asked quietly from his corner by the stove.

Maureen nodded her head and said nothing.

Merle queried the child for a few moments, discovered that she was not lost, that her momma knew where she was, and that she had never seen anyone fish through the ice before. "Well, you just sit still with me," he told her, "and before long your momma or somebody else from the park will be out here looking for you. It's snowing here and ought to be there, too. That'll bring 'em out to get you."

By now she had her snowsuit off and was seated cross-legged on the bunk. She had said very little, answering Merle's questions with yes or no and nothing more.

Her silence seemed to please him. "You're a nice kid," he said, and for the first time in months, he smiled.

After a while, Maureen lay back on the bunk against the old man's blanket roll and fell asleep. Outside, the wind moaned and drove the snow across the ice, piling it in long, soft drifts along the shore. The sky had closed in, and even though it was still early in the afternoon, it seemed like evening. Every now and then, Merle tossed a chunk of wood into the stove, lit his pipe, took a sip of whiskey, and checked his lines.

It was dark outside and snowing heavily, when the door was suddenly shoved open, and Maureen's mother, her boyfriend, Claudel, right behind her, stepped into the tiny chamber, filling the crowded space to overflowing, so that Claudel had to retreat quickly. There were others outside, their heads bobbing and craning behind Doreen for a look.

Merle had lit the kerosene lantern and had prepared a supper of fried bass fillets, boiled greens pulled from the lake bottom, and tea in his only cup for the child, whiskey from the bottle for himself.

Doreen, in her hooded parka crusted with snow, embraced her child. "Thank God you're all right!" The little girl pulled away. "I don't know what got into me!" Doreen cried. "Letting you out of my sight for a minute on a day like this!"

Maureen stared down at the holes in the ice, which were dark now.

"She insisted on coming out here to visit you, Mr. Ring, and I said no, but the second my back was turned so I could do the laundry, she was gone. It never occurred to us that she'd come out *here*, till later this afternoon, when the snow started building up. I thought she was just playing around the park somewhere."

Merle went on eating, quite as if the woman weren't there.

"She's probably been telling you all *kinds* of stories!"

Merle said nothing.

"Did you, honey?" she asked her daughter. "Have you been telling Mr. Ring all kinds of stories about us?"

The child pouted and shook her head from side to side. "No," she said. "I just wanted to watch him fish. I fell asleep," she added, as if to reassure her mother.

The door swung open, letting in a blast of cold air and blowing snow. It was Terry's face this time, and he said in a rush, "Listen, we're freezing out here, we got to get moving or we're gonna freeze to death. Everything okay?" he asked, peering at Doreen, at the child, and at Merle. "You know," he said to Doreen, winking. "Everything okay?"

Behind him, Bruce's face bobbed up and down as he tried to get a glimpse of the interior, and, behind Bruce, several more figures moved about impatiently.

"Yes, yes, Terry, for Chrissakes!" Doreen hissed. "Just give me a minute, will ya?" She pushed against the door to close it, but another hand from the other side shoved it back.

It was Captain Knox. In the gentle light cast by the lantern, his square face, scarlet and angry inside the fur-lined hood of his parka, was clenched like a fist. "Ring," he barked. "This time you've gone too far! Kidnapping! A federal offense, Ring."

"Get the hell outa here!" Doreen shouted. Merle, wide-eyed and silent, watched from the far corner. Someone grabbed the Captain from behind and pulled him away, and Doreen slammed the door shut again. The sound of bodies bumping violently against the walls of the bob-house, shouts, cries—all got caught in the steady roar of the wind and borne away.

"The goddamn old fool!"

"Let me talk to him, let *me!*"

"Get off! Get off my legs, goddamnit!"

The door was flung open yet again, and this time it was Marcelle who was shouting, her voice high and full of fear and anger. "Doreen, get the kid dressed, and get the hell out of here, so I can talk sense to this crazy old man!" She pushed her way through the doorway, her bulk against the wall. Maureen started to cry, then to shriek, and finally to wail. Leon LaRoche called to her, "Little girl, little girl, don't cry!" and pushed his way in behind Marcelle, only to have Terry throw an arm around his neck and drag him backward onto the ice.

"Asshole!" Terry snarled.

"Get off my legs, young man!" It was the Captain shouting at Bruce.

Noni Hubner started screeching, "This is insane! You're all insane!" while her mother, Nancy, pulled Terry away from Leon and cried, "That's all you people know, violence!"

"Get your hands off him!" Carol warned. "And what the hell do you mean, 'you people'?" she said, bringing her face up close to Nancy's.

Nancy slapped the woman's face, then started to bawl and, tears freezing on her cheeks, collapsed to the ice, moaning, "Oh, my God, I'm sorry! I'm so sorry!"

The door to the bob-house, held back by the press of the people inside, was wide open now, and the light from inside cast a flickering, orange glow over the ice. Claudel, a pint bottle in his hand, clearly drunk, sat a ways from the others with his legs splayed as if he had been thrown there from above. He got himself up on his feet, wobbled for a second, and made for the bob-house, holding his bottle out before him. "Hey! Merle! Lemme talk to him! Let's have a drink, Merle, an' we'll get this whole fuckin' thing all straightened out! Lemme talk to him. Me an' Merle understand each other," he said, pawing at Marcelle's shoulder.

Marcelle turned and shoved Claudel back, and he careened into the darkness. "You just want to get on his good side, you leech!" she shrieked. Bruce tried to slide through the doorway and past the woman's large body, but she bumped him against the jamb with her chest. "Just hold it, pal."

"No, man, let me cool things out, give me a few minutes," he whined.

"Keep the hippie away from him!" bellowed Captain Knox.

". . . safekeeping . . . ," came a wail from Nancy Hubner. "Just for safekeeping."

"Mother's right! Listen to my mother!"

"Get the cigar box!" Leon LaRoche shouted. "It's in the cigar box!"

Terry was on his hands and knees, squeezing between Bruce's and Marcelle's legs, one long arm snaking behind Doreen, and then he had it, the cigar box, the money.

Doreen saw him. "Gimme that thing!" She reached for the box.

"I'll take it!" Marcelle cried. "I'm the manager, I'm the one who's responsible for everything!"

Bruce made a grab at the box, grimly and silently. Behind him, Leon had reached in, and the Captain had his hand extended, palm up, while the others, Nancy, her daughter Noni, the nurse Carol, and poor, drunk Claudel, tugged at people's shoulders and backs, trying to pull them away from the door. The wind howled, and the people shouted and swore, and the child wept, and Merle watched, wide-eyed and in silence, while the cigar box went from hand to hand, like a sacred relic, until, as it passed through the doorway, it flapped open, and spilled its contents into the wind, scattering the suddenly loose bills into the darkness. People screamed and grabbed at the bills that, in a second, were gone, driven instantly into the darkness by the wind. Scrambling after the money, the people quickly slipped on the ice and fell over one another and cursed one another, and then were suddenly silent. The box lay open and empty in the circle of light outside the door. The people lay all sprawled on the ice in the darkness just beyond. At the door, holding it open, stood Merle and the little girl.

Here is what happened afterwards. All the residents of the trailerpark, except Merle, went back to their trailers that night. By dawn, they all, except for Merle, were out on the ice again, searching for the money. They worked alone and as far from one another as possible, poking through snowdrifts along the shore, checking among the leafless bushes and old dead weeds, the bits of driftwood frozen into the lake, rocks and other obstructions, all the likely places. No doubt, many or even all the residents of the trailerpark found money that day, and the next and the next, until one morning, as if by prearrangement, no one showed up on the ice. The people who had jobs went back to them; those who ordinarily stayed home did so. No one ever told anyone else whether he or she had been lucky enough to find some of the lost, windblown hundred-dollar bills, so it's possible that no one, in fact, had been that lucky. More likely, some were and some weren't, but all were ashamed of having tried to acquire it. Besides, everyone had seen up close what happens when your neighbors find out that you have been luckier, even by a little, than they have been.

Merle stayed on at the bob-house for the few weeks of winter that remained. In early March, the ice began to soften and turn mushy in places. Gauzy fogs hung over the wet, pearlescent surface of the lake, obscuring the bob-house from the trailerpark and erasing the opposite shore altogether. Before long, V's of Canada geese were passing north-ward overhead, and then, at the weirs, a narrow wedge of open water appeared. Long, shallow ponds of water lay resting on top of the ice, swelling and spreading in the sunlight, while, beneath the ice, deep, dark, slowly warming water chewed its way patiently toward the sur-face, which gradually got blotchy and pale green and then actually broke away from itself in places, making fissures and wide, tipping plates.

No one knew the exact day when Merle left the bob-house, but one morning there was a sheet of open water where the bob-house had been, dark water sparkling under the morning sun, and Merle himself was seen by several people that same day outside his trailer somberly scraping the bottom of his old, dark green rowboat.

Firewood

Nelson Painter is a man who is old, but doesn't know it yet. The dates and names of events he remembers and—though they're private and not that reliable on their own—his memories themselves all tell him that he's not an old man, not yet, not this early in the game. Everything but his body tells him it's impossible to come up only sixty-one and old, and even his body is ambiguous about it, because it's impossible, for instance, for a truly old man to be out of bed as he is every morning of the year at six, even on a Sunday in midwinter, when it's still dark as night and snow is lightly falling and the temperature's stuck at fifteen below as he slides his slippers and bathrobe on in the dark so as not to wake the wife and moves to the bathroom to pee in a hurry and then, hands stuck in the pockets of the robe because the house is so cold, he gets quickly downstairs, with the lights on now, follows his breath down the stairs that creak a familiar tune under his feet as he descends to the living room, crosses to the door of the kitchen, unlatches the low gate, and greets with a nod the dog, stiff between her dysplastic hips, a seven-year-old Great Dane with one yellow and one brown eye.

The dog clatters its nails on the linoleum floor and waits at the door for the man to switch on the overhead light, latch back the gate to the living room, where the thick furniture and carpeting sit sanctified

93

and permanently new, as in a department store window display, and finally open the outside door and the aluminum storm door and release the huge, lumbering dog to the yard. Nelson stands a moment behind the silvery frosted glass and tries to remember his dream of a moment ago. It was years ago, in the dream. It was like most of his dreams that way, a phenomenon that goes on disturbing him, irritating him, actually, infuriating him sometimes, because you ought to be able to move on in your dreams, just as you move on in your life. Your kids grow up, you marry another woman, you move away, come back, change, and change again. You'd think your dreams would know that and would somehow deal with that. He knows he's not thinking the same thoughts he thought ten and twenty years ago. Why the hell, then, is he dreaming the same dreams? Not exactly, of course, but almost—and in tone and atmosphere and most of the settings and many of the people, too, his dreams now are the same as his dreams when he was a young man of thirty and forty and his kids were kids and he was married to their mother.

His life then was loud and boisterous and quarrelsome most of the time, "a goddamned pressure cooker," he called it, but not all bad, surely not as bad as his first wife said and as he thought then, though he was not wrong to leave her and the kids and move on to another life, another woman, who doesn't fight him so hard all the time, who seems to like him better than his first wife liked him, or rather, seems to like the aspects of his character that he himself likes, or believes he likes. Or wants to like. His humor, for instance. He is funny, quick, and sarcastic in an intelligently cruel way that surprises people and makes most of them laugh. And his being so principled, which you might call an unwillingness to compromise, or intolerance, if, like his first wife, who did not understand a lot of things about him, you didn't understand his belief in his own beliefs. And then there is his independence, his insistence that he needs no one's love, though he claims to be pleased by what he's given and says he has plenty of love of his own to give back. Still, at bottom, when push comes to shove, as he says, he does not *respect* love, which fact pleases him.

He can't see the snow falling, but he knows it's coming down—perhaps he can hear it, flecks of white ticking the frozen ground. When you've lived a lifetime or nearly so within fifty miles of where you were born, your body responds to shifts in weather well ahead of your mind, so that to predict the weather you consult your body and not the weather itself. As the pressure drops, one's skin tightens, one smells moisture in the air, hears snow flurries falling in the dark, and one knows what's coming. The body of Nelson Painter this early morning in mid-January in central New Hampshire knows the barometer is falling, the humidity and temperature are rising, and there is a snowstorm coming from the southwest, a blizzard maybe, and as a result Nelson knows that the cord of firewood, two-foot-long chunks of maple and birch dumped in a heap in his yard beside the driveway a month ago, will be covered in a foot or two of snow by noon, which disgusts him, because the boy should have come over and picked up the wood two or more weeks ago, or even before Christmas, the day Nelson called him and told him about the wood, his Christmas present to his son. There wasn't any snow then, and the ground, frozen solid since November, was as hard as steel plate, and the wood, dumped unceremoniously from an old stake-bodied truck by the same local man who sold Nelson his winter's wood every year, ten cords of it, had bounced and rolled over the ground, a sprawl of a pile that instantly looked ugly to Nelson. But he thought his son would drive right over from Concord in his Japanese pickup and haul it home, so he left it there on the frozen lawn by the driveway. Then, after Christmas there was a thaw, the annual January Thaw, and the yard turned to muck, the wood sank under its own weight, and it rained, and then there came a freeze again, a hard freeze, and now the wood is glued to the yard, as if molecules of maple and birch have been welded to molecules of frozen, dead grass and dirt.

Nelson looks into the silver layer of frost covering the storm door before him and knows that it's lightly snowing on the other side, and he says to himself, I'll have to call the bastard and get him over here to haul away his own damn Christmas present, or else I'll have to see it there in the spring, coming up out of the melting snow like a damn boneyard. He closes the inner door and steps away, and a moment later he's on his knees in front of his woodstove, a cast-iron Ranger from Sears, low and deep enough for two-footers. He crumples last Sunday's *Union Leader* into balls and twists of paper, chucks sticks of kindling split off maple logs, scratches a match against the tray in front of the stove, tosses it in and clanks the door shut, and, rolling back on his heels, listens to the stove sigh and moan as the flames inside begin to catch and feed and grow.

A moment later, Nelson stands up slowly, shambles from the stove to the sink, reaches into the overhead cabinet on the right, next to the small square window that looks into the darkness of the backyard and field and woods beyond, and he draws out the bottle of vodka. With his other hand he reaches into the overhead cabinet on the left and plucks a juice glass from a stack and places it on the drainboard. His right hand trembling only slightly, he fills the glass with vodka, recaps the bottle, and places it back inside the cabinet, and now he enjoys his first drink of the day, a deliberate, slow act as measured and radiant as a sacrament, as sweet to him as the sun rising over the winter-burnt New Hampshire hills, as clean as new frost. That first drink is the best drink of the day. It's as if all the others he drinks from now until he falls back into his bed tonight he drinks solely to make this first drink wonderful. Without them and the need they create in his blood, this first drink would be as nothing, a mere preliminary to preliminaries. With them, it's the culmination of Nelson's day. He sips at the vodka steadily, as if nibbling at it, and his gratitude for it is nearly boundless, and though he appears to be studying the darkness out the window, he's seeing only as far as the glass in his hand and is thinking only about the vodka as it fits like a tiny, pellucid pouch into his mouth, breaks into a thin stream, and rolls down his throat, warming his chest as it passes and descends into his stomach, where the alcohol enters his blood and then his heart and brain, enlarging him and bringing him to heated life, filling the stony, cold man with light and feeling and sentiment, blessing him with an exact nostalgia for the very seconds of his life as they pass, which in this man is as close to love as he has been able to come for years, maybe since childhood.

Outside, the dog scratches feebly at the door, almost apologetically, and Nelson, after first rinsing the glass and placing it back into the cabinet, finally turns and lets the cold animal in. She's abject and seems eager to stay out of the man's way, which is difficult, since both of them are large and the room is small, but when he crosses to check on the woodstove, the dog limps quickly away and stands by the sink until he returns, and then she moves back by the door, where she watches, waiting until he sets the coffeepot on the electric range and sits down at the Formica-topped table at the far wall. Finally, as Nelson unfolds yesterday's paper and begins to read, the dog circles and lies down next to the woodstove, arranging herself in an ungainly heap of legs and tail, neck, muzzle and ears, a collapsed, fawn-colored tent.

The sound an hour later of Nelson dialing the telephone wakes the dog. She lifts her heavy head and watches him at the table dial the phone on the wall beside him. The room is filled with white light now and smells of coffee and toasted bread and woodsmoke. Nelson holds the receiver loosely to his ear and lets it ring, eight, nine, ten times, until his son answers.

"H'lo?"

"Good morning."

"Oh, hi, Dad."

"Wake you up?"

"Well—yeah. It's what, eight? No. Jesus, it's not even seven-thirty. What's up?"

"You, now. Want me to call back later? You alone? You got some-body there?"

"Ha. Not very likely. Yeah, I'm alone, all right. No, no, you don't need to call back, I can talk, I'm awake. I was just up late last night, that's all," he says. Then, with great heartiness, "So—what's happening? How're you doing?"

Nelson says fine and comes right to the point of his call: "You got a cord of firewood sitting out here in my yard, Earl, and the snow's start-ing to fly already, so if you want to burn any of that stuff this winter, you better drive over here and get it out this morning."

Earl says damn, but quickly assures his father that he'll be over in a few hours. "Be good to see you, anyhow," he adds. "I haven't seen you since what, Christmas?"

"Before."

"Right, before. Well—we got to catch up."

Nelson agrees, and the men say good-bye and hang up. Then Nel-son gets stiffly up from the table and tosses a log from the woodbox into the stove, goes to the cabinet over the sink, and brings down the vodka bottle and juice glass and pours his second drink of the day. The dog watches, her yellow and brown eyes drooping from the heat. Then she closes her eyes and sleeps.

The woman in Nelson Painter's dream is sometimes his first wife, Adele, who lives out in San Diego now, alone, and sometimes she's Allie, his second wife, who lives with him in this house, where as town clerk she runs her office from the room he made out of the shed that connects the house to the barn. In the dream, it doesn't seem to matter, Adele or Allie; they behave the same way—they scream at him, a roar, high and

windy, a frightening mix of rage and revulsion that blames him for everything in general and nothing in particular. The dream always takes place
in New Hampshire, though sometimes it's set in the tenements and trailers he shared with Adele when they were young and raising their three
kids, when Nelson was an apprentice and then a journeyman carpenter,
working out of the Catamount local; and sometimes the dream is set in
this house, a renovated nineteenth-century farmhouse that he bought
when he married Allie and started making good money running work for
the state and large, out-of-state contractors building New Hampshire
dams, hospitals, and now the Seabrook nuclear power plant. Nelson is no
longer running work, of course, no longer a foreman, for it has gotten too
complicated for someone without an engineer's degree, and he can't concentrate like he used to, but even so, he is making good money, thirty-six
grand last year, more than Earl with his schoolteaching in Catamount,
more than that bastard Georgie down in Rhode Island, working for the
state as a fancy-pants counselor but never writing his own father, never
returning calls. He acts like the old man is dead, for God's sake. What's
wrong with a kid like that, a man in his thirties who won't speak to his
own father? At least Earl deals with him, more or less, though you'd have
thought, if one of the boys was going to hate the father, it would be Earl,
the elder, who was so much closer to his mom and was twelve when Nelson left them and thus probably was her confidant during those years
when she was mad at Nelson for leaving them and not sending more
money. But Georgie, he was always the easy one, the friendly one. It didn't
make sense. Any more than his dream made sense, the dream in which
Nelson strolls into the room—a kitchen, a bedroom, it's one or the other—
and the woman, Adele or Allie, looks up from her work, ironing, putting
away dishes, unpacking clothes from a trunk, and recognizing him, she
points and starts screaming at him, as if to say, "He's the one! He's the one
who killed me, murdered my baby, slew my mother, father, sister, brother!
Him! Him!"

Despite its insane fury, the dream doesn't weigh on Nelson so much as it angers him. He knows it's about guilt, not redemption, and he's said to himself at least a hundred times that of *course* he feels guilty for the way he's treated people over the years, his wives, his children, others, too, old friends who won't talk to him anymore, sisters, brothers-in-law, bosses, even strangers, guys he meets in bars after work and drinks late with and then somehow gets to arguing with, and before he knows how it happens, it has happened again, and there he is, being pulled off some guy and hustled out the door or picked up off the floor and aimed by strangers toward his car. Then he weaves across the lot to his car, gets it started, and drives slowly home, where for years Adele and now Allie wait for him, wait to shout at him, or if not to shout, then to glare and snub him and show him her back, until he gets mad all over again and wrecks the careful affection he's built up between them since the last time. Oh, sure, he knows that once every few years he loses control and hits his wife across the face or pushes her away too hard. But he isn't a *wife beater*, one of those guys who takes out his frustrations on someone who can't defend herself. No, he just loses control once in a while, once in a *great* while, dammit, when he's been hounded, nagged, criticized, picked at, until he just can't stand it anymore, so he lashes back, pushes her away, gets himself left alone, for God's sake, so he can *think*.

Around eight, Nelson takes his third drink. Then, passing from the kitchen through Allie's cluttered office, he goes into the cold, dark barn, where his ten cords of wood are stacked in neat, head-high rows along the near wall from the front to the back of the large building. When he returns, chilled, with an armload of wood, he sees his wife at the range, boiling water for tea. Her short, blue-gray hair is wet from her shower and slicked back like a boy's, and she's dressed in her usual western clothes, jeans too tight around her big hips and legs and a red-and-white-checked shirt with pearl buttons. Her clothing annoys him, though he never says so directly. "You dress like you want people to think you keep horses," Nelson has told her. With most people (though no longer with him), Allie affects a manliness that Nelson finds disturbing—a hearty, jocular way of speaking. She's a back slapper, a shoulder puncher, characteristics that, when he first took up with Allie, attracted Nelson. Long before that, he'd come to despise Adele's whine, her insecurity and depression, so that Allie's good-natured teasing, her tough talk, released him from guilt for a while, maybe a year, maybe two, until he began to see through the bravado to the strangely fragile woman inside, and when he hurt her with his hard, unexpected words and once in a while with his hands, too, he began to feel guilty again, just as with Adele. You think a woman's strong, that she can take it, so you treat her as an equal, and before you know it she can't take it, and suddenly you're forced to tiptoe around her as if a single hard step would break her into a thousand weeping pieces. More and more, Nelson believes that being alone is the only clear route to his happiness. It's coming to seem the only way to avoid hurting other people, which in his experience is what gives them power over you. Look at Georgie, his son. The boy has a power over Nelson that comes from his belief that he was hurt by Nelson over twenty years earlier, when the boy was only ten. Earl, now—he's different. Earl's made of tougher stuff. You can't really hurt him; he's like his dad that way. He won't let you close enough to hurt him, and consequently he never obtains any power over you, either. That's the kind of love Nelson both understands and respects. It's what he had with his second wife in the first year or two of their marriage and what he misses in her now.

"You're up, eh," he says to Allie's back and dumps the wood into the woodbox, startling the dog awake.

"Yep." The dog gets to her feet and crosses to Allie, shoves her head against the woman's hand until she strokes it between the long, floppy ears. "Ah, you big baby," Allie says. The dog leans her weight against Allie's thigh, and she goes on patting the tall, ungainly animal. It's

Allie's dog, not Nelson's—he insists that he doesn't like animals. He's been this way for as long as he can remember. He doesn't know why he is this way, and he doesn't care anymore, if he ever did. It's too late to care. It's how he's survived, and thus it's who he is. Let other people adjust to him—Allie, Earl, Georgie, everyone. If, like Georgie, they aren't willing to adjust, then fine, go away, leave him alone. Alone to think.

"Paper come yet?" Allie asks him.

"You feel like going out to get it, it's there." Nelson has sat back at the table and faces the woodstove, rubbing his hands before it, to get rid of the chill. He's a large, fleshy man, and he looks like a bear cleaning its paws after eating.

"You gonna get dressed?" she asks.

"Eventually. It's Sunday."

"I know. I just—"

"What?"

"Nothing." She walks to the refrigerator, pulls a tube of frozen orange juice from the freezer, and goes to the sink to prepare it.

"Earl's coming by," he says. "He can bring the paper in from the mailbox."

"Oh? He coming for the wood? It's snowing."

"That's the point. He don't get it now, it'll be there in April." Suddenly, he stands up, and the dog clatters away from the sink, and Allie looks over at him.

"What?" she says.

Nelson is looking intently out the window next to the stove, staring at the driveway and yard, where his son's wood is heaped up.

"What?" she repeats. "Who is it?"

"Leave me alone. For God's sake, leave me alone. I'm trying to think." He moves closer to the window and peers out, as if searching for someone in the snowy distance.

Allie goes back to breaking the frozen orange juice into a green plastic pitcher, and the dog sits on rickety haunches and watches Nelson at the window. "Maybe I should get dressed," he says in a low voice. "So I can help Earl crack that wood loose and load it. Stuff's frozen into the ground, most of it."

Allie says nothing.

"Maybe I'll call him again. See if he's left yet."

"It takes a half hour in good weather. He'll be an hour today," Allie says without looking at him. "You got no hurry." She speaks carefully, slowly, in a deliberately quiet voice.

Nelson dials his son's number, sits down, and lets it ring. On the fourth ring, Earl answers. "Hello?"

"Good morning," Nelson says.

"Oh, hi, Dad."

"I was just wondering . . ."

"Yeah, look, I'm sorry. I got sidetracked here, some people came by and we got talking. Listen, you gonna be there all day today? I can come by later more easily, if that's okay?"

"Well, the snow . . ."

"Yeah, I know. You're right. That is good wood. Be nice to get it home here, before it gets buried and all."

They are silent for a few seconds, then Earl says to his father, "How about I come out there next Sunday? Or maybe an afternoon this week after school. Yeah, that'd be better all around for me. Though you won't be there then—but we can get together some other time, right?"

"It don't matter much to me one way or the other how you do it—it's your wood, not mine."

"Right."

"All right, then," Nelson says in a voice that's almost a whisper.

"You okay, Dad?"

Nelson hesitates a second, ten seconds, twenty. He opens his mouth to speak.

"Dad? You okay?"

"Yeah. I'm . . . I'm fine." His thoughts are burning and whirling, as if there were a fire inside his head. "I . . . I wanted to ask you something," he says.

"Sure. What about?"

"I guess about your brother. About Georgie. You. Your mother. Your sister."

"Fine," Earl says. "Shoot."

"No. I mean, not— Well, maybe we oughta talk about this stuff over a few beers or something, you know?"

Earl says, "Hey, fine with me. Anything you say, Dad."

"Well, I was wondering, see, about Georgie. About why he's so mad with me," Nelson blurts, and the fire inside his head roars in his ears, stings his eyes, fills his nostrils and mouth with smoke and ash.

His son says, "You should be asking him that. Not me."

"Yes. Right, of course. You," he says, "you're not mad at me like that, are you? For leaving your mother and all? You know . . . you know what I mean. All that."

Earl inhales deeply, then slowly exhales. "This is weird. This is a weird conversation for us to be having, Dad. I mean, you— Look, I made my peace with all that years ago, and Georgie hasn't, that's all. From his point of view, you ruined his life or something. But that's only how he sees it."

"I didn't, though. I didn't ruin anybody's life. You can't ruin a person's life. I just left, that's all."

"Yeah. It's only a figure of speech."

"I didn't ruin anybody's life."

"Yeah."

"Not your mother's. Not Louise's. Not yours, Earl. Not Georgie's, either."

"No, Dad, not mine. You can be sure of that. Listen, I got to get off, okay? There's people here. I'll be over to dig that wood out sometime this week, some afternoon this week, okay?"

Nelson says fine, that's fine with him, but Earl will have to do it alone, because he is home only on weekends, now that winter's here. "I been staying the week down at Seabrook lately," he says.

"No kidding. Where?"

"I got a room in a motel over in Hampton. It's nice. Color TV. You know. Kitchenette."

"Nice," Earl says.

Nelson says, "I . . . I'm sorry, about that other business, Georgie and all."

"Hey, no sweat, Dad. Look, I gotta go," he says. "Talk to you later, okay?"

"Fine."

"Love to Allie," he says, and then good-bye, and the phone is dead, buzzing in Nelson's hand.

He looks up and sees that his wife is staring at him. He places the receiver on the hook and walks to the sink, pours himself another vodka, only a few ounces, half the glass, and drinks it down with a single swallow. This time he leaves the glass in the sink and the bottle on the drainboard.

"How many's that?" Allie asks in a flat, matter-of-fact voice, as if asking him the date. She sips at her tea and over the rim of her cup watches him ignore her. Then she says, "Earl's off in his own world. Don't let him bother you."

"He doesn't bother me. That damn wood bothers me. That's what bothers me."

"Earl doesn't really need it, you know. He lives in town, he just has that little bitty fireplace of his—"

"That's not the *point!*" The point, he tells himself, is that the pile of wood looks like hell out there in the yard, and under the snow it looks somehow worse, because it's no longer clearly firewood but may as well be merely trash or sand or brush or landfill, the dumb, shapeless residue of a job halted when winter came on. Abruptly, Nelson unlatches the gate, passes into the cool, dim living room, and walks upstairs to the bedroom. In a short while, he is dressed in heavy, green twill pants and wool shirt and snow boots and has returned to the kitchen, where he pulls his mackinaw on, then his black watch cap and thick work gloves.

"You getting the paper?" Allie asks from the table. The dog has settled at her feet.

"Yeah," Nelson grunts. Quickly, he walks out to the barn, where, with the door to Allie's office closed tightly behind him, he shoves open the large, sliding door at the front, flooding the darkness with sudden white light and swirls of blowing snow. For a moment he stands, hands sunk in his pockets, staring down the driveway to the road, his back to the green rear deck of his Pontiac station wagon and the gloomy darkness of the cavernous barn beyond. He moves around the car to the front door on the driver's side and opens it, reaches under the seat, and draws out a half-full pint of vodka. Unscrewing the cap, he tips the bottle up and drinks. It makes no difference—he feels no better or worse after having taken the drink. All he has done is avoid feeling as bad as he would have felt without it. When he has replaced the bottle under the car seat, he turns and bumps against the chopping block, a stump with a steel splitting wedge and single-edged ax driven into its corrugated top. He laughs at himself, and his voice sounds strange to him, an old man's voice—Ho, ho, ho!—mixed with a drunkard's voice—Har, har, har! Hesitating a second at the door, he turns back again, retrieves the bottle from under the car seat, and slides it into his mackinaw pocket. He leaves the barn and, like an Arctic explorer setting out for the North Pole, plunges into the snow.

It's deeper than he expected, eight or ten inches already and drifting, a heavy, wet snow driven by a hard northeast wind and sticking to every surface that faces it, trees, houses, barns, chimneys, and now Nelson Painter, working his way down his driveway from the huge open door of the barn, a man turning white, so that by the time he reaches the woodpile he's completely white, even his face, though he's pulled his head down into his coat as far as he can and can barely see through the waves of wind-driven snow before him.

He leans over and with one gloved hand grabs at a chunk of wood, yanks at it, but it won't come. He brushes snow away, grabs at another, but it, too, won't give. Standing, he kicks at the first log, and it breaks free of the pile and rolls over in the snow. He picks it up, lays it against his chest, and kicks at the second log. He kicks twice, three times, but it won't come loose, so he takes the first stick, and holding it by one end, whacks it against the second, until it breaks free. He's out of breath, sweating inside his coat, cursing the wood. He picks up the two sticks and goes to work on a third, which he eventually kicks loose of the pile and picks up and stacks in his arms, and then, when he kicks at a fourth piece of wood, he loses his balance, slips, and falls, and the pieces roll into the snow. Slowly, on his hands and knees, puffing laboriously now, he gathers up the three logs and stands, his left hip burning in pain where he fell against it, and starts back toward the barn.

Halfway there, retracing his nearly filled tracks, he sees on his left the door to the house push slowly open against the blowing snow, and Allie steps onto the sill and waves an arm at him, indicating that she wants him to come inside, to the kitchen. He can't make out her face, but he knows her look, he's seen it lots of times before, a mixture of anger, hurt, and concern, and he can't hear her because of the wind, and his cap pulled down over his ears, but he knows what she is shouting to him: "Come inside, for God's sake, Nelson! You're drunk! You're going to hurt yourself!" The dog appears beside her and, not recognizing Nelson, bounds outside, barking ferociously at him, leaping eagerly through the snow toward him, barking with great force at the snow-covered stranger in the yard, and when Nelson turns to avoid the animal's rush, he slips on the wet snow and falls again, dropping the wood and scattering it. Suddenly, the dog recognizes him and retreats swiftly to the kitchen. Nelson reaches into his coat pocket, pulls out the bottle, works the cap off, and takes a long drink. Recapping the bottle, he places it in his pocket and looks back toward the door, but it's closed. He's alone again. Good. Slowly, he retrieves his three sticks of wood one by one and stands and resumes his trek to the barn. It seems so far away, that dark opening in the white world, miles and years away from him, that he wonders if he will ever get there, if he will spend years, an entire lifetime, out here in the snow slogging his way toward the silent, dark, ice-cold barn, where he can set his three pieces of firewood down, lay one piece of wood on the floor snugly against the other, the start of a new row.

Quality Time

Tires crunch against the crushed stone driveway, and a flash of head-lights crosses Kent's bedroom window, waking him from a light sleep. But he wasn't asleep, he tells himself. Merely resting, eyes closed. Listening. Just as, when Rose was still in high school, he lay in bed after midnight and listened for the sound of a car—his, or the current boyfriend's, her girlfriend's father's car, sometimes even his ex-wife's car—bringing Rose home to his house, where she spent the weekend, Kent's every-other-weekend, or her spring-break week, or her two-week midsummer visit. In his house in his town, his turn to be the custodial parent.

Quality time, they called it. He would greet her at the door and make sure she wasn't drunk or high or sad, and when she was suffering from any of those conditions, he tried to treat her condition rationally, calmly, realistically. Kent was a physician, a trained scientist, as he thought of it, and also a man of the world. He knew what kids were dealing with out there. He sympathized. Even today, a decade later and more of an administrator now than a physician, Kent still sympathizes.

He hears the thump of Rose's clunky Doc Martens against the front deck, the jingle of the house key, and the slammed door. In three months Rose will be thirty, and she still slams the door when she comes in, no matter how late the hour. And Kent still checks the car for scratches and dents the morning after she borrows it. Especially this car, his brand-new Audi, silver and sleek—his sixtieth birthday present to himself. He's already reminding himself to examine the car in the morning before he leaves for the office, so he won't discover the ding in the fender or the broken taillight late in the afternoon in the clinic parking lot, which is where she'll insist it must have happened, since she has absolutely zero recollection of any fender-bender occurring on her watch. He'll accept that. He'll have to. He turns on the bedside lamp, gets out of bed, and walks to the closet. But she'll be lying. Or worse, she won't really know one way or the other how it happened, and won't care, either. He pulls his bathrobe over his pajamas and pads barefoot down the hall to the kitchen.

"Hey, babe. Nice time?" he says and plucks a bunch of purple grapes from the fruit bowl on the breakfast table. She's sprawled at the table, thoughtfully drinking milk from a half-gallon container. Kent likes this kitchen, the only truly up-to-date, architect-designed room in the house. It's an orderly arrangement of stainless steel, ceramic tile, overhead pot racks, and butcher-block islands. He had it renovated top to bottom back when he first got serious about gourmet cooking and enjoys telling people that the kitchen is state-of-the-art. The rest of the house is more or less the way it was when he bought it fifteen years ago, the year after the divorce. Since then, though he's enjoyed several long-term romances with women, good women his own age, marriageable women, he's not shared his house with anyone—except his daughter. Hasn't wanted to. A nineteen-fifties, midlevel mafia capo's suburban ranch, is how Kent likes to describe the house to strangers.

He pops the grapes one by one into his mouth. He's been unmarried now for nearly as long as he was married, and the fact freshly surprises him. He drops the grape stem into the trash compactor.

"I wish you'd use a glass," he says evenly. Julia, his ex-wife, gave her that habit—drinking orange juice, milk, whatever, straight from the carton.

"Sorry, Pops, I forgot. It's been a while," Rose says. She shrugs and smiles up at him, sheepishly, or maybe mockingly, he's not sure which. It hasn't been that long since she last visited him, has it? Barely half a year.

She stands and crosses to the glassware cabinet, where she takes out a tumbler and fills it, leaving the carton on the counter. Rose is a tall, large-boned woman with burgundy-colored, shoulder-length hair. Her skin comes from her mother—skin so smooth and strikingly pale it seems washed in a hazy blue light. When Julia was Rose's age, he remembers, she tied her hair back the same way and in summer favored sleeveless, V-neck blouses. Julia then, like her daughter now, showed as much face, throat, and arms as possible. If you've got it, she used to say, show it.

Kent doesn't know how Julia does her hair now or if her skin is still as beautiful—he hasn't seen her close-up in over seven years. He imagines that she's changed in that time as much as he and in most of the same ways. In seven years your whole body replaces itself, cell by cell.

He picks up the milk carton and returns it to the refrigerator. "So how was it tonight, with your old pals?"

"Okay," she says. "It was fun." Then, "Not, actually. Not okay. Not fun."

"Oh? Why?"

"Eddie and Jeanette and Tucker and Sandy? They're not my old pals. Not really. And they're married, they're couples, et cetera. And they're definitely on the boring side. Tep-id."

"They are?" he says in a low, sad voice. He wants to let his disappointment show without having to say it.

"Yeah. I didn't even know them, you know, till after the divorce. I mean, I knew them, we hung out a lot when we were teenagers, but it was mostly summers, Dad. A few weeks at a time."

He understands. It has to be hard for her, five hours on a Trailways bus to visit the old man every six months or so for a long weekend or maybe a week. Then being alone with him at his house (her house once, as he often points out, but, as she insists, not hers anymore), until he fears he's holding her against her will, so he starts pushing her to go out on her own, go ahead, borrow the Audi, visit some of her old pals. Most of the local people her age, because they've not left this small, upstate town for more promising climes, have married one another and have settled for much less than Rose wants for herself. She's right. They *are* boring.

Rose is an artist, a sculptor who has already had two one-person shows of her work, the first at Skidmore in Saratoga Springs, where she went to college, and the other at a small gallery in Litchfield, Connecticut, where Julia lives. Julia and her second husband, Thatcher Clarke, the executive director of the clock and watch museum there, helped arrange it. When Julia first met Thatcher, a few months before her divorce from Kent became final, he was the director of the Adirondack Arts Council and had already been hired to run the clock and watch museum down in Litchfield, one hundred twenty miles to the south. Within weeks of the divorce, Julia followed him there. Rose went with her. Because of the schools. That's when the need for quality time arrived.

Kent honestly believes that Ol' Thatch, as he calls him, is perfect for Julia, and he's been a good stepfather for Rose. He's a hale fellow well-met, in Kent's words, and a liberal New England Republican. Kent, on the other hand, is proud to be neither. He spoke with Ol' Thatch briefly at Rose's high school graduation, renewed their slight acquaintance when she graduated from Skidmore, and saw him a third time last fall at the Skidmore show.

Julia didn't attend the opening. She was at a health spa in New Mexico, Rose explained. Was she okay? Health-wise? "Oh, sure," Rose assured him. "It's about weight. As usual." Julia had mailed the spa her fif-teen-hundred-dollar deposit months earlier and didn't want to lose it, so Rose told her to go, for heaven's sake. She could see Rose's new work on her own anytime. Two months later, Rose had the show in Litchfield.

Rose kisses her father on the cheek, says good night, and saunters down the hall toward her room, flipping off lights as she goes. Her bed-room is situated on the opposite end of the house from Kent's master bedroom. It was originally meant to be guest quarters, but the first weekend Rose spent with him in his new house, when she was fifteen, Kent turned the guest bedroom, dressing room, and bath over to her. He did it casually, as if it were something that occurred to him only when it was happening, but it was long-planned and for him a memo-rable event. It was his first chance to feel like a father, a real father with a house large enough to give his teenage daughter her own bedroom suite, where she could play her music and watch TV and talk on her own phone without interfering with his music, TV, and phone. He was no longer a middle-aged single guy subletting a semifurnished garden apartment in a complex filled with young professionals. He'd hated that. He was a proper family man now. His house, his daughter's rooms, and her regular, ongoing presence at his house proved it.

He needed that visible evidence of paternity, and he believed that Rose did, too. The divorce was harder on her, he feels, than either Julia or Rose herself is willing to acknowledge—Julia because she still feels guilty for the several careless little love affairs that led up to the divorce and ostensibly caused it, and, too, because she was the one who after-wards moved away; and Rose because she doesn't want her parents to worry about her any more than they already do.

It wasn't Julia's dalliances, though, that caused the divorce, or her removal to Litchfield that heightened the pain of it for Rose. And Kent knows it. As the years pass, some things in life do get simpler, and Kent's divorce from Julia was becoming one of those things. No, it all came down to the simple fact that he grew up, and she didn't, and then wouldn't. And because she had plenty of inherited money, she's never had to. She didn't need Kent's money or proximity to raise their child, she could do it on her own, and, mostly, that's what she did. There's no way, of course, that he can tell this to Rose or Julia. Not now. They'd think he was criticizing them, and he wasn't.

Kent washes Rose's milk glass in the sink, places it into the dish rack, and switches off the overhead light. He steps into the darkened sitting porch just off the kitchen—he can't remember if he locked the door to the backyard. The flagstone floor is cold against his bare feet, when suddenly it's as if he's walking on gravel or broken peanut shells. Popcorn, maybe. Beads from a broken necklace? He gropes beside him in the dark, until his hand finds a floor lamp.

It's birdseed! A wide trail of sunflower and wildflower seeds and cracked corn spills from the pantry behind him, where he stores a hundred-pound bag of mixed birdseed in a large galvanized trash can. The trail crosses the porch to the door leading outside. Mornings over his second cup of coffee and evenings over his first Scotch and soda, Kent often sits out here on the glider and watches the birds flutter greedily over the three large bird feeders hanging from the maple tree. There are finches, both purple and gold, pine siskins and grosbeaks, cardinals and phoebes. Once he saw an indigo bunting and was so excited he shouted, "Look!" but he was alone. His shout, even through the glass, scared the bunting, and it flew away and didn't return.

He stares down at the birdseed scattered over the slate floor, and he feels his neck and ears redden. She must have refilled the feeders sometime earlier tonight, and instead of bringing the feeders into the pantry and filling them there, which is how he does it and has demonstrated for her any number of times, she carried the seeds, scoop by scoop, across the porch and out the door, spilling as she went. That's so damned typical! And, of course, since she never sees disorder anyway and didn't see the stuff scattered across the floors of the porch and pantry, she didn't think to clean it up. Never crossed her mind. He strides down the hall to Rose's end of the house, snapping on lights as he goes.

He knocks firmly on her door. Not with anger, for while he is exasperated, he's not angry. He's confused. He can admit that much. After all these years, he still doesn't understand why she can't or won't remember what he tells her to do, what he asks her to do, what he wants her to do, when she's in his house. When she's in his *life*, for heaven's sake. She acts as if, for her, his life doesn't exist, or if it exists at all, it doesn't have any meaning. He can't bear that.

She opens the door. She's wearing green-and-blue-plaid flannel pajamas and has her toothbrush and toothpaste in hand. "You haven't gone to sleep yet, have you?" he asks evenly.

"I haven't made my evening ablutions yet," she says, smiling. Then she sees his expression. "What's the matter?"

"The birdseed, Rose. You spilled it all over the porch floor."

She wrinkles her brow and stares at her father's face, not quite getting what he's after. "I did?"

"Yes."

"Sorry. I . . . I wasn't aware . . . ," she trails off. "The bird feeders were almost empty. You want me to clean it up . . . now?"

"If you don't mind."

She sighs audibly. "O-kay."

Kent turns and walks purposefully back to his side of the house, not stopping until he's inside his bedroom and has closed the door, extinguished the light, and has got himself under the covers in bed. He's breathing rapidly, as if he's just climbed three flights of stairs. His heart is pounding, and adrenaline is rushing through his body. He knows what's happening to his body, he's a doctor, after all. But *why* is it happening? Why is he fuming over such a trivial offense? Why even view it as an offense in the first place? Must he take *personally* every-thing his daughter does wrong?

In the morning, Kent leaves for the office before Rose wakes. There are no dents or scratches on his Audi. He feels guilty for last night, not because he did or said anything to hurt her, but because he *was* angry, when clearly something else was called for. He's not sure what, but he knows that anger was useless to them both. Useless and therefore offensive somehow. Around ten, he telephones the house, and she picks up. "I wondered if you'd like to meet me for lunch downtown," he says, a little shy and stiff.

"Sounds great!" She's chewing food, he can tell, and is probably still in bed in her pajamas, flopped in front of the TV, working her way through the lox and bagels he bought especially for her visit.

"Want me to come by the house and pick you up?"

"No, I'll ride the bike! It's gorgeous out, and I need the exercise. I've been a lump all week."

They agree to meet at his office at one. At a quarter to one, Kent walks out the door of the clinic, leans against the railing of the front steps, and looks along the street uphill to his right, where he knows that Rose in a few moments will come into view pedaling her old bike, the blue Raleigh three-speed that he bought for her the summer she turned fourteen. She already owned a bike, a present on her twelfth birthday from both Mom and Dad, but he bought her the Raleigh him-self so that, after the divorce, she could ride from her mother's house to his whenever she wanted. Then Julia moved. Or from his house to the office, he assured her, where they could meet for lunch on Saturdays when he had to work. She rode from his house on Ash Street to Main and then cruised ten blocks along Main to the long, curving hill that flattened and straightened where it passed in front of the clinic. He remembers October leaves skidding across the sidewalks and streets, and the sky was deep blue. He liked to wait on the steps outside, just as he is doing today, and every time he saw her pedal around that far curve with a wide, excited grin on her face and her auburn hair flying behind her in the rippling sunlight, his chest filled with joy and with an inescapable sadness, and he could barely keep his eyes from flooding with tears. He knew what gave him the joy—she did; he loved her, and the joy proved it—but he did not know what caused the sadness.

Here she comes now, a beautiful young woman in jeans and mint green sleeveless T-shirt, wearing sunglasses, and smiling broadly at the sight of her father. He stands on the clinic steps with arms folded, still a hundred yards away from her, and she lifts her right hand high in the air and waves.

He waves back, smiles, and feels his chest tighten and buckle with emotion. He has never felt as proud of Rose as he does at this moment. It's the simplicity of her beauty and her sincerity, he decides. That's what makes him proud of her. They are qualities of body and character, qualities of *self*, that for unknown reasons have been invisible to him until this moment. He doesn't ask why he never saw them before. Instead, he wonders why they should have suddenly become visible.

Because she is at hand, yet still far away, is his answer. But coming nearer by the second, and nearer, when suddenly, to avoid hitting something on the road that he can't see, a piece of broken glass, perhaps, she swerves the bike out into the middle of the street and puts herself between an oncoming UPS truck and a Volvo station wagon bearing down behind her. Kent reaches toward her with both arms, his mouth wide open as if to shout, but he can't break his silence, he can't even say her name, and she swerves a second time, this time cutting in front of the UPS truck and off Main Street onto a narrow lane on the opposite side, where she disappears.

The UPS truck passes Kent nonchalantly, as if the driver has noticed nothing out of the way, as if he's not seen anyone in danger for a very long time, and the Volvo station wagon passes in the other direction as normally as cars have passed all day, the woman driver chatting with the passenger, her husband, perhaps, or a client to whom she's about to show a house. Then, on his right and across the street, Rose emerges from behind a high hedge on the corner of Main, pedaling her blue Raleigh with ease and obvious pleasure. She's still smiling and is close enough now to call to him and be heard. "Hey, Dad! What a day, huh?"

Kent rushes across the street and grabs her bicycle by the handlebars and stops it dead. Rose's face drops and tightens. Her father is panting, red-faced, sweating.

"Jesus, Dad, what's the matter?" she asks, her voice rising in fear. "Are you okay?"

"*Why*? Why do you do this to me? To *yourself*! Why do you do it to yourself?"

Rose lets go of the handlebars. She reaches forward and places her hands on her father's shoulders, as if she is the parent and he the reckless child. "Dad," she says. "Stop."

"Why?"

Then, calmly, patiently, with a detachment that's incomprehensible to him, she explains. "I do it because what you do is violent, and it makes me violent, too. That's why." The two of them stand there with the blue bicycle between them, traffic whizzing by in the background.

"What? It's *my* fault?"

She sighs, and then she tells her father what he needs most to know, but has always seemed incapable of knowing: that his kindness and intimacy draw her close to him, but only for him to reject her—because of her sloppiness, her carelessness, her disorder. She reminds him of last night's confrontation over the spilled birdseed. She tells him that he should have let it go till morning. "I'm twenty-nine, Dad. Leave me a note. I'd have cleaned it up this morning." He spoiled their earlier moment in the kitchen, she says, which, if he had left her alone, would have helped her deal with her little failure later in a useful way. "In a way that wouldn't have scared you. You don't know, but it's what I've been doing for years," she says.

"What have you been doing for years?"

"Things that would scare you, Dad. Only this time you saw it."

Side by side, they walk along the sidewalk, uphill away from the office. Rose keeps one hand on the handlebars, steering the bike, and the other on her father's slumped shoulder. "I'm not angry at you," she says, sounding distant and almost scientific. "Not anymore." She understands his needs. Her needs, however, are different, and it's her mother, she says, who's shaped her needs. Not him.

"Your mother?"

"Dad, Mom is like my hollow double," she says. "My absent self. Not you. You're my father." All these years he's treated her as if she were like him, she explains, instead of like her mother. And consequently he's dealt with her as if she had his needs instead of her mother's. Rose smiles at him, but from a great height.

It's only a flash of awareness, as if a darkened room were lit for a second and then dropped into darkness again, but Kent sees how vain and cruel he's been. He sees that he's been a man completely opposed to the man he thought he was. And as surely as he lost her mother fifteen years earlier, he has lost Rose now, and for the same reason. He knows nothing of his daughter's needs, because he knew nothing of her mother's.

He says to Rose, as they turn off Main Street onto Ash, "Was I wrong, to divorce your mother? To leave you?"

"No," she says. "You weren't. But you shouldn't have tried to keep her through me. And me through her," she says. "Now you've lost us both."

"You'll never come to visit me again, will you?"

She shakes her head no. "I'm sorry. I think this has been the end of everything between us. But we'll see." She tells him to go on back to his office. She'll leave the bicycle in the garage and call a cab to take her to the Trailways station.

He stops, and she continues on.

The Lie

A ten-year-old boy—maybe eleven, maybe nine, but no older and certainly no younger—kills his buddy, one Alfred Coburn, while the two are enemy espionage agents engaged in a life-or-death struggle in the middle of the wide, perfectly flat, tarred roof of an American-owned hotel in Hong Kong. The young killer, whose name is Nicholas Lebrun, stabs his good buddy in the chest just below the left nipple, slicing deftly between two ribs, thence through the taut pericardium, plunging unimpeded into the left ventricle of the heart—stabs his friend with an inexpensive penknife manufactured by the Barlow Cutlery Corp., of Springfield, Massachusetts. This knife has a plastic, simulated-wood grip and a two-and-a-half-inch steel blade. Also a one-and-a-half-inch smaller, narrower blade.

Alfred, poor wide-eyed Alfred, squeaks in surprise and falls; Nicholas understands what has happened and runs home.

A distance of approximately one city block separates the Transilex parking lot that has been serving as the roof of an American-owned hotel in Hong Kong and the asbestos-shingled, wood-framed, mid-Victorian house that has been serving as the Lebrun home and hearth for over forty years—ever since Nicholas's paternal grandfather was a young, newly wedded, still childless man. Nicholas's grandfather was named Ernest, but he was called Red because of the color of his thick, short-cropped hair and mustache. A clockmaker and a good one, too, Ernest learned his trade (he would have said craft) in his hometown of Hartford, Connecticut. Later, when the time industry shifted to Waltham, Massachusetts, shortly before the outbreak of World War II, he followed it and went to work for the Waltham Watch Company. A French Protestant and native New Englander, Ernest Lebrun: thrifty, prudent, implacably stable, high-minded and honorable, incorruptible, intelligent, organized, good-humored—all resulting in his having become well-liked and financially secure well before he was forty years old. He died in a dreamless sleep shortly after World War II had finally ground to a halt and sometime during the year that commenced with his grandson Nicholas's birth and winked out with the child's first birthday, a fact surely of considerable moment for Ernest (Red): hanging on to shreds of life until after the birth of his first male grandchild, the son of an only son, assured finally and at the very end of the continuation of the name, et cetera.

It is because of the distance between the Transilex parking lot and home and because he ran all the way home that Nicholas is out of breath, panting, and red-faced when he turns into the scrubby yard and arrives safely at what appears to be and what later turns out to be heaven.

Robert Lebrun, the boy's middle-aging, auburn-haired father, a paid-in-full member of the United Association of Plumbers and Pipe-fitters (AFL-CIO), Local 143, is comfortably swinging on the porch glider, smoking an after-supper cigar in the orange evening light and from time to time reading from the tabloid newspaper spread on his lap.

Abruptly, Nicholas parks himself next to his father, upsetting with his momentum the glider's gentle vacillation, and the father asks the son, his only child, heir to his ancient name and lands, Why is he running? The lad tells his father why he is running. Not, of course, without considerable encouragement from the father—whose cigar goes slowly out during the telling.

Young Nicholas does not forget to mention the fact that just as he steps off the flat, square expanse of tar that has been serving as the Transilex parking lot—now almost innocent of parked automobiles—and onto the narrow sidewalk of Brown Steet, he happens to glance back at his little friend's fallen body, that small heap of summer clothing and inert flesh already used up and thrown out, dropped in the middle of the great black square. A crumpled pile of stuff lying next to the front tire of a bottle green British Ford sedan. And in that fraction of a second, Nicholas realizes that the owner of the bottle green sedan—a man who lives in the neighborhood and who unfortunately is notoriously effeminate, a practicing pederast, in fact, mocked to his face by all the neighborhood kids and behind his back by the parents—is strolling blithely across the lot, is approaching his car from the side opposite Nicholas and the car's right front tire.

It's possible that the man, whose name is Toni Scott, catches a glimpse of Nicholas in flight, but that possibility shall have to remain equivocal. The facts which follow shall demonstrate why this is so.

Toni, who has worked as a waiter in an attractively decorated Boston cocktail lounge of socially ambiguous, though not inconsiderable fame for several years now, has been saving at least five dollars a month by parking his car illegally in the Transilex parking lot, always taking care to remove his car well before the 9:00 P.M. departure of the Transilex cafeteria second shift and—because of his nighttime working hours—usually managing to slip the innocuous little sedan back into the lot sometime between the 4:00 A.M. unlocking and 5:00 A.M. arrival of the cafeteria first shift. However, this particular summer evening ritual removal of his car from its stolen space definitely, even though only partially and from afar, is observed over young Nicholas Lebrun's fleeing shoulder (fateful, damning, backward glance!) just before the rigorously bathed, meticulously groomed, idly smiling Toni Scott, filled to the eyes with sweet memories and still sweeter anticipation, discovers Alfred Coburn's hard, sun-haired body by accidentally smashing its rib cage, sternum, and spine with the right front tire of his bottle green car.

He cuts the wheel hard to the left, revs up the tiny four-cylinder motor, and spins the car backwards, swinging the front of the car around in an arc to the right—so that he can make his exit from the lot by the very gate Nicholas has used just seconds earlier.

It is at this point in the boy's narrative that Robert Lebrun interrupts his son and compels him to insist that no one saw him stab his playmate. He makes the boy reassure him that he (Nicholas) did not extract the penknife from Alfred's chest—an unnecessary reassurance, for Toni's right front tire has already torn the knife from its nest of flesh, bone, and blood, has ground it against pavement, paint, white pebbles in the tar, has smashed the plastic simulated-wood grip and removed all fingerprints. Then Lebrun makes Nicholas repeat several times the part of his narrative that has to do with Toni Scott's arrival on the scene, and finally, after telling his son in clear, exact, and step-by-step terms just what he intends to do, Lebrun stomps into the house and, yelling *Emergency, Police!* to the telephone operator, he calls the cops.

Speaking rapidly, he whispers practically that he is Robert Lebrun of number forty-eight Brown Street and his son and another neighborhood kid have just been sexually molested by the neighborhood fag and his son broke away from the guy but the other kid is still with the sonofabitch in his car, which is parked in the Transilex parking lot, the one that used to be the old Waltham Watch factory lot, and he (Lebrun) is leaving right now to kill that filthy sonofabitch with his bare hands so if they want Toni Scott alive they have about three minutes to get to him. He makes one other call—to Alfred Coburn, Senior, over on Ash Street, some three blocks farther from the parking lot than is the Lebrun house—and using that same rapid, whispery voice, he tells Alfred Coburn, Senior, what he has just related to the cops.

Then Lebrun lunges for the parking lot, while Toni Scott, who dials the police department from the public phone booth that stands luminous in a dark corner of the lot, hears through the glass walls the rising shrieks of approaching sirens before he has even completed dialing the number.

In this story everyone who lies and knows that he lies does so effectively. That is, he is believed. Furthermore, everyone who lies and yet knows not that he lies—meaning, for example, Evelyn Lebrun (Nicholas's adoring mother) and poor Alfred Coburn, Senior, and the two or three neighborhood ladies who claim they saw Toni Scott talking to the boys from inside his green foreign car, heard the awful thing call the tykes from their play, saw him smilingly offer them candy if they would get into his car—these people also manage to lie effectively: they are believed by the police, the rest of the people in the neighborhood, the newspapers, the district attorney, the psychiatrists testifying for the prosecution, the psychiatrists testifying for the defense, the defense attorney himself (although he pretends not to believe), the judge, the jury, and the U.S. Court of Appeals.

Everyone who tells the truth—meaning Toni Scott, the thirty-eight-year-old, fatting, balding homosexual—tells the truth stupidly, inconsistently, alternately forgetting and remembering critical details, lying about other unrelated matters, and so on into the night. Toni Scott is not believed, although now and then he is pitied. . . .

*   *   *

Thus the compassionately prompt arrival of the police at the scene of
Alfred Coburn's beastly murder—slain savagely by a scorned and therefore enraged deviate—plucks Toni Scott from the huge pipe fitter's
hands of Robert Lebrun, only to set him down again one year later in
Walpole State Prison (life plus ninety-nine years).

It may have been noticed that the original lie originated with Nicholas's
dad. It was not mentioned, however, that once the lie had been designed
and manufactured, once it had been released to the interested public,
Robert Lebrun began to have certain secret misgivings about the way
the lie was being used. The cause of these hesitant, shadowy misgivings
was not, as one might suppose, the cruel fate of Toni Scott. Rather, it was
the consummate skill, the unquestioning grace of movement from bla-
tant truth to absolute falsehood that consistently, repeatedly, and under
the most trying of circumstances was demonstrated by Robert Lebrun's
only begotten son, the young Nicholas Lebrun. It was almost as if for
Nicholas there was no difference between what actually happened and
what was said to have happened.

"What happened, Nickie?" his father asks. "Why the hell you running in this heat? You never run like that when you're called, only
when you're being chased."

"Nobody's chasing me," the kid answers. "But something really
awful happened."

"What?"

"I don't know actually. Me and Al was just playing around, see, and
he got cut with a knife, only I didn't mean it, it was an accident, honest.
You gotta believe me, Pa." The boy uses the same name for his father
that Robert Lebrun was taught to use for his.

This is the point at which Lebrun begins shuffling fearfully
through his memories and imagination for an alibi. The fear of retribu-

tion, which he now believes to be dominating his son's entire consciousness (even to the boy's physical perceptions—of the scaly white glider, the splintery porch floor catching against the corrugated bottoms of his U.S. Keds, the cooling air laden with the smell of freshly cut grass, the cold zinc smell of his father's dead cigar, the sounds of his mother's sleek hands washing dishes in warm soapy water), this fear is in reality now the father's very own.

The father attributes to his son the overwhelming quality of fear that he knows would have to be his were he ten or nine or eleven years old and faced with "something really awful," "an accident," a wounding that occurs without warning, absolute and in its own terms as well. Right in the middle of a game.

The father's now: the force behind the knife as it buries a two-and-a-half-inch steel blade in the playmate's bony chest; then comes the realization that the boy is dead absolutely and forever, no joke, no pretense, no foolish vain imitation of the absence of existence; his now: the flight from the body's silent accusation, away from this gusty hotel rooftop deserted and stark in the midst of ragged, teeming, Oriental architecture; and his: the image seen through tinted, wraparound glass of the figure of Toni Scott strolling across the lot toward his green sedan.

And thus Robert Lebrun lies, not to save his son, but to save himself. His own father, Ernest (Red) Lebrun, would have found the dynamic reversed from the beginning of the lie to the end, and, no doubt, Robert at some point along the progression was aware of this, knew that his own father, were *he* placed in a similar circumstance, would not have been able to credit *his* son with possessing an overpowering fear of retribution, and thus the child's experience would have remained intact, still his very own, unmolested by the rush of the father's consciousness of himself. And, no doubt, this awareness of how Ernest Lebrun would have responded to a similar set of circumstances, circumstances in which he, Robert Lebrun, would have been the lonely, unmolested son, was a critical factor in making it impossible even now for Robert to become anything other than that lonely, unmolested son. The redheaded Ernest gave to his young son an absolute truth and an absolute falsity, and for that reason Robert was forever a child. Robert to his son gave relative truth and relative falsity, and for that reason Nicholas was never a child.

The question of responsibility, then, seems not to have been raised in at least three generations.

Indisposed

Lie in bed. Just lie there. Don't move, stare at the ceiling, and don't blink. Keep your fingers from twitching. Let your weight press into the mattress. Take shallow, slow breaths, so that the covers neither rise nor fall. Feel the heavy, inert length of your body. The whole of it, from your head to your feet, like the trunk of a fallen tree moldering and sinking slowly into the damp, soft ground of the forest.

For that is how he likes you best—your husband, William. You are Jane Hogarth, wife to the painter, keeper of his house and bed. He sees you as a great, tall tree that he is too short to climb, except when you are prone, cut down by the ax of his temper or drawn down by his words, his incessant words, and the needs that drive them.

It's now midmorning. You are indisposed and have remained here in bed, as if it were a choice, a decision not to rise at dawn, empty the pots, wash and dress, brush out your hair, descend the stairs to the kitchen, build the fire and start preparing the day's food, send Ellen to the market, organize the wash, beat the carpets, sweep and wash the floors, the two of you—the big, slow-moving, careful woman and her helper, that skinny, nervous, rabbitlike girl, Ellen.

You're a poor combination, you and that girl. Together you seem to break more crockery, waste more time, do more work than either of you would do alone. You follow each other around as if setting right what the other must have done wrong. You never should have agreed to take her in, but she is your cousin, a Thornhill, and her family could not hold her at home in the country any longer. It was the only way to keep the girl from becoming a harlot. William insisted on it. Absolutely insisted.

Of course, he insisted, you reflect. They're just alike, he and that tiny, quick girl. They probably have the same appetites. If he did not have this house and you to run it, to keep it clean and comfortable and filled with food and drink for him and his friends, he would have long ago died a rake's miserable death. And he knows it. He saw that girl and recognized the temperament and he knew the way she would go, if you did not take her in. He sat there in his short-legged chair in the corner, the only chair in the house that lets his feet rest flatly on the floor, and his eyes and hands and mouth would not stop moving until you relented.

We can't set her onto the streets, and your uncle won't let her return home, and her mind seems set on the city life, and on and on he chattered, while his hands moved jerkily across the paper on his lapboard, and his eyes jumped like blue fleas, and the girl wrung her hands and spun around, dropping her bonnet, stooping to retrieve it, knocking over the water pitcher and basin on the table next to her, all the while apologizing and blathering as much family gossip into your face as she could think of, probably making most of it up, just to keep on reminding you that you, too, are a Thornhill and that she is the daughter of your famous father's country brother.

Maybe my father—, you tried to say, but he wouldn't let you finish. *No, no, no, no, no!* he said, his eyes still hopping over the girl, leaping from her clear face to her fresh young bosom to her slender hips and back again, as she spun and wrung and bumped into things. *No, your father's house is already too crowded. All those apprentices, maids, children, patrons, hangers-on. And how many cousins already in from the country? Even he himself, your father, couldn't say. No, our house is quite large enough, she should stay here with us. After all, there's only the two of us. And you need a helper,* he said, suddenly turning his gaze on you, as if you had just entered the room.

His eyes filled wetly with sympathy for you. You nodded your head slowly up and down, and his eyes went swiftly back to the girl, his hands to the drawing on his lap. Then, the matter settled and the drawing finished, he stopped, folded the sheet of paper in half, stood up, and went out the door to the street, calling over his shoulder as he rounded the corner that he wouldn't be back till later this evening.

Which you knew. No reason for him to say even that much anymore. He'll come home sometime after midnight, smelling of wine and beef fat and whores, humming downstairs in the kitchen while he rummages for a piece of cake or slice of cold meat. Then he'll bump his way up the stairs, and he'll be on you, climbing up and over you with his nervous, little body, already stiff and pressing against you with it, prodding, poking, groping, his hands yanking at your breasts, his wet mouth jammed against your dry throat, until finally, to stop him from jabbing himself against you, you spread your large thighs and let him enter you, and for a few moments, as if searching for your womb, he leaps around inside you.

Then, at last, he sighs and releases his grip on your breasts and slides out of you and off. You hear him standing in the darkness buttoning himself up. He wobbles unsteadily from the room and down the hallway to his own room. A few minutes pass in silence, and he begins to snore. And you lie in your bed and stare blankly into the sea of darkness that surrounds you.

Now, this morning, when Ellen comes to your door and asks what should she do today, you say that you are indisposed, meaning that you cannot come down today—as if it were a choice, a decision. You almost remind the rabbitlike girl that after three months in the house she should know what to do. You remember that you yourself knew after three months what was expected. And you had no patient, calm, competent, older woman to teach you the intricacies of housekeeping. Ellen walks off with her chamber pot in hand, and you lie there in your bed, preferring to have the girl think you have decided to stay in bed today, like a lady of leisure, than that she know the truth.

The truth is that you have made no decision at all. Not to rise, and not to stay abed. When you woke at dawn, it was as if you had not wakened at all. You had merely slipped from sleep into a world where neither sleep nor wakefulness existed, where you could neither act nor not act. And so you lie here, hoping that by imitating a corpse you will at least seem to be in the same world as the people around you. They will think you are present, even if only as a corpse.

But you are not present. You are absent, gone from this house, its clutter of beds, pots, chairs, tables, bottles, linens, carpets, dogs, and clothes, and gone from the people who live here, that taut, young woman downstairs in the kitchen and the man who went out to his studio early this morning, as always, that man, that chattering, growling, barking, little man, his bristling red hair and bright little eyes, his jerky hands and his sudden switches of mood, words, movement, direction. You are absent from them both. Gone. Your large, strong, smooth-moving body. Your barren body.

And so, helpless, you lie in bed. You can't move. You stare at the ceiling, and you cannot blink your eyes, even as the shadows fade and the afternoon light scours the plaster to a white glare. You feel your weight press steadily into the mattress. You take shallow, slow breaths, and the covers neither rise nor fall. You feel the heavy, inert length of your long body, from the crown of your head to the soles of your feet, as if it were the trunk of a fallen tree moldering and sinking slowly into the damp, soft ground of the forest.

Suddenly, he is in the room, standing next to the bed. Your husband, William Hogarth, the famous painter and engraver. You stare at the ceiling, but you know he is standing there beside you. You can hear his quick, gulping breaths, can smell his sweat and his mouth, the kidney pie and ale he had for lunch. He is asking questions, making demands for answers. His voice barks at you. Leaning over you, blocking your view of the ceiling, he peers into your eyes, and his expression changes from that of an annoyed man to that of a wondering man. But he is not happy when he is a wondering man, and his expression swiftly changes back to one of annoyance.

It occurs to you that he will beat you again, will double those hard, small fists of his and throw them at you, as if you were in a pit and he were stoning you from above. You are not afraid. Not now. Not anymore. You are absent now, and though he may bury you in this pit with his stony fists, he will bury only your barren body, as if he were pummeling a pile of some poor woman's old clothes.

As suddenly as he came, he is gone. You are alone again. The shadows on the ceiling, long gray wedges, have returned. Falling—, you are falling and flying away at the same time, from this thick body, from the bed, its four carved posts, from the room itself, the clutter, the babble of furniture, crockery, clothes, and carpets, away from the house and the crowd standing wide-eyed on the narrow street in front, gaping skyward as you fly and fall away from them. It's what he would want. You are pleasing him at last. You have left behind what he wants—your large, slow body, your silence, and your acceptance of his blows, his words, his pushing, stiff little body, his seed. You are pleasing him at last.

You watch him return to the house with the doctor in tow. They are both out of breath and red-faced as they come through the door and enter the bedroom. It is dusk. The doctor asks for light, and, in a few seconds, Ellen appears next to them with a lit candle. The doctor, a short man, almost as short as your husband, but older, rounder, dirtier, takes the candle from the girl and holds it near your face. You watch them all—the somber, wheezing doctor with the stained fingers, the fair-haired, pink-faced girl, her new breasts popping above her bodice like fresh pears, and your husband, bobbing nervously behind, talking, talking, making suggestions, asking quick questions, recalling similar cases. From time to time, he looks at the girl's breasts and goes silent.

You watch them all, including the one they are examining, the body on the bed. It is the largest body in the room, the strongest, the only healthy body in the room. The doctor's lungs are bad, his face is red and blotched with purple islands and broken veins, and his hands are stunted and bent from arthritis. The girl, though young, is nervous and cannot eat without suffering great stomach pain. Her blond hair has started to fall out in thatches when she brushes it in the morning. And your husband, when he rises, coughs bits of blood, suffers from excruciating headaches, and has had three attacks of gout in this one year. Your body, though, lying there below you, is an athlete's, unblem-ished, bulky, powerful, and smooth. That's what they're trying to save, that's what they believe they can save—your big, healthy body. They need it, but it lies on its back, like a wagon without wheels. They are all annoyed. Why won't it work? they ask each other. What's wrong with this big, strong, in all observable ways healthy body?

The doctor asks the girl what were the exact words your body uttered this morning when she came to the room to check on it, to see why it was not performing its usual tasks.

Indisposed. It said it was indisposed, the girl tells the man. *Nothing more, sir. No complaints or anything.* The girl's hands are in fists jammed against her hips.

The doctor takes a small vial from his case and with one hook-like hand prods open the mouth of your body. With the other he empties the vial into it. Then he closes the mouth, massages the muscular throat, forcing the body to swallow. It swallows the thick, salty fluid, and the doctor releases the throat, content.

He wipes the mouth of the gray vial with his fingers and places it neatly into his case. *I've given it a purgative,* he says to your husband. *By morning, it should be back to normal again. You can do without it till then, can't you?* the physician asks him, winking.

Your husband grins and looks at Ellen's breasts. *Of course!* he says, and invites the doctor downstairs for a drink and something to eat. The girl Ellen runs ahead to prepare the table for the men.

Now your body lies alone in the darkening chamber. You watch it from above, from a place touching the ceiling. The body hears the doctor laugh, a rumble of voices, chairs against the floor. Then the sound of the doctor's hearty departure. Laughter of your husband and Ellen. A door between rooms somewhere downstairs opens and clicks closed. Carriages pass in the streets, a pair of harlots argues with a vendor. Someone calls to a departing friend.

The body shudders slowly. A bubble grows inside the belly and then bursts. The body shudders again, this time more violently. It is the gray purgative working. Then the body erupts with rumbling noises from its several orifices, and its surface ripples with muscular contractions. It is wet with sweat, yet goes on shivering as if chilled. The body continues barking and erupting with noise, sounds of air under pressure being suddenly released. The sheet is wet, at first with sweat, soaked, but with urine now as well. Then a watery stool trickles from between the buttocks and spreads, foul-smelling, beneath the thighs.

The body hears the call of your husband downstairs as he opens the door to the street and informs the girl Ellen that he won't be home till later. Then the sounds of evening drift up the stairs and seep under the closed door of the bedroom—the creak of the pump, dishes being washed, the sound of cupboard doors being opened and closed, and, after a while, the clicking steps of Ellen past your closed door and up the stairs beyond to her tiny room in the attic. Then—except for an occasional passing carriage, a cry from the street, a barking dog—silence.

The body lies motionless in its waters and extrusions, quiet now, the heart beating slowly, regularly, peacefully, the bladder, the kidneys, and intestines emptied and at rest, the lungs expanding and contracting with perfect symmetry and ease. For the first time that you can remember, you look down at your large, slow body, and you pity it. For the first time, you pity your body. Until this moment, you have felt either indifference or dislike, annoyance. For it has made you the plain daughter of a famous and demanding father, the one passed over in favor of your smaller, prettier sisters when the young artists and budding courtiers came to call at the home and studio of the grand and official court painter, the newly knighted Sir James Thornhill. It was the body presented at last to that persistent, abrasive one, the tiny man with the grandiose ambitions, given over to him almost as a joke, as a way of getting him to go away and cease his incessant talking. Hogarth wants a Thornhill, eh? Well, let him have Jane, let him have the body we call Jane, the cumbersome one, the one that's larger than most men. Let him wake every morning and be reminded of his smallness. Ho, ho, she may turn out to be barren. A good joke on a desperate man, and a solution to the problem posed by a daughter too large and too plain to marry off easily.

You did not pity it then, you were angry with it, annoyed that it should get caught so helplessly in other people's designs for themselves. But you pity it now, tonight, as it lies there below you like a great and dignified beast trapped in quicksand, resigned, yet with all its systems functioning efficiently in the darkness, as close to a state of rest as a living organism can come without descending into death. Stasis. You pity it for its very presence in the world, its large and pathetic demands on space, the way it tries and constantly fails to avoid being seen. And the way it has at last given up that attempt, has at last agreed to be seen, to be wholly present. You pity it, and finally you understand it. You understand the body of Jane Hogarth.

From below comes the abrupt noise of your husband returning from the company he keeps, drunkenly bumping furniture and walls as he makes his way in darkness up the narrow stairs. He stops outside your room, where your body lies in its cold juices. He pauses for a second, then moves down the hallway. At the attic stairs he stops again. Slowly he ascends to the attic. His feet scuffle overhead, like rats.

Your body stirs, then rises, and plucks itself gracefully from the sopped and stinking bed. At the sideboard there is a china pitcher of water and a basin. With a wet cloth and soap, your body slowly washes itself. Delicately, lovingly, the hands move over the shoulders, breasts, and belly, across the buttocks and thighs. Even the feet are washed and carefully dried. Then it slips a clean, white, linen gown on, and, relighting the candle left by Ellen on the sideboard, your body takes its leave of the room, as if the body were a queen leaving her private chambers for court. The body turns left at the door and stops at the bottom of the attic stairs, turns left and mounts the stairs to the attic.

There they are, the man atop the girl in her narrow bed in the corner. They are twined together in a tangle of limbs, blotches of hair, bedclothes in a snarl. You watch as your hands place the candle on a stool by the door and reach across to the man, who, suddenly aware of the presence of your body in the low room, filling it with bulk and swiftness, turns from the girl's shut face and faces yours, as your huge hands grab his shoulders as if they were chunks of mutton and yank him away from the girl's clinging legs. The little man is hefted into the air, and the girl screams. He groans helplessly and is pitched across the room against the wall. Your left hand grabs his throat, lifts him to a standing position, and your right hand, balled into a fist, crashes into his face. Your hand releases his throat and lets his body collapse on the floor, a marionette with its strings cut, where he moans and spits in pain and fear. When your gaze turns back to the girl, the man scuttles for the door and clatters down the stairs to the hallway below, and, while the girl pleads for her life, he flees through the darkened house for the street, howling through his broken mouth like a dog kicked by a horse. Your right hand slaps the girl powerfully across the side of her small head, then in one continuous motion sweeps through the air to her wicker satchel next to the bed, draws it up and hurls it at her. Her wardrobe is wrenched open and its contents spilled onto the floor, then thrown at the sobbing girl on the bed.

Calmly, with dignity, your tall, broad, powerful body turns and leaves the room, descends the stairs, and somberly returns to your bedroom. A new candle is lit, and the bedding is removed and swiftly replaced with clean linen. Then the body slides into the cool, broad bed, covers itself against the chill of the late summer night, and soon falls into an even sleep.

The morning will come, and though many things will still be the same, some things will be different. The girl, Ellen, will be gone, on the streets of the city or else returned to her father's home in the country. Your husband, his mouth tender for weeks, will be silent, but brooding and filled with the resentment that feeds on fear. He will go on behaving just as before, and in time he will forget this night's fury and your immense power, and his fear will abate, and drunkenly one night he will climb onto your prone body to take his pleasure from it. People will still smile when they see you in the company of your diminutive husband, and it will irritate him, as always, and he will hurriedly walk several paces in front of you. You will remain childless.

But never again, for as long as you live, will you be indisposed. You will live in your body as if it were the perfect mate, the adoring father, the admiring handmaiden, and the devoted child of your devotions. You will live in your body as if it were your own.

The Child Screams and Looks Back at You

When your child shows the first signs of illness—fever, lassitude, aching joints and muscles—you fear that he is dying. You may not admit it to anyone, but the sight of your child lying flushed and feverish in bed becomes for an instant the sight of your child in his coffin. The nature of reality shifts, and it's suddenly not clear to you whether you are beginning to dream or are waking from a dream, for you watch the child's breath stutter and stop, you cry out and then struggle to blow life back into the tiny, inert body lying below you. Or you see the child heave himself into convulsions, thrash wildly in the bed and utter hoarse, incoherent noises, as if he were possessed by a demon, and horrified, helpless, you back to the door, hands to mouth, crying, "Stop, stop, please, oh, God, please stop!" Or, suddenly, the bed is sopped with blood pouring from the child's body, blood seeping into the mattress, over the sheets through the child's tangled pajamas, and the child whitens, stares up pitifully and without understanding, for there is no wound to blame, there is only this blood emptying out of his body, and you cannot stanch its flow, but must stand there and watch your child's miraculous, mysterious life disappear before you. For that is the key that unlocks these awful visions—your child's being simply alive is both miracle and mystery, and therefore it seems both natural and understandable that he should be dead.

Marcelle called her boys from the kitchen to hurry and get dressed for school. One of these mornings she was not going to keep after them like this, and they would all be late for school, and she would not write a note to the teacher to explain anything, she didn't give a damn if the teacher kept them after school, because it would teach them a lesson once and for all, and that lesson was when she woke them in the morning they had to hurry and get dressed and make their beds and get the hell out to the kitchen and eat their breakfasts and brush their teeth and get the hell out the door to school so she could get dressed and eat her breakfast and go to work. There were four of them, the four sons of Marcelle and Richard Chagnon. Joel was the oldest at twelve, and after him, separated by little more than nine months, came Raymond, Maurice, and Charles. The father had moved out, had been thrown out of the apartment by Marcelle's younger brother, Steve, and one of Steve's friends nearly nine years ago, when the youngest, Charles, was still an infant, and though for several years Richard tried to convince Marcelle that she should let him move back in with them and let him be her husband and the father of his four sons again, she had never allowed it, for his way of being a husband and father was to get drunk and beat her and the older boys and then to wake ashamed and beg their forgiveness. For years she had forgiven him, because to her when you forgive someone you make it possible for that person to change, and the boys also forgave him—they were, after all, her sons, too, and she had taught them, in their dealings with each other, to forgive. If you don't forgive someone who has hurt you, he can't change into a new person, she told them. He is stuck in his life with you at the point where he hurt you. But her husband and their father, Richard, after five years of it, had come to seem incapable of using their forgiveness in any way that

allowed him to stop hurting them, so finally one night she sent her oldest boy, Joel, down the dark stairs to the street, down the street to the
tenements where her brother, Steve, lived with his girlfriend, and Joel
found Steve sitting at the kitchen table drinking beer with a friend and
said to him, "Come and keep my daddy from hitting my mommy!" That
night marked the end of Marcelle's period of forgiveness, for she had
permitted outsiders, her brother and his friend, to see how badly her
husband, Richard, behaved. By that act she had ceased to protect her
husband, and you cannot forgive someone you will not protect.
Richard never perceived and understood that shift. If you don't know
what you've got when you've got it, you won't know what you've lost
when you've lost it. Marcelle was Catholic, and even though she was
not a diligent Catholic, she was a loyal one, and she never remarried,
which is not to say that over the years she did not now and again fall in
love, once even with a married man, only briefly, however, until she
became strong enough to reveal her affair to Father Brautigan, after
which she broke off with the man, to the relief of her sons, for they had
not liked the way he came sneaking around at odd hours to see their
mother and talked with her in hushed tones in the kitchen until very
late, when the lights went off, and an hour or two later he left. When in
the morning the children got up and came out to the kitchen for breakfast, they talked in low voices, as if the married man were still in the
apartment and asleep in their mother's bed, and she had deep circles
under her eyes and stirred her coffee slowly and looked out the window and now and then quietly reminded them to hurry or they'd be
late for school. They were more comfortable when she was hollering at
them, standing at the door to their bedroom, her hands on her hips, her
dressing gown flapping open as she whirled and stomped back to the
kitchen, embarrassing her slightly, for beneath her dressing gown she
wore men's long underwear, so that, by the time they got out to the
kitchen themselves, her dressing gown had been pulled back tightly

around her and tied at the waist, and all they could see of the long underwear beneath it was the top button at her throat, which she tried to cover casually with one hand while she set their breakfasts before them with the other. On this morning, however, only three of her sons appeared at the table, dressed for school, slumping grumpily into their chairs, for it was a gray, wintry day in early December, barely light outside. The oldest, Joel, had not come out with them, and she lost her temper, slammed three plates of scrambled eggs and toast down in front of the others, and fairly jogged back to the bedroom, stalked to the narrow bed by the wall where the boy slept, and yanked the covers away, to expose the boy, curled up on his side, eyes wide open, his face flushed and sweating, his hands clasped together as if in prayer. Horrified, she looked down at the gangly boy, and she saw him dead and quickly lay the covers back over him, gently straightening the blanket and top sheet. Then, slowly, she sat down on the edge of the bed and stroked his hot forehead, brushing his blond hair back, feeling beneath his jawbone as if for a pulse, touching his cheeks with the smooth backside of her cool hand. "Tell me how you feel, honey," she said to the boy. He didn't answer her. His tongue came out and touched his dry lips and went quickly back inside his mouth. "Don't worry, honey," she said, and she got up from the bed. "It's probably the flu, that's all. I'll take your temperature and maybe call Doctor Wickshaw, and he'll tell me what to do. If you're too sick, I'll stay home from the tannery today. All right?" she asked and took a tentative step away from the bed. "Okay," the boy said weakly. The room was dark and cluttered with clothing and toys, model airplanes and boats, weapons, costumes, tools, hockey equipment, portable radios, photographs of athletes and singers, like the prop room of a small theater group. As she left the room, Marcelle stopped in the doorway and looked back. Huddled in his bed, the boy looked like one of the props, a ventriloquist's dummy or a heap of clothes that, in this shadowy half-light, only resembled a human child for a second or two; then, looked at from a second angle, came clearly to be no more than an impatiently discarded costume.

Most people, when they call in a physician, deal with him as they would a priest. They say that what they want is a medical opinion, a professional medical man's professional opinion, when what they really want is his blessing. Information is useful only insofar as it provides peace of mind, release from the horrifying visions of dead children, an end to this dream. Most physicians, like most priests, recognize the need and attempt to satisfy it. This story takes place in the early 1960s, in a small mill town in central New Hampshire, and it was especially true then and there that the physician responded before all other needs to the patient's need for peace of mind, and only when that need had been met would he respond to the patient's need for bodily health. In addition, because he usually knew all the members of the family and frequently treated them for injuries and diseases, he tended to regard an injured or ill person as part of an injured or ill family. Thus it gradually became the physician's practice to minimize the danger or seriousness of a particular injury or illness, so that a broken bone was often called a probable sprain, until X rays proved otherwise, and a concussion was called, with a laugh, a bump on the head, until the symptoms—dizziness, nausea, sleepiness—persisted, and the bump on the head became a possible mild concussion, which eventually may have to be upgraded all the way to fractured skull. It was the same with diseases. A virus, the flu that's going around, a low-grade intestinal infection, and so on, often came to be identified a week or two later as strep throat, bronchial pneumonia, dysentery, without necessarily stopping there. There was an obvious, if limited, use for this practice, because it soothed and calmed both the patient and the family members, which made it easier for the physician to make an accurate diagnosis and to secure the aid of the family members in providing treatment. It was worse than useless, however, when an over-optimistic diagnosis of a disease or injury led to the patient's sudden, crazed descent into sickness, pain, paralysis, and death.

Doctor Wickshaw, a man in his middle forties, portly but in good physical condition, with horn-rimmed glasses and a Vandyke beard, told Marcelle that her son Joel probably had the flu, it was going around, half the school was out with it. "Keep him in bed a few days, and give him lots of liquids," he instructed her after examining the boy. He made house calls, if the cry for help came during morning hours or if it was truly an emergency. Afternoons he was at his office, and evenings he made rounds at the Concord Hospital, twenty-five miles away. Marcelle asked what she should do about the fever, one hundred four degrees, and he told her to give the boy three aspirins now and two more every three or four hours. She saw the man to the door, and as he passed her in the narrow hallway he placed one hand on her rump, and he said to the tall, broad-shouldered woman, "How are things with you, Marcelle? I saw you walking home from the tannery the other day, and I said to myself, 'Now that's a woman who shouldn't be alone in the world.'" He smiled into her bladelike face, the face of a large, powerful bird, and showed her his excellent teeth. His hand was still pressed against her rump, and they stood face-to-face, for she was as tall as he. She was not alone in the world, she reminded him, mentioning her four sons. The doctor's hand slipped to her thigh. She did not move. "But you get lonely," he told her. She had gray eyes, and her face was filled with fatigue, tiny lines that crossed her smooth, pale skin like the cracks in a ceramic jar that had broken long ago and had been glued back together again, as good as new, they say, and even stronger than before, but nevertheless fragile-looking now, and brittle, more likely to break a second time, than when it had not been broken at all. "Yes," she said, "I get lonely," and with both hands, she reached up to her temples and pushed her hair back, and holding on to the sides of her own head she leaned it forward and kissed the man for several seconds, pushing at him with her mouth, until he pulled away, red-faced, his hand at his side now, and moved self-consciously sideways toward the door. "I'll come by tomorrow," he said in a low voice. "To see how Joel's doing." She smiled slightly and nodded. "If he's better," she said, "I'll be at work. But the door is always open." From the doorway, he asked if she came home for lunch. "Yes," she said, "when one of the boys is home sick, I do. Otherwise, no." He said that he might be here then, and she said, "Fine," and reached forward and closed the door on him.

Sometimes you dream that you are walking across a meadow beneath sunshine and a cloudless blue sky, hand in hand with your favorite child, and soon you notice that the meadow is sloping uphill slightly, and walking becomes somewhat more difficult, although it remains a pleasure, for you are with your favorite child, and he is beautiful and happy and confident that you will let nothing terrible happen to him. You cross the crest, a rounded, meandering ridge, and start downhill, walking faster and more easily. The sun is shining, and there are wildflowers all around you, and the grass is golden and drifting in long waves in the breeze. Soon you find that the hill is steeper than before, the slope is falling away beneath your feet, as if the earth were curving in on itself, so you dig in your heels and try to slow your descent. Your child looks up at you, and there is fear in his eyes, as he realizes he is falling away from you. "My hand!" you cry. "Hold tightly to my hand!" And you grasp the hand of the child, who has started to fly away from you, as if over the edge of a crevice, while you dig your heels deeper into the ground and grab with your free hand at the long grasses behind you. The child screams and looks back at you with a pitiful gaze, and suddenly he grows so heavy that his weight is pulling you free of the ground also. You feel your feet leave the ground, and your body falls forward and down, behind your child's body, even though with one hand you still cling to the grasses. You weep, and you let go of your child's hand. The child flies away.

That night the boy's fever went higher. To one hundred five degrees, and Marcelle moved the younger boys into her own room, so that she could sleep in the bed next to the sick boy's. She bathed him in cool water with washcloths, coaxed him into swallowing aspirin with orange juice, and sat on the edge of the bed next to his and watched him sleep, although she knew that he was not truly sleeping, he was merely lying there on his side, his legs out straight now, and breathing rapidly, like an injured dog, stunned and silently healing itself. But the boy was not healing himself, he was hourly growing worse. She could tell that. She tried to move him so that she could straighten the sheets, but when she touched him, he cried out in pain, as if his spine or neck were broken, and, frightened, she drew back from him. She wanted to call Doctor Wickshaw, and several times she got up and walked out to the kitchen where the telephone hung on the wall like a large black insect, and each time she stood for a few seconds before the instrument, remembered the doctor in the hallway and what she had let him promise her with his eyes, remembered then what he had told her about her son's illness, and turned and walked back to the boy and tried again to cool him with damp cloths. Her three other sons slept peacefully through the night and knew nothing of what happened until morning came.

When your child lives, he carries with him all his earlier selves, so that you cannot separate your individual memories of him from your view of him now, at this moment. When you recall a particular event in your and your child's shared past—a day at the beach, a Christmas morning, a sad, weary night of flight from the child's shouting father, a sweet, pathetic supper prepared by the child for your birthday—when you recall these events singly, you cannot see the child as a camera would have photographed him then. You see him simultaneously all the way from infancy to adolescence to adulthood and on, as if he has been moving through your life too rapidly for any camera to catch, and the image is blurred, grayed out, a swatch of your own past pasted across the foreground of a studio photographer's carefully arranged backdrop.

When her son went into convulsions, Marcelle did not at first know it, for his voice was clear and what he said made sense. Suddenly he spoke loudly and in complete sentences. "Ma, I'm not alone. I know that, and it helps me to not be scared. For a while I thought I was alone," he declared. Marcelle sat upright and listened alertly to him in the darkness of the bedroom. "Then I started to see things and think maybe there was someone else in the room here with me, and then I was scared, Ma. Because I didn't know for sure whether I was alone or not. But now I know I'm not alone, and knowing it helps me not be scared." She said that she was glad, because she thought he was talking about her presence in the room, and she took his recognition of her presence as a sign that the fever had broken. But when she reached out in the darkness and touched his neck, it was burning, like an empty, black pot left over a fire, and she almost cried out in pain and might have, had the child not commenced to shout at her, bellowing at her, as if she were a large, ugly animal that he wished to send cowering into the far corner of his room.

Most people, when they do what the physician has told them to do, expect to be cured. When they are not cured, they at first believe it is because they have not done properly what they have been told to do. Sickness is the mystery, the miracle, and the physician understands such things, we say, whereas we, who are not physicians, all we understand is health. This is not the case, of course, for health is the mystery and the miracle. Not sickness. Sickness can be penetrated, understood, predicted. Health cannot. The analogy between the physician and the priest will not hold, for sickness and injury are not at all like divine protection and forgiveness. Sadly, most people and most physicians and most priests do not know this, or if they do, they do not act as if they know it. It's only in dealing with our children that we treat life as if it were indeed the miracle, as if life itself were the mystery of divine protection and forgiveness, and in that way, it is only in dealing with our children that most people are like priests serving God, making it possible for poor sinners to obtain grace.

Doctor Wickshaw hurried into the boy's bedroom and this time knew that the boy had contracted meningitis, probably spinal meningitis, and he also knew that it was too late to save the boy, that if the boy did not die in the next few days, he would suffer irreparable damage to his central nervous system.

Marcelle knew that by her son's death she was now a lost soul. She did not weep. She went grimly about her appointed rounds, she raised her three remaining sons, and each of them, in his turn, forgave her and protected her. The one who died, Joel, the oldest, would never forgive her, never shield her from judgment, never let grace fall on her. Late at night, when she lay in bed alone, she knew this to the very bottom of her mind, and that knowledge was the lamp that illuminated the mystery and the miracle of her remaining days.

Sarah Cole: A Type of Love Story

I

To begin, then, here is a scene in which I am the man and my friend
Sarah Cole is the woman. I don't mind describing it now, because I'm a
decade older and don't look the same now as I did then, and Sarah Cole
is dead. That is to say, on hearing this story you might think me vain if
I looked the same now as I did then, because I must tell you that I was
extremely handsome then. And if Sarah were not dead, you'd think I
was cruel, for I must tell you that Sarah was very homely. In fact, she
was the homeliest woman I have ever known. Personally, I mean. I've
seen a few women who were more unattractive than Sarah, but they
were freaks of nature or had been badly injured or had been victimized
by some grotesque, disfiguring disease. Sarah, however, was quite normal, and I knew her well, because for three and a half months we were
lovers.

Here is the scene. You can put it in the present, even though it took
place ten years ago, because nothing that matters to the story depends
on when it took place, and you can put it in Concord, New Hampshire,
even though that is indeed where it took place, because it doesn't matter where it took place, so it might as well be Concord, New Hampshire,
a place I happen to know well and can therefore describe with suffi-

cient detail to make the story believable. Around six o'clock on a Wednesday evening in late May, a man enters a bar. The bar, a cocktail lounge at street level, with a restaurant upstairs, is decorated with hanging plants and unfinished wood paneling, butcher-block tables and captain's chairs, with a half dozen darkened, thickly upholstered booths along one wall. Three or four men between the ages of twenty-five and thirty-five are drinking at the bar and, like the man who has just entered, wear three-piece suits and loosened neckties. They are probably lawyers, young, unmarried lawyers gossiping with their brethren over martinis so as to postpone arriving home alone at their whitewashed town-house apartments, where they will fix their evening meals in microwave ovens and afterwards, while their TVs chuckle quietly in front of them, sit on their couches and do a little extra work for tomorrow. They are, for the most part, honorable, educated, hardworking, shallow, and moderately unhappy young men.

Our man, call him Ronald, Ron, in most ways is like these men, except that he is unusually good-looking, and that makes him a little less unhappy than they. Ron is effortlessly attractive, a genetic wonder, tall, slender, symmetrical, and clean. His flaws—a small mole on the left corner of his square, not-too-prominent chin, a slight excess of blond hair on the tops of his tanned hands, and somewhat underdeveloped buttocks—insofar as they keep him from resembling too closely a men's store mannequin, only contribute to his beauty, for he is beautiful, the way we usually think of a woman as being beautiful. And he is nice, too, the consequence, perhaps, of his seeming not to know how beautiful he is, to men as well as women, to young people (even children) as well as old, to attractive people (who realize immediately that he is so much more attractive than they as not to be competitive with them) as well as unattractive people.

Ron takes a seat at the bar, unfolds the evening paper in front of him, and, before he can start reading, the bartender asks to help him, calling him "Sir," even though Ron has come into this bar numerous times at this time of day, especially since his divorce last fall. Ron got divorced because, after three years of marriage, his wife chose to pursue the career that his had interrupted, that of a fashion designer, which required her to live in New York City while he had to continue to live in New Hampshire, where his career got its start. They agreed to live apart until he could continue his career near New York City, but after a few months, between conjugal visits, he started sleeping with other women, and she started sleeping with other men, and that was that. "No big deal," he explained to friends who liked both Ron and his wife, even though he was slightly more beautiful than she. "We really were too young when we got married. College sweethearts. But we're still best friends," he assured them. They understood. Most of Ron's friends were divorced by then, too.

Ron orders a Scotch and soda with a twist and goes back to reading his paper. When his drink comes, before he takes a sip of it, he first carefully finishes reading an article about the recent reappearance of coyotes in northern New Hampshire and Vermont. He lights a cigarette. He goes on reading. He takes a second sip of his drink. Everyone in the room—the three or four men scattered along the bar, the tall, thin bartender, and several people in the booths at the back—watches Ron do these ordinary things.

He has got to the classified section, is perhaps searching for someone willing to come in once a week and clean his apartment, when the woman who will turn out to be Sarah Cole leaves a booth in the back and approaches him. She comes up from the side and sits next to him. She's wearing heavy, tan cowboy boots and a dark brown, suede cowboy hat, lumpy jeans, and a yellow T-shirt that clings to her arms, breasts, and round belly like the skin of a sausage. Though he will later learn that she is thirty-eight years old, she looks older by about ten years, which makes her look about twenty years older than he actually is. (It's difficult to guess accurately how old Ron is; he looks anywhere from a mature twenty-five to a youthful forty, so his actual age doesn't seem to matter.)

"It's not bad here at the bar," she says, looking around. "More light, anyhow. Whatcha readin'?" she asks brightly, planting both elbows on the bar.

Ron looks up from his paper with a slight smile on his lips, sees the face of a woman homelier than any he has ever seen or imagined before, and goes on smiling lightly. He feels himself falling into her tiny, slightly crossed, dark brown eyes, pulls himself back, and studies for a few seconds her mottled, pocked complexion, bulbous nose, loose mouth, twisted and gapped teeth, and heavy, but receding chin. He casts a glance over her thatch of dun-colored hair and along her neck and throat, where acne burns against gray skin, and returns to her eyes, and again feels himself falling into her.

"What did you say?" he asks.

She knocks a mentholated cigarette from her pack, and Ron swiftly lights it. Blowing smoke from her large, wing-shaped nostrils, she speaks again. Her voice is thick and nasal, a chocolate-colored voice. "I asked you whatcha readin', but I can see now." She belts out a single, loud laugh. "The paper!"

Ron laughs too. "The paper! The *Concord Monitor*!" He is not hallucinating, he clearly sees what is before him and admits—no, he asserts—to himself that he is speaking to the most unattractive woman he has ever seen, a fact that fascinates him, as if instead he were speaking to the most beautiful woman he has ever seen, so he treasures the moment, attempts to hold it as if it were a golden ball, a disproportionately heavy object which—if he does not hold it lightly, with precision and firmness—will slip from his hand and roll across the lawn to the lip of the well and down, down to the bottom of the well, lost to him forever. It will be a memory, that's all, something to speak of wistfully and with wonder as over the years the image fades and comes in the end to exist only in the telling. His mind and body waken from their sleepy self-absorption, and all his attention focuses on the woman, Sarah Cole, her ugly face, like a warthog's, her thick, rapid speech, her dumpy, off-center wreck of a body. To keep this moment here before him, he begins to ask questions of her, he buys her a drink, he smiles, until soon it seems, even to him, that he is taking her and her life, its vicissitudes and woe, quite seriously.

He learns her name, and she volunteers the information that she spoke to him on a dare from one of the two women sitting in the booth behind her. She turns on her stool and smiles brazenly, triumphantly, to her friends, two women, also homely (though nowhere as homely as she), and dressed, like her, in cowboy boots, hats, and jeans. One of the women, a blond with an underslung jaw and wearing heavy eye makeup, flips a little wave at her, and, as if embarrassed, she and the other woman at the booth turn back to their drinks and sip fiercely at straws.

Sarah returns to Ron and goes on telling him what he wants to know, about her job at Rumford Press, about her divorced husband, who was a bastard and stupid and "sick," she says, as if filling suddenly with sympathy for the man. She tells Ron about her three children, the youngest, a girl, in junior high school and boy-crazy, the other two, boys, in high school and almost never at home anymore. She speaks of her children with genuine tenderness and concern, and Ron is touched. He can see with what pleasure and pain she speaks of her children; he watches her tiny eyes light up and water over when he asks their names.

"You're a nice woman," he informs her.

She smiles, looks at her empty glass. "No. No, I'm not. But you're a nice man, to tell me that."

Ron, with a gesture, asks the bartender to refill Sarah's glass. She is drinking White Russians. Perhaps she has been drinking them for an hour or two, for she seems very relaxed, more relaxed than women usually do when they come up and without introduction or invitation speak to Ron.

She asks him about himself, his job, his divorce, how long he has lived in Concord, but he finds that he is not at all interested in telling her about himself. He wants to know about her, even though what she has to tell him about herself is predictable and ordinary and the way she tells it unadorned and clichéd. He wonders about her husband. What kind of man would fall in love with Sarah Cole?

2

That scene, at Osgood's Lounge in Concord, ended with Ron's departure, alone, after having bought Sarah a second drink, and Sarah's return to her friends in the booth. I don't know what she told them, but it's not hard to imagine. The three women were not close friends, merely fellow workers at Rumford Press, where they stood at the end of a long conveyor belt day after day packing TV Guides into cartons. They all hated their jobs, and frequently after work, when they worked the day shift, they put on their cowboy hats and boots, which they kept all day in their lockers, and stopped for a drink or two on their way home. This had been their first visit to Osgood's, however, a place that, prior to this, they had avoided out of a sneering belief that no one went there but lawyers and insurance men. It had been Sarah who asked the others why that should keep them away, and when they had no answer for her, the three decided to stop at Osgood's. Ron was right, they had been there over an hour when he came in, and Sarah was a little drunk. "We'll hafta come in here again," she said to her friends, her voice rising slightly.

Which they did, that Friday, and once again Ron appeared with his evening newspaper. He put his briefcase down next to his stool and ordered a drink and proceeded to read the front page, slowly, deliberately, clearly a weary, unhurried, solitary man. He did not notice the three women in cowboy hats and boots in the booth in back, but they saw him, and after a few minutes, Sarah was once again at his side.

"Hi."

He turned, saw her, and instantly regained the moment he had lost when, two nights ago, once outside the bar and on his way home, he had forgotten about the ugliest woman he had ever seen. She seemed even more grotesque to him now than before, which made the moment all the more precious to him, and so, once again, he held the moment as if in his hands and began to speak with her, to ask questions, to offer his opinions and solicit hers.

I said earlier that I am the man in this story and my friend Sarah Cole, now dead, is the woman. I think back to that night, the second time I had seen Sarah, and I tremble, not with fear, but in shame. My concern then, when I was first becoming involved with Sarah, was merely with the moment, holding on to it, grasping it wholly, as if its beginning did not grow out of some other prior moment in her life and my life separately, and at the same time did not lead into future moments in our separate lives. She talked more easily than she had the night before, and I listened as eagerly and carefully as I had before, again with the same motives, to keep her in front of me, to draw her forward from the context of her life and place her, as if she were an object, into the context of mine. I did not know how cruel this was. When you have never done a thing before and that thing is not simply and clearly right or wrong, you frequently do not know if it is a cruel thing, you just go ahead and do it. Maybe later you'll be able to determine whether you acted cruelly. Too late, of course, but at least you'll know.

While we drank, Sarah told me that she hated her ex-husband

because of the way he treated the children. "It's not so much the money," she said, nervously wagging her booted feet from her perch on the high barstool. "I mean, I get by, barely, but I get them fed and clothed on my own okay. It's because he won't even write them a letter or anything. He won't call them on the phone, all he calls for is to bitch at me because I'm trying to get the state to take him to court so I can get some of the money he's s'posed to be paying for child support. And he won't even think to talk to the kids when he calls. Won't even ask about them."

"He sounds like a sonofabitch."

"He is, he is!" she said. "I don't know why I married him. Or stayed married. Fourteen years, for Christ's sake. He put a spell over me or something. I don't know," she said, with a note of wistfulness in her voice. "He wasn't what you'd call good-looking."

After her second drink, she decided she had to leave. Her children were at home, it was Friday night, and she liked to make sure she ate supper with them and knew where they were going and who they were with when they went out on their dates. "No dates on school nights," she said to me. "I mean, you gotta have rules, you know."

I agreed, and we left together, everyone in the place following us with his or her gaze. I was aware of that, I knew what they were thinking, and I didn't care, because I was simply walking her to her car.

It was a cool evening, dusk settling onto the lot like a gray blanket. Her car, a huge, dark green Buick sedan at least ten years old, was battered almost beyond use. She reached for the door handle on the driver's side and yanked. Nothing. The door wouldn't open. She tried again. Then I tried. Still nothing.

Then I saw it, a V-shaped dent in the left front fender, binding the metal of the door against the metal of the fender in a large crimp that held the door fast. "Someone must've backed into you while you were inside," I said to her.

She came forward and studied the crimp for a few seconds, and when she looked back at me, she was weeping. "Jesus, Jesus, Jesus!" she wailed, her large, frog-like mouth wide open and wet with spit, her tongue flopping loosely over gapped teeth. "I can't pay for this! I *can't!*" Her face was red, and even in the dusky light I could see it puff out with weeping, her tiny eyes seeming almost to disappear behind wet cheeks. Her shoulders slumped, and her hands fell limply to her sides.

Placing my briefcase on the ground, I reached out to her and put my arms around her body and held her close to me, while she cried wetly into my shoulder. After a few seconds, she started pulling herself back together, and her weeping got reduced to snuffling. Her cowboy hat had been pushed back and now clung to her head at a precarious, absurdly jaunty angle. She took a step away from me and said, "I'll get in the other side."

"Okay," I said, almost in a whisper. "That's fine."

Slowly, she walked around the front of the huge, ugly vehicle and opened the door on the passenger's side and slid awkwardly across the seat until she had positioned herself behind the steering wheel. She started the motor, which came to life with a roar. The muffler was shot. Without saying another word to me or even waving, she dropped the car into reverse gear and backed it loudly out of the parking space and headed out of the lot to the street.

I turned and started for my car, when I happened to glance toward the door of the bar, and there, staring after me, were the bartender, the two women who had come in with Sarah, and two of the men who had been sitting at the bar. They were lawyers, and I knew them slightly. They were grinning at me. I grinned back and got into my car and, without looking at them again, left the place and drove straight to my apartment.

3

One night several weeks later, Ron meets Sarah at Osgood's, and after buying her three White Russians and drinking three Scotches himself, he takes her back to his apartment in his car—a Datsun fast-back coupe that she says she admires—for the sole purpose of making love to her.

I'm still the man in the story, and Sarah is still the woman, but I'm telling it this way because what I have to tell you now confuses me, embarrasses me, and makes me sad, and consequently I'm likely to tell it falsely. I'm likely to cover the truth by making Sarah a better woman than she actually was, while making me appear worse than I actually was or am; or else I'll do the opposite, make Sarah worse than she was and me better. The truth is, I was pretty, extremely so, and she was not, extremely so, and I knew it, and she knew it. She walked out the door of Osgood's determined to make love to a man much prettier than any she had seen up close before, and I walked out determined to make love to a woman much homelier than any I had made love to before. We were, in a sense, equals.

No, that's not exactly true. I'm not at all sure she feels as Ron does. That is to say, perhaps she genuinely likes the man, in spite of his being the most physically attractive man she has ever known. Perhaps she is more aware of her homeliness than of his beauty, for Ron, despite what I may have implied, does not think of himself as especially beautiful. He merely knows that other people think of him that way. As I said before, he is a nice man.

Ron unlocks the door to his apartment, walks in ahead of her, and flicks on the lamp beside the couch. It's a small, single-bedroom, modern apartment, one of thirty identical apartments in a large brick building on the Heights just east of downtown Concord. Sarah stands nervously at the door, peering in.

"Come in, come in," Ron says.

She steps timidly in and closes the door behind her. She removes her cowboy hat, then quickly puts it back on, crosses the living room, and plops down in a blond easy chair, seeming to shrink in its hug out of sight to safety. Behind her, Ron, at the entry to the kitchen, places one hand on her shoulder, and she stiffens. He removes his hand.

"Would you like a drink?"

"No . . . I guess not," she says, staring straight ahead at the wall opposite, where a large, framed photograph of a bicyclist advertises in French the Tour de France. Around a corner, in an alcove off the living room, a silvery gray twenty-one-speed bicycle leans casually against the wall, glistening and poised, slender as a thoroughbred racehorse.

"I don't know," she says. Ron is in the kitchen now, making himself a drink. "I don't know . . . I don't know."

"What? Change your mind? I can make a White Russian for you. Vodka, cream, Kahlúa, and ice, right?"

Sarah tries to cross her legs, but she is sitting too low in the chair and her legs are too thick at the thighs, so she ends, after a struggle, with one leg in the air and the other twisted on its side. She looks as if she has fallen from a great height.

Ron steps out from the kitchen, peers over the back of the chair, and watches her untangle herself, then ducks back into the kitchen. After a few seconds, he returns. "Seriously. Want me to fix you a White Russian?"

"No."

Again from behind and above her, Ron places one hand on Sarah's shoulder, and this time she does not stiffen, though she does not exactly relax, either. She sits there, a block of wood, staring straight ahead.

"Are you scared?" he asks gently. Then he adds, "I am."

"Well, no, I'm not scared." She remains silent for a moment. "You're scared? Of what?" She turns to face him, but avoids his blue eyes.

"Well . . . I don't do this all the time, you know. Bring home a woman I . . . ," he trails off.

"Picked up in a bar."

"No. I mean, I like you, Sarah. I really do. And I didn't just pick you up in a bar, you know that. We've gotten to be friends, you and me."

"You want to sleep with me?" she asks, still not meeting his steady gaze.

"Yes." He seems to mean it. He does not take a gulp or even a sip from his drink. He just says, "Yes," straight out, and cleanly, not too quickly, either, and not after a hesitant delay. A simple statement of a simple fact. The man wants to make love to the woman. She asked him, and he told her. What could be simpler?

"Do you want to sleep with *me*?" he asks.

She turns around in the chair, faces the wall again, and says in a low voice, "Sure, I do, but . . . it's hard to explain."

"What? But what?" Placing his glass down on the table between the chair and the sofa, he puts both hands on her shoulders and lightly kneads them. He knows he can be discouraged from pursuing this, but he is not sure how easily. Having got this far without bumping against obstacles (except the ones he has placed in his way himself), he is not sure what it will take to turn him back. He does not know, therefore, how assertive or how seductive he should be with her. He suspects that he can be stopped very easily, so he is reluctant to give her a chance to try. He goes on kneading her doughy shoulders.

"You and me, Ron . . . we're real different." She glances at the bicycle in the corner.

"A man . . . and a woman," he says.

"No, not that. I mean, different. That's all. Real different. More than you think. You're nice, but you don't know what I mean, and that's one of the things that makes you so nice. But we're different. Listen," she says, "I gotta go. I gotta leave now."

The man removes his hands and retrieves his glass, takes a sip, and watches her over the rim of the glass, as, not without difficulty, the woman rises from the chair and moves swiftly toward the door. She stops at the door, squares her hat on her head, and glances back at him.

"We can be friends, though, okay?"

"Okay. Friends."

"I'll see you again down at Osgood's, right?"

"Oh, yeah, sure."

"Good. See you," she says, opening the door.

The door closes. The man walks around the sofa, snaps on the television set, and sits down in front of it. He picks up a TV *Guide* from the coffee table and flips through it, stops, runs a finger down the listings, stops, puts down the magazine, and changes the channel. He does not once connect the magazine in his hand to the woman who has just left his apartment, even though he knows she spends her days packing TV *Guides* into cartons that get shipped to warehouses in distant parts of New England. He'll think of the connection some other night, but by then the connection will be merely sentimental. It'll be too late for him to understand what she meant by "different."

4

But that's not the point of my story. Certainly, it's an aspect of the story, the political aspect, if you want, but it's not the reason I'm trying to tell it in the first place. I'm trying to tell the story so that I can understand what happened between me and Sarah Cole that summer and early autumn ten years ago. To say we were lovers says very little about what happened; to say we were friends says even less. No, if I'm to understand the whole thing, I'll have to say the whole thing, for, in the end, what I need to know is whether what happened between me and

Sarah Cole was right or wrong. Character is fate, which suggests that if a man can know and then to some degree control his character, he can know and to that same degree control his fate.

The next time Sarah and I were together we were at her apartment in the south end of Concord, a second-floor flat in a tenement building on Perley Street. I had stayed away from Osgood's for several weeks, deliberately trying to avoid running into Sarah there, though I never quite put it that way to myself. I found excuses and generated interest in and reasons for going elsewhere after work. Yet I was obsessed with Sarah by then, obsessed with the idea of making love to her, which, because it was not an actual *desire* to make love to her, was an unusually complex obsession. Passion without desire, if it gets expressed, may in fact be a kind of rape, and perhaps I sensed the danger that lay behind my obsession and for that reason went out of my way to avoid meeting Sarah again.

Yet I did meet her, inadvertently, of course. After picking up shirts at the cleaner's on South Main and Perley Streets, I'd gone down Perley on my way to South State and the post office. It was a Saturday morning, and this trip on my bicycle was part of my regular Saturday routine. I did not remember that Sarah lived on Perley Street, although she had told me several times in a complaining way—it's a rough neighborhood, packed-dirt yards, shabby apartment buildings, the carcasses of old, half-stripped cars on cinder blocks in the driveways, broken red-and-yellow plastic tricycles on the cracked sidewalks—but as soon as I saw her, I remembered. It was too late to avoid meeting her. I was riding my bike, wearing shorts and T-shirt, the package containing my folded and starched shirts hooked to the carrier behind me, and she was walking toward me along the sidewalk, lugging two large bags of groceries. She saw me, and I stopped. We talked, and I offered to carry her groceries for her. I took the bags while she led the bike, handling it carefully, as if she were afraid she might break it.

At the stoop we came to a halt. The wooden steps were cluttered with half-opened garbage bags spilling eggshells, coffee grounds, and old food wrappers to the walkway. "I can't get the people downstairs to take care of their garbage," she explained. She leaned the bike against the banister and reached for her groceries.

"I'll carry them up for you," I said. I directed her to loop the chain lock from the bike to the banister rail and snap it shut and told her to bring my shirts up with her.

"Maybe you'd like a beer?" she said as she opened the door to the darkened hallway. Narrow stairs disappeared in front of me into heavy, damp darkness, and the air smelled like old newspapers.

"Sure," I said, and followed her up.

"Sorry there's no light. I can't get them to fix it."

"No matter. I can follow along," I said, and even in the dim light of the hall I could see the large, blue veins that cascaded thickly down the backs of her legs. She wore tight, white-duck Bermuda shorts, rubber shower sandals, and a pink, sleeveless sweater. I pictured her in the cashier's line at the supermarket. I would have been behind her, a stranger, and on seeing her, I would have turned away and studied the covers of the magazines, TV Guide, People, the National Enquirer, for there was nothing of interest in her appearance that in the hard light of day would not have slightly embarrassed me. Yet here I was inviting myself into her home, eagerly staring at the backs of her ravaged legs, her sad, tasteless clothing, her poverty. I was not detached, however, was not staring at her with scientific curiosity and, because of my passion, did not feel or believe that what I was doing was perverse. I felt warmed by her presence and was flirtatious and bold, a little pushy, even.

Picture this. The man, tanned, limber, fit, wearing red jogging shorts, Italian leather sandals, a clinging net T-shirt of Scandinavian design and manufacture, enters the apartment behind the woman, whose dough-colored skin, thick, short body, and homely, uncomfortable face all try, but fail, to hide themselves. She waves him toward the table in the kitchen, where he sets down the bags and looks good-naturedly around the room. "What about the beer you bribed me with?" he asks.

The apartment is cluttered with old, oversized furniture, yard sale and secondhand stuff bought originally for a large house in the country or a spacious apartment on a boulevard forty or fifty years ago, passed down from antique dealer to used furniture store to yard sale to thrift shop, where it finally gets purchased by Sarah Cole and gets hauled over to Perley Street and shoved up the narrow stairs, she and her children grunting and sweating in the darkness of the hallway—overstuffed armchairs and couch, huge, ungainly dressers, upholstered rocking chairs, and, in the kitchen, an old flat-topped maple desk for a table, a half dozen heavy, oak dining room chairs, a high, glass-fronted cabinet, all peeling, stained, chipped, and squatting on a dark green linoleum floor.

The place is neat and arranged in a more or less orderly way, however, and the man seems comfortable there. He strolls from the kitchen to the living room and peeks into the three small bedrooms that branch off a hallway behind the living room. "Nice place!" he calls to the woman. He studies the framed pictures of her three children arranged as if on an altar atop the buffet. "Nice-looking kids!" he calls out. They are. Blond, round-faced, clean, and utterly ordinary-looking, their pleasant faces glance, as instructed, slightly off camera and down to the right, as if they are trying to remember the name of the capital of Montana.

When he returns to the kitchen, the woman is putting away her groceries, her back to him. "Where's that beer you bribed me with?" he asks again. He takes a position against the doorframe, his weight on one hip, like a dancer resting. "You sure are quiet today, Sarah," he says in a low voice. "Everything okay?"

Silently, she turns away from the grocery bags, crosses the room to the man, reaches up to him, and, holding him by the head, kisses his mouth, rolls her torso against his, drops her hands to his hips and yanks him tightly to her and goes on kissing him, eyes closed, working her face furiously against his. The man places his hands on her shoulders and pulls away, and they face each other, wide-eyed, amazed and frightened. The man drops his hands, and the woman lets go of his hips. Then, after a few seconds, the man silently turns, goes to the door, and leaves. The last thing he sees as he closes the door behind him is the woman standing in the kitchen doorframe, her face looking down and slightly to one side, wearing the same pleasant expression on her face as her children in their photographs, trying to remember the capital of Montana.

5

Sarah appeared at my apartment door the following morning, a Sunday, cool and rainy. She had brought me the package of freshly laundered shirts I'd left in her kitchen, and when I opened the door to her, she simply held the package out to me, as if it were a penitent's gift. She wore a yellow rain slicker and cap and looked more like a disconsolate schoolgirl facing an angry teacher than a grown woman dropping a package off at a friend's apartment.

I invited her inside, and she accepted my invitation. I had been reading the Sunday New York Times on the couch and drinking coffee, lounging through the gray morning in bathrobe and pajamas. I told her to take off her wet raincoat and hat and hang them in the closet by the door and started for the kitchen to get her a cup of coffee, when I stopped, turned, and looked at her. She closed the closet door on her yellow raincoat and hat, turned around, and faced me.

What else can I do? I must describe it. I remember that moment of ten years ago as if it occurred ten minutes ago. The package of shirts on the table behind her, the newspapers scattered over the couch and floor, the sound of windblown rain washing the side of the building outside, and the silence of the room, as we stood across from one another and watched, while we each simultaneously removed our own clothing, my robe, her blouse and skirt, my pajama top, her slip and bra, my pajama bottom, her underpants, until we were both standing naked in the harsh, gray light, two naked members of the same species, a male and a female, the male somewhat younger and less scarred than the female, the female somewhat less delicately constructed than the male, both individuals pale-skinned with dark thatches of hair in the areas of their genitals, both individuals standing slackly, as if a great, protracted tension between them had at last been released.

6

We made love that morning in my bed for long hours that drifted easily into afternoon. And we talked, as people usually do when they spend a half day or half a night in bed together. I told her of my past, named and described the people whom I had loved and had loved me, my ex-wife in New York, my brother in the Air Force, my mother in San Diego, and I told her of my ambitions and dreams and even confessed some of my fears. She listened patiently and intelligently throughout and talked much less than I. She had already told me many of these things about herself, and perhaps whatever she had to say to me now lay on the next inner circle of intimacy or else could not be spoken of at all.

During the next few weeks, we met and made love often, and always at my apartment. On arriving home from work, I would phone her, or if not, she would phone me, and after a few feints and dodges, one would suggest to the other that we get together tonight, and a half hour later she'd be at my door. Our lovemaking was passionate, skillful, kindly, and deeply satisfying. We didn't often speak of it to one another or brag about it, the way some couples do when they are surprised by the ease with which they have become contented lovers. We did occasionally joke and tease each other, however, playfully acknowledging that the only thing we did together was make love but that we did it so frequently there was no time for anything else.

Then one hot night, a Saturday in August, we were lying in bed atop the tangled sheets, smoking cigarettes, and chatting idly, and Sarah suggested that we go out for a drink.

"Out? Now?"

"Sure. It's early. What time is it?"

I scanned the digital clock next to the bed. "Nine forty-nine."

"There. See?"

"That's not so early. You usually go home by eleven, you know. It's almost ten."

"No, it's only a little after nine. Depends on how you look at things. Besides, Ron, it's Saturday night. Or is this the only thing you know how to do?" she said and poked me in the ribs. "You know how to dance? You like to dance?"

"Yeah, sure . . . sure, but not tonight. It's too hot. And I'm tired."

But she persisted, happily pointing out that an air-conditioned bar would be as cool as my apartment, and we didn't have to go to a dance bar, we could go to Osgood's. "As a compromise," she said.

I suggested a place called the El Rancho, a restaurant with a large, dark cocktail lounge and dance bar located several miles from town on the old Portsmouth highway. Around nine the restaurant closed, and the bar became something of a roadhouse, with a small country-and-western band and a clientele drawn from the four or five villages that adjoined Concord on the north and east. I had eaten at the restaurant once, but had never gone to the bar, and I didn't know anyone who had.

Sarah was silent for a moment. Then she lit a cigarette and drew the sheet over her naked body. "You don't want anybody to know about us, Ron. Do you?"

"That's not it. . . . I just don't like gossip, and I work with a lot of people who show up sometimes at Osgood's. On a Saturday night especially."

"No," she said firmly. "You're ashamed of being seen with me. You'll sleep with me, all right, but you won't go out in public with me."

"That's not true, Sarah."

She was silent again. Relieved, I reached across her to the bed table and got my cigarettes and lighter.

"You owe me, Ron," she said suddenly, as I passed over her. "You owe me."

"What?" I lay back, lit a cigarette, and covered my body with the sheet.

"I said, 'You owe me.'"

"I don't know what you're talking about, Sarah. I just don't like a lot of gossip going around, that's all. I like keeping my private life private, that's all. I don't *owe* you anything."

"Friendship you owe me. And respect. Friendship and respect. A person can't do what you've done with me without owing her friendship and respect."

"Sarah, I really don't know what you're talking about," I said. "I am your friend, you know that. And I respect you. I do."

"You really think so, don't you?"

"Yes. Of course."

She said nothing for several long moments. Then she sighed and in a low, almost inaudible voice said, "Then you'll have to go out in public with me. I don't care about Osgood's or the people you work with, we don't have to go there or see any of them," she said. "But you're gonna have to go to places like the El Rancho with me, and a few other places I know, too, where there's people I know, people I work with, and maybe we'll even go to a couple of parties, because I get invited to parties sometimes, you know. I have friends, and I have some family, too, and you're gonna have to meet my family. My kids think I'm just going around barhopping when I'm over here with you, and I don't like that, so you're gonna have to meet them, so I can tell them where I am when I'm not at home nights. And sometimes you're gonna come over and spend the evening at my place!" Her voice had risen as she heard her demands and felt their rightness, until now she was almost shouting at me. "You *owe* that to me. Or else you're a bad man. It's that simple, Ron."

7

The handsome man is overdressed. He is wearing a navy blue blazer, taupe shirt open at the throat, white slacks, white loafers. Everyone else, including the homely woman with the handsome man, is dressed appropriately—that is, like everyone else—jeans and cowboy boots, blouses or cowboy shirts or T-shirts with catchy sayings or the names of country-and-western singers printed across the front, and many of the women are wearing cowboy hats pushed back and tied under their chins.

The man doesn't know anyone at the bar or, if they're at a party, in the room, but the woman knows most of the people there, and she gladly introduces him. The men grin and shake his hand, slap him on his jacketed shoulder, ask him where he works, what's his line, after which they lapse into silence. The women flirt briefly with their faces, but they lapse into silence even before the men do. The woman with the man in the blazer does most of the talking for everyone. She talks for the man in the blazer, for the men standing around the refrigerator, or, if they're at a bar, for the other men at the table, and for the other women, too. She chats and rambles aimlessly through loud monologues, laughs uproariously at trivial jokes, and drinks too much, until soon she is drunk, thick-tongued, clumsy, and the man has to say her good-byes and ease her out the door to his car and drive her home to her apartment on Perley Street.

This happens twice in one week and then three times the next—at the El Rancho, at the Ox Bow in Northwood, at Rita and Jimmy's apartment on Thorndike Street, out in Warner at Betsy Beeler's new house, and, the last time, at a cottage on Lake Sunapee rented by some kids in shipping at Rumford Press. Ron no longer calls Sarah when he gets home from work; he waits for her call, and sometimes, when he knows it's she, he doesn't answer the phone. Usually, he lets it ring five or six times, and then he reaches down and picks up the receiver. He has taken his jacket and vest off and loosened his tie and is about to put his supper, frozen manicotti, into the microwave oven.

"Hello?"

"Hi."

"How're you doing?"

"Okay, I guess. A little tired."

"Still hungover?"

"Naw. Not really. Just tired. I hate Mondays."

"You have fun last night?"

"Well, yeah, sorta. It's nice out there, at the lake. Listen," she says, brightening. "Why'n't you come over here tonight? The kids're all going out later, but if you come over before eight, you can meet them. They really want to meet you."

"You told them about me?"

"Sure. Long time ago. I'm not supposed to tell my own kids?"

Ron is silent.

She says, "You don't want to come over here tonight. You don't want to meet my kids. No, you don't want my kids to meet *you*, that's it."

"No, no, it's just . . . I've got a lot of work to do . . ."

"We should talk," she announces in a flat voice.

"Yes," he says. "We should talk."

They agree that she will meet him at his apartment, and they'll talk, and they say good-bye and hang up.

While Ron is heating his supper and then eating it alone at his kitchen table and Sarah is feeding her children, perhaps I should admit, since we are nearing the end of my story, that I don't actually know that Sarah Cole is dead. A few years ago, I happened to run into one of her friends from the press, a blond woman with an underslung jaw. Her name, she reminded me, was Glenda; she had seen me at Osgood's a couple of times, and we had met at the El Rancho once when I had gone there with Sarah. I was amazed that she could remember me and a little embarrassed that I did not recognize her at all, and she laughed at that and said, "You haven't changed much, mister!" I pretended to recognize her then, but I think she knew that she was a stranger to me. We were standing outside the Sears store on South Main Street, where I had gone to buy paint. I had recently remarried, and my wife and I were redecorating my apartment.

"Whatever happened to Sarah?" I asked Glenda. "Is she still down at the press?"

"Jeez, no! She left a long time ago. Way back. I heard she went back with her ex-husband. I can't remember his name, something Cole. Eddie Cole, maybe."

I asked her if she was sure of that, and she said no, she had only heard it around the bars and down at the press, but she assumed it was true. People said Sarah had moved back with her ex-husband and was living for a while with him and the kids in a trailer in a park near Hooksett, and then, when the kids, or at least the boys, got out of school, the rest of them moved down to Florida or someplace because he was out of work. He was a carpenter, she thought.

"He was mean to her," I said. "I thought he used to beat her up and everything. I thought she hated him."

"Oh, well, yeah, he was a bastard, all right. I met him a couple times, and I didn't like him. Short, ugly, and mean when he got drunk. But you know what they say."

"What do they say?"

"Oh, you know, about water seeking its own level and all."

"Sarah wasn't mean, drunk *or* sober."

The woman laughed. "Naw, but she sure was short and ugly!"

I said nothing.

"Hey, don't get me wrong," Glenda said. "I liked Sarah. But you and her . . . well, you sure made a funny-looking couple. She probably didn't feel so self-conscious and all with her husband," she said somberly. "With you, all tall and blond, and poor old Sarah . . . I mean, the way them kids in the press room used to kid her about her looks, it was embarrassing just to have to hear it."

"Well . . . I loved her," I said.

The woman raised one plucked eyebrow in disbelief. She smiled. "Sure, you did, honey," she said, and she patted me on the arm. "Sure you did." Then she let the smile drift off her face, turned, and walked away from me.

When someone you have loved dies, you accept the fact of her death, but then the person goes on living in your memory, dreams, and reveries. You have imaginary conversations with her, you see something striking and remind yourself to tell your loved one about it and then get brought up short by the fact of her death, and at night, in your sleep, the dead person visits you. With Sarah, none of that happened. When she was gone from my life, she was gone absolutely, as if she had never existed in the first place. It was only later, when I could think of her as dead and could come out and say it, *My friend, Sarah Cole, is dead,* that I was able to tell this story, for that is when she began to enter my memories, my dreams and reveries. In that way, I learned that I truly did love her. And now I have begun to grieve over her death, to wish her alive again, so that I can say to her the things I could not know or say when she was alive, when I did not know that I loved her.

8

The woman arrives at Ron's apartment around eight. He hears her car with the broken muffler blat and rumble into the parking lot below, and he crosses quickly from the kitchen and peers out the living-room window and, as if through a telescope, watches her shove herself across the seat to the passenger's side to get out of the car, then walk slowly in the dusky light toward the apartment building. It's a warm evening, and she's wearing her white Bermuda shorts, pink, sleeveless sweater, and shower sandals. Ron hates those clothes. He hates the way the shorts cut into her flesh at the crotch and thigh, hates the large, dark caves below her arms that get exposed by the sweater, hates the sucking noise made by the sandals.

Shortly, there is a soft knock at his door. He opens it, turns away, and crosses to the kitchen, where he turns back, lights a cigarette, and watches her. She closes the door. He offers her a drink, which she declines, and, somewhat formally, he invites her to sit down. She sits carefully on the sofa, in the middle, with her feet close together on the floor, as if being interviewed for a job. He comes around and sits in the easy chair, relaxed, one leg slung over the other at the knee, as if he were interviewing her for the job.

"Well," he says, "you wanted to talk."

"Yes. But now you're mad at me. I can see that. I didn't do anything, Ron."

"I'm not mad at you."

They are silent for a moment. Ron goes on smoking his cigarette.

Finally, she sighs and says, "You don't want to see me anymore, do you?"

He waits a few seconds and answers, "Yes. That's right." Getting up from the chair, he walks to the silver-gray bicycle and stands before it, running a fingertip along the slender crossbar from the saddle to the chrome-plated handlebars.

"You're a sonofabitch," she says in a low voice. "You're worse than my ex-husband." Then she smiles meanly, almost sneers, and soon he realizes that she is telling him that she won't leave. He's stuck with her, she informs him with cold precision. "You think I'm just so much meat, and all you got to do is call up the butcher shop and cancel your order. Well, now you're going to find out different. You *can't* cancel your order. I'm not meat, I'm not one of your pretty little girlfriends who come running when you want them and go away when you get tired of them. I'm *different*! I got nothing to lose, Ron. Nothing. So you're stuck with me, Ron."

She sits back in the couch and crosses her legs at the ankles. "I think I *will* have that drink you offered."

"Look, Sarah, it would be better if you go now."

"No," she says flatly. "You offered me a drink when I came in. Nothing's changed since I've been here. Not for me and not for you. I'd like that drink you offered," she says haughtily.

Ron turns away from the bicycle and takes a step toward her. His face has stiffened into a mask. "Enough is enough," he says through clenched teeth. "I've given you enough."

"Fix me a drink, will you, honey?" she says with a phony smile.

Ron orders her to leave.

She refuses.

He grabs her by the arm and yanks her to her feet.

She starts crying lightly. She stands there and looks up into his face and weeps, but she does not move toward the door, so he pushes her. She regains her balance and goes on weeping.

He stands back and places his fists on his hips and looks at her. "Go on, go on and leave, you ugly bitch," he says to her, and as he says the words, as one by one they leave his mouth, she becomes the most beautiful woman he has ever seen. He says the words again, almost tenderly. "Leave, you ugly bitch." Her hair is golden, her brown eyes deep and sad, her mouth full and affectionate, her tears the tears of love and loss, and her pleading, outstretched arms, her entire body, the arms and body of a devoted woman's cruelly rejected love. A third time he says the words. "Leave me now, you disgusting, ugly bitch." She is wrapped in an envelope of golden light, a warm, dense haze that she seems to have stepped into, as into a carriage. And then she is gone, and he is alone again.

He looks around the room, searching for her. Sitting down in the easy chair, he places his face in his hands. It's not as if she has died; it's as if he has killed her.

Assisted Living

Mother and son entered the restaurant talking, their statements overlapping, "I'm sorry, no, Teddy, it wasn't like that at all," she said, and he said, "The only way the two things make sense, *moral* sense, is if they're cause and effect. The old man used you, Mom, he used you pure and simple."

Caught at the door by everyone, they stopped talking, smiled, nodded good morning to Della behind the counter and the several customers they recognized. And looked hard into one another's face.

"That'll be enough out of you," Emily said, and smiled. A joke.

Teddy touched his lips with an index finger, bowing to her authority. His joke. He towered over her, bulky as a bear in his camel hair coat and silk scarf.

Emily loved Teddy and was grateful to him but sometimes felt he should just let things go, or let her go. She poked her bladed nose and chin up at him like a fist. The woman was eighty-one, and the events were nearly a half century old—she didn't even think they were interesting anymore, let alone connected. On her own she never would have connected them. Fine, if he wanted to worry over the distant past as if it explained his and her present, but he shouldn't make her do it, too.

Teddy was very intelligent, though, and knew a lot more about the world and men—his father included—than she. He was a man himself, after all, and a college-educated professional, a pharmacist who owned his drugstore and the minimall that contained it. Teddy had moved his mother up here to New Hampshire barely a year ago from her house in Somerset, Massachusetts, where, after her divorce from Teddy's father, Wayne, and after Teddy and his younger brother and sister finished their educations and married and raised children and even after their divorces and remarriages, she'd stayed on alone. She had grown old in that modest, suburban house, the cookie-cutter ranch that she first saw back in the fall of 1953, when it was freshly built, the paint barely dry, and the yard and neighborhood still a raw construction site.

She and Wayne had sat in the green Studebaker he liked so much and stared at the house from the unpaved street. She was behind the wheel, and he was in the passenger's seat; they were peering out her open window. "It's too small," she said. "We'll never fit."

He reached over and wrapped her shoulders in his thick arm and smiled at the house as if appraising a villa. "Not to worry, m'dear. The place itself will grow, until we do fit."

He was mostly right. A more than competent carpenter, Wayne that first year built a large screened porch off the kitchen and the following year added an el with a master bedroom and second bathroom. Emily and the kids planted grass and maple saplings and a boxwood hedge. Before long, the tract house had become a proper American home in the suburbs, the envy of the preceding generation of Americans and the desire of the one that followed. Then came the divorce from Wayne—because of his drinking and womanizing, and she was better off without him anyhow, everyone said so—and the kids left home for college, secretarial school, the military, and Emily's sixties arrived and went, and she grew ever more alone, and her seventies passed, when most of her friends died. Until she turned eighty, and it became evident to Teddy, and to Emily, too, that, even though she was still relatively healthy and clearheaded, she could no longer manage basic household tasks. She had the early signs of Parkinson's and what she said was a leaky heart and claimed to have had a stroke, although her own doctor doubted it: she seemed to have suffered no lasting effects from it, except an occasional loss of peripheral vision, and called it *my* stroke, not *a* stroke.

Of her three children, Teddy was the custodial child and the one, at least in his siblings' eyes, with the money. His brother was still in the Army, a noncommissioned officer ready to retire, and his sister was an administrative assistant for a college dean. With their easy approval and Emily's reluctant consent, Teddy had moved their mother to this town, his town, the neat, self-contained village in southern New Hampshire where he had settled with his newly begun second marriage a decade ago, and installed her in an efficiency apartment in an assisted-living facility. Teddy paid all her bills and let her use her small social security check for pin money. The facility offered nutritious, balanced meals in a dining hall on the first floor, regularly scheduled entertainment and recreation periods, laundry service, and housecleaning. And, as Teddy often reminded her, a comprehensive "life-care" health plan with a clinic and visiting physician right there on the premises. "If you broke your hip and needed round-the-clock medical care for months, you could stay right here at St. Hubert's," he said. "Down there in Somerset, all alone, you'd have to go straight into a nursing home."

She agreed. Old age was dangerous, and assisted living looked like the best protection available.

Sometimes, however, the place seemed little more than an oversized boardinghouse filled with nearly mindless, disabled old people, a trio of cold-eyed nurses, and a cadre of bored, cigarette-smoking attendants who'd rather be working in a prison. It seemed those times a strange way to live, with nothing natural about it. Whenever

Emily wondered what she was doing in such a place and how had she come to choose it, she recited back to herself the sequence of small, sharply determined steps that had brought her here, starting with her report to Teddy on the phone eighteen months ago that she could no longer lug home her week's groceries and lived too far from a store that delivered and thus had begun to ride the bus downtown and back daily for her food.

She missed her ranch house in Somerset and her longtime independence and possibly her solitude and wanted them back. Or if not that, then at least to be free to complain about their absence. But she couldn't even complain. "Consider the alternatives, Mom," Teddy kept reminding her. "This is not just what's best for you, it's your only option. You really can't live alone anymore."

True enough, she supposed, and also true that in some ways it was a relief to let Teddy take control of her life and a luxury not to have to worry ever again about anything.

Except, unexpectedly, this—this what? This *mystery*, which had been nothing at all, a nonexistence in her life. Until this morning, until Teddy, driving her to the diner in his new Lincoln Towncar, created it. In all these years, Emily had not thought to put the two together—her husband Wayne's car accident down in New Bedford and his sudden decision a few weeks later to sell the partially renovated Victorian house in New Hampshire and buy the barely finished ranch house down in Somerset, Massachusetts. In a matter of days, Wayne had uprooted Emily and their children and replanted them in a fly-by-night housing development a hundred miles to the south. At the time, the accident, which she knew only from Wayne's account, seemed to have happened to someone other than her husband, to a total stranger, and not to her and her three kids. The move from New Hampshire to Somerset, however, seemed to have happened only to her and the kids, and not to Wayne.

"Look, the connections, Mom, are obvious," Teddy said. With one hand he stirred nonfat creamer into his coffee and with the other set the empty plastic thimble neatly into the tray of unopened creamers. It was the occasion of their weekly breakfast at the Cascades Diner; a ritual marked and silently honored by the waitresses and the regulars. Teddy Holmes was a good son. A man nearly sixty years old, a local businessman with plenty of responsibilities and a second wife and grown family of his own, yet he still managed to find time once a week to take his elderly mother out for breakfast.

"Not obvious to me," Emily said. "Not then, and not now, either."

Della, their waitress, bellied up to the booth, pen poised and order pad out, and asked if they knew what they wanted.

"Yes!" Emily exclaimed and with helpful precision listed small grapefruit juice, two poached eggs medium-soft, toasted English muffin. "With *ba-con*," she growled, expressing anticipated pleasure, and added, "Extra crispy, please," and fluttered her eyelashes.

Della gave her a promissory wink and turned to her son, who ordered his usual scrambled eggs, bacon, and hash browns. Slowly he stirred his coffee. As if to reassure him, Emily rested her hand on his, and he ceased stirring, lifted his cup with his free hand, and took a sip.

"Sometimes I neglect how hard it was for you kids," she said. "Before my divorce, even."

Teddy's father—her late ex-husband, as Emily referred to him—had been a willful man and charming, and in moving them he'd gone against everyone, especially the children, who, after months of anxious resistance, had finally settled into their third school and home in the seven years since Teddy started school. She remembered that Teddy more than the others had hated the move. And though she herself had truly resented living apart from her husband and raising their kids practically on her own, Emily hadn't wanted to move, either. She loved that small New Hampshire town, the broad, tree-lined streets and large white homes, the grassy commons downtown, and the easy availability of roles that she could fill—church bake-sale chairperson, PTA vice president, Boy Scout mother, Girl Scout mother, member of the women's auxiliary to the fire department, to the VFW, the Elks. Emily liked small-town organizations and associations—she was the type of woman who is happiest when presented with a clear-cut role in life, when *chosen*. And she liked the house they'd bought there, a long-neglected, four-bedroom Victorian. After stripping half its walls and woodwork of generations of wallpaper and paint, she had begun to glimpse unexpected possibilities of gentility.

But down in Massachusetts, Wayne told her, they'd finally be living close to where his work was located, and he could sleep in his own bed on weeknights for a change. It wasn't his fault that he resided with his wife and kids only on weekends. He hated it as much as they did. He particularly hated the long drives home on Friday night and back on Sunday. Wayne was a shipyard welder, and he'd followed the construction of the first generation of nuclear submarines south along the New England coast from Portland, Maine, to Portsmouth, New Hampshire, where he'd worked on the *Thresher*, which so famously sank. From there he'd transferred to Charlestown, Massachusetts, and, after six months, signed on in New Bedford. Which was where the accident happened.

"Times like this," Teddy said, "I wish the old man was still around. So I could ask him."

"Ask him what?"

"About the accident. The move. All of it."

"It wouldn't matter," she said. "Your father lied about everything when he was alive, and he'd lie about it dead, too. Lie, lie, lie. The worst thing, Teddy, is he lied to me knowing all the while it would only make me lie unintentionally to you kids." She gave him a soulful, hurt look.

Teddy feigned sympathy and inwardly smiled. Recently, to his mild surprise, he'd found his mother's turns of phrase amusing, and sometimes on the phone with his brother or sister he had tried to share his pleasure by repeating some typically disjointed exchange with her. They, however, were not amused. Since high school they had deliberately lived as far from New England and their shared past as possible; both claimed that their mother's characteristic turns of phrase were merely flags for her self-absorption, her shallow, craven need for attention, and her self-serving ignorance. Teddy's siblings, when younger and between marriages, had described their childhoods at length and in detail to psychotherapists and had separately concluded that their mother was a fully flowered narcissist. To them, therefore, whatever she unintentionally revealed of herself solely concerned her present, not their past. They weren't interested.

Teddy, however, was. His mother was his very close neighbor now, and he'd seen much more of her in the last year alone than any of them had in the previous forty, and he was freshly revising many of his earlier assumptions about her character. Leading him to revise certain assumptions about his childhood and youth, and to rethink his memories of his father.

"It wouldn't matter what he told you, dead or alive, he'd still be lying," she repeated. "No matter what he described, the point would be to keep me from finding out about some woman he was seeing at the time. There would be one woman for the car accident in New Bedford, and another for the move to Somerset. In those days, women and me not finding out about them are what connected everything in that man's life."

Teddy shook his head no, and waited for Della to set their breakfast platters in front of them. Emily stared eagerly at her food, checked out his plate as if comparing portions, and commenced eating. There was more to it than that, he was certain. For one thing, it was the same woman, not two different women, who lurked behind the accident and who was also somehow the direct cause of their having to leave New Hampshire. He was sure of it.

He hadn't reflected on these memories in decades. All through his adolescence and even after college, Teddy remembered that long-ago summer and fall only in shifting pieces shaded and half-hidden behind a gauze curtain. He had a specific memory of running from the kitchen of their house in New Hampshire to the woods. Of hiding in the woods until after dark, while the family and even some of their neighbors hollered his name and searched for him. Of the peepers shrieking in the dark; of the smell of damp earth and leaves rotting underfoot. He had no memory of being found or of returning to the house or of the actual move to Somerset. There was no sequence to his memories, no clear chronology, no *sense* to them. His father came home to New Hampshire from New Bedford late one Friday night as usual, and that Sunday morning, whistling and full of good cheer, griddled pancakes for the three children, and when their mother arrived at the table, still in her nightdress and bathrobe, her eyes red and puffy from crying, he announced to the three that they were moving to a new house, a ter-rific, brand-new house down in Massachusetts, and he would be com-ing home from work every night, like other daddies did. Teddy remem-bered his father saying that he hated lawyers, every damned one of them, even his own lawyer. His mother wept; Teddy heard her from his bedroom in the new house, the room that he shared now with both his brother and sister, who were asleep, he was sure, and couldn't hear their mother crying first in the living room, then in the kitchen, then out-side on the back steps, calling, *Wayne, Wayne, I'm sorry, I didn't mean what I said!* as his father strode angrily into the suburban night. He wanted to wake his brother and sister, but decided not to. He remembered when he walked into his parents' bedroom on a snowy Sunday morn-ing and said to them, *Who's Brenda? What're you guys talking about?* his father had looked at him crossly and said, *Teddy, for Christ's sake, get lost!*

His father couldn't drive them in his car anywhere anymore. The men that he worked with picked him up on Sunday nights and drove him to New Bedford two hours away and brought him home again on Friday nights late. The family had moved to Massachusetts, but his father still came home only on weekends. He came home drunk. He told them that one of these days he'd be working in the Charlestown Navy Yard again, which was close to Somerset, and then he'd come home every night in time for supper. *Won't that be great, kids?* His mother, who was driving the Studebaker in the middle of the week one afternoon, said, *Daddy was in an accident and has lost his driver's license for a year. It upsets him to talk about, so don't notice it in front of him, okay?*

For years, like an archaeologist attempting to reassemble a piece of pottery from a handful of shards, he'd turned the memories over in his mind, trying to construct a coherent narrative, a story with a beginning, middle, and end that would explain the intensity of emotion that he associated with that brief period of his life. He finally gave it up. It was adolescence, that's all. These emotions, like his brother's and sister's overall feelings toward their mother, were displaced from some other, still unexamined part of his life. There was no story here.

Until this morning, when he picked up his mother at St. Hubert's Assisted Living Facility. The Home, she insisted on calling it. She hitched herself into the passenger seat and with her usual twists and grunts had so much difficulty fastening the seat belt that at last he had to lean over and snap it for her himself. She responded with a sincere, almost blissful smile. Her great pleasure was in being attended to, and it didn't matter who it came from or whether the attention was large or small: the degree of pleasure it gave was the same. Then she said, "I dreamed about the house in Somerset last night. It was lucky, you know, that Wayne made me put it in my name."

Teddy said, "He did what?"

In her dream, she rode the bus home from Teddy's drugstore with a bag of groceries, and after a long walk, when she felt utterly lost in a strange city, she finally found the house, but when she tried to open the door it was locked. Then she noticed a for sale sign on the front lawn, which frightened her. "I said to myself, 'It's lucky Wayne made me put the house in my name,' and then woke up, feeling very relieved that he'd done that. What do you think that means?" she asked. She knew Teddy enjoyed explaining people's dreams, but she took his interpretations no more seriously than she took her daily horoscope in the newspaper. Still, it flattered Teddy to be asked, and they were *her* dreams, after all, and her horoscope, so the form of the inquiry was familiar and pleasing to them both.

"That you were relieved?"

"I *know* why I was relieved. He put the house in my name is why. No, the other."

"But that's the most intriguing detail in the dream."

"It wasn't just in the dream, Teddy. It was real."

"What was?"

"Your father putting the house in my name."

Teddy looked across at her, puzzled and suddenly troubled. "Why the hell would Dad do that? In reality, I mean. I can understand in a dream why, but not in reality."

Wayne hadn't even attended the closing at the bank, she told him. She'd gone alone. He was too busy, had to work that day, something. She couldn't remember. Anyhow, since it was going to be in her name—the deed, the mortgage, the insurance, everything—there actually was no reason for him to go. The car, too, she said, his Studebaker: he'd transferred title of the car to her a few weeks before they passed papers on the house. That's why it was so much easier later, she explained, when they got divorced, for her to hold on to the house and car. And probably why he felt he didn't owe her any alimony, either, and didn't have the guilt of a normal man who wasn't making his child support payments on time.

"So, yes, I guess there was a negative side to it, as well as a positive," she said. "Maybe I wasn't so lucky after all."

"There's only one reason he'd sign everything over to you," Teddy announced.

"The paperwork," she said quickly. "Your father always hated paperwork. I was the one who paid the bills and corresponded, you know."

"He must've been on the losing end of a lawsuit."

"No, no. He was just too busy, and he hated paperwork, that's all. Do you mind if I have some heat?" she asked. "Would you turn the heater on?"

Teddy ignored her. He was remembering his father's car accident, realizing for the first time that it had occurred close to the time of their move from New Hampshire south to Somerset, the one event in his childhood that Teddy associated with the beginning of disruption, loss, and fear: he believed that, for him, there began the end of family life. Up to that point, Teddy hadn't noticed the rapidly widening gap between other people's family lives and his. But from then on, from the autumn of his thirteenth year, the gap defined him.

Teddy's memories of his father's accident were as sketchy and unreliable as his memories of the move to Somerset, and his mother was as reluctant to talk about both events now as she had been back when they occurred. Teddy, however, was not in the slightest reluctant to reconstruct the events of that summer and fall of 1953 and then to substitute for his tattered memory of the original his closely woven reconstruction.

It was a warm June weeknight on the south shore of Cape Cod. Wayne Holmes and his lady friend were out for the evening in Wayne's green Studebaker, heading down Route 28 from a roadhouse in Hyannis to a tavern in Falmouth. As they entered the village proper, Wayne reached to tune the car radio, trying to pick up Vaughn Monroe and his orchestra, broadcast live from the Norumbega Ballroom all that week.

He took his eyes off the road for a second, when a child, a boy maybe ten years old or possibly as old as Teddy, stepped between two parked cars, and Wayne's right front fender caught the boy and tossed him into the air. There were screams, shouts, tires squealing—and then an awful silence, except for Vaughn Monroe's theme song, "Racing with the Moon."

The boy was killed instantly. The middle son of a Portuguese fisherman, he was on his way home from the butcher shop where he worked part-time as a delivery boy. Wayne's lady friend had slammed her head against the dashboard, causing a concussion and possible fracture, and her neck and back had been seriously injured by whiplash, but she would in time recover from her injuries completely. Wayne was drunk. He could walk and talk coherently, but he had consumed half a dozen Manhattans in the Hyannis roadhouse and a bottle of beer on the drive to Falmouth. Arrested at the scene, he was thrown into jail for the night and released the next morning on bail posted by his union shop steward at the New Bedford shipyard.

Teddy didn't know the name of his father's lady friend, but he thought it might be Brenda. To the police, to his insurance company's lawyers, to the lawyer for the parents of the dead boy, and to the judge and jury, Wayne denied that he had been drinking—the police at the scene were wrong, that's all. There were no breath tests then, no proof, and Brenda, perjuring herself, backed him up. The charge of driving-while-intoxicated was dropped, and because the boy had stepped into moving traffic at midblock, Wayne was found not responsible for his death, which should have ended the case.

Except that Wayne reneged on his promise to divorce Emily and marry Brenda. He didn't even visit Brenda in the hospital to comfort her or to thank her for testifying falsely on his behalf. The accident had frightened Wayne deep in his bones and made him decide temporarily to give up drinking and womanizing. Besides, he'd lost his driver's license for a year, an automatic penalty when the driver of a moving vehicle causes a fatality, and his car insurance policy had been canceled, and he was going to need the help of his wife and friends just to get back and forth between work in Massachusetts and home in New Hampshire. It was time to end the affair.

Brenda disagreed. She loved him and had lied for him at considerable risk to herself and did not expect to be repaid with abandonment and indifference. She had spent three weeks in the hospital and now suffered recurrent migraines, serious and continuing back and neck pain, and so on, a long list of complaints and deprivations that he would have to pay for. It was going to cost him tens of thousands of dollars. She promised she'd strip him of everything he owned.

Brenda revealed her intentions to Wayne in New Hampshire one Saturday afternoon in July. He was in the living room half asleep on the sofa, listening to a Red Sox game on the radio, when the phone rang. Emily, passing through the room at that moment, answered it, handed the receiver to him, and said, "It's a woman for you." She then went into the kitchen and sat at the window and stared dry-eyed out at her children playing in the yard.

A few moments later, Wayne entered the kitchen and stood behind her. He placed his heavy, wide hands on her shoulders and said, "We're going to have to sell the house and move. Out of state. And I've got to put the car in your name, along with everything else I own or we own jointly. It's because of the accident, Emily. The parents of the kid, they're suing me for everything I own."

Emily nodded, accepting his explanation, but not believing it, either. The truth, whatever it was, would wreck her life and the lives of her children. The truth would have to wait.

"Teddy, please," Emily said, "may I have the heat turned up? It's quite cool in here."

"Sorry," he said and flicked the heater switch and set the thermostat at seventy-two degrees. The big, gray Lincoln still impressed Teddy, even after owning it for a year, and he took particular pleasure in operating its onboard electronic systems. Emily, too, liked the car and whenever she was a passenger, for the duration of the ride, ran her fingertips lovingly along the seams of the soft leather upholstery. She'd never noticed the habit, but her son had. So far he'd not mentioned it to her, because he knew that if he brought her pleasure to her attention, she would abandon it.

Emily looked out the car window at the large, white houses crowding the broad, tree-lined street. "It wasn't the way you say, Teddy. The accident and all. That had nothing to do with our decision to move to Somerset. And there was never anyone he promised to marry. Your father didn't want a divorce from me, not even later. I was the one who wanted it. Well, not really," she said. "I did it because of you kids."

"Us? You've got to be kidding, Mom."

"You know what I mean, Teddy. Please, honey, just leave me alone. This is all water under the dam." She paused, and they drove on in silence. "We don't have to rehash everything these many years later, do we?" she asked him.

"I just want to know the truth," he answered as he pulled the car into the parking lot of the diner.

"The truth about what?"

"The connections. Cause and effect. I need to know if the old man moved us out of our house and home for a reason, no matter how tawdry and selfish. Or was it just on a whim? If it *was* for a reason, if the one thing, his accident and so forth, caused the other, then I guess I can forgive him. But if there wasn't any reason, well . . ." He shut off the engine and opened his door. "I think that's what's terrified me for years, Mom. Since it happened, actually, I've been afraid that he did it on a whim. That he did it, not because he thought he *had* to, but because he *wanted* to! If that turns out the case, I don't think I'll spit on his grave, exactly. . . . But you, of all people, should know how I'd feel. I'd sure *want* to spit on his grave!" He saw that his mother was struggling with her seat belt again, and he reached over and released her.

She smiled up at him, as if she hadn't heard a word he'd said. "They don't make these things for old people, do they?"

He didn't answer. They walked side by side to the entrance of the diner, and once again he stated his need to believe that his father had torn the family from their beloved home to protect himself from the wrath of a spurned woman.

Emily said, as they came through the door, "I'm sorry, no, Teddy, it wasn't like that at all."

And he said, "The only way the two things make sense, *moral* sense, is if they're cause and effect. The old man used you, Mom, he used you pure and simple."

Now they were leaving. While Teddy paid the check at the cash register, Emily walked alone to the car. The conversation had left her sadder than she could remember feeling in years. Since her divorce, really. And even then she hadn't felt this sad. She hadn't had the time back then to take the measure of her sadness, not with so much happening, so many crises large and small. Her heart in her chest felt changed by the sadness from flesh to stone, fossilized.

Why, she asked herself, was Teddy so obsessed and troubled by the move away from New Hampshire those many long years ago? He had settled in a town very like the town they'd been forced to leave and had made himself a full new life here, almost as if he'd resided and worked here since childhood. He had even taken to calling it his hometown. And he'd bought a house that was in many ways a replica of the Victorian house they'd had to sell for the tacky little ranch in Somerset. Teddy had repaired the breach in *his* life.

Emily, though, had nothing that was as beautiful and strong and in its proper place as Teddy's hometown and house. And she never would.

She had nothing that could repair or replace the life that her husband had stolen from her that long-ago summer when he decided her life and their children's were actually his. The children, in time, had taken their lives back, all three of them, especially Teddy. But she had gone on without hers for so long that she had nearly forgotten it ever existed at all—until this morning, when Teddy started questioning her. Now she saw that all she had for a life was the Home, St. Hubert's Assisted Living Facility. And she knew that the Home wasn't really hers, either. It was Teddy's, not hers. He was doing to her what his father had done to him, only softly and slowly, and the person he was lying to was himself.

Teddy came up behind her and opened the car door for her. When she spoke, she turned away, so he wouldn't see her tears. "You're right, Teddy. About your father. And that woman, Brenda something. It was like you said, your father didn't do it on a whim, Teddy. He didn't. He had his reasons."

He looked at her now and saw that she was crying. "Oh, Mom, I'm sorry," he said, but he knew instantly that it was too late. He had done a thing that could not be undone.

She patted his hand. "You're a good boy, Teddy," she said. "A good boy."

The Neighbor

The idea was to watch his gaunt wife, seated on the sulky, drive the chocolate-colored mare down the dirt road to the general store, to make a small purchase there, and return. He was a black man in his fifties, she a white woman the same age, his children (from a previous marriage) were black, her children (also from a previous marriage) were white. Everyone else in town was white, also. Many of them had never seen a black man before this one. That's probably why he had this idea about the sulky and his wife and the store.

On the other hand, he may have had it because he and his wife and all their children were incompetent and, in various ways, a little mad. The madness had got them kicked out of the city, but here, after three years in a small farm-community north of the city, it was the incompetence that had angered the people around them. Country people can forgive madness, but a week ago, the family's one immediate neighbor, a dour young man in his late twenties, walked out his back door and saw for the tenth time one of their chickens scratching in his pathway to the woodpile. He rushed back into his house and, returning with an Army .45 handgun, fired eight bullets into the chicken, making a feathered, bloody mess of it.

That same night, the black man with his two teenage daughters and his two teenage stepsons and his wife drove to the racetrack and bought for one hundred dollars an unclaimed trotter, an eighteen-year-old mare named Jenny Lind. They rented a van and lugged her home and put her in the barn with the goats, sheep, chickens, and the two Jersey heifers. The farm, the huge barn, the animals—except for the mare—were all part of an earlier idea, the idea of living off the land. But the climate had proved harsh, the ground stony and in hills, the neighbors more or less uncooperative—and there was that incompetence.

It was the end of summer, and every morning as the sun rose the black man got up and before his breakfast walked the mare along the side of the dirt road in the low, cold mist. Behind him, in layers, were the brown meadow and the clumpy rows of gold and ruby-colored elm trees and the dark hills and the mist-dimmed orange sun. Every morning he paraded Jenny Lind the length of the route he had planned for his wife and the sulky—his shining arm raised to the bridle, his face proudly looking straight ahead of him as he walked past his neighbor's house, his mind reeling with delight as he imagined his wife in her frail-wheeled sulky riding to the store, where she would buy him some pipe tobacco and some salt for the table, a small package to be wrapped in brown paper and tied with string, and then, after she returned along the curving dirt road to the house, one of her sons or one of his daughters would run out and hold the reins for her and help her step graciously down. In that way, the horse received its daily exercise—for no one in the family knew how to ride, because, as the father pointed out to them, no one in the family had yet been to a riding academy, and, besides, Jenny Lind was a trotter.

They searched all over the state for a sulky they could afford, but no one would sell it to them. Finally, he phoned the man at the racetrack who had sold them the horse and learned of a good, used sulky for sale in a town in the far southwest corner of the state. That morning, after exercising the mare, he and his wife got into the pickup truck and drove off to see about the used sulky.

All day long, the two teenage sons and the two teenage daughters
rode the mare bareback up and down the dirt road, galloping past the
neighbor's house, braking to a theatrical stop at the general store, and
galloping back again. A hundred times they rode the old horse full-
speed along the half-mile route. Silvery waves of sweat covered her
heaving sides and neck, and her large, watery eyes bulged from the
exertion, and late in the afternoon, as the sun was drifting down
behind the pines in back of the house, the mare suddenly veered off the
road and collapsed on the front lawn of the neighbor's house and died
there. The boy who was riding her was able to leap free of the collapsing bulk, and astonished, terrified, he and his brother and stepsisters
ran for their own house and hid in a loft over the barn, where, eating
sandwiches and listening to a transistor radio, they awaited the return
of their parents.

The neighbor stood in his living room and, as darkness came on,
stared unbelieving at the dead horse on his lawn. Finally, when it was
completely dark and he couldn't see it anymore, he walked onto his
front porch and sat on the glider and waited for the black man and his
wife to come home.

Around ten o'clock, he heard their pickup clattering along the road.
The truck stopped beside the enormous bulk of the horse. With the pale
light from the truck splashed across its dark body, the animal seemed of
gigantic proportions, a huge equestrian monument pulled down by van-
dals. The neighbor left his porch and walked down to where the horse
lay. The black man and his white wife had got out of their truck and
were sitting on the ground, stroking the mare's forehead.

The neighbor was a young man, and while a dead animal was nothing new to him, the sight of a grown man weeping and a woman sitting
next to him, also weeping, both of them slowly stroking the cold nose
of a horse ridden to death—that was something he'd never seen before.
He patted the woman and the man on their heads, and in a low voice

told them how the horse had died. He was able to tell it without judging the children who had killed the animal.

Then he suggested that they go on to their own house, and he would take a chain and, with his tractor, would drag the carcass across the road from his lawn to their meadow, where tomorrow they could bury it by digging a pit next to it. Close enough, he told them, so that all they had to do was shove the carcass with a tractor or a pickup truck and it would drop in. They quietly thanked him and got up and climbed back into their truck and drove to their own house.

The Rise of the Middle Class

Weary, half-defeated by history, and almost as wary of those you have spent your life's energies and treasure to make free as you are of their iron-minded oppressors, you are the middle-aging Simón Bolívar, and less than a month ago you arrived here in Kingston, Jamaica, in desperate flight from Venezuela, arrived with a Spanish price on your head and a pack of rabid assassins dogging your trail down from the mountains of Colombia to the sea, always hoping you would stupidly trust someone you should not. You did not, and, happily, the assassins seem not to have followed you here, at least not yet.

It is the afternoon of the seventh of June, 1815. Your friend, Mr. Henry Cullen, has invited you to leave Kingston and visit with him at his plantation in Falmouth, a Great House situated on a limestone cliff overlooking Jamaica's tranquil north shore, and you have gratefully accepted. The effort of trying to convince agents of the English king to support you and your ragtag rebellions against the Spanish king has angered and exhausted you. And neither anger nor exhaustion becomes you. Your pale, delicate face and frame, your intelligence, your exquisitely refined, yet passionate sensibility, these become clouded and only vaguely felt, by you or anyone else, when you are angry; and when you are exhausted, you fear that you resemble an aesthete, a type of human being you abhor.

Yes, my dear friend, you write to Cullen, scratch-scratch against the parchment. *I shall arrive one week from tomorrow, probably rather late in the day, for your Jamaican roadways are not much smoother or straighter than my beloved Venezuelan mountain paths.*

You put down the pen, and the first of the assassins to reach the island, one López Martínez Martínez, springs through the open door from the balcony outside, grabs you by the ruffled collar of your shirt, and raises his knife. You note absurdly that he smells of goat cheese and wet canvas. Though you are the victim and he the killer, he grins in fear, his tongue afloat in his toothless mouth.

When your shirt tears in his grip, you yank yourself away from him, knocking over the escritoire, and your letter to Cullen falls to the parquet floor like a leaf, slips onto the balcony and off, drifting to the sunny courtyard below, where it is seen by a black man, an English slave named Jack, commonly called Three-Fingered Jack, for two fingers of his right hand were chopped off in childhood as punishment. He squints and stares up, as if to see where the paper might have come from. He could, if he wished, peer across the balcony outside your room and through the open doors and could watch you struggle with the assassin.

Jack says nothing. He walks slowly over and picks up your unfinished letter to Cullen, folds it carefully in half and half again, and slides it between his sweaty belly and leather belt. Jack does not worry about your welfare. He knows that you are an important man, that you have two British soldiers from Fort Charles posted outside your door, and that they will hear your struggle with Martínez Martínez and will save you. Jack wants your piece of paper. Paper is useful and not cheap.

Later in the day, you look around your room for your letter to Cullen. You search under the bed and the dresser, even inside the mahogany wardrobe. It's nowhere to be seen. Where could it have flown to? Curious.

Finally, you sit down at the escritoire and begin again, even more wearily and gratefully than when you wrote the first letter. *My dear Henry, your kind offer to remove me from the swelter and the crowds of Kingston to the refreshing luxury of your Great House has been received here with delight and great relief, for I was beginning to believe that I. . . .*

When you have completed the letter and have sealed it with wax, you rise from the table, go to the door of your chamber, and hand the letter to the guard outside, instructing him to post it immediately to Falmouth. Then, feeling both enervated and oddly agitated—because of Martínez Martínez, you tell yourself, in spite of the fact that he is now quite dead, a chunk of meat with a mouth shuddering with flies—you walk to the balcony and peer down into the courtyard.

The packed earth is the color of cream. A black man works alone down there, raking away the tracks of the horses, smoothing the grounds, pulling slowly on his split-bamboo rake, moving the riffles and ripples in the dirt, clods kicked loose by the horses, droppings, and the leaf or stalk that may have idly fallen to the ground after having been blown into the courtyard from beyond the walls by an errant puff of wind off the bay. Slowly, tediously, he pulls these tiny disturbances in gradually closing, concentric circles. From above, you examine the circles closely, and eventually you realize that they are spirals, coils, moving toward a still center which, with a wide, square-bladed shovel, the black man will remove and deposit outside the gate. The design will be gone. Without the center, there will be no spiral, no coil.

You study the man for a moment. He is a slave. A man wholly inside history, you reflect. No one will assassinate him. He can only be murdered. To be assassinated, you must first step outside history; you have to be guilty of trying to affect history from outside. Like God. The slave, by definition, can never obtain that prerogative, you observe. You envy him. More and more often, in recent months, you have found yourself envying people you regard as being wholly determined by the sweep of history. The shepherd in Peru. The Inca baby outside the cathedral in Bogotá. The sailor on the British frigate that brought you to Kingston. And now this one, a slave.

You think: That man probably has my letter to Cullen, the first one. He probably saw it skitter out the open door to the balcony, the very door that the assassin entered. He probably saw the assassin climb the tile drain to the narrow ledge and watched him crawl along the ledge to the balcony, saw him swing his legs over the balcony rail, open the door an inch wider, and stroll into my room, the knife already in his hand.

Even so, you bear the slave no malice. Quite the contrary. No, to be free to stand there below and watch one man attempt to assassinate another, and to be able to do nothing—what a respite! You squint and look closely, and you realize that the black man has seen you staring down at him. He is staring back. He probably envies me, you think. What an irony. To envy the man who envies you.

It is late. The sun drifts closer to the horizon above the bay and the flatlands to the west of Kingston. Beyond the fortress walls lies the turquoise sea, now smeared red by the setting sun. You are growing morose, so you "pull yourself together," as the English say, and in your mind compose the first sentence of yet another letter to the editors of the Kingston newspapers, The Royal Gazette and The St. Jago Gazette. Here is the sentence: *Sir: To the everlasting credit and glory of His Royal Majesty King George III and the Royal Governor of Jamaica, the Duke of Manchester, it is true today that the lowliest blackamoor in this paradise, a three-fingered Negro slave named Jack, is more to be envied than the founder of a Republic torn from the darkly bleeding heart of the mighty South American continent.*

You believe that the English will believe that this is true; you know that at this moment, for you, it is true; and you also know that Three-Fingered Jack, if he could read your letter, would laugh. But the obligation to shape a future history forbids you to say what is true for everyone. That crude freedom would only allow you to doodle and dribble, to waste time and paper while sitting here in a fortress by the sea, help-lessly waiting for the Spanish Empire to crack at its feeble feet and drop its heavy head down parapets, cliffs, palisades, campaniles. You think of equestrian statues toppling from building-sized bases. You think of armored Arab horses stumbling on the pampas and shattering their thin, brittle legs. You think of cashew trees sprawling heavily across spindly trunks. You think of a waterspout. "If only," you murmur, and the images of collapse multiply.

It is dark. The room is filled with maroon and purple wedges of shadow. Again, you stroll to the balcony and look into the courtyard. Down there it is now wholly dark. You can see nothing definite. A pit of blackness. Noise of leather moving against leather, of horses breath-ing, of a man's callused hand moving across his forearm against the hairs—these carefully rise through the silence to you.

He's still down there. You know he's down there, buried in the dark-ness the same way he's buried in history. You light the lantern behind you and place it on the escritoire. You step in front of it to the edge of the balcony. You show yourself in sharp profile. A shot rings out.

The Burden

Because of the shabby character of the boy's mother and also that of the man she married the same day she found herself legally divorced and able to marry again, and because the two had determined to live far away from New Hampshire without even bothering to send him their address until several years later, Tom had raised Buddy practically by himself. And he had seen his son through hard times, especially as the boy got older, such as when he was in the service for one year and later when he got himself beat up by the guy with the baseball bat and spent six months flat on his back in Tom's trailer learning how to talk again. So, of course, when Tom walked into the Hawthorne House for a beer, even though, after the bright afternoon sunlight outside, he wasn't used to the darkness inside, he recognized the boy right away. You can do that with your children, you can tell who they are even in darkness and all you can see of them is their height and the position they happen to be standing in. You just glance over, and you say, Oh, yeah, there's my son.

Tom didn't know the girl with him, though. Not even when he drew close to her and could see her face clearly in the dim light of the bar. She was sitting alone in the booth next to the jukebox where Buddy stood studying the songs. Tom could tell she was with Buddy and not alone because of the way she watched him while he studied the names of the songs on the jukebox. It was the way girls always watched Buddy, as if they couldn't believe he wasn't going to disappear from in front of them any second—just poof! and he'd be gone, a curl of smoke hanging in the air where a second ago he had been smiling and chattering in that circular way of his. Nobody knew where Buddy got it from, his good looks and that way he had of talking so interestingly that people hated to see him come to a stop or ask a question, even. His mother, Maggie, Tom's ex-wife, had been pretty (back when she was Buddy's age, that is) but she had never been as outstandingly good-looking as Buddy was, and Tom, even though he had a square and regular-featured face, was not the kind of man you'd compliment for his looks, and neither Tom nor his ex-wife owned what you'd call a gift of gab, especially not Tom, who usually seemed more interested in listening than in talking, anyhow.

Tom walked past the girl, who looked around twenty-five, which made her four years older than Buddy and which was also usual for him. The girl was dark-haired and pretty, but actually more stylish than pretty, when you got up close, with a round face and a grim little mouth. Her short hair was all kinked up in a way that was fashionable just then, which made her somewhat resemble a dandelion, until you looked into her eyes and saw that she was awfully worried about something. You couldn't tell what it was, actually, but it was clear that she was not at peace with her circumstances.

Tom stopped behind his son and next to the bar, and, as he moved on to the bar, he reached out and absently tapped his son on the shoulder, and the boy turned around and smiled nicely. Tom didn't smile back, he didn't even look at Buddy. He looked across at Gary, the bartender who also owned the place, and ordered a bottle of beer.

"You're keeping your door locked now, Dad," Buddy said, as if Tom didn't realize it.

"I know." Tom turned around and faced him.

Buddy reached out and shook his father's hand. "This here's Donna," he said, nodding toward the girl. "Donna picked me up hitching outside Portland on the Maine Pike, and we sorta got to be friends in a very short order, which is certainly nice for me, because I'm nothing special, and you can see that she is."

Donna gave Tom a thin smile and did not look like a person who was glad to find herself where she had found herself, stopped in a dingy New Hampshire mill town barroom to have a chat with her new boyfriend's father. Tom didn't give a damn about her, though, one way or the other. If she wanted to drive all over the countryside just because she thought Buddy looked good beside her, it didn't matter to Tom, because women were always doing things like that, and so were men.

"How long you in town this time?" Tom asked his son. Gary delivered the bottle of beer, and Tom turned back to the bar and drank off half the bottle. He was feeling weighted down and metallic inside, as if his stomach were filled with tangled stovepipe wire, because even though Buddy was his son and he could recognize him in the darkness, he didn't like it when he saw him. Not anymore.

"So, Dad, you're keeping your door locked nowadays," he said again.

Tom was silent for a few seconds and did not look at the boy. "That's right. Ever since you left and took with you every damned thing of mine you could fit into that duffel of yours. My tape deck, tapes. You even took my cuff links." He looked down at his shirt cuffs. "I must be stupid." He finished off the bottle of beer, and Gary automatically slid a second over. Gary was a tall, skinny, dark-haired man with a toothpick in his mouth that made him look wiser than he probably was. He was the fourth owner of the bar in the last ten years.

Once again, Buddy smiled in that easy way he had, like a summer sun coming up, and Tom felt his stomach clank and tangle. "C'mon, Dad, I only *borrowed* that stuff. I only planned to be gone for the weekend, me and Bilodeau, that kid from Concord. It was a weekend, the weather suddenly got warm, you probably don't remember, but it did. And we were planning to chase some girls Bilodeau knew over on the coast near Kittery. But things just got screwed up, and before the weekend was over, we ended up going in different directions with different people. You know how it goes." He showed Tom both his palms, as if to prove he wasn't hiding anything.

"That was last April." Tom knew his son was lying, and there was no damned sense trying to catch him out or somehow prove the boy was lying or get him to admit it, because he'd just go on lying, topping one lie with another, canceling one out with a new one, on and on, until, out of fatigue and boredom, you just gave up. Buddy was one of those people who are always ready to go a step further than anyone else, and after a while you could see that about him, so you'd stop, and he'd be standing there just ahead of you, smiling back. It was almost as if he didn't know the difference between right and wrong.

"April?" the girl said. She lit a cigarette and looked at Buddy through the smoke. "So what's been happening since April? This is June," she observed, as if she had just got a glimpse, from the conversation between the father and the son, of what might be in store for her if she went ahead with her plans and hooked up for a while with this good-looking, smooth-talking, slender young man. It probably started out as a whim, picking up and spending the weekend with a guy she'd seen hitchhiking in Maine. It would make a funny story she could tell on herself to friends in Boston or Hartford or wherever she had originally been headed. But now things were starting to look a little off-center to her, not quite lined up, which is how it always was with Buddy, how it always had been. He was so damned good-looking, all white teeth and high cheekbones and quick-sloping, narrow nose and deep blue eyes, the American dream-boy, and he talked sweetly and in a strangely elaborate way, all in circles and curls that kept you listening, so that pretty soon you forgot what it was you were planning on doing, and instead you plugged into his plans, not your own, but then, someplace down along the line, things started to look a little bit off-center, as if a couple of basic pieces hadn't been cut right. And you couldn't tell which pieces were off, because the whole damned thing was off.

Buddy peered down at her as if he couldn't quite place her. "What's been happening since April?" he asked. "You really want to know?"

"No. Not really. It just seemed a funny thing, that's all . . ."

"Funny. What's funny?" Buddy asked. Tom watched the two carefully from the bar.

"Nothing," the girl said. "Forget it." She closed her eyes for a second, and when she opened them, her expression had changed, as if she had turned Buddy into a stranger, as if she were seeing him for the first time all over again, but this time with the knowledge that she had gained since morning, when she first saw him at the Portland exit with his thumb out and his duffel and suitcase on the road beside him.

"Forget funny?" Buddy said, smiling broadly. "Who can forget funny?" He turned away from the girl and faced his father and suddenly started talking to him. "Listen, Dad, that's why I stopped down at the trailer, before I came up here. To give your stuff back, I mean. Hey, I couldn't do it way the hell up there in Maine among the trees and lakes, and then Donna here was nice enough to drive all this distance out of her way just to help me drop these things off at your place, before we resume our wanderings. Listen, Dad, since April I've been way the hell out on a narrow neck of land in northern Maine, working on this lobster boat." He laid a hand on his father's shoulder.

Tom didn't believe a word the boy said. He had decided long ago, as policy, not to believe anything his son told him. And that, he told himself, was one of the reasons he kept his trailer locked now for the first time in his entire life. You're supposed to love your son and trust him and protect him, and that had always been easy for Tom, but this new way of treating him was a burden, and he hated it. For years, Tom had loved his son and trusted him and protected him, behaving precisely the way he knew the boy's mother, his ex-wife, Maggie, would not have behaved. Maggie would have let the boy down. Maggie wouldn't have been home the night the state troopers brought him in all drunk and raving, and the boy would have ended up in jail. Maggie wouldn't have known how to handle it when he got his head bashed in by that guy with the baseball bat in Florida. She would have let him rot in that charity ward in the Florida hospital, before she'd have brought him home, set him up on the living-room couch in front of the TV, and then every night for six months taught the boy how to talk again, until finally he could make those looping, charming sentences of his again, and people would sit back in their chairs and listen with light smiles on their faces to see such a clever, good-looking young man perform for them. Maggie never would have borne up under the weight of Buddy, Tom knew. The proof of her weakness, as if he needed proof, he'd obtained the summer Buddy turned twelve, when he had taken the boy by Greyhound all the way to Phoenix, Arizona, to visit his mother, at her request. Tom took a two-week holiday alone farther west, visiting Disneyland, Knott's Berry Farm, and Universal Studios and watching the surfers at Huntington Beach, the only time he had ever seen real-life surfers. When the two weeks were up and Tom called back at Phoenix for his son, things had changed, and he left the boy in Phoenix, at the boy's request, presumably for good (at least that was Maggie's and her husband's intention and Buddy's as well). Tom returned to New Hampshire and didn't hear anything from his son until September, when the boy showed up at the trailer. Maggie had put him alone on a Boston-bound bus in Phoenix connecting to another bus to Concord, New Hampshire, and the boy, more travel-wise by now than he'd been in June, had hitchhiked the final twenty-five miles home to Catamount. No, for Maggie it was the love and the trust and the protection that made the burden. For Tom, the burden was in withholding that love, trust, and protection. That's what he believed.

For it wasn't simply Buddy's stealing his father's belongings that had turned the man against him, though that helped. And it wasn't that the boy seemed incapable of telling the truth about anything—he would lie when there was nothing to be gained by it, he lied for the sheer pleasure of lying, or so it seemed, and if you asked him was it raining outside, he'd look out the window, see that it was raining, and say no, not yet, and when you stepped out the door into the rain, you'd turn around and look at Buddy, and he'd say with great delight that it must have started raining that very second. And it wasn't that the boy was reckless and troublesome, that he seemed incapable of avoiding the kind of person who happened at that moment to want to hurt someone, especially someone young and pretty and mouthy. Buddy would find himself in a bar, the Hawthorne House, say, next to a crossed-up truck driver or some hide-stacker from the tannery, and he would do everything he could think of to make himself look even younger, prettier, and mouthier than he was, and he'd end up getting himself thrashed for it. And then somehow he'd find his way back to the trailerpark, and he'd drag himself to the door, swing open the door, and fall into the living room, where his father would be sitting in front of the TV with a can of beer in his hand and the open newspaper on his lap.

"Buddy! What the hell's happened?"

"Oh, Daddy, did I ever get myself into one this time! They got some mean and dirty-fighting, rattle-snaking, bad-ass cowboys hanging out nowadays at the Hawthorne House. It's just not your family restaurant anymore."

It wasn't any of those actions and attitudes and incapacities that turned Tom against his son and made him lock his door against his boy. In fact, if anyone had asked him why, after all those years of standing by him, had he suddenly gone and turned against his boy, Tom would not have been able to answer. All he knew was that it began for him about a week after Buddy left this last time, back in April. Right off, Tom noticed that his son had taken with him his tape deck, tapes, a bottle of Canadian Club whiskey, his cuff links, two shirts, and probably a dozen more possessions that he wouldn't find out about until he needed them and went looking for them. He merely observed that, once again, his son had made off with everything of his that he could lay his hands on, and he was, once again, glad that none of it was irreplaceable. Nothing Tom owned was irreplaceable, even though that was not by intention. In recent years he had worked off and on as an escort driver for a mobile home manufacturer in Suncook, hiring out with his own pickup truck and CB radio, usually as the lead man, the one with the sign, WIDE LOAD FOLLOWING, on the front of his truck, and before that he had driven an oil delivery truck, so while he had always made enough to house and feed and clothe himself and his one child, he hadn't made much more than that. Certainly, he had never made enough to buy anything that was irreplaceable.

But about a week after Buddy left this time, Tom began to feel something he had never felt before—at least with regard to Buddy he had never felt it before. He felt relieved. Relieved that the boy was gone from him, was not at home in front of the TV set or coming in late all drunk and bashed up or slamming cupboard doors in the morning in search of food. He was glad, for the first time he could remember, that he did not have to see the boy's face across the table from him; he discovered that he enjoyed eating alone. And then, once he admitted to himself that he was relieved to have the boy gone from him, it was as if he had released a flood of bad feelings about the boy, so that his face darkened every time Buddy's name was mentioned or every time he walked into some evidence of the boy's ever having lived with him, his dirty clothes in that final week's laundry, for example, or a letter that came to him three days after he left, a letter in a woman's handwriting, Tom could tell, because of the careful, large, rounded letters. And then even his memories of the boy's childhood began to turn sour and ugly, and he couldn't remember something he'd once enjoyed with the boy without feeling his stomach tighten and grow heavy, so that he would turn away from the memory and think about something more immediate. For instance, he taught Buddy to ice-skate when he was only four or five and taught him to shoot a hockey puck into a makeshift goal he set up on the lake behind the trailerpark not far from shore and within sight of his own trailer. Buddy developed the basic skills quickly and soon was obsessed with practicing the sport, especially the part that had him skating full speed to a spot twelve or fifteen feet in front of the goal and firing the puck a few inches off the ice into the goal, then coasting forward, stick raised to celebrate the score, retrieving the puck, and looping back out to make the run over again. For hours in the late afternoons that winter, the boy skated alone and shot goals, and his father looked out the window of the trailer as it grew swiftly dark outside and watched the tiny figure of his son move back and forth across the gray surface of the ice, until after a while it seemed the boy was floating in a dark haze, and then Tom stepped outside to the frozen ground and hollered for him to come in for supper. And the image of his son that he held in his mind as he called his name into the darkness was of his small, struggling figure afloat in a haze between the ice below and the sky above, as if sky and ice had merged and had become an ether, as if the firmament had been erased. Remembering this now, as he often did when, by accident, he happened to look out the window in the kitchen that showed him a wide expanse of the open lake, he winced and held on to the edge of the counter as if to regain lost balance, and he thought about getting some new tiles to replace the half dozen that were lifting from the floor in front of the sink.

Tom didn't understand this shift in his feelings, this great relief, as if a huge burden had been lifted from his back. He was ashamed of it, which only replaced one burden with another. For it seemed wrong to him, wrong to feel glad that his son was gone away, wrong to hope that he would never come back, and it seemed shameful to him that memories of his son made him wince, that signs of his son's life made him look away with irritation, that questions from friends about his son's whereabouts and welfare made him grit his teeth and answer abruptly and vaguely. But he couldn't help himself. It was out of his control. Buddy had even started entering his dreams in the same irritating way, turning a pleasant dream sour, a peaceful dream turbulent, a funny dream grim.

He knew Buddy eventually would come back, would show up in town again, probably down at the trailer, and if not there, then up here at the Hawthorne House, where Buddy knew his father could be found almost every afternoon drinking three or four beers and listening to Gary and the locals who stopped in after work. That's when Tom had taken to locking his door whenever he left the trailer, something he had never done before, not in all the years he had lived at the trailer-park. In recent years most people in the park had taken to locking their doors, mainly because of rumors of theft (though no one actually knew firsthand of any thievery), and until now Tom had refused to go along with the trends, saying that he had nothing worth stealing anyhow, so why try to protect it? Then one morning he had walked out the door to his truck, about to leave for a two-day job escorting a sixty-seven-foot Marlette from Suncook to just outside Syracuse, New York. He got into the truck, started the engine, peered back at the powder blue trailer, and thought, The door. He got out, walked quickly across to the cinder-block steps, reached up, and locked the door. That was that. And he had locked it, whenever he left the trailer, ever since.

The girl Donna was gone. She had got up as if going to the ladies' room, and she hadn't come back.

"Where's Donna, Dad?" Buddy asked, looking hurt and slightly bewildered. He sat down in the booth where she had been sitting earlier.

"Gone, maybe." Tom turned away from his son and faced the bar, standing between two barstools as if he were in too much of a hurry to sit down and relax.

Buddy sat in the booth looking half dazed, but it was the wrong way to look, or so it seemed to Tom, so Tom said nothing, even though he thought about it, about how the boy should be acting at a time like this. After all, a new girlfriend got spooked and slipped out the door and drove off in her car, and she might have taken all Buddy's belongings with her, even including his father's tape deck and tapes and cuff links. Why, then, wasn't the boy racing outside to see if the girl at least had tossed his bags out of her car before driving off? And why wasn't he cursing her? Or maybe even laughing, at himself, at the girl, at his fate? Instead, he sat in the booth, languid, head lolling back, eyes half closed. Tom glanced down at the boy, then turned swiftly away again. The sight of his son sitting like that made him tighten inside and caused his shoulders and the small of his back to stiffen.

"You think she tossed your bags out before she took off?" he asked the boy in a low voice.

Gary looked across at Buddy and chuckled. He apparently didn't see anything wrong with the way the boy was acting. He craned his neck so he could see out the window to where the girl's car had been parked. "Buddy, you're in luck this time. She left your gear. It's sitting out there in the lot." He looked at Tom and grinned and winked.

Tom didn't respond. Instead, he sighed and turned away from the bar and came and sat opposite his son in the booth, saying as he slid into the seat, "Well, Buddy, what are your plans now? Where you headed for now?"

Buddy smiled warmly, as if noticing his father's presence for the first time. "I was thinking about staying here for the summer, you know, maybe get some work locally, drilling wells or as a carpenter's helper. Then in the fall see if I can't work something out down at the university, maybe get the government to help me pay for a couple of engineering drawing courses or something. You know, with the GI Bill, so I could get a better job next year and gradually work my way to the top, become a captain of industry, maybe even run for governor or open up a car dealership or start a tree farm . . ."

"Buddy, I'm serious."

"So'm I, Dad. I'm serious." And suddenly he looked it, his mouth drawn tightly forward, his blue eyes cold and grim, his hands clenched in fists in front of him on the table.

In a soft voice, Tom reminded the boy that the government wouldn't help him pay for anything, not with his kind of discharge from the Army—he'd spent more than half his one year in the Army locked up in the stockade, usually for trivial offenses, but offenses committed so compulsively and frequently that finally they gave up on him and sent him home to his father. Tom told the boy, again, that he couldn't take courses down at the university until he first finished high school, and he told him, again, that with his reputation for trouble it was almost impossible for him to get work around here anymore, unless he was willing to work the night shift down at the tannery stacking hides. And he told his son that he didn't want him to live with him in his trailer. Not anymore. Not ever.

Quickly, as if startled, Buddy looked at his father, and his blue eyes filmed over with tears. "You're kicking me out?" His lip trembled. Tom saw that the boy was terrified and was about to cry, and he was shocked to see it.

He got up from the booth quickly. "C'mon, we'll talk about this outside," he said gruffly, and he hurried away from the booth, tossing Gary a pair of dollar bills as he passed the bar. Buddy followed silently.

Outside, in the brightness of the parking lot, they stood facing each other at the tailgate of Tom's pickup truck. Nearby, Buddy's duffel and battered brown canvas suitcase lay in a heap on the pavement.

"Dad, maybe I could just stay till I got on my feet. You know, just till I saved a little money, enough to rent my own place. . . ."

Tom looked at the boy steadily. They were the same height and build, though Tom, twenty years older, was slightly heavier and thicker through the shoulders and arms. Behind them a lumber truck changed gears, braked, and slowed, passed through the town on its way south. Tom cleared his throat. "You got to take care of yourself now," he said slowly.

The boy walked to his bags and dragged them toward Tom's truck, lifted them and tossed them into the back. He was smiling again. "C'mon, Dad, just a few days. I'll get hold of Donna, I got her number down in Boston, she gave it to me, and I'll call her and set something up with her. She just took off because she had to be in Boston by tonight, and she could see I wanted to stay here awhile and visit alone with you, sort of to reestablish contact."

Tom reached over the tailgate into the truck and pulled out the bags and dropped them onto the pavement behind Buddy. His face grew long and heavy, and the boy stared down at the bags as if not understanding what they were doing there, and, when his gaze came back, Tom saw that the boy was about to weep again.

Another lumber truck approached the Hawthorne House, changed gears as it neared the curve and slope from the bar to the tannery below. "You could pick up a ride on one of those trucks this afternoon and be in Boston tonight, if you wanted to," Tom said.

"Daddy . . ."

It had turned into a low, gray day, dark and heavy and cool, not sunny and warm as it had been an hour earlier. The streets of the town were nearly empty. No cars passed. Generally, in a mill town people don't move about much except early in the day and late.

"Daddy . . . c'mon, I'm broke," Buddy said quietly, and his voice cracked and tears rolled down his cheeks, and he looked like a small boy standing before his father, open-faced, weeping, his shoulders slanting toward the ground, his hands hanging uselessly down. "I need some money . . . before I can take off on my own. Please help me, Daddy. I need some money. I won't cause you any more trouble, I promise."

Tom looked away from the sight of his son and up at the gray sky, and he could see that it would rain soon. Then he looked away from the sky and down the hill toward the dam and the red-brick tannery and then finally at the boy's duffel and suitcase. "I've heard promises," he said. "And I've had to make up my mind, regardless."

"I can't go off alone . . ."

"You just did, from last April."

"Yes!" the boy cried. "But I thought I could come back! I didn't know you'd lock your door against me!"

Tom studied the boy's face carefully, as if seeing something there he had never seen before. When you love someone for years, you lose sight of how that person looks to the rest of the world. Then one day, even though it's painful, you push the person away, and suddenly you can see him the way a stranger sees him. But because you know so much more about him than a stranger can, you are frightened for him, as frightened as you would be for yourself, if you could see in yourself, as you see in him, that you're not quite right, that you don't quite fit into the place the world has tried to make for you.

Tom stopped looking at his son and instead looked at the ground. He took a deliberate step past his son and picked up the two bags, turned, and pitched them into the back of the truck. Slowly, as if exhausted, he walked around to the driver's side and got in.

"C'mon," he said in a low voice and started the engine.

The boy brightened and, instantly transformed, ran around to the other side and slid in next to his father. "Oh, hey, listen, Dad," he said, "I promise I won't cause you any more trouble! I'll even pay you room and board, I'll get a job tomorrow down at the tannery, stacking hides! Just like you said!" He stuck his right arm out the open window and slapped the side of the truck with the flat of his hand, making a loud noise, and repeated it with sudden, erratic exuberance. "I'll get a car, a good used car, and then I'll be able to rent my own place, Dad. Hey, maybe rent a trailer at the park near you, there's always a couple of vacancies . . ." He went on banging the side of the truck.

Tom didn't answer. He dropped the truck into reverse, waited as another lumber truck passed, backed into the street, and turned left and headed downhill toward the tannery, following the lumber truck.

Buddy ceased banging the door and peered out the open window at the stores and houses and then the dam and old mill, with the tannery buildings on the left. "Where we going, Dad? The trailerpark's the other way."

Tom said nothing. He shifted down a gear as they came up close behind the lumber truck, which was laboriously making its way up the hill on the far side of the dam. At the top of the hill, the road straightened and widened, and Tom pulled out and passed the truck, giving a toot and a wave to the driver as he passed. Driving fast, he soon was ahead of the truck by a quarter mile or more, and two miles down the road from the dam, with rolling green fields of new corn spreading away from the road, he came to the entrance ramp to the Turnpike, where he pulled over and stopped the pickup. The lumber truck was drawing slowly behind him.

Buddy said, "You sonofabitch."

"You get out and stick your thumb out, and that driver'll pick you up."

Buddy wrenched open the door and stepped out of the pickup and slammed the door shut behind him. Slinging his bags quickly to the ground, he waved at the driver of the truck hissing to a stop by the ramp and showed him his thumb. The driver waved him up, and Buddy climbed aboard. Tom let the truck pass, turned slowly around in the road, and headed back to town.

Mistake

In the spring of 1960, I turned twenty. By June, I'd be married, so I was working at a second job, selling women's shoes at a Thom McAn's in a shopping center out in West St. Petersburg. Driving home late six nights a week in my shaky '48 Studebaker, I cast wary glances out the open window at the causeway that looped across the bay north to Tampa, a string of lights over dark water that somehow made me think of New York City, and for a few terrifying seconds each night I wondered if I was making the biggest mistake of my life.

Days I worked as a window trimmer for Webb's City, after I'd been let go at Maas Brothers. Webb's City was an early cut-rate department store parked on an invisible line that separated the neighborhood where middle-class blacks lived from the neighborhood where poor whites lived. There were eight of us in the Display Department, as it was called—art school dropouts, alcoholic ex-stagehands, sign painters and me—and from the small warehouse on the edge of the Webb's City parking lot where we toiled through the long, hot, Florida day building frames, cutting and stretching paper, carving homosote, painting signs, and repairing old mannequins, we looked out the open door one way and watched the black people stroll their streets, turned and looked out the door on the opposite side and watched the white people, mostly runaway Georgia farmers and their wives and skinny children, pass their days on the broken-down porches of rented bungalows.

It could have been depressing, but I was twenty years old and going to be married soon to a very pretty eighteen-year-old blond girl with green eyes that made me feel crazy. Also, I was thought to be unusually talented at this business of decorating department store windows. I had a future. When you think you have a future, you're not easily depressed.

My roommate at the time, Martin Schram, who worked with me at Webb's City, did not think he had a future. He was thirty-one, had spent two years in Cleveland studying art, then had joined the Navy. He learned to paint signs and after four years on an aircraft carrier went back for four more, until he got frightened by what he seemed to be doing to his life, so he came home to Cleveland, where he found that he'd already done it, and moved to Florida.

We shared a railroad flat that was half a bungalow. Martin, since he was older, claimed the more desirable front room, which had windows and a door to the porch. I got the middle room, which was small and dark, a damp, hot cavern between Martin's room and the kitchen and bath in back. I figured that, with my two jobs, I wasn't home much, anyhow, and besides, by the time I got married to Eleanor I'd have enough money saved to buy a whole house. As a result, I didn't complain about the darkness and the heat and the occasional slugs that inched their way up the gray walls, fell back to the floor, and after a while started over again.

Martin envied me because Eleanor loved me. "I don't mean that I'm in love with your Eleanor or anything," he said the night this all came out. "I don't even particularly like her." It was past midnight, a Friday in late April, and I had come home from Thom McAn's exhausted, as I'd been working five days and nights straight, angry, because I still had another night to go, and more than usually frightened, for I'd endured an especially horrifying vision of the causeway lights over Tampa Bay on the drive home, had felt my legs turn to water, because the awful question did not go away when I forced my gaze back to the white line in the road ahead of me, and I almost cracked and cried out, *Yes, yes, I am about to make the biggest mistake of my life!*

We were drinking beer. Colt 45 was new then, and I liked the snow-covered mountains and blue sky on the label, especially when it was hot and like tonight had recently rained and the live oak trees and Spanish moss were still dripping noisily onto the muddy front yard and sidewalk beyond. I stripped as I passed through my room, walked shirtless and barefoot out to the dark kitchen, and swung open the refrigerator, let the pale, cool light wash the room, and there on the top shelf, frosty and brilliant, was a pair of unopened six-packs of blue-white-and-gold cans of beer.

By the time he told me that he envied me, Martin and I had finished the first six-pack and were halfway through the second. Martin Schram could drink beer. He was German and thick-bodied, built like an overstuffed sofa. He had dark, short hair that he was losing, a heavy brow and large, square chin, and a grim, thin mouth. His blue eyes, though small, were the most expressive and easily read part of his face, and when I wanted to know what he was thinking, which wasn't all that often, I looked at his eyes. Tonight, however, we were out on the unlit porch, bare feet on the wooden rail, seated side by side in plastic-and-aluminum folding chairs, and I could not see his eyes and had to ask him what he meant.

He sighed.

"No, I mean it. What do you mean, you envy me because of Eleanor?"

"Forget it, kid," he said. He emptied the can and crunched it with one hand. The light-weight cans had just come out, and we liked smashing them as if they were the rigid cans that took two hands to crush.

"Kid," I said.

That's when the noise next door started. A man and woman lived there, the Smiths, known to me and Martin only by the nameplate on the door next to ours and by sight, when they went out to work in the morning and returned at night. They spent the rest of the time inside their apartment, no matter how hot it got, which left the porch entirely to us, a circumstance we did not complain of. We figured they stayed inside because the man was deformed. Mr. Smith's arms were like flippers, half as long as normal arms and dwindled at the wrists and hands. Evidently, he was able to drive, and judging from the way he dressed—sport coat altered especially for his arms, slacks, dress shirt and tie—he held a decent job. Mrs. Smith was normal-looking. Actually, she was on the attractive side (as was he, except for the arms) and went out every morning dressed like a salesgirl at a first-class department store, Maas Brothers, say, a place that wouldn't hire any of the short, dumpy, gum-chewing, acne-covered women and girls who could get work at Webb's City. My fiancée Eleanor worked at Maas Brothers, in beachwear.

We had heard noises from next door on several occasions that year, always late at night, and always Friday, payday. It was the sound of a man beating a woman. More precisely, it was the sound of a woman hollering that she was being beaten by a man, something that we, of course, discounted, because we could not imagine how he could do it. There would be a thump and a bang or two, then a shriek, a wail, some long drawn-out sobs, and some more thumps. Then quiet. That was it. If both Martin and I happened to be home and in the same room at the same time, he would look over at me and shake his head and smile. "Sonofabitch's at it again."

"Can't really be hurting her, though."

"No. She's as big as he is, and she's got regular arms."

"Yeah! It's just probably something they do."

"You can never tell what people like."

"Yeah!"

This time, though, was different. The noises went on too long, and they got louder. Mr. Smith sounded drunk, and we could hear him snapping and snarling like a dog in a dogfight, and she was wailing, a high, unbroken keening sound, like an old Greek woman who'd been told her favorite son was dead.

"Jesus Christ," Martin said. "They're really going at it tonight."

"What do you think?" I said. I got up from my chair and walked across the porch and faced the closed door to their apartment. "Maybe the bastard's hitting her with a stick or something."

"Naw, they're like a coupla alley cats, that's all. Forget it." I heard Martin crack open another beer. Three left. If I didn't open a fresh one now, he'd get two, and I'd get one. But then I'd have two warm beers instead of one cold one. Hard to choose.

"I don't know, I think we oughta do something," I said.

"Like what? Call the cops? I don't believe in that. Husband and wife, they got to work these things out themselves. You'll see."

I opened the screened door to our apartment and went back to the kitchen and got myself a cold beer. When I came out to the porch, I put the unopened can on the floor next to my chair and went on drinking from the open one.

Then Mrs. Smith started screaming. "No, no, no!" Mr. Smith's voice was muffled, but it sounded like he was threatening to kill her, over and over.

"I think he's trying to kill her," I said.

"No," Martin said, but he got up from his chair and joined me in front of their door.

"What if he's got a gun?" I asked.

"I don't think the bastard can shoot it. All he's got is those little grippers, for Christ's sake."

"Yeah, but the sonofabitch can drive a car!"

"True."

"You think we should do something?" I asked.

"He's just a crippled little guy taking it out on his wife. It's just something they do," Martin said, and he moved slowly away and down the steps to the front yard.

"Where you going?"

"I want to see if maybe I can see inside," he said from the darkness. "They got all the blinds drawn."

"I heard a gun!"

"What? I didn't hear it."

"No, a click. I heard it click, like maybe he's only clicking it at her. You know?"

Martin came back onto the porch and sat himself heavily into the folding chair. "Look, if the gun goes off, then I'll worry. Not before." He took a long pull from his beer. "'Clicks.'" He laughed lightly.

Mrs. Smith screamed, and I reached forward and pushed the doorbell. Silence on the other side of the door. I waited a few seconds and pushed the bell again, a long, loud buzz, and slowly the door opened, and I saw Mr. Smith standing there in T-shirt and slacks, panting, red-faced. Without a gun.

"What do you want?" He was several inches shorter than I and slender, almost delicate-looking. His lank blond hair had fallen across his face, and his mouth was working angrily, as if trying to rid itself of something objectionable. His tiny, shriveled arms hung at his sides like the wings of a newly hatched bird. He looked pathetic, but very angry, and I was surprised to find myself afraid of him, afraid of his intensity, his breathlessness and flushed face and hard eyes, the desperation these things signified to me. I had none of it, and, until that moment I had not known it even existed in the world, despite the signals I had been getting every night on my drive home from the shoe store. And despite Martin Schram, whose envy of me I understood so feebly that I could barely hide my lack of interest.

"We heard a lotta noise," I said gruffly.

He looked me over with care, without apology. "You trying to sleep?"

"No . . . but we were wondering . . ."

"Who's that?" Mrs. Smith called from somewhere behind him. I could see furniture overturned beyond the man, rugs rippled and out of place, an empty quart beer bottle, still rolling. The light in the room cut a blond swath across the far wall at an oblique, useless angle, as if a table lamp had been placed on its side on the floor. I imagined Mrs. Smith lying in a corner of the room, holding mournfully to her rib cage, her legs splayed out in front of her, and I forgot my fear and was glad I had interrupted them.

"It's just the kid next door," Mr. Smith said, as if disappointed.

"Are you all right?" I called.

"Get the hell out of here," he said. "Mind your own damned business."

I drew open the screened door. "Are you all right, Mrs. Smith?"

She entered the living room from the darkness of a further room and leaned against the doorframe there, wearing a filmy, pink nightgown, her bare arms crossed over her breasts, her legs crossed at the ankles. She looked bored, impatient, and irritated all at once.

I took a single step toward her and, halfway into the room, said to her, "I'm sorry. I just . . . I thought he . . ."

Suddenly, the man was shoving me back with his tiny arms, pushing them against my chest, astonishing me with the hard force of the shoves. "Get outa here! G'wan, get the fuck outa here!"

I leapt out of his way and yelled, "Leave her alone, you sonofabitch! Leave the woman alone!"

Then Martin was behind me, grabbing me from behind and yanking me away from the door.

"Close your door!" he said to Smith. "And shut the hell up. For God's sake."

Smith closed the door, and Martin turned to me. His face in the brown light off the shaded windows had collapsed in on itself, and I saw him as I'd never seen him before. He was frightened and very sad and deeply, painfully weary of me. His small eyes were watered over, and his thin lips trembled.

I took a step backward, turned, and sat down. Martin came around and sat down next to me, and I could tell, even without looking at him, that his whole body was shaking.

I was stone-cold calm. "I'm sorry," I said. I leaned over and plucked the unopened can of Colt 45 from the floor and opened it and took a slug.

"You . . . ," he said.

"What?"

"You don't know a damned thing. About anything."

"You're right."

"You just say that. You say it so easy," he said. He lit a cigarette. The rain had stopped a long time before, and now the dripping from the trees and Spanish moss had stopped too. Crickets started up. I heard trucks on Route 19, three blocks away, change gears.

"You're right about that too," I said. "I say it so easy." I stood up, leaned against the railing, and looked at his silhouette. "But I mean it."

"You probably do," he said, as if he no longer cared. It was too late to matter to him. He got up then and went inside and lay down on his bed and fell asleep.

I did marry the girl with the green eyes, Eleanor from beachwear, and it was not the biggest mistake I ever made, even though it was, of course, a mistake. Two weeks before the wedding, I was hired as display director for the Montgomery Ward's store in Lakeland, youngest display director in the state of Florida, and moved out of the apartment I shared with Martin Schram.

"You better come to the wedding, pal," I said. We were on the porch, a midafternoon, with a rented trailer behind my Studebaker, all my worldly belongings inside.

"I'll be there," he said, and he clapped me on both shoulders. "You'll be okay, kid."

"You will too," I said.

"Right."

We shook hands, and I left.

Plains of Abraham

Had he known everything then that he'd know later, Vann still would have called it a coincidence, nothing more. His was a compact, layered mind with only a few compartments connected. He had been married three times and was unmarried now, and this morning he couldn't shake Irene, his second wife, from his mind. He shaved and dressed for work, tightened the covers, and slid the bed back under the sofa, all the while swatting at thoughts of Irene, the force of his swipes banging doors and walls, making him feel clumsy and off-balance. *Thinking about problems only aggravates problems,* but the way these random scraps of memory, emotion, and reflection flew at him—even now, four years after the divorce from Irene, with the lump of a whole third marriage and divorce in between—was strange. Vann and Irene had not seen or spoken to each other in person once in those years.

It was a coincidence, that's all, and would have been one even if Vann *had* known that on this particular morning, a Wednesday in November, Irene, who was forty-eight years old and close to a hundred pounds overweight and suffering from severe coronary disease, who normally would herself be getting ready for work, was instead being prepared at Saranac Lake General Hospital for open-heart surgery. The procedure, to be performed by the highly regarded vascular surgeon,

Dr. Carl Ransome, was to be a multiple bypass. It was a dangerous, although not an uncommon operation, even up here in the north-country, and had Irene not collapsed in pain two days earlier while grocery-shopping at the Grand Union in Lake Placid with her daughter Frances, the procedure would have been put off until she had lost a considerable part of her excess weight. Too late for that now.

"Jesus," Dr. Ransome had said to the night nurse, after visiting Irene in her room for the first time, "this'll be like flaying a goddamned whale." The nurse winced and looked away, and the young surgeon strode whistling down the corridor.

Vann stirred a cup of instant coffee and wondered if he ever crowded Irene's mornings the way she did his. Probably not. Irene was tougher than he, a big-bellied joker who had seemed nothing but relieved when he left her, although he himself had been almost surprised by his departure, as if she had tricked him into it.

"Good riddance," she liked saying to Frances, her daughter. "Never marry a construction man, doll baby. They're hound dogs with hardhats," she said.

Vann wasn't quite that bad. He was one of those men who protect themselves by dividing themselves. He regarded love and work as opposites—he loved to work but had to work at love. Yet, with Irene, what Vann thought of as love had come easy, at least at first. When they married, Irene and Vann had been in their mid-thirties, lonely, and still shaky from the aftershocks of belligerent first divorces, and for a few years they had managed to meet each other's needs almost without trying. Vann was a small man, wiry, with muscles like doorknobs, and back then he had liked Irene's size, her soft amplitude. He had regarded her as a large woman, not fat. And she had liked and admired his crisp, intense precision, his pale crew-cut hair, his tight smile.

To please her, and to suit himself, too, he had come in off the road and for a while kept his tools in the trunk of his car and worked locally.

He started his own one-man plumbing and heating business, limited mostly to small repairs and renovations, operating out of an office and shop that he built into the basement of Irene's house in Lake Placid. Frances, who was barely a teenager then, had resented Vann's sudden, large, hard presence in her mother's life and home and stayed away at boarding school, except for holidays, which was fine by Vann, especially since Irene's first husband was paying the tuition.

Irene quit her job at the real estate office and kept Vann's books. But after four barely break-even and two losing years in a row, his credit at the bank ran out, and the business collapsed, and Vann went on the road again. Soon he saw his needs differently. He guessed Irene saw her needs differently then, too. He knew he had disappointed her. He allowed himself a couple of short-term dalliances, and she found out about one. He told her about one other. He drank a lot, maybe too much, and there were some dalliances he barely remembered. Those he kept to himself. A year later, they were divorced.

Vann had known from the moment he and Irene first spoke of marriage that if he failed at this, his second shot at romance and domestic bliss, he would have to revise his whole view of life with women. This was going to be his second and probably last chance to get love and marriage right. Vann knew that much. You can't make a fresh start on anything in life three times. By then, if a man gets divorced and still goes on marrying, he's chasing something other than romance and domestic life, he's after something strictly private. Vann had gone on anyhow. And now, in spite of the third divorce, or perhaps because of it, whenever he told himself the story of his life, the significance of his second marriage remained a mystery to him and a persistent irritant. Vann remembered his ten years with Irene the way men remember their war years: the chapter in the story of his life so far that was both luminous and threatening and loomed way too large to ignore.

He picked up his coffee cup and went outside and stood on the rickety, tilted porch of the cottage, where he deliberately studied the smear of pink in the eastern sky and the rippling ribbons of light on the small, manmade lake in front of him. *Lake Flower. Weird name for a lake.* He decided that it was going to be a fine day. Which pleased him. He'd scheduled the ductwork test for today and did not want to run it in a nasty, bone-chilling, autumn rain. Vann was field superintendent for Sam Guy, the mechanical contractor out of Lake Placid, on the addition to the Saranac Lake General Hospital. Tomorrow, if today's test went smoothly—he had no reason to think it wouldn't—he'd have the heat turned on in the new wing. After that they'd be working comfortably inside.

It was still dark—dark, and cold, a few degrees below freezing—when he got into his truck and drove from the Harbor Hill Cottages on Lake Flower out to the hospital, and despite his studied attempts to block her out, here came Irene again. He remembered how they used to sit around the supper table and laugh together. She had a loose, large face and no restrictions on distorting it to imitate fools and stupid people. Her tongue was rough as a wood rasp, and she had a particular dislike of Sam Guy, who, the day after Vann's business folded, had hired him and sent him back on the road. "That man needs you because without you he can't pour pee from a boot," she'd declare, and she'd yank one of her own boots off and hold it over her head and peer up into it quizzically.

Vann had never known a woman that funny. Toward the end, however, she had started turning her humor on him, and from then on there was no more laughing at Irene's comical faces and surprising words. His only recourse had been to slam the door behind him, while she shouted, "G'wan, go! Good riddance to bad rubbish!"

He switchbacked along tree-lined streets, crossing the ridge west of the narrow lakeside strip of hotels, motels, stores, and restaurants, and entered a neighborhood of small wood-frame houses and duplexes. The pale light from his headlights bounced off frost that clung like a skin to yellowed lawns, glassed-in porches, and steeply pitched rooftops. Gray strands of smoke floated from chimneys, and kitchen lights shone from windows. *Jesus, family life.* Which, despite all, Vann still thought of as normal life. *And a proper breakfast.* Vann could almost smell eggs and bacon frying. Moms, dads, and kids cranking up their day together: he could hear their cheerful, sleepy voices.

Vann had lived that sort of morning, but not for nearly fifteen years now; and he missed it. Who wouldn't? Way back in the beginning, up in Plattsburgh, with his own mom and dad, he'd been one of the kids at the table; then later, for a few years, with his first wife, Evelyn, and the boys, he had been the dad. But family life had slipped from his grasp without his having noticed, as if, closing his eyes to drink from a spring, he'd lost a handful of clear water and was unable afterwards to imagine a way to regain it. The spring must have dried up. A man can't blame his hands, can he?

Instead, he'd learned to focus his thoughts on how, when he was in his twenties and married to Evelyn and the boys were young, he simply had not appreciated his good luck. That was all. Evelyn had remarried happily and wisely right after the divorce, and the boys, Neil and Charlie, raised more by their stepfather than by Vann, had turned into young men themselves—gone from him forever, or so it seemed. A postcard now and then was all, and the occasional embarrassed holiday phone call. Nothing, of course, from Evelyn—his child bride, as he referred to her—but that, especially as the years passed, was only as it should be.

The way he viewed it, Vann's main sin in life had been not to have appreciated his good luck back when he had it. If he had, he probably would have behaved differently. His was a sin of omission, then. To reason that way seemed more practical to him and more dignified than to wallow in regret. It helped him look forward to the future. It had helped him marry Irene. And it had eased his divorce from Inger, his third wife. *The Norwegian*, was how he thought of her now.

At the variety store where Broadway turned onto Route 86, he picked up a *Daily Enterprise* and coffee to go and a fresh pack of Marlboros. He was driving one of Sam Guy's company pickups, a spruce green three-quarter-ton Jimmy, brand-new. It had been assigned to him directly from the dealer, and though he liked to pretend, at least to himself, that the vehicle belonged to him and not his boss, Vann would not have said aloud that it was his. That wasn't his style. He was forty-nine, too old to say he owned what he didn't. And too honest.

Besides, he didn't need to lie: he was making payments to the Buick dealer in Plattsburgh on a low-mileage, two-year-old, black Riviera that he'd bought last spring to celebrate his divorce from the Norwegian. She'd gotten sole ownership of the house he'd built for them in Keene Valley, but she was also stuck with the mortgage, which gave him some satisfaction. His monthly payments for the car had worked out to six dollars less than his monthly alimony checks, a coincidence Vann found oddly satisfying and slightly humorous, although, when he told people about it, no one else thought it funny or even interesting, which puzzled him.

The Norwegian had gotten his previous car, a rusted-out AMC Eagle, but she was welcome to that, too. The Riviera was loaded. A prestige car. It cheered Vann to be seen driving it, and he hoped that over the summer the Norwegian, who was a legal aide for the Adirondack Park Agency in Ray Brook, had accidentally spotted him in the Riviera once or twice. He didn't particularly want to see her, but he sure hoped that she had seen him and had noted that Vann Moore, yes indeedy, was doing just fine, thanks.

Out on Route 86 a few miles west of town, he turned right at Lake Colby and pulled into the hospital parking lot, drove to the rear of the three-story brick building, and passed along the edge of the rutted field to the company trailer, where he parked next to a stack of steel pipe. From the outside, the new wing, a large cube designed to merge discreetly with the existing hospital building, appeared finished—walls, roof, and windows cemented solidly into place. Despite appearances, however, the structure was little more than a shell. The masons hadn't started the interior walls yet, the plumbers hadn't set any of the fixtures or run the aboveground water, vacuum, and air lines, and the electricians were still hanging overhead conduit. The painters hadn't even hauled their trailer to the site.

The ductwork for the air-conditioning and heat was finished, though. Three days ahead of schedule. Vann was a good super. He'd risen in the ranks from journeyman pipe fitter to foreman to super. He'd run his own business and could read drawings and engineering specs, could do estimates for new work in Sam Guy's office in Lake Placid when the weather turned bad and everyone else got laid off. And he was a good boss, respected and liked by his men. Sam Guy regarded Vann as his right hand and had no compunctions about saying so, and he paid him appropriately. To people who wondered about Vann's way of life, and there were a few, Sam said that if Vann hadn't been tagged over the years with alimony payments and hadn't lost three houses, one to each wife, he'd be living well on what he earned as a super. He wouldn't be renting furnished rooms and shabby, unused vacation cottages, following the work from town to town across the northcountry. To Vann, however, the opposite was true: if he hadn't followed the work, he'd not have been divorced three times.

Inside the hospital, in the physicians' scrub room, Dr. Ransome and his assistant this morning, Dr. Clark Rabideau, the resident cardiologist who was Irene's regular physician, and Dr. Alan Wheelwright, the anesthesiologist, were discussing the incoming governor's environmental policies while they slowly, methodically washed their hands and arms.

Their patient, Irene Moore, dozy with sedatives, her torso shaved from chin to crotch, was being wheeled on a gurney down the long, windowless, second-floor hallway from her room to the main operating room at the end. Her twenty-year-old daughter Frances sat alone by the window in Irene's room, flipping through a copy of *Cosmopolitan*. Frances was a tall, big-hipped girl, a second-year student at Saint Lawrence University, planning to major in psychology. Her straight, slate-colored hair fell limply to her shoulders, and her square face was tight with anxiety.

With her mother unconscious, or nearly so, Frances felt suddenly, helplessly alone. *I'm over my head in this,* she said to herself, *way over,* and quickly turned the pages, one after the other. *What the hell am I supposed to be thinking about? What?*

It was nearly daylight. In the northeast, the flattened sky over Whiteface Mountain was pale gray. In the southeast, over Mounts Marcy and Algonquin, a bank of clouds tinted pink was breaking apart, promising a clear day. The other workers were rumbling onto the job site, electricians, masons, plumbers, steamfitters, driving their own cars and pickups, while the foremen and supers arrived in company vehicles. It was light enough for Vann, smoking in his truck, sipping his coffee, to read the front page of the paper and check the NFL scores. It got his mind finally off Irene.

He folded his paper and left the warm truck, but as he crossed to the trailer, key in hand, he glanced out across Lake Colby at the pink morning sky and the dark line of pines below, and the scenery sent him drifting again. He remembered an afternoon four years ago, shortly after the divorce. He was running the public high school job over in Elizabethtown and living in the Arsenal Motel on Route 9N at the edge of town, and one Friday when he drove in from work, a large flat package was waiting for him at the front desk.

Vann knew at once that it was from Irene—he recognized her

handwriting and the return address, their old Lake Placid address. He lugged the crate back to his room and lay it flat on the bed and studied it for a while. What the hell kind of joke was she playing on him this time?

Finally, he pried open the crate and removed several layers of brown paper and plastic bubble wrap from the object inside. It was a large, framed picture. He recognized it instantly, and felt a rush of fear that made his heart pound, as if he had unwrapped a bomb. It was a signed color photograph by a well-known local photographer of Adirondack scenery. Very expensive, he knew. A few years back, when they were still happily married, he and Irene had strolled into a Lake Placid crafts shop, and Vann had glanced up at a picture on the wall and had felt himself leap straight up and into it, as if into someone's dream. It was called *Plains of Abraham* and the scene was of a late summer day, looking across a field of tall grasses and wildflowers toward Mount Algonquin. The golden field, wide and flat, lay in sunshine in the fore-ground at eye level. A dark, jagged line of trees cut across the middle, and the craggy, plum-colored mountain towered in the distance, a pure and endless blue sky behind and above it.

This was the first and the only picture that Vann had ever wanted to own. He asked the saleswoman how much, figuring he could maybe spring for a hundred bucks.

"Twenty-two hundred dollars," she said.

He felt his ears and face flush. "Pretty pricey," he said and moved quickly on to the maple cutting boards and ceramic bowls.

For months afterwards, Irene had teased him about it, imitating his high, thin voice and pursed lips. "Pretty-pricey," she chirped, checking out a restaurant menu. Or speculating about local real estate: "Pretty-pricey." But she had seen the strange, distant, pained look on her husband's face as he gazed at the picture on the wall of the crafts shop. And now here it was before him, as if staring at him from his bed, while he stood over it, confused, frightened, stubbornly resisting awe. He no more wanted to live with that picture than he wanted to live with the woman who had sent it to him. It made him feel invaded, trapped, guilty. Just as she did. If he kept it, what was he supposed to do, write her a thank-you note? What he *should* do, he thought, is return the picture to the crafts shop and pocket the money himself. Serve Irene right.

He took down the large print of an antlered deer that hung above his bed in the motel room and replaced it with *Plains of Abraham* and stepped back to examine it. It was like a window that opened onto a world larger and more inviting than any he had ever seen. No, the picture was too personal between him and Irene and too mysterious to return for cash, he decided. He would wrap it up and recrate the thing and mail it back to her tomorrow. She's so damned smart, let *her* figure out why she sent it to him.

He washed and changed out of his work clothes and went for supper and a few drinks at the Ausable Inn in Keene Valley, where he'd arranged to meet Inger, the Norwegian, whom at that time he'd not quite decided to marry, although he was sleeping with her three and four nights a week. He didn't return to the motel until halfway through the next day, Saturday, and by then, hungover, fuddled with sex and sleeplessness, he had all but forgotten the picture. But when he entered the small room and saw the photograph hanging above his bed, he remembered everything. He sat down on the chair facing it, and his eyes filled with tears. He could not believe that he was actually crying. Crying over what? An overpriced picture of some *scenery*? A damned *divorce*? An *ex-wife*?

He took down the photograph and rehung the deer print. Carefully, he wrapped the picture, returned it to its crate, and stuck the crate into his closet, where it remained more or less forgotten for the entire summer. When the school job was finished and Vann moved seventy miles south to Glens Falls, where a shopping mall was going in, he lugged the picture along and stashed it in the back of his motel room closet down there. He still owned the thing, although it remained in its crate, and the crate stayed in his closet, hidden, barely acknowledged by Vann, except when one job was over and he packed to move to the next. He'd pull it out and sit on the bed and study Irene's original mailing label as if it could somehow tell him why he couldn't seem to get rid of the damned thing.

To Irene, her mind and body muffled by sedatives, the washed-out blue tile walls of the operating room looked almost soft, as if covered with terry cloth. The operating table, shaped like a cross, was in the middle of the room under a bank of white lights. Irene felt her body being eased off the cart by a female nurse and the two male attendants who had brought her here. They arranged themselves alongside her in a line and slid her smoothly onto the table. Her body felt like cold butter. She could see what was happening, but it seemed to be going on elsewhere, in a room beyond glass, and to someone else. Her arms were extended and strapped down, and a long, dark blue curtain was drawn around her upper and lower parts, leaving only her enormous trunk exposed.

"We're outa here, Dale," one of the attendants said, and Irene heard the squeaky wheels of the cart and the swish of the closing door.

Hidden behind her, Alan Wheelwright, the anesthesiologist, in a blue cotton gown and cap and white surgical mask, stood at the head of the table preparing bags of blood for transfusion, while the nurse, her flecked green eyes expressionless above her mask, swabbed Irene's belly with orange antiseptic, covering her mounded body from hip to throat, back to front, humming as she worked, as if she were home alone painting her toenails. Then, into each of Irene's thick, chalk white arms, the nurse inserted an intravenous catheter.

Irene saw a man's face, which she recognized, despite the mask, as Dr. Rabideau's, and next to him another man, taller, with bushy white eyebrows, whom she did not recognize but felt she should. There were more nurses now, and the room suddenly seemed crowded and small. A man laughed, genuinely pleased. Someone sang, *I'm forever blowing bubbles.*

She wondered where in the room Vann was standing. Maybe he was one of the people in the masks. She looked at the eyes; she knew Vann's eyes. Her own eyelids seemed to be semitransparent sheets, shutting over and over, in layers. She blinked and left a film; then another. She wondered if her eyes had been shut for a long time already.

What we have here, folks, is hard labor.

Vann's eyes were sapphire blue and crinkly at the corners, even when he wasn't smiling, like now.

Break out the retractors, Dale. We have liftoff.

Vann was down in the dim basement of the new wing, a huge, cold, open space cluttered with cinder blocks, unused rolls of pink insulation, and stacks of conduit. It took him several tries, but finally he got the gas-powered Briggs & Stratton compressor chugging smoothly. The pump was tied to the overhead ductwork through a three-quarter-inch gate valve with a pressure gauge, which Vann had installed strictly for the purposes of the test. He had a kid, Tommy Farr, to help him, but Vann made the connections himself, using Tommy to hand him the tools as he needed them—hose clamps, screwdriver, pipe joint compound, stillson wrench. His bare hands were red and stiff from the cold; Vann didn't like working with gloves.

The rest of his crew was scattered over the first and second floors of the wing, installing plumbing fixtures in the lavatories and running the vacuum and oxygen lines. The sheet-metal guys had been released for a new job, a supermarket in a minimall over in Tupper Lake. He figured if any blowouts or blocks in the ductwork showed up, he and Tommy could locate and fix them themselves. He wasn't worried. It was a routine test under fairly low pressure, twenty-five pounds per square inch. It wasn't as if the ducts were going to carry water. Just heated air from the large, dark furnace that sat ready to be fired in a shadowed corner of the basement and cooled air from the crated air-conditioning units that had been lifted to the rooftop by crane a week ago.

"All right, Tommy," Vann said, and he stood away from the valve and handed the skinny kid the wrench. "You wanna do the honors?" Vann lit a cigarette, clenched it between his lips, and inhaled deeply and stuck his chilled hands into his jacket pockets.

"Just turn the sucker on?"

"Let 'er rip. When you hit twenty-five PSI's on the gate valve gauge, close 'er up."

The kid knelt down and with one large hand slowly opened the valve and released a jet of compressed air into the pipeline that led to the threaded gate valve soldered to the side of the sheet-metal duct directly overhead. That duct in turn led from the cold furnace behind them to elaborate crosses and intersections at several places in the basement, which split into smaller ducts that passed through the reinforced concrete ceiling on to the floors above. At each floor the ducts split again and snaked between and above the yet-to-be installed walls and ceilings of the new rooms and corridors. These ducts, carefully blocked and baffled at the openings, turns, T's, and Y's, eventually crossed out of the new wing into the old hospital and tied into its system, which carried heated air from the outdated but still adequate furnace in the basement of the main wing of the hospital to the one hundred fifty private and semiprivate rooms and wards, the scrub rooms and surgeons' dressing rooms, the physical therapy center, the operating rooms, the emergency room, the maternity ward and nursery, and all the large and small, public and private lavatories, the janitors' closets, kitchens, dining rooms, nurses' lounges, computer center, labs, billing offices, administrative offices, and the gift shop and florist shop, which was closed this early in the day, and the nearly empty waiting

rooms, and even into the large, glass-fronted lobby, where Frances, the
daughter of Irene Moore, was at this moment strolling from the hospital, down the steps to the parking lot. Frances was on a run into town
for some small present to greet her mom when she woke, something
sentimental and silly, like a teddy bear, that her mom would pretend to
hate, the way she always did, but Frances knew that her mom would
store the gift in a secret drawer so that she could take it out and look
at it whenever she wanted to realize anew how much her daughter
loved her.

Something was going wrong. The first sign was a cool puff of air that
carried a gray plume of ash—probably cigarette ash—from a wall register into the cafeteria on the first floor of the old wing. A janitor leaned
against his mop and with some annoyance watched the gray powder
float onto his clean floor.

In a laboratory on the second floor, bits of dirt fell from the ceiling
vent onto the head and shoulders of a puzzled technician, causing her to
jump from her seat and stare at the vent for a moment. When no further
debris fell, she sat back down and resumed cataloging urine samples.

Then along one corridor after another and in the maternity ward
and in several of the private rooms, on all three floors of the hospital,
nurses, doctors, maintenance people, and even some patients began to
see tiny scraps of paper, ashes, shreds of pink insulation, metal filings,
sawdust, and unidentifiable bits of dirt fly from the registers and ceiling
vents, float through the air, and land on sheets and pillows, sterilization
cabinets, stainless steel counters, computers, desks, spotless equipment
and tools of all kinds, dusting hairdos, nurses' caps, starched white uni-
forms, and even falling onto the breakfast trays. Nurses, doctors, administrators, and staff people strode up and down hallways and made phone
calls, trying to locate the cause of this invasion of flying debris. Attendants grabbed sheets and blankets and covered the newborn infants in

the nursery and patients in the wards, shouting orders and firing angry questions at one another, while patients pressed their buzzers and hollered for help and brushed the floating bits of dirt and trash away from their faces, bandages, casts, and bedding. Those patients who were mobile ran, limped, and rolled in wheelchairs from their rooms and wards to the hallways and nurses' stations, demanding to know what was happening, had there been an explosion? Was there a fire?

In the operating room, Dr. Rabideau shouted, *Close her up! For Christ's sake, close her up and get her the hell out of here!*

Down in the cold basement of the new wing, Vann stood in the light of a single bulb and puzzled over the gauge on his compressor. He rubbed his cigarette out on the cement floor.

"She's not holding any pressure at all now. Not a damn bit," he said to Tommy Farr. "Something's open that shouldn't be. Or else we've got one hell of a blowout someplace," he said and reached up and shut off the air to the main duct. He switched off the compressor motor, and the basement was suddenly silent.

"How we gonna find out what's open?" Tommy asked.

"We got to check everything that's supposed to be closed. One of you guys must've left a cap off one of the register openings."

"Hey, not me! I ain't no sheet-metal guy. I was in the trailer counting fittings all day Friday."

"I know, I know. I just need somebody to blame," Vann said smiling. He clapped the kid on the shoulder. "C'mon, let's get the drawings from the trailer. We'll go room to room and check every vent until we find the missing cap. Then we'll cap 'er and try again."

Vann had done his job the way he was supposed to, and his men had done theirs. He could not have known what had occurred beyond the thick fire wall that separated the new wing from the old, could not have known that over there, when he finally shut his compressor down, the debris had instantly ceased to fall. And he could not have known that seconds after Doctors Ransome, Rabideau, and Wheelwright in a panic had closed their incisions and rushed her from the operating room, his ex-wife Irene had gone into cardiac arrest in the recovery room. They had managed to get her heart pumping again and her blood pressure back, but an embolism had formed in her left carotid artery and had started working its way toward her neck. Shortly after noon, a blood vessel between the left temporal and parietal lobes of her brain burst, and Irene Moore suffered a massive stroke and immediately lapsed into a coma.

The only surgeon in the area capable of removing the clot from her brain was driving over from Plattsburgh. They hoped to have the operating room cleaned up and ready for him by early evening. With her heart condition, however, and the trauma inflicted on her by the interrupted surgery this morning, and the likelihood of still more embolisms, the anticoagulants, and now the stroke, "I'm sorry, but it truly does not look good," Dr. Rabideau told Frances.

She did not know where to turn for consolation or advice. She was the only one left in the world who loved her mother, and her mother was the only one left who loved her. Frances's father, Irene's long-gone first husband, had his new life, a new wife and new kids out in California. Irene's second husband, Vann, had his new life, too, Frances supposed. He and Frances had never liked each other much, anyhow.

A little after lunch, the supervisor of maintenance in the hospital found Vann on the second floor of the new wing, still tracing the overhead ducts with Tommy Farr. The supervisor, Fred Noelle, was a man in his mid-sixties who had worked for the hospital since high school. He knew every inch of the old building, every valve, switch, pump, and fitting, and had been an especially useful consultant when they were designing the addition. Cautiously, Fred asked Vann if earlier this morning he might have done something in the way of connecting the heat and ventilation ducts of the new wing to the ducts of the old. Tied them together, say, and then opened them up, maybe. Fred knew there were lawsuits coming. A lot of finger-pointing and denials.

"No," Vann said. "Why? You got problems over there?"

"Have we got problems? Yes, we've got problems. We'll be cleaning the place up for the rest of the year." He was a balding, heavyset man with a face like a bull terrier, and he looked very worried.

"What the hell happened?" Vann asked him.

Fred told him. "They got crap on patients, in the labs, all over. Even in the operating rooms."

Vann was silent. Then he spoke slowly and clearly, directing his words to the kid but speaking mainly for Fred Noelle's benefit. "It couldn't have been us. There are baffles between the two systems, blocks, and they don't come out till after we get everything installed and blown out and balanced and the whole wing is nice and clean and ready for use. Then we open it to the old system. And that won't be till next summer," he said, his voice rising. He knew he was telling the truth. He also knew that he was dead wrong.

Somewhere, somehow, one of the baffles between the two networks had not been installed by his men, or else had been left off the drawing by the mechanical engineer who had designed the system for the architect. Either way, Vann knew the fault was his. This morning, before cranking up the compressor, on the off chance that one of his sheet-metal guys had screwed up, he should have checked the baffles, every damned one of them. No one ever did that, but he should've.

He placed the drawing on the floor and got down on his hands and knees to examine it. "See," he said to Fred. "Take a look right here. Baffle. And here. Baffle. And here," he said, pointing to each of the places where the ducts crossed through the thick wall between the two wings of the hospital.

But then he saw it. No baffle. The mechanical engineer had made a terrible mistake, and Vann, back when they'd installed the ducts, hadn't caught it.

Fred got down beside him, and he saw it, too. "Uh-oh," he said, and he placed his fingertip where a barrier should have been indicated and where, instead, the drawing showed a main duct flowing through the old exterior wall and connecting directly to the heat and ventilation system of the hospital. A straight shot.

Tommy squatted down on the other side of Vann and furrowed his brow and studied the drawing. "Bad, huh, Vann?"

Vann followed Fred Noelle out of the structure and across the parking lot and through the main entrance of the hospital. They went straight to the large carpeted office of Dr. Christian Snyder, the hospital director. Fred made the introductions, and Dr. Snyder got up and shook Vann's hand firmly.

"We think we got this thing figured out," Fred said. Dr. Snyder was a crisply efficient fellow in his early forties with blond, blow-dried hair. He wore a dark, pin-striped suit and to Vann looked more like a down-state lawyer than a physician. Fred unrolled the drawing on Dr. Snyder's large mahogany desk, and the three men stood side by side and examined the plan together, while Fred described Vann's test and how it was supposed to work and how it had failed.

"You're the subcontractor for the sheet-metal work?" Dr. Snyder said to Vann.

"No. No, I'm just the field super for him. Sam Guy, he's the subcontractor."

"I see. But you're responsible for the installation."

"Well, yes. But I just follow the drawings, the blueprints."

"Right. And this morning you were testing the new ductwork, blowing compressed air through it, right?"

"Yes, but I didn't realize . . ."

Dr. Snyder cut him off. "I understand." He went around his desk, sat down heavily and picked up a pencil and tapped his teeth with it. "Fred, will you be able to attend a meeting here this evening? Seven-thirty, say?"

Fred said sure, and Dr. Snyder reached for his phone. Vann picked up the drawing and started to roll it up. "Please, leave that here," Dr. Snyder said, and then he was speaking to his secretary, "Celia, for that meeting with Baumbach, Beech, and Warren? Fred Noelle, who's in charge of maintenance, he'll be joining us."

He glanced up at Vann as if surprised to see him still standing there. "You can go, if you want. Thanks for your help. We'll be in touch," he said to Vann, and went back to his telephone.

Outside in the lobby, alone, Vann pulled out a cigarette and stuck it between his lips.

"Sir! No smoking!" the receptionist barked at him, and he shoved the cigarette back into the pack and made for the door.

On the steps he stopped and lit up and looked across the road at Lake Colby and the pine trees and hills beyond. There was a stiff, cold breeze off the lake, and it was starting to get dark. Vann checked his watch. Three thirty-five. Off to his left he saw a woman with her back to him, also smoking and regarding the scenery. Vann couldn't remember when he had done anything this bad. Not at work, anyhow. In life, sure—he'd messed up his life, messed it up lots of ways, most people do. But, Jesus, never at work.

The woman tossed her cigarette onto the parking lot below and turned to go back inside, and Vann recognized her—Frances, his ex-wife's daughter. He realized that he was glad to see her and blurted, "Hey, Frances! What're you doing here?" Startled, she looked up at him, and he saw that she was crying. "Wow, what's the matter, kid? What's happened?" he said, and took a step toward her. She was taller than he remembered, a few inches taller than he, and heavier. Her face was swollen and red and wet with tears. "Is it your mom?"

She nodded yes, like a child, and he reached out to her. She kept her arms tight to her sides but let him hold her close. He was all she had; he would have to be enough.

"Come on inside and sit down, honey, and tell me what's happened," Vann said, and with one arm around her, he walked her back into the lobby, where they sat down on one of the blond sofas by the window. "Jeez," he said, "I don't have a handkerchief."

"That's okay, I got a tissue." She pulled a wrinkled tissue from her purse and wiped her cheeks.

"So tell me what happened, Frances. What's wrong with your mom?"

She hesitated a second. Then she inhaled deeply and said, "I don't understand it. She's in a coma. She went in for open-heart surgery this morning, and something happened, something went wrong, and they had to bring her out in the middle of it."

"Oh," Vann said. "Oh, Jesus." He lowered his head. He put his hands over his face and closed his eyes behind them.

"There were complications. She had a stroke. The doctors don't think she'll come out of it," she said, and started to cry again.

Vann took his hands away from his face and sat there staring at the floor. The beige carpet was decorated with the outlines of orange and dark green rectangles. Vann let his gaze follow the interlocking colored lines from his feet out to the middle of the room and then back again. Out and back, out and back. There were six or eight other people seated in the sofas and chairs scattered around the lobby, reading magazines or talking quietly with one another, waiting for news of their mothers and fathers, their husbands and wives and children in the rooms above.

"Do you think maybe could I go and see her?" he said in a low voice.

"I don't think so. She's in intensive care, Vann. She won't even know you're there. I saw her a little while ago, but she didn't know it was me in the room."

Slowly Vann got to his feet and moved away from Frances toward the receptionist by the elevator. He wanted to see Irene. He could say it to himself. It didn't matter if she knew he was there or not, he had to see her. He needed to fill his mind with her actual, physical presence. No fading memories of her, no tangled feelings of guilt for things done and undone, no dimly remembered hurts and resentments. Too late for all that. He needed to look at her literal existence, see her in the here and now, and take full-faced whatever terrible thoughts and feelings came to him there.

"I need to see my wife," he said to the receptionist. "She's in intensive care."

The woman peered at him over her horn-rimmed glasses. "Who's your wife?"

"Irene. Irene Moore."

He signed the book that the woman pushed at him and stepped quickly toward the elevator. "Third floor," she said. He got into the elevator, turned, and saw Frances seated across the lobby looking mournfully at him. Then the door slid closed.

At the nurses' station outside the intensive care unit an elderly nurse pointed him down a hallway to a closed door. "Second bed on the right. You can't miss her, she's the only one there."

The room was dark, windowless, lit only by the wall lamp above the bedstead. Irene's body was very large; it filled the bed. Vann didn't remember her as that big. She made him feel suddenly small, shrunken, fragile. There were IV stands and oxygen tanks and tubes that snaked in and out of her body and several thick black wires attached to cabinet-sized machines that blinked and whirred, monitoring her blood pressure, heart, and breathing.

For a long time he stood at the foot of the bed peering through the network of tubes and wires at his ex-wife's wide, round body. She was covered to her neck by a sheet. Her thick arms lay limp and white outside the sheet. A tube dripped clear liquid into a vein at one wrist. On the other wrist she wore a plastic identification band.

No wedding ring, he noticed. He looked down at his own left hand. No wedding ring there, either. *Irene, you're the one I loved.* He said the words silently to himself, straight out. *And I'm only loving you now. And, Jesus, look at what I've done to you, before I could love you.*

What's that love worth now, I wonder. To you or me or anybody?

He felt a strong wind blow over him, and he had to grab hold of the metal bedframe to keep from staggering backwards. The wind was warm, like a huge breath, an exhalation, and though it pummeled him, he wasn't afraid of it. He turned sideways and made his way along the bed. The wind abated, and he found himself looking down at Irene's face. There was a tube in her slightly open mouth and another in one of her nostrils. Her eyes were closed. Somewhere behind her face, Irene was curled in on herself like a child, naked, huddled in the darkness, alone, waiting.

Vann slipped his hands into his jacket pockets and stood with his feet apart and looked down on the woman he had been able to love for only a moment. He stood there for a long time, long after he had ceased to love her and had only the memory of it left. Then he turned away from her.

When he emerged from the elevator to the lobby, he quickly looked around for Frances and found her seated in a far corner of the room, slumped in a chair with her head on one arm and her eyes closed as if asleep. He sat down next to her, and her eyes fluttered open.

"Did you see her?" Frances asked.

"Yeah. I did. I saw her."

"She didn't know you were there, did she?"

"No. No, she didn't," he said. "But that didn't matter."

"Where're you going now, Vann? From here."

"Well, I don't know. I thought maybe I'd wait here, Frances. Keep you company. If you don't mind, I mean."

The girl didn't answer him. They both knew that Irene was going to die, probably before morning. Like a father, Vann would wait here with her and help the girl endure her mother's death. He thought of the big framed picture that Irene had sent him and that he had carted around with him these last few years from one job to the next, wondering what to do with the thing. *Plains of Abraham. What kind of name was that, anyhow? The picture was of a mountain.* Maybe he would give it to Frances. He'd just give it to her and say that her mother had bought it for him years ago because she knew he loved it, and he hoped that Frances liked it enough to hang it where she could see it every day, and he could see it sometimes, too, if she'd let him.

People coming into the lobby were brushing snow off their shoulders and hats. Vann looked out the window at the parking lot and the lake. It had been snowing for a while, and the cars in the lot were covered with powdery white sheets. Sam Guy would fire him, no doubt about it, and both Vann and Sam would be lucky if no one sued them. Vann would go back to working locally out of his car, like he'd done when he first married Irene. He was coming in off the road, too late, maybe, to make anyone happy, but here he was anyhow, trying.

Theory of Flight

Her first day at Kitty Hawk, she stayed at the cottage with her mother and father and explained to them why she was leaving Roger. As if speaking into a tape recorder, the three adults stared straight ahead and talked to one another. They sat on the beach in canvas and aluminum chairs and watched the children play with shovels and buckets at the edge of the water. The sun was white, unencumbered, untouched, in a cloudless sky, burning at the center of the dark blue, circular plane.

Bored with buckets and shovels, the two little girls—daughters and granddaughters—put the toys down and moved closer to the water to dodge the waves, tempting them, dodging again. At first laughing gaily, then, whenever a wave shoved their ankles and knees or as it receded caught them from behind, their laughter suddenly, momentarily, turned manic, and their small, brown faces shifted to gray, mouths gaping, eyes searching the beach for Mamma.

"Jesus," Janet said. "It's like Greece, this sky and that sun!"

"All week," her father said. "It's been like this all week. Can you believe it?" With his leathery, tanned skin, bony face, and round, wrinkle-rimmed eyes, he looked like a giant sea turtle thrown into a canvas beach chair. He lay there, rather than sat, staring at his granddaughters, fingertips nervously drumming knobby knees, toes digging into the hot white sand. "Maybe you can give it one last chance," he said. "You've got the children to think about, you know."

"All I've *done*, for God's sake, is think about the children! I mean, please, figure it out for yourself, Daddy. Are they better off with one parent who's reasonably sane and more or less happy than with two parents, both of whom are crazy and miserable and blaming their craziness and misery on each other? Which would *you* have preferred? For that matter, which do you think I would have preferred?" Chewing her upper lip, she still did not look at him. She wondered about herself, her thirties: Would she become idly cruel?

Her father started to stammer, then inhaled deeply, a reversed sigh, and talked rapidly about his own mother and father, reminding himself, his wife, and his daughter that at least once in this life there had been a perfect marriage. In the middle of his eulogy, his wife got up from her chair, wiped clinging grains of sand from her calves and hands, and walked back to the cottage.

"Do you want a drink, Janet?" she called over her shoulder. The turquoise straps of her bathing suit were cutting into reddened loaves of flesh.

"God, no, Mother! It's only three o'clock!"

"What about you, Charles?"

"Gin and tonic. You know."

The mother turned and waded through the deep sand, over the low ridge to the cottage. The daughter and the father continued to sit in the low-slung chairs, side by side, watching the girls play. For several minutes, the old man and the young woman said nothing.

Then the man sighed loudly and said, as if to a friendly bartender, "Jesus, what a goddamn shame."

She turned slowly and looked at him. "A shame that it took me eight years. That's all I'm ashamed of!" she snapped. She got up from her chair and jogged down to the water, pounding through the surf until she was waist-deep, and dove into a breaking wave, disappearing and after several seconds popping up beyond the wave in smooth, dark green, deep water.

She poked one hand up in the air and waved to her father. He lifted a skinny brown arm and slowly waved back.

Stalking past the bunch of teenage boys and men in T-shirts with sleeves rolled up to show off biceps and tattoos, Janet hurried to a place about halfway down the Fish Pier. Out at the end of the pier, the serious fishermen had gathered, fifteen or twenty of them, red-faced white men in duck-bill caps, short-sleeve shirts, and Bermuda shorts, all of them leaning like question marks over the waist-high wood railing, peering out and down at their lines, silently attentive.

Janet was what they used to call a looker—neat, trim, sexy if tanned and wearing carefully selected clothes, a fashionably casual haircut, and minimal makeup (but not without makeup altogether), the kind of woman whose attractiveness to men depended greatly on the degree to which she could reveal that men were attractive to her. If, when it turned out that for whatever reason or length of time she was not interested in a particular man, her boyish, physical intensity was capable of frightening him, and on such occasions she was sometimes thought to be a lesbian, which, on these occasions, pleased her. It'd serve the bastards right, she thought.

Slipping in between two small groups of black people, men and women, she found a spot at the rail and broke out her fishing gear. She stuffed a cold, slumbering bloodworm onto a hook, leaned over the rail, and flipped the tip of the rod, casting underhanded, sending the weighted hook and worm forty or fifty feet out and twenty feet down into the dark water. Slowly, she reeled the line back in, watching the people around her as she worked.

"How you doin' today?" a man with an enormous head asked her. He flashed a mouthful of gold-trimmed teeth.

"Can't tell yet. I just got here," she said. She heard the words clicking in a hard, flat, Boston accent. She never heard her own accent, except when speaking with black people, regardless of where they were from. Southern whites, strangely, only made her conscious of *their* accent, not her own. The same was true for Hispanics. The man was with two women, both of whom seemed to be older than he, and two men, also older than he. None of the others was fishing. Instead, they drank beer and ate fried chicken legs and chattered with each other and with the various people passing by and standing around them. The man fishing was, by comparison, a solitary. He carefully ignored the others. His very large head was almost startling to look at, all the more, for a white person, because of his shining blackness. Janet didn't realize she was staring at him, at his head, the considerable force of it, until, smiling easily at her, he said, "You know me, Miss?"

"No. No, I guess not. I just thought, I . . . you do look familiar to me, that's all."

"You prob'ly seen me around," he said, almost bragging.

"Yes." She noticed that whenever he spoke to her the others imme-diately lapsed into silence—but only for as long as he was speaking. When she answered him, they went back to their own conversations, not hearing her. It was as if she had said nothing, as if she were a crea-ture of his imagination. It made her nervous.

Nevertheless, the two continued talking idly to one another while they fished, with long periods of thoughtful silence between exchanges, and soon she no longer noticed that the others watched her in attentive silence when he spoke, then switched off and ignored her altogether when she responded. Suddenly, they both finally started catching fish—spots, small, silvery white fish with a thumbnail-sized black dot over each gill. "The tide comin' in," he explained. "We gonna get us a mess of fish now, you wait," he said, and as he spoke, she felt the deliberate tug of a fish on her line. She yanked with her left hand and reeled with her right, swiftly pulling in a small fish that glistened in the sun as she drew it up to the pier and over the rail. The fish she caught, one after another, were only a bit larger than her hand, but the man declared that they'd be the best fish she'd ever caught. "You fry up a mess of them little spots in the mornin' an' that'll be your best break-fast!" he promised and grinned at her and reeled in another for himself, slipped it off the hook, and shoved it into the burlap sack at his feet.

She let her own caught fish accumulate inside the tin tackle box she had brought, her father's. She could hear them rattling around inside, scattering the hooks, sinkers, and lures in the darkness. Her heart was pounding, from the work as much as from the excitement. She pictured the large, gray blossoms of sweat that she knew had spread across her back and under her arms. Her arms and legs were feathery and full of light, as she felt the shudder and the familiar, hard tug of one fish after another hitting the bait, felt it pull against the steady draw of the reel, then fly through the air, up and over the rail onto the pier. She wanted to laugh out loud and yell to the man next to her, Hey! I got *another* one! and *another* one!

But she said nothing. They both worked steadily in silence, grabbing the flopping, hooked fish off their lines, jamming fresh worms onto the hooks, reaching over the rail and casting the lines underhanded in long arcs back down into the water, feeling the weighted hooks hit the water and sink a foot or two into it, feeling them get hit again, and then reeling the fish back toward the pier, lifting them free of the water into the air and drawing them up to the pier and the rail again, and again, until, sweat rolling across her face, her arms began to ache, the muscles of her right hand between thumb and forefinger to cramp, and still the fish kept on hitting the lines. There was a grim, methodical rhythm to their move-ments, and they were working together, it seemed, the young white woman in blouse and shorts and blue tennis shoes and the middle-aged black man in T-shirt and stained khaki trousers and bare feet.

And then, as suddenly as it had begun, it was over. Her line drifted slowly to the bottom and lay there, inert, as if tied to a rock. His line, five feet away from hers, did the same. The two of them leaned further out and watched, waiting. But nothing happened. The fish were gone. The tide had moved them closer to the beach, where the school had swirled and dispersed in silvery clouds, swimming with the current along the beach, away from the pier and parallel to the breaking waves. She watched surf casters scattered up the beach one by one begin to catch fish, their long poles going up like tollgates as the schools moved rapidly along.

She lay flat on her back in the sand, no blanket or towel beneath her, feeling her skin slowly darken, tiny, golden beads of sweat gradually stringing her mouth along her upper lip and over her chin, crossing her forehead just above her eyebrows, puddling in the gullies below her collarbones and rib cage, between her small breasts, and drifting, sliding in a thin, slick sheet of moisture down the smooth insides of her thighs. It was close to noon, and the sun, a flat, white disc, was almost directly overhead, casting practically no shadow.

"Mommy, you're really getting red," Laura quietly said. She stood over her mother for a moment, peering down with a serious, almost worried look on her face. She was the older daughter, temperamentally more serious than her sister. They had always called her Laura, had never tried giving her a nickname. The other child, named Eva, was called Bootsie, Bunny, Noosh, and Pickle—depending on the parent's mood and the expression on the face of the child. Most people found the two girls attractive and likable—as much for the differences in their personalities as for their physical similarities. Four-year-old Eva was in appearance a smaller version of seven-year-old Laura, and both girls looked exactly like their mother.

This morning the three of them wore purple two-piece bathing suits, and while the mother sunbathed, the daughters, with their pails and shovels, played in the hot sand beside her. The grandmother had driven into the village for groceries and mail, and the grandfather was on his regular morning walk, three miles up the beach to the old Coast Guard station and back.

"Look, Mommy, *sharks!*" Laura cried. Janet propped herself up on her elbows and squinted against the hard glare of sand and mirror-like water. Then she saw them. Porpoises. Their gray backs slashed the water like dark knives.

"They're not sharks, they're porpoises, Laura."

"Are they dangerous?"

"No. They're supposed to be very bright and actually friendly to humans."

"Oh," she said, not believing.

Janet lay down on her back again and closed her eyes. She studied the backs of her eyelids, a yellow-ocher sheet with a slight, almost translucent scratch, like a thin scar, in front of the lid, between her eyeball and the lid. Every time she tried to look at the scar—which seemed to ride across the surface, moving slowly, like a twisted reed floating on still water—it jumped and disappeared off the edge of her circle of vision. A tiny scratch on the retina, she decided. The only way she could actually see it was if she tried not to look at it, but looked past it, as if at something else located in the same general region. Even then, however, she found herself eager to see the line (the scar or scratch or whatever it was), and she searched for it, caught a glimpse of it, and, chasing with her gaze, watched it race ahead of her and out of sight.

Janet realized that the girls were no longer close beside her. She sat up and looked around for them. A small flock of gulls loped over the water, dipping, dropping, lifting, going on. The porpoises still sliced the water a few hundred yards from the beach. As far as she could see in both directions, the beach was deserted. She called, "Laura!" Then called again, louder, and stood up, looking back toward the cottage.

"Listen, Mommy, wake up! You're really getting a terrible sunburn!" Janet opened her eyes and looked into Laura's worried face. Eva was sitting a few yards away, humming to herself while she buried her feet in a knee-deep hole she had dug in the sand. "Did you fall asleep?" Laura asked.

"No." She stood up and brushed the sand off the backs of her slender legs, shoulders, and arms. "C'mon, let's walk up the beach and meet Grandpa," she said cheerfully. She reached a hand to Laura, leaned down, and helped Eva pull herself free. The three of them started down the beach toward the Coast Guard station. Offshore, the porpoises cruised alongside, headed in the same direction, and, above them, the gulls.

The third night in the cottage, listening to the radio, a top 40 station from Elizabeth City, Janet drank alone until after midnight. She situated herself on the screened porch, gazed out at the ridge of sand that lay between the cottage and the beach, milky white until almost ten o'clock, when it slowly turned gray, then black, against the deep blue, eastern night sky. She drank Scotch and water, and each new drink contained less water and proportionately more Scotch than the previous, until her face felt like a plaster mask slipping forward and about to fall into her lap.

She was alone. Her mother and father had done their drinking before dinner, as was their habit, and had gone to bed by nine-thirty, also their habit. Janet had almost forgotten their routines, and a flood of sour memories swept over her, depressing her, separating her from her own life sufficiently to make her feel self-righteous sitting there on the porch with the bottle of Teacher's, a pitcher of water, a tub of ice cubes, and a small transistor radio on the floor beside her. She poured and drank one glassful of Scotch and water after another, letting the sweetly sad songs from that summer's crop swarm over her past and present lives. At one point she told herself that she was very interested in the differences between the way her parents drank and the way she drank—meaning that she was interested in making sure that there were differences.

As the land behind her cooled, the wind blew steadily and strongly, and the sound of the waves crashing in darkness on the packed, wet sand filled all the space that lay behind the sound of the radio. Janet thought in clumsy spirals backwards in time, of her husband, Roger, his years in graduate school, and their town house in Cambridge, where the children were born, and the years before that, when she and Roger were in college, the years she'd endured while in high school in Connecticut, living at home with her parents, and then she was a very young girl visiting her grandparents, here, at Kitty Hawk, where the family had been coming for summers for as long as she could remember and before she was born. And now here she was again, back where she had started, where they had started, too, her parents, and she was placing her own daughters where she had been placed, even to the point of sleeping them in the same room she had used at their age. Her chest and throat filled with a hard knot of longing. And as soon as she was aware of its presence, the knot loosened and unraveled and regathered as anger—anger at her life, as if it were an entity distinct from her, for all the cunning ways it had trapped her and her children.

Momentarily satisfied with this object for her emotion, she flicked off the radio, stood slightly off-balance, rocked on the balls of her feet like a losing prizefighter, and wound her way back into the living room, bumping curtly against the maple arm of the couch, grabbing at the light switches, dumping the house finally into darkness, and made her way down the hall to the stairs and up the stairs to her bedroom, the "guest room" at the end, moving in spite of the darkness with pugnacious confidence, but off-balance, inept.

*   *   *

Over on the western side of the Outer Banks, the sound side, the water was shallow and most of the time calm. The fourth morning at Kitty Hawk, Janet decided to take the girls to one of the small inlets where they could wade and even swim safely. They were excited by the prospect, though they didn't quite understand how it could be so different only a few miles away. If here by the cottage there was an ocean with huge, dangerous waves and undertows and tides, how could they get into the car and go to the same salty water a few miles away and have it be like a shallow lake?

Driving fast along the narrow road north of Kitty Hawk—deep sand on both sides, witchgrass, sea oats, and short brush, with high dunes blocking any possible views of the ocean—Janet slowed suddenly and carefully pulled her father's green Chrysler station wagon over and picked up a hitchhiker. He was slight and not very tall, an inch or two taller than Janet. About twenty-two or -three, with long blond hair, almost white, that hung straight down his back, he moved with an odd, precise care that was slightly effeminate and, to Janet, attractive. As he came up beside the car, he smiled. He had even white teeth, good-humored blue eyes, a narrow nose. He pitched his back-pack into the rear of the car, where the girls sat, nodded hello to them, and climbed into the front seat next to Janet.

"How far you goin'?" he asked.

"Out beyond Duck, to the Sound. Four or five miles, I guess. Will that get you where you want?"

"Yeah," he answered. He slid down in the seat, folded his hands across his flat belly, and closed his eyes, obviously enjoying the smooth luxury of the car, the insulating comfort of the air conditioner, as Janet drove the huge vehicle swiftly along the road, floating over bumps, gliding flatly around curves and bends in the road.

"Connecticut plates," the young man said suddenly, as if remembering a name he'd forgotten. "Are you from Connecticut?" He was unshaven, but his cheeks weren't so much bearded as covered with a soft, blond down. He was tanned, wearing jeans, patched and torn, faded and as soft-looking as chamois, and a dark green T-shirt. He was barefoot. Slipping a bit further down in the seat, his weight resting on the middle of his back, he placed his feet onto the dashboard in front of him gingerly, with a grace and care that made it seem natural to Janet.

She explained that she was from Cambridge, that the car was her father's, her parents were the ones who lived in Connecticut. Manchester, outside Hartford. And she was just down here for a while, she and her daughters, visiting them at their cottage. Though she herself hadn't been down here in years, not since her childhood. Because of summer camps and school and all. . . .

"Yeah, right," he said, peering casually around, taking in the girls in the back, who grinned soundlessly at him, and the Styrofoam floats in the far back of the car, beach towels, a change of clothes for each of them, a bag with sandwiches and cookies in it, a small cooler with ice and a six-pack of Coke inside. "You going swimming in the Sound?" he asked.

"Yes, for the kids, y'know?" She started to explain, about the waves, the undertow, the tides, how these presented no problem over on the Sound and children their ages could actually swim and enjoy themselves, not just sit there digging in the sand, which was about all they could do over on the sea side—when she realized that she was talking too much, too rapidly, about things that didn't matter. She asked him, "What about you? Are you staying down here for the summer? Or what?"

"I'm just kind of passing through. I may stay on for the summer, though," he added softly. His accent identified him as a Northerner, but that was about all.

"Are you living here? In Kitty Hawk, I mean?"

"I made like this camp out on the dunes a ways, beyond where the road ends. It's a fine place, so long as they don't come along and move me out. Nobody's supposed to be camping out there."

"Do you have a tent?" she asked, curious.

"They'd spot that as soon as I pitched it. I just sort of leaned some old boards and stuff together, pieces of wood I found along the beach and in the dunes. Last night, when it rained, I bet I stayed as dry as you did. It's the best place I've had all year. Up north, even in summer, there's no way you can be comfortable drifting around like this. But down here, it's easy, at least till winter comes. I work a couple of days every couple of weeks pumping gas at the Gulf station in Manteo, for groceries and stuff. That's where I'm comin' from now. I got my two weeks' groceries an' stuff in my pack. I just spend the rest of my time, you know, out on the dunes, sitting around in my shack, playing a little music, smoking some good dope, fishing on the beach. Stuff like that."

"Oh," she said.

The road ahead was narrower and, on both sides, dunes, and beach beyond dunes, and no vegetation except for brown grasses scattered sparsely across the sands, and as they rounded a curve, the road ended altogether. There was a paved cul-de-sac at the end where, without much trouble, one could turn a car around, and Janet steered the big Chrysler into this area and parked it. She shut off the motor, opened the door, and stepped out quickly.

The young man got out and walked around to the back, where he flopped the tailgate down, pulling his pack out first, then the kids' floats, the lunch bag and cooler, and the towels and clothes. The girls scrambled past him, leaped down from the tailgate, and ran for the water. They were already in their bathing suits and didn't break stride as they hit the quietly lapping water and raced in, quickly finding themselves twenty or thirty feet from shore and the water not yet up to their knees. Janet had come around to the back of the car, but by the time she got there the man was already closing the tailgate, lifting it slowly. Smiling, she came and stood beside him, to help lift the heavy tailgate, brushing his bare arm with her hand, then moving tightly toward him, touching his thigh with the front of hers. They lifted the slab of metal together, slamming it shut, and moved at once away from the car and from each other. She peered easily into his face, and he answered with a slight smile.

"Want to come up and see my shack?" He stood about eight feet away from her, one hand resting on his pack.

"Where is it?" She tossed her head and slung a wisp of hair away from her eyes. She leaned over and picked up the two coffin-shaped floats, hating the touch of the things against her hands, their odd weightlessness.

He waved a hand toward the seaside. "A couple hundred yards over that way. Just walk over those dunes there, and when you get to the beach, go along for maybe a hundred yards and cut in toward the dunes again, and then you'll see my shack. It'll look like a pile of driftwood or something to you at first, but when you get closer, you'll see it's a pretty cool place to live," he said, showing his excellent teeth again. "I got some good smoke, too, if you care for that."

She looked down at the clothes lying in the sand, the paper bag and ice chest, the beach towels, then back at the bony youth in front of her.

"Well, no. I don't think so. I have my daughters here. They haven't had a chance to swim, really, not since we got here, and I promised them this would be it. A whole day of it. But thanks," she said.

He answered, "Sure," lifted his pack onto his back and jabbed his arms through the straps and started across the pale sand, through slowly waving lines of sea oats, leaving deep, drooping tracks behind him.

She stood at the back of the car for a few moments, watching him depart, then turned and dragged the Styrofoam floats down to the edge of the water.

"You coming in, too, Mamma?" Eva asked her.

"Yeah, Pickle. I'm coming in, too."

"What were you talking about, you and that man?" Laura wondered, looking anxious. She stood knee-deep in the tepid water, about twenty feet from shore.

"Nothing much, really. He wanted me to come and see the way he lives. I guess he's proud of the way he lives. Some people are proud of the way they live. I guess he's one."

"Are you?" Laura asked.

"No," Janet said. Then she went back to the car for the rest of their gear.

When she woke the next morning, the first thing she knew was that it was raining—a soft, windless, warm rain, falling in a golden half-light—and she couldn't decide if it had just begun or was about to end.

Dressing quickly, she shoved a brush through her hair and walked out to the hall, heard her daughters talking behind the door of their bedroom, saw that the door to her parents' room was still closed, and, judging it to be early, probably not seven yet, walked downstairs to the living room. Immediately, upon entering the room, she felt the dampness of it. In the mornings here, the living room and kitchen seemed strangely inappropriate to her—wet, chilled, smelling of last night's supper—which made her eager to get a pot of coffee made, bacon frying, the new day begun.

As she moved about the small kitchen, from the Formica-topped counter to the stove to the refrigerator, she gradually realized that the rain had stopped, and the golden haze had been replaced by a low, overcast sky that cast a field of gloomy, pearl-colored light. She stopped work and looked out the window toward the ocean. A gull, as it swept up from the beach, ascending at the ridge between the cottage and the water, seemed to burst from the ground. Its belly was stained with yellow streaks the color of egg yolk, and she realized that the seagulls—

scavengers, carrion eaters, filthy, foul-smelling creatures—were beautiful only when seen from a distance. Suddenly, the force of the day, the utter redundancy of it, the closure it represented and sustained, hit her. She was unwilling to believe that her life was going to be this way every day, unwilling to believe it and yet also unable to deny it any longer: a lifetime of waking to damp, smelly couches and chairs, to rooms filled with cold furniture, to preparing food again, for herself, for her children, of waking to sudden gray skies and stinking birds searching for garbage, and on through the day more meals, more messes to make and clean up afterwards, until nightfall, when, with pills or alcohol, she would put her body to sleep for eight or ten hours, to begin it all over again the next morning. It wasn't that she believed there was nothing more than this. Rather, she understood that—no matter what else there was—she would never get away from this. Anything she might successfully add to her life could only enter it as background to this repeated series of acts, tasks, perceptions, services. She was thirty years old, not old, and it was too late to begin anything truly fresh and new. A new man, a new place to live, a new way of life, a profession, even—the newness would be a mockery, a sad, lame reaction to the failure of the old. There had been the promise, when she left Roger, of sloughing off her old life the way a snake sloughs off an old skin, revealing a new, lucid, sharply defined skin beneath it. But the analogy hadn't held.

And she was trapping her own children. The terms of her life had become the terms of theirs, and thus they, too, would spend the rest of their lives in relentless, unchanging reaction to patterns she could not stop establishing for them. None of them, not she, not her daughters, was going to get free. Once again, she'd been fooled, but this time, she knew, it was for the last time. She felt a dry bitterness working down her throat. Walking to the bottom of the stairs, she quietly called her daughters down for breakfast.

*　　*　　*

"Look, it's going to be a lousy day all day, so instead of waiting around here hoping the sun will come out, is it okay if I take your car and spend the day with the kids, just driving around and taking in the sights?" She lit a cigarette, flicked the match onto the floor, saw it lying there, a thin tail of smoke ascending from one end, and quickly plucked it back. And wondered what the hell made her do that. She held the burnt match carefully between her thumb and forefinger, while her father tried to answer her first question.

It was difficult for him, mainly because he wanted her to know, on the one hand, that he was eager for her to use his car, that, in fact, he was eager to be able to help her in any way possible (going for his wallet as the thought struck him), but also, he wanted her to know that he and her mother would be forced to endure her and the children's day-long absence as a painful event—wanted her to know this, but didn't want that knowledge to coerce her into changing her mind and staying at the cottage or leaving the children here while she took the car and went sight-seeing alone. After all, he reasoned with himself, they were *her* children, and right now they must seem extra-precious to her, for, without Roger, she must need to turn to them for even more love and companionship than ever before. He imagined how it would have been for Anne, his wife, if they had gotten divorced that time, years back, when Janet was not much older than Laura was now.

Yes, but what would this day be like for him and for Anne, with Janet and the children gone? A gray blanket of dread fell across his shoulders as he realized that five minutes after the car pulled away, he and his wife would sit down, each of them holding a book, and wait impatiently for the sound of the car returning. After lunch, they would take a stroll up the beach, walking back quickly so as not to miss them, if Janet and the children decided to return to the cottage early, and, because, of course, they would not have come back early, he and Anne would spend the rest of the afternoon in their chairs on the porch, holding their books, he a murder mystery, she a study of open class-rooms in ghetto schools. Well, they could drink early, and maybe Anne could think of something special to fix for dinner, blue shell crabs, and could start to work on that early, and he could rake the beach again, dig-ging a pit for the trash he found, burying it, raking over the top of the pit carefully, removing even the marks left by the teeth of the rake.

"*Sure* you can take the car, that's a *fine* idea! Give us a chance to take care of some things around here that need taking care of anyhow. How're you fixed for cash? Need a few dollars?" he asked without look-ing at her, drawing out his billfold, removing three twenties, folding them with his second finger and thumb and shoving them at her in such a way that for her to unfold and count it would be to appear slightly ungrateful. She could only accept.

Which she did, saying thanks and going directly into the living room, switching off the television as she told her daughters to hurry up and get dressed, they were going out for a ride, to see some exciting things, the Wright Brothers Memorial, for one thing, and maybe a shipwreck, and some fishing boats and a lighthouse, and who knows what else. She looked down at her hand, found that she was still hold-ing the burnt match. She threw it into an ashtray on the end table next to the couch.

She drove fast, through the village of Kitty Hawk—several rows of cot-tages on stilts, a few grocery stores and filling stations, a restaurant, a bookstore, and the Fish Pier—and south along Highway 158 a few miles, to Kill Devil Hills. The overcast sky was breaking into shreds of dirty gray clouds, exposing a deep blue sky. Though the day was warm, the sun was still behind clouds. The hard light diminished colors and softened the edges of things, making it seem even cooler than it was. Janet switched the air conditioner off and lowered the windows oppo-site and beside her, and warm, humid air rushed into the car. In the back, the girls had taken up their usual posts, peering out the rear window, finding it more satisfying to see where they had been than to seek vainly for where they were going.

On her right, in the southwest, Kill Devil Hill appeared, a grassy lump prominent against the flattened landscape of the Outer Banks, and at the top of the hill, a stone pylon that, from this distance of a mile, resembled a castle tower.

"We're almost there," she called to the girls. "Look!" She pointed at the hill and the tower.

"Where?" Laura asked. "Where are we going?"

"There. See that hill and the tower on top? Actually, it's not a tower. It's only a stone memorial to the Wright Brothers," she explained, knowing then why she had never come here before and simultaneously wondering why the hell she was coming here now.

"The Wright Brothers?" Laura said. "Are they the airplane men?"

"The men who invented the airplane."

"Oh."

"Mamma, look!" Eva chimed in. "A castle! Are we going to the castle? Can we go to the castle?"

"Yes."

"How many brothers were there?"

"Two. Wilbur and Orville."

"Only *two*?"

"Yes."

"Will there be a king and queen at the castle?"

"No . . . yes. Sure."

"Laura, there's going to be a king and queen at the castle!"

"Stupid! That's not a castle."

"Let her call it a castle, Laura. It looks like one."

Off the highway, they drove along the narrow, winding approach to the memorial, passing the field and the low, flat-roofed, glass-walled structure that housed the various exhibits and the scale model of the aircraft, past the two wooden structures at the northern end of the field where, she remembered reading once years ago, the brothers had stored their device and had worked and slept while preparing it for flight. Janet was surprised to find herself oddly attracted to the place, to the hill, round and symmetrical, like an Indian mound, and, atop it, the pylon that, even up close, looked the way as a child she had pictured the Tower of London.

Janet parked the Chrysler in the small parking lot on the west side of the hill. The three of them got out and walked quickly along the paved pathway that methodically switchbacked to the top. In seconds, the girls had run on ahead, and Janet was alone. The sky was almost clear now, a bright, luminous blue, and the sun shone on her face as she climbed. She was sweating and enjoying it, feeling the muscles of her back and legs working hard for the first time in weeks. The sense of entrapment she had felt a few hours ago she could recall now only with deliberate effort. She still perceived it as the primary fact of her life, but merely as if it were a statistic. Ahead of her, Laura and Eva darted about the base of the tower, scurrying around the thing as if looking for an entrance. In a few moments, she arrived at the crest, breathing hard, sweating, and the girls ran to meet her.

"It's a castle all right!" Eva cried happily. "But we can't get in, the door's locked!" She pulled Janet by the hand to a padlocked, steel door. "The king and the queen had to go to work, I guess. They aren't home."

"I guess not, Pickle," Janet said. They walked slowly around to the other side, where they sat on the ground and peered down the slope that the two bicycle mechanics had used for launching their strange machine. Then, as if a wonder were unfolding before her eyes, filling her with awe, Janet saw a large, clear image of the two men from the Midwest and their clumsy wire, wood, and cloth aircraft and the sustained passion, the obsession with making it work, and their love for it and for each other. It was like discovering a room in her own house that she'd never suspected existed, opening a door that she'd never opened, looking in and seeing an entirely new room, unused, unknown, altering thoroughly and from then on her view of the entire house.

The image was of her own making, but that didn't lessen the impact. She saw the brothers as having released into their lives tremendous energy, saw it proceed directly, as if from a battery, from their shared obsession and their mad, exclusive love for each other—a positive and negative post, the one necessitated by the presence of the other. They had not permitted themselves, she decided, to live as she feared she was condemned to live: curled up inside a self that did not really exist.

For her, the image was perceived by her body as much as by her mind, and she felt lightened by it, as if she could fly, like a deliberately wonderful bird, leaping from the lip at the top of the little hill, soaring from the height of land first up and then out, in a long, powerful glide across the slope and then over the field that aproned it, drifting easily, gracefully, slowly to the ground, coming to rest at the far end of the field, where the two workshops were located, where, she decided, she would pitch herself into the task of making a machine that could fly, making it out of wires and shreds of cloth and odd remainders of wood and rough pieces of other machinery—the junk of her life so far. Her daughters careened uphill past her, mocking and singing at each other, asserting their differences to each other, and she knew, from the way her face felt, that she would be tireless.

Standing, she turned and waved for the girls to follow, and the three of them descended the hill, holding hands, and talking brilliantly.

Comfort

Leon LaRoche, the bank teller, tried to tell this story once to his friend and neighbor, Captain Dewey Knox (U.S. Army, ret.). Leon was in his late twenties when he made the attempt, and he had been drinking beer with the Captain in the Captain's trailer for several hours, so he was slightly drunk, or he probably would not have tried to tell it at all. When drunk, it's your judgment about the sayable that goes, not your inhibitions.

The two men had been talking about a kid who used to live at the trailerpark, Buddy Smith, who had been a thief and a liar and whose father, Tom Smith, had finally thrown him out of the trailer he'd shared with his son for most of the kid's life. Six months after the son departed, the father shot himself, and nobody understood any of it. Buddy Smith never showed up in Catamount again, not even for the funeral, and that had been the end of the matter, except when folks now and then wondered whatever happened to him and wondered why his father, a sociable, though utterly private man, had killed himself. Most people believed that by now the kid was locked up in jail somewhere out West, where his mother was supposed to live, and that Tom Smith had shot himself in the mouth with his shotgun because, since he had been living alone, his drinking had got out of hand, and too much drinking alone can make you depressed. Nobody thought the two events, the son's departure and the father's suicide, were connected. At least not in such a way as to think the suicide could have been avoided, which is to say, at least not in such a way as you could blame the son for the death of the father.

"I liked Buddy," Leon said, gazing into his glass. "I really did." The two men were seated at the Captain's kitchen table, the television set still rumbling behind them in the living room, for when Leon knocked on the door and offered to share a six-pack of beer with him, the Captain had been watching the evening news and in his pleasure had neglected to shut the machine off. The older man was grateful for the interruption—it was a frosty November night, and people generally don't go calling on people uninvited on nights like this—and when the first six-pack was drunk, the Captain started offering beer from his refrigerator, until they found themselves working their way through a third six-pack. The Captain said he didn't mind, it was a Friday night anyhow, and he was restless and felt like having company, so what the hell, crack open another, Leon, and relax, for Chrissakes, you're too uptight, boy. "You remind me of myself when I was your age," he told Leon. "Some people have to learn to relax, have to force themselves to do it, and then after a while it comes naturally," he said laughing, as if to prove how finally it had come naturally to him.

"No, I really liked Buddy, although I can't say I knew him very well. He was a chess player. I never knew that, until this one night after work, and I went into the Hawthorne House for a drink, because I was angry, pissed off, from having been yelled at once too often by Bob Fosse at the bank. You wouldn't believe that man, I don't believe that man. After what, seven years, and he still treats me like shit. Anyhow, I went into the Hawthorne House, which is unusual for me, because that place can be kind of rough, you know, and I hate the *smell* of it, like urine and old beer, but like I said, I was angry at Bob Fosse and needed a drink to calm down.

"Buddy was playing one of the pinball machines, alone, as usual. He never seemed to have friends in town, even though there are plenty of kids his age in town, too many of them, if you want my opinion, who don't seem to do anything except hang around drinking beer and flexing their muscles and getting themselves tattooed. Buddy was like that, too, or at least he seemed like that, except that he kept pretty much to himself. Also he didn't exactly *look* like those guys. I mean, he was always clean-looking, and he wore his hair short, and he took good care of his clothes. He looked like an Army recruit home on leave from boot camp. Even so, he never seemed to do much except hang around the trailerpark or up at the Hawthorne House, as if waiting for someplace far away and very different from this place. Those other guys his age, they were made in Catamount, New Hampshire, to stay in Catamount, New Hampshire, and eventually to die in Catamount, New Hampshire. It was stamped all over their faces, all over their bulky muscles, all over the way they talked and laughed and punched each other around."

The Captain knew the type. He shoved his paw across his white crew cut and sighed. "Bring back the draft," he intoned, "and in a year the streets of America will be cleared of that type and safe to walk in again."

"Buddy had spent a year in the service, actually. The Marines, I think he told me, and just as he was about to be shipped overseas to Germany or someplace, he was in a motorcycle accident that put a metal plate into his head and got him discharged. He told me this while we were sitting at the bar, but I don't think I believed him, because while he was telling me all this, he kept smiling at me and watching my eyes, as if he was putting me on, just to see if I'd believe some lie.

"He was a chess player. He said he wasn't very good, but he liked to play, which is true for me, too, so I said we should get together to play chess sometime, and he thought that was a great idea. He didn't know anyone around here who played chess, he said, and neither did I. He had a way of watching the point of his cigarette while he smoked that was unusual. I bought him a second beer, and we talked about how hard it was, living in a small town in New Hampshire, how boring it was, and how mean-minded the people were. He said as soon as he got some money that was owed him by a guy in the Marines he was leaving for the West Coast, and then he asked me why I stayed here, living in Catamount, going back and forth every day from the trailerpark to the bank. I explained how my mother lives in Concord, where I grew up, and this was the best job I could find when I got out of New Hampshire Commercial College, and I go to Boston sometimes on weekends, I told him. He was curious about that, about what I do in Boston on weekends, and I told him the truth, that I go around to the bars and maybe take a meal at a fancy restaurant and go to a movie. That's all. He didn't believe me, but he was very nice, very cheerful and friendly. He said I probably stayed home every weekend and watched TV.

"By then the place was filling up and had got pretty noisy. The juke-box was playing, and two or three couples were dancing, and you had to holler to be heard, so I asked Buddy to come back to my place for some supper and a few games of chess. He asked me if I had anything to drink, apologizing as he asked, explaining that he was broke or else he'd offer to buy the beer. I had plenty of beer in the fridge plus a bottle of Scotch I keep around, and I had planned to go on home and cook up a couple of hamburgers for myself, anyhow. I hadn't played any chess in over a year, not since my brother was back East visiting my mother two Thanksgivings ago. Buddy said fine, so I paid, and we left in my car.

"When we got to the trailer, he opened a beer and set up the chess-board in the living room, while I cooked hamburgers. He had the tele-vision on and was watching it and drinking beer and seemed very relaxed to me. But he seemed sad, too. It's hard to explain. He probably reminded me of myself, somehow, sitting there alone, with the television set on and a chessboard set up in front of him. I walked into the living room to say something to him, I don't know what, just something that wouldn't make him seem so sad and alone to me, maybe, and when I passed behind his chair, I lay my hand on his shoulder in a friendly way. You know. Just lay my hand on his shoulder as I passed behind his chair.

"What happened then was . . . embarrassing. I don't know why I'm telling this to you, I've never told anyone else. But it's bothered me ever since. He grabbed at my hand as if it were an insect, a spider or something, and threw it off his shoulder. When he stood up and turned to face me, he was red-faced and enraged, sputtering at me, calling me a fairy, all kinds of names. He knocked over the chessboard, made a few wild moves around the room like he was trying to find a way out without passing me, and finally went by me like I had some kind of disease he could catch, and slammed the door."

The Captain was at the refrigerator and had drawn out a pair of beers. He let the door shut on its own and stood facing it. "Well," he said. "Well, then . . . so he decided you had . . . unnatural desires, eh?"

"Apparently. Yes, he did. But I didn't."

"Of course not." The Captain was still facing the closed refrigerator door.

"It was just that he looked so sad and alone there. So pitiful. I can't describe it. Sometimes you can have a feeling toward a person that makes you want to do that, to place a hand on him and that's all, just to comfort him, even though he doesn't know he needs comfort—no, especially because he doesn't know he needs comfort. But I don't know why I'm telling you this. I must need comfort myself and not know it or something," Leon said, and he laughed lightly, nervously.

The Captain laughed with him and turned and sat back down at the table. Leon, his face pinched in thought, opened the bottle and filled his glass, then studied the glass carefully, watching the bubbles rise inside and the moisture drip down the outside. The Captain filled his pipe from a brown leather pouch and lit it, drawing in the smoke rapidly, until he had it going on its own. Then he asked Leon if it was true, was he a fairy?

Leon slowly looked up at the older man, the way you would look at a falling tree if you had got unexpectedly caught beneath it. It was too late to step out of its path. "Yes," he said. "A fairy. I suppose I am."

The Captain smiled and said that he had always thought so, but Leon was not to worry, because his secret was safe with him. He understood that sort of thing, it happened all the time in the service. Well, not all the time, but often enough that you had to learn to be tolerant, so long as people kept these things to themselves. He continued talking a few seconds longer, but Leon was already standing and pulling on his jacket, moving for the door.

At the door, he apologized for having drunk so much of the Captain's beer, and quickly stepped outside to the cold night air. It was a clear sky, with falling stars and a crescent moon that looked like a narrow streak against the dark blue sky.

Success Story

After high school, I attended an Ivy League college for less than one term. A year later, I was married and living in central Florida. This was 1958 and '59. General Dwight Eisenhower was our President, and Dr. Fidel Castro, hunkered down in the mountain passes southeast of Havana, was getting praised for his integrity and good looks by *Time* magazine and *Reader's Digest*.

I'd been a whiz kid in high school, rewarded for it with an academic scholarship. In this Ivy League school, however, among the elegant, brutal sons of the captains of industry, I was only that year's token poor kid, imported from a small New Hampshire mill town like an exotic herb, a dash of mace for the vichyssoise. It was a status that perplexed and intimidated and finally defeated me, so that, after nine weeks of it, I fled in the night.

Literally. On a snowy December night, alone in my dormitory room (they had not thought it appropriate for me to have a roommate, or no one's profile matched mine), I packed my clothes and few books into a canvas duffle, waited until nearly all the lights on campus were out, and sneaked down the hallway, passed through the service entrance, and walked straight down the hill from the eighteenth-century cut-stone dormitories and classroom buildings to the wide boulevard below, where huge, neoclassical fraternity houses lounged beneath high, ancient elms. At the foot of the hill, I turned south and jogged through unplowed snow, shifting my heavy duffle from one shoulder to the other every twenty or thirty yards, until I passed out of the valley town into darkness and found myself walking through a heavy snowstorm on a winding, narrow road.

A month later—with the holidays over and my distraught mother and bewildered younger brother and sister, aunts, uncles, and cousins, all my friends and neighbors and high school teachers, as well as the dean and director of admissions at the Ivy League college, convinced that I not only had ruined my life but may have done something terrible to theirs, too—I turned up in St. Petersburg, Florida, with seven dollars in my pocket, my duffle on my shoulder, and my resolve to join Castro in the Sierra Maestra seriously weakening.

I'd spent Christmas and New Year's at home, working days and nights as a salesman in a local men's clothing store, trying hard to behave as if nothing had happened. My mother seemed always to be red-eyed from weeping, and my friends from high school treated me coolly, distantly, as if I had dropped out of college because of a social disease. In some ways, my family was a civic reclamation project—the bright and pretty children and pathetic wife of a brute who, nearly a decade ago, had disappeared into the northern woods with a woman from the post office, never to be heard from again. As the oldest male victim of this abandonment, I was expected by everyone who knew the story to avenge the crime, mainly by making myself visibly successful, by rising above my station, and in that paradoxical way show the criminal how meaningless his crime had been. For reasons I was only dimly aware of, my story was important to everyone.

Leaving them behind, then, abandoning my fatherless family in a tenement and my old friends and the town I had been raised in, was an exquisite pleasure, like falling into bed and deep sleep after having been pushed beyond exhaustion. Now, I thought the morning I left—

stepping onto the ramp to Route 93 in Catamount, showing my thumb to the cars headed south—*now* I can start to dream my own dreams, not everyone else's.

The particular dream of joining Castro died easily. It started dying the moment I got out of the big, blue Buick sedan with Maryland plates that had carted me straight through all the way from Norfolk, Virginia, to Coquina Key in St. Petersburg, where the elderly man who drove the car had a "fiancée," he told me, with a suite in the Coquina Key Hotel.

"You, you're a smart kid," he said to me, as I slid from the car and hauled out my duffle from the back. "You'll do all right here. You'll catch on." He was a ruddy, white-haired man with a brush cut that he liked to touch with the flat of his hand, as if patting a strange dog. "Forget Cuba, though. No sense getting yourself killed for somebody else's country." He was a retired U.S. Army captain, named Knox, "like the fort," he'd said, and he gave advice as if he expected it to be taken. "Kid like you," he said, peering across at me from the driver's seat, "smart, good-looking, good personality, you can make a million bucks here. This place," he said, looking warmly around him at the marina, the palm trees, the acres of lawn, the flashy bougainvillea blossoms, the large new cars with out-of-state plates, the tall, pink Coquina Key Hotel with the dark red canopy leading from the street to the front entrance, "this place is *made* for a kid like you!"

"Yeah. Well, I got plenty of time for that." I took a step away from the car, and Knox leaned farther across the front seat. I said to him, "I don't need to make a pile of money just yet."

"No? How much you got?"

"Not much. Enough." I lifted my duffle to my shoulder and gave the man a wave.

"If you don't need money, kid, what *do* you need, then?"

"Experience, I guess." I tried to smile knowingly.

"Listen. I've been coming down here every goddamned winter for eight years now, ever since I retired. I've *got* experience, and lemme tell you, this place is gonna be a boom town. It already is. All these old people from the North, and there's gonna be more of 'em, son, not less, and all of 'em got money to spend, and here you are on the ground floor. I'd give all my experience for your youth. Son, forget Cuba. Stay in St. Pete, you'll be a millionaire before you're twenty-five."

I was sorry now that I'd told Knox the truth back in Virginia, when he'd asked me where I was going. I'd said Cuba, and he'd laughed and asked why, and I had tried to tell him, but all I could say was that I wanted to help the Cuban people liberate themselves from a cruel and corrupt dictator. We both knew how that sounded, and neither of us had spoken of Cuba again, until now.

I stepped away from the car to the curb. "Well, thanks. Thanks for the advice. And the ride. Good meeting you," I said.

He called me by my name. I hadn't thought he'd caught it. "Look, if you need some help, just give me a call," he said and stuck a small white card out the window on the passenger's side.

I took the card and read his first name, Dewey, his address back in Chevy Chase, Maryland, and a post office box here in St. Petersburg. "Thanks," I said.

"I stay at the hotel," Knox said, nodding toward the high, pink, stuccoed building. "With my fiancée. Her name's Sturgis, Bea Sturgis. Bea's here all the time, year round. Nice woman. Give a call anytime."

"I'm okay," I said. "Really. I know what I'm doing."

He smiled. "No," he said. "You don't." Then he waved good-bye, dropped the Buick into gear, and moved off slowly toward the hotel garage.

It was not quite nine in the morning, and it was already hot. I peeled off my jacket, tied it to the duffle, and strolled across the street to the park by the marina and sat down on a bench facing the street. Behind me, charter fishing boats and yachts rocked tenderly against the narrow dock, where pelicans perched somberly on the bollards. Across the street, men and women in short-sleeved, pastel-colored blouses and shirts and plaid Bermuda shorts drifted in and out of the hotel. New cars and taxis and limousines drove people by and let people off and picked people up. A light breeze riffled quietly through the royal palm trees that lined the street. Everyone and everything belonged exactly where it was.

I was suddenly hungry and realized that I hadn't eaten since the night before at a Stuckeys in North Carolina. A few minutes passed, and then I saw Knox emerge from the parking garage at the left of the hotel and walk briskly along the sidewalk toward the hotel, his gaze straight ahead of him, businesslike. He reached the canopy, turned under it, and entered the building, nodding agreeably to the doorman as he passed through the glass doors to the dark, cool interior.

I stood up slowly, grabbed my duffle, crossed the street, and followed him.

I never saw Knox again. I called him from the house phone in the lobby, and he laughed and called the manager, who met me at the front desk and gave me a note to take to the concierge, who put me to work that very day as a furniture mover.

I was the youngest and the healthiest of a gang of seven or eight men who set up tables and chairs for meeting rooms and convention halls, decorated ballrooms for wedding receptions, moved pianos from one dining room to another, dragged king-sized mattresses from suite to suite, unloaded supplies from trucks, delivered carts of dirty linen to the basement laundry, lugged sofas, lamps, cribs, and carpets from one end of the hotel to the other. Paid less than thirty dollars a week for six ten-hour days a week, we worked staggered shifts and were on call seven days a week, twenty-four hours a day. We were given room and board and ate in a bare room off the hotel kitchen with the dishwashers and slept two to a tiny, cell-like room in a cinder-block dormitory behind the hotel.

Most of the kitchen help was black and went home, or somewhere, at night. We furniture movers were to a man white and, except for me, over forty, terminally alcoholic, physically fragile, and itinerant. It took me a few days to realize that we were all a type of migrant worker, vagrants, wanderers down from the cold cities and railroad yards of the North, and that the day after payday most of this week's crew would be gone, replaced the next day by a new group of men, who, a week later, would leave, too, for Miami, New Orleans, or Los Angeles. No one else wanted our jobs, and we couldn't get any other. We were underpaid, overworked, and looked down upon by chambermaids, elevator operators, and doormen. Like certain plumbing tools, we were not thought to exist until we were needed.

Even so, less than two weeks into this line of work, I decided to succeed at it. Which was like deciding to succeed at being a prisoner of war, deciding to become a *good* prisoner of war. I believed that I could become so good at moving furniture that I'd be irreplaceable and shortly thereafter would be made boss of the furniture movers, and then my talent for organization, my affection for the hotel, and the warmth of my personality would be recognized by the concierge, who would promote me, would make me his assistant, and from there I'd go on to concierge itself, then assistant manager, until, before long, why not *manager*? In the distant future, I saw a chain of hotels linking every major city on the Gulf of Mexico (a body of water I had not actually seen yet) that I would control from a bank of telephones here on my desk in St. Petersburg at the Coquina Key, which, since it was where I got my start, would become the central jewel in my necklace of hotels and resorts, my diadem, a modest man's point of understandable pride. I would entertain world leaders here—Dr. Fidel Castro, President Dwight Eisenhower, Generalissimo Chiang Kai-shek. People would congratulate me for having dropped out of an Ivy League college after less than one term, and my mother and brother and sister would now realize the wisdom of my decision, and friends from high school would call me up, begging for jobs in one of my many hotels. Late at night, lying in my narrow bunk, my temporary roommate snoring in the bunk below, I imagined testimonial dinners at which I would single out my old friend Dewey Knox from Chevy Chase. He'd be seated alongside his lady, Bea Sturgis, at the head table, just beyond the mayor of St. Petersburg and the governor of Florida. "It all started with Knox," I'd say. "He told me this place was made for a guy like me, and he was right!"

Furniture movers came and went, but I stayed. The fourth person in five weeks with whom I shared my grim cell was named Bob O'Neil, from Chicago, and when he found out that I'd been a furniture mover at the Coquina Key for longer than a month, he told me I was crazy. I'd come back from setting up a VFW luncheon in the Oleander Room, hoping to sneak a few hours' sleep, as I'd been up most of the night before, taking down the tables and chairs and cleaning up the hall after an all-state sports award banquet. My previous roommate, Fred from Columbus, a fat, morosely silent man whose hands trembled while he read religious tracts, which he wordlessly passed on to me, had got his first week's pay two days before and had taken off for Phoenix, he said, where his sister lived.

My new roommate, when I arrived, had already claimed the bottom bunk and removed my magazines and was now lying stretched out on it. I closed the door, and he sat up, stuck out his hand, and introduced himself. "Hi," he said, "I'm Bob, and I'm an alcoholic." He was in his early or late forties; it was hard to tell which. His face was broad and blotched, with broken veins crisscrossing his cheeks and large red nose. He was bright-eyed and had a cheerful, loose mouth and a wash of thin, sandy-gray hair.

I removed his open, nearly empty, cardboard suitcase from the only chair in the room and sat down. I said, "How come you tell people you're an alcoholic, Bob?" and he explained that he was required to by Alcoholics Anonymous, which he said he had joined just yesterday, after years of considering it.

"That's what you *got* to say," he said. "You got to admit to the world that you're an alcoholic. Put it right out there. First step to recovery, kid."

"How long before you're cured?" I asked. "And don't have to go around introducing yourself like that?"

"Never," he said. "Never. It's like . . . a condition. Like diabetes or your height. I'm allergic to booze, to alcohol. Simple as that."

"So you can't touch the stuff?"

"Right. Not unless I want to die." He swung his feet around to the floor and lit a cigarette. "Smoke?"

"No, thanks," I said. "The bottom bunk's mine."

"You're kidding me," he said, smiling broadly. "Look at you—what're you, eighteen? Twenty?"

"Eighteen. Almost nineteen."

"Eighteen. Right. And here I am, an old, sick man, an alcoholic, and you can jump up there like a pole vaulter. And you're saying that bottom bunk's yours." He sighed, coughed, lay back down, and closed his eyes. "You're right. It's yours."

"No, go ahead. I'll sleep on top."

"No, no, no! You're right, you got here before me. First come, first served. That's the law of the land. I understand, kid."

I climbed up the rickety ladder at the end of the bunk and flung myself face-forward onto the bed.

"You sure you don't mind?" he asked, sticking his head out and peering up at me.

"No."

"How long you been here, anyhow?"

"Little over five weeks," I said. More than half as long as I went to college, I noticed.

"Five weeks!" He laughed and told me I was crazy, said it in a high, amused voice. "Well," he said, yawning, "you must be getting real good at it."

"Yeah."

Nobody worked these jobs more than a week or at the most two, he explained. "You're like a prisoner, never see the light of day, never make enough money to make a difference in your life, so what you gotta do, you just gotta get your pay and leave. Get the hell out. Find a place or a job that does make a difference. Smart, good-looking kid like you," he said, "you can do better than this. This is America, for Christ's sake. You can do real good for yourself. How much money you got saved up?"

"Not much. Little over sixty bucks."

"Well, there you go," he said, as if presenting a self-evident truth.

I thanked him for the advice, explained that I was tired and needed sleep. I was on the night shift that week and had been told to fill in for a guy who'd left the morning crew, something that was happening with increasing frequency, which I had taken as a sure sign of imminent success.

Over the next few days, whenever we talked, which was often, as he was garrulous and I was lonely, we talked about Bob's alcoholism and my refusal to take his advice, which was to leave the hotel immediately, rent a room in town, get a job in a restaurant or a store, where people could see me, as Bob explained, because, according to him, I had the kind of face people trusted. "An *honest* face," he said, as if it communicated more than merely a commitment to telling the truth, as if intelligence, reliability, sensitivity, personal cleanliness, and high ambition all went with it. "You got an *honest* face, kid. You should get the hell out there in the real world, where you can *use* it."

For my part, I advised him to keep going to his AA meetings, which he said he did. He was tempted daily to drink, I knew, by the flask toters in our crew, and often he'd come into the room trembling, on the verge of tears, and he'd grab me by the shoulders and beg me not to let him do it. "Don't let me give in, kid! Don't let the bastards get to me. Talk to me, kid," he'd beg, and I'd talk to him, remind him of all he'd told me—

his broken marriages, his lost jobs, his penniless wanderings between Florida and Chicago, his waking up sick in filthy flophouses and pan-handling on street corners—until at last he'd calm down and feel a new determination to resist temptation. I could see that it was hard on him physically. He seemed to be losing weight, and his skin, despite the red blotches and broken veins, had taken on a dull gray pallor, and he never seemed to sleep. We were both on the night shift that week, and all day long, except when he went out for what he said were his AA meetings, I'd hear him in the bunk below, tossing his body from side to side in the dim afternoon light as he struggled to fall asleep, eventually giving up, lighting a cigarette, going out for a walk, returning to try and fail again.

One afternoon, a few days before his first payday, he reached up to my bunk and woke me. "Listen, kid, I can't sleep. Loan me a couple bucks, willya? I got to go get a bottle." His voice was unusually firm, clear. He'd made a decision.

"Bob, don't! You don't want that. Stick it out."

"Don't lecture me, kid, just loan me a coupla bucks." This time he was giving me an order, not making a request.

I looked into his eyes for a few seconds and saw my own stare back. "No," I said and turned over and went defiantly to sleep.

When I woke, it was growing dark, and I knew I'd almost missed supper, so I rushed from the room and down the long tunnel that con-nected the dormitory to the hotel kitchen, where the night dishwash-ers and furniture movers were already eating. Bob wasn't there, and no one had seen him.

"He's working tonight!" I said. "He's got to work tonight!"

They shrugged and went on eating. No one cared.

A half dozen rooms on the fourteenth floor were being painted, and we spent the night moving furniture out and storing it in the base-ment, and there was a chamber of commerce breakfast that we had to set up in the Crepe Myrtle Room. By the time I got back to my room, it was daylight. Bob was there, sound asleep in the bottom bunk.

I looked around the room, checked the tin trash can, even peered into the dresser drawers, but found no bottle. He heard me and rolled over and watched.

"Lookin' for something?"

"You know what."

"A bottle?"

"Yeah. Sure."

"Sorry, kid."

"You didn't drink?"

"Nope." He sat up and smiled. He looked rested for the first time, and his color had returned. He lit a cigarette. "Nope, I didn't break. Close, though," he said, his blue eyes twinkling, and he held his thumb and index finger a pencil width apart. "Close."

I grinned, as if his triumph were mine. "You really got through it, huh? What'd you do? Where were you all night?"

"Right here. While you were working, I was sleeping like a baby. I got back here late from the AA meeting. It was a long one, and I was burnt, man. So I just told 'em I was sick, they could dock my pay, and then I came back here and slept the night away."

"Wow! That's great!" I shook his hand. "See, man, that's what I've been telling you! You got to keep going to those AA meetings!"

He smiled tolerantly, rubbed out his cigarette, and lay back down. I pulled off my shirt and trousers, climbed up to my bed, and when I heard Bob snoring, I fell asleep.

That afternoon, when I woke, Bob was gone again. I got down from my bed and noticed that his cardboard suitcase was gone, too. His drawer in the dresser was empty, and when I looked into the medicine cabinet above the tiny sink in the corner, I saw that he'd taken his shaving kit. He'd moved out.

I was confused and suddenly, unexpectedly, sad. I stood in front of the mirror and shaved, the first time in three days, and tried to figure it all out—Bob's alcoholism, which did indeed seem as much a part of him as his height or the color of his eyes, and my caring about it; his persistent advice to me, and mine to him; his vain dream of not drinking, my dream of . . . what? Success? Forgiveness? Revenge? Somehow, Bob and I were alike, I thought, especially now that he had fled from the hotel. The thought scared me. It was the first time since that snowy night I left the college on the hill that I'd been scared.

I wiped off the scraps of shaving cream, washed my razor, and opened the cabinet for my bottle of Aqua Velva. Gone. A wave of anger swirled around me and passed quickly on. I sighed. Oh, what the hell, let him have it. The man left without even one week's pay; a morning splash of aftershave would make him feel successful for at least a minute or two. The rest of the day he'll feel like what he is, I thought, a failure.

I picked up my shirt and pants and slowly got dressed, when, leaning down to tie my shoe, I saw the pale blue bottle in the tin trash can between the dresser and the bed. I reached in, drew it out, and saw that it was empty.

Chucking it back, as if it were a dead animal, I looked around the gray room, and I saw its pathetic poverty for the first time—the spindly furniture, the bare cinder-block walls and linoleum floor, the small window that faced the yellow-brick side of the parking garage next door. Knox's blue Buick was probably still parked there. I looked at my half dozen paperback books on the dresser—mysteries, a Stendhal novel, an anthology of *Great American Short Stories*—and my papers, a short stack of letters from home, a sketchbook, a journal I was planning to write in soon. I'd brought it for Cuba. Then I pulled my old canvas duffle out from under the bed and began shoving clothes inside.

I rented a room from an old lady who owned a small house off Central Avenue in downtown St. Petersburg, a quiet neighborhood of bungalows and tree-lined streets that was beginning to be devoured at the edges by glass-and-concrete buildings housing condominiums, insurance companies, and banks. The room was small, but bright and clean, in the back off the kitchen, with its own bathroom and separate entrance. With the room went kitchen privileges, but I would have to eat in my bedroom. There were strict house rules that I eagerly agreed to: no visitors, by which I knew she meant women; no smoking; no drinking. I'd been meaning to give up smoking anyhow, and since the only way I could drink was more or less illegally, it seemed more or less a luxury to me. Especially after Bob O'Neil. As for women in my room, based on my experience so far, the old lady might as well have said no Martians.

"I'm a Christian," she said, "and this is a Christian home." Her name was Mrs. Treworgy. She was tiny, half my size, and pink—pink hair, pink skin, pink rims around her watery eyes.

"I'm a Christian too," I assured her.

"What church?"

I hesitated. "Methodist?"

She smiled, relieved, and told me where the nearest Methodist church was located; not far, as it turned out. She herself was a Baptist, which meant that she had to walk ten blocks each way on Sundays. "But the preaching's worth it," she said. "And our choir is much better than the Methodist choir."

"I'm sure."

"Maybe you'd like to come with me some Sunday."

"Oh, yes, I would," I said. "But I'll probably try the Methodist church first. You know, it being what I'm used to and all." What I was used to was sleeping till noon on Sundays, and before that, back when my mother made me go, dozing through mass.

"Yes, of course." Then she asked for the first and last months' rent in advance. Eighty dollars.

"All I've got to my name is sixty-seven dollars," I said and confessed, as if to a crime, that I had just quit my job at the Coquina Key Hotel and briefly described the conditions there, as if they were extenuating circumstances. "It was a very . . . unsavory atmosphere," I said, looking at the floor of her living room. The room was small, crowded with large, dark furniture and portraits of Jesus, close-ups and long shots, seated by a rock at prayer and ascending like Superman into heaven.

She looked at me carefully. "You have an honest face," she pronounced. "And I'm sure you'll find a new job right away. Whyn't you just pay me the first month's rent, forty dollars, and we'll go from there."

"Oh, thank you, Mrs. Treworgy. Thank you. And you wait," I said, "I'll have a job by tomorrow!"

Which I did. Following at last the advice of my ex-roommate Bob O'Neil, I applied for a job where I could be seen, as a menswear salesman at the fashionable downtown Maas Brothers Department Store. On the application form, however, under hobbies, I wrote "drawing and painting" and was instead hired to work in the Display Department as an assistant window trimmer.

The Display Department was located in the basement of the large, modern building, and as an assistant I was expected to build and paint the backdrops for the interior and window displays designed and installed by a tall, thin, Georgia man named, appropriately, Art, and a bulky, middle-aged, black-haired woman named Sukey, who wore turquoise and silver Indian jewelry and hand-printed muumuus. Art was an agreeable man in his forties who'd worked in advertising in Atlanta until a decade ago, when his ulcers erupted and sent him to the hospital for the third time in one year, after which he'd quit and moved to Florida. He popped antacid tablets all day, and his mouth was perpetually dry and white-lipped, but he joked and smiled easily, teased Sukey for her artistic pretensions, me for my youth and ignorance, and Ray, the obese, bald sign painter, for his weight and baldness.

It was a cheerful, easygoing place, especially after the Coquina Key

Hotel, and I enjoyed the work, which was not difficult. I built lightweight wood frames, usually four feet by eight feet, covered them with colored paper or foil, painted screens and backdrops, cleaned brushes and swept the floor of the shop. Afternoons, I delivered signs for Ray to the department heads upstairs, ate lunch with the salespeople and the rest of the staff in the company cafeteria on the first floor, and after work went out for beers with Art, Sukey, and Ray, and then walked whistling back to my room at Mrs. Treworgy's, where, after supper, I drew pictures, usually somber self-portraits, read, and prepared to write in my journal.

I turned nineteen that spring, and there were pink, white, and yellow hibiscus blossoms everywhere and sweet-smelling jasmine, oleander, and poinciana trees in bloom. Palm trees fluttered in the warm breezes off the Gulf, and tamarind trees clacked their long dark pods, while citrus trees in backyards produced huge, juicy oranges for the plucking. I wore short-sleeved shirts, light cotton trousers, sandals, and felt my body gradually cease cringing from the remembered New England cold and begin to expand and move out to meet this strange new world. I was tanned and well fed, muscular and extremely healthy, and my mind, naturally, began turning obsessively to thoughts of women.

Even though it was only a respite, for the first time since the previous December I felt free of guilt for having failed at life without having first tried to succeed. Freed from such a complex, burdensome guilt, I was trapped instantly by lust. Not ordinary lust, but late-adolescent, New England virginal lust, lust engendered by chemistry crossed with curiosity, lust with no memory to restrain and train it, lust that seeks not merely to satisfy and deplete itself, but to avenge itself as well. For the first time in my life, I seemed to be happy and consequently wanted only to make up for lost time and lost opportunities, to get even with all those Catholic schoolgirls who'd said, "Stop," and I stopped, all those passionate plunges frozen in agonizing positions in midair over car seats, sofas, daybeds, carpeted living room floors, beach blankets, and hammocks, all those semen-stained throw pillows on the asbestos tile floors of pine-paneled basement dens. This was lust with a vengeance.

The male of the species ceased to exist. Walking to work in the morning, I saw only women and girls getting on and off buses, step-ping from parked cars, long brown legs drawing skirts tightly against tender thighs, blouses whose sole function seemed to be to draw my attention to breasts. At lunch in the cafeteria, I looked watery-eyed and swollen across the food counter at the black women, the first I'd seen up close, all shades of brown and black, from pale gold and cof-fee to maple red and mahogany, their dark eyes looking straight through me, as if I were invisible, and when I tried to smile, to be seen, and now and then succeeded, I quickly dropped my eyes and moved down the line to the cash register, where, as I paid, I searched the cafeteria for the girl who'd been standing next to me in line, a salesgirl I'd once heard talking to Sukey in the basement shop about eye makeup and had watched from then on every chance I got, always from a safe distance, however, as she had strawberry blond, wavy, shoulder-length hair that made my hands open and close involuntarily, large green eyes that made my lips dry out, a soft Southern accent that made my breath come in tiny packets.

It was as if my awareness of my surroundings were determined by a glandular condition. After work, I sat with Art, Sukey, and Ray in the bar on the corner across from the store, and while they spoke to one another and to me, I watched, like a panther about to pounce, the girls from the store, watched them smoke their cigarettes and talk, slender wrists flicking, gold bracelets catching light and bouncing it through smoke off the walls, moist red lips nipping at the air, parting for white teeth, pink wet tongues, little cries of laughter. I began to wonder what Sukey looked like under her throat-to-ground muumuu and pictured hot loaves of flesh. Delivering signs for Ray to swimwear on the second floor, I rode the escalator up from the first and sniffed the air eagerly and caught the scent of perfume, lipstick, shaved underarms, and nearly tripped at the top. I went to church with Mrs. Treworgy, got lost watching the teenage girls in the choir, and as we left I inadvertently crossed myself, which I knew Protestants did not do, though I told Mrs. Treworgy that we Methodists sometimes did. I was invited by Art to have dinner with him and his wife, and throughout the meal wondered how Art would take it if I had a brief love affair with his dark, bouffant-haired wife, who asked me if people from New England really did say, "Pahk the cah in Hahvahd Yahd," and if so, why didn't I talk that way? I told her they did and I did, and for the rest of the evening I did.

To save myself from abject humiliation and worse, I did what men usually do in this situation. I went back to guilt and became obsessed with my work. I decided to succeed in this new trade, to become the best assistant window trimmer that had ever worked at Maas Brothers. It was time, I decided, for me to make my move. In my room at night, I drew window displays—anything to keep my mind and hands busy at the same time. Some of the designs were for windows that exhibited spring dresses, but more often they portrayed less agitating merchandise, like air conditioners, men's shoes, lawn mowers, and lamps. Many of them were inventive and well-drawn designs that the next day I left lying around Art's workbench and Sukey's easel, even leaving my pad open next to Ray's brushes when I went upstairs for his midmorning snack. I figured that once I was permitted to design and install my own window, my talent would be recognized and I'd be promoted. On my way. With a new kid hired to replace me as assistant, Art or Sukey would be moved to the larger store in Tampa or shifted to the Maas Brothers about to open in Miami. I'd follow a few years later, only to pass them by, moving swiftly up the ladder of window trimming to where the only moves left would be horizontal, into management, vice president in charge of advertising, and on up from there.

Then it happened. One morning in May, I came whistling cheerfully into the shop, as was my habit, and Art called me aside and said that there was going to be a fashion show in swimwear that afternoon and they needed a tropical-island floor display right away. "Sukey and me're all tied up getting them damned Memorial Day windows done," he drawled. "Whyn't you-all try your hand on the tropical island?"

"Why, sure," I said. I flipped open my sketchbook. "What've you got in mind, Art? I'll work up some sketches."

"Just some kind of backdrop, some grass or sand, a mannequin in a swimsuit, maybe a coupla colored spots. You can do it. I seen your drawings lying around. Now's your opportunity to show us what you can do on your own." He smiled down at me and winked.

I made my sketches, a four-by-eight-foot panel with broad streaks of rose, silver, and orange to signify a tropical sunset, three or four long palm fronds on the upper left corner of the panel, and two women, one standing, looking mournfully out to sea, her hands at her eyes, as if watching eagerly for her lover's return, the other seated, resigned to his absence, contemplating the pink and white gauze blossoms that I planned to scatter over the earth. The two faces of Penelope, thought, waiting for Odysseus, me.

I cut two-by-fours for the frame, instead of the usual one-by-twos, nailed them together with eightpenny nails, cross-braced it horizontally and vertically, cut and nailed on plywood triangles to square the corners, and covered both sides with tautly drawn metallic paper, stapling back and hiding the seams neatly, so that, finished, it resembled nothing so much as a solid block of sea blue steel. They'll use this panel for years, I gloated, and indeed, when I stood the panel up, it was like a well-made house, an oak tree, a piece of public sculpture that would outlive the culture that had produced it.

The others went up to lunch, but I stayed down in the shop, painting streaks of cloud and sunlight on my panel. "Don't fuss with that thing too long now," Art called back. "You got to have that display done and installed by two. The fashion show starts up at two."

"No sweat!" I hollered. I had everything I needed out and arranged neatly before me: the two mannequins, wigs, one blond, one brunette, gauze blossoms, palm fronds, colored spots and extension cords, and the tools I'd need to set them up—hammer, screwdriver, screws, and angle iron to fasten the panel to the island, tape, staple gun, and so on. All I needed now was the bathing suits.

I telephoned swimwear from Art's office. One of the salesgirls answered, and instantly, though she said nothing more than "Swimwear," I recognized the voice. Two notes, and I knew the entire tune. It was the girl I'd overheard talking to Sukey about eye makeup, the strawberry blond I'd studied from a distance in the cafeteria, the green-eyed beauty in the crowd at whom I'd aimed my hunter's gaze from the corner booth after work.

I cleared my throat and stammered that I needed a pair of bathing suits for the fashion show display.

"Okay," she sang. "We're trying on bathing suits right now, for the show and all, so whyn't you come on up and just pick out what you-all want?"

"Sure, fine. Sure, that's great, a great idea. Ah . . . who'll I ask for? What's your name?"

"Eleanor," she said, and the word rose in my mind like an elegant seabird against a silver moon over dark Caribbean waters.

"Sure. Fine. Eleanor, then. Okay, then . . ."

"G'bye," her voice chimed in my ear.

I put down the phone and decided to take my panel to the second floor right away, to set it up first and then see which bathing suits matched the colors of my sunset before I made my selection. It was surprisingly heavy. In fact, I could barely lift it. I tipped it, got leverage, lifted, and carried the panel out of the shop, ducking at the door to keep it from scraping, and managed to get it all the way up the wide stairs from the basement to the first floor, before I had to stop and rest a minute. The store was jammed with lunch-hour shoppers, women mostly, many of whom gazed with what I took to be admiration at my blue panel, which I now regarded as very nearly a work of art.

The escalators were located at the center of the large, crowded floor, where the ceiling swooped and opened up to reveal the second floor as a kind of mezzanine. I could see young women strolling about in bathing suits up there, bare shoulders, naked arms and legs, bare feet, pink arches, toes.

I hefted my panel, got it balanced, and moved carefully through the throng of shoppers to the escalator and got in line. By the time I stepped onto the metal stairs, the panel had grown heavy again, so I set it down, placing one corner on the step. I peered around it and up and caught a glimpse of the girl named Eleanor, wearing a two-piece bathing suit, blood red it was, and very revealing, for in that instant I saw that she had large, high breasts, and a navel, my God, a female navel—when I noticed something falling lightly past my face like sprinkles of dust. I heard a loud, grinding noise from overhead, screams from below, and debris started falling all about me. I looked up and saw that the top edge of my panel was digging a trench into the ceiling, a gouge that ripped away plaster, wires, pipes, and tubes, and the higher we rode on the escalator, my panel and I, the deeper into the ceiling it dug, relentlessly, as if with rage, while women above and below me, pushing and grabbing one another in fear, shrieked and ran to escape falling chunks of ceiling.

I let go of the panel, but it held there, rigid, like a plow blade, jammed now between the metal tread of the escalator and the ceiling above, which curved lower and lower as we neared the second floor, until the ceiling was almost low enough for me to reach up and touch, when the top of the panel ground against the reinforced-concrete floor of the mezzanine itself, and promptly the metal stair began to give. The panel, however, refused to give. It creaked, bowed a little, but it held. The escalator kept on moving, while the noise level rose—screams, shouts, cries for help, falling debris, wood grinding against concrete, metal bending under wood—until, at last, the ceiling curved up and away from the stairwell, and my panel sprung free, rising like a mainsail, floating over the rail, and tumbling onto the adjacent down escalator, where people ran in horror as it bounced heavily end over end toward glass counters filled with cosmetics, notions, jewelry, perfumes.

Up above, still riding the escalator, I watched with almost scientific detachment as the stair, bent by the panel into a shallow V, neared the slot in the floor where the stairs in front of it one by one flattened neatly and slid away. I saw the bent stair hit the slot, felt the whole escalator beneath my feet buckle and jump, heard the motor grind on stubbornly, until at last it stopped.

All the electricity in the building had gone off. We were in a dusky haze, as if after a terrorist's attack. It was silent, with smoke and dust hovering in the air. A chunk of rubble rolled into a corner. Water splashed aimlessly from a broken pipe. A fluorescent light fixture held by a single wire broke loose and fell to the floor. A woman sobbed. A mother called her child.

I was at the top of the stairs, facing swimwear. Before me stood several girls in bathing suits, their hands fisted in horror before open mouths, their eyes wild with fear. One or two wept quietly. I saw the girl named Eleanor among them, and I turned and ran blindly back down the way I had just ridden to the top, leaping over rubble and shoving my way past terrified shoppers, stunned men in business suits, janitors, salesgirls, crunching over broken glass toward the door and away from the crowd that had emerged from the cafeteria, past a white-faced Art and Sukey, and out, finally, to the street. My chest heaved furiously, my ears rang, and still I ran, charging through traffic without looking, as fire trucks and police cars with sirens wailing pulled up at the store.

I was in a small park, walking slower and slower along a white crushed-stone pathway that curved around flower beds. There were live oak trees overhead with Spanish moss hanging down, and small birds flitted in and out of the pale green leaves. Finally, I stopped. I sat down on a bench and put my head in my hands. I believed that my life had all but ended. I was wrapped entirely in shame, as if in a shroud. It was a new feeling, a horrible one, for it surrounded me, enveloping my mind and body totally.

There was no way out of it. In those few moments in the park in St. Petersburg, immolated by endless shame, I was every man who had failed, who had run out on job, family, children, friends—who had run out on *opportunity*. I was Bob O'Neil, drunk and lying about it in Florida; I was my father, silent and withdrawn in northern New Hampshire. I was the boy who went up the hill and then, inexplicably, turned around and came back empty-handed. I was Little Boy Blue asleep with his horn, while the sheep roamed the meadow, and the cows ate the corn. I was ashamed for all of us, every one.

Then, gradually, I felt the presence of a hand on my shoulder. I sat up and turned and followed the delicate, white hand on my shoulder out to a woman's arm. It was Eleanor's, and her green eyes were filled with pity, endless pity that matched perfectly my endless shame. She was wearing the dark red bathing suit that I had loved, and she reached forward and placed her naked arms around my chest and laid her head on my shoulder. I smelled her hair, felt her smooth skin against mine.

We stayed like that for a long time, I on the bench, she standing behind me, both of us weeping silently, me in shame and she in pity, until it was almost dark. And that is how I met my first wife, and why I married her.

Cow-Cow

We were living in the same double-wide up on Spruce Hill as we had since before we got married, before we had any kids, even, and this one night last August me and Larry are heading home from the Spread, not shitfaced, but pretty buzzed, lifted a little, I guess you could say, which was a fairly typical condition for us then. It's only been not quite a year, and I'm completely aware that I could get back there in a minute if I wasn't watching myself. Larry I can't speak for. Not anymore. His drinking is his problem now, mine is mine.

So we're just pulling into the driveway in Larry's old bucket-of-rust Taurus—he's driving, and I'm enjoying the view, so to speak, as there was an almost full moon, and the woods and fields and the roofs of the houses and barns were covered with silver-gray light like frost—when Larry says, "Shit, the cow's out!" This was not a small thing, nor was it a thing that hadn't happened to us numerous times already, especially with that particular cow. We raise and butcher all our meat. Or we used to. And there are bears up there on Spruce Hill and wild dogs, which I did not especially want to see eat our cow before we did. Besides, cows can get into all kinds of trouble on their own, break their legs on old fencing or fall down an open well or quarry, and by the time you got to it it'd be dead and rotted and useless to butcher for meat.

She wasn't a fancy cow, a Hereford or Black Angus or something, just a cow-cow. But she was important to us, as we never had much for cash income, except summers, when Larry could get work house painting or the odd job that came his way from the tourist industry, from summer people and the such. Come winter, that cow was food on the table for us and the kids. Protein, was how I looked at her, and consequently, since we only raised one at a time, Protein was the name I gave to all our cows, so as not to get too attached to the beast. So as not to forget the reason for its existence, I explained to the kids.

Although it didn't really work for them. They always ended up thinking of the cow as a member of the family, practically. To them, Protein was a word like any other and could be turned into a name as easily as Bossy or Elsie. Or my name, even, or Larry's. For that reason we butchered our animals only on days when the kids were in school or up to my mother's or sleeping over at a friend's house. To spare them the actual dispatching and final departure of the cow. If the kids didn't have to watch it in person, they had no problem with killing animals and butchering them, and they could talk about how they missed old Protein even as they sat at the table chewing on one of her steaks. Kids are like that. They can hold contrary opinions or opposite feelings in their heads without the slightest sense of illogic.

The barnyard gate was wide open, which is how Larry knew the cow was out. Typically, in a hurry to get to the Spread, he'd probably neglected to latch it after he fed and watered her. I'd been inside, putting the kids down. "Hold your horses, for Christ's sake, I'm coming!" I told him when I got into the car.

"Just 'cause it's still light out don't mean it ain't late," he grumbled.

"No, Larry, it doesn't," I said, and sighed so he could notice. "It certainly does not." I don't think I was any more pissed at Larry than usual, but it did feel different to me that night. Heavier somehow, like the force of gravity was dragging my feelings to the ground and staking them there. Although I didn't pay any heed to it at the time. I'd gotten used to him long ago. Larry's not a bad man, not as-such, anyhow, and he wasn't behaving that night any differently than the way he always behaved. Impatient, distracted, self-centered, and critical—that was Larry for as long as I'd known him. But sentimental, too, and, for a man, weepy. Sorrowful is a word I would use. I think that's what kept me around so long. His sorrow. And I think he knew it.

I went into the house to check on the kids, while Larry went to the barn and in the moonlight, too late now, closed the gate. I watched him from the window of the darkened kitchen. He made sure this time that it was latched. He moved slowly and deliberately, as if he needed to keep telling himself where he was and what he was doing there. The movements of a drunk man. The kids were all in bed asleep, except for Lydia, who was watching Letterman and had to be reminded that she had school tomorrow so get the hell to bed. "Right now!" I said, and she skulked off, angry and wounded, the way only a thirteen-year-old girl can be. Larry hit the car horn a couple times, and I went out to shut him up so the kids wouldn't wake. He had the motor running and the car turned around in the driveway, heading out.

"Where're you going?" I asked him.

"The cemetery. She's probably gone there again, same as last time. Cows are stupid. They keep going back to the same place they got caught last time. Get in," he said. "It's dark, I'll need you to shine the headlights while I catch her."

"You bring a bucket of grain?"

"Yes, I brought a bucket of grain." Sarcastic.

"Flashlight?"

He didn't answer. I got into the car beside him. "What about your gun? You got your gun?"

"No. Why?"

"Get your gun, Larry. Jesus!"

"Why?"

"To shoot her, for Christ's sake! Get your gun! Get your fucking gun!" I don't know why I was hollering, but I was.

He got out of the car and went into the house and came back a minute later with his twelve-gauge. "I don't see the point of shooting her," he said, laying the gun on the backseat.

"You need to shoot her, Larry, because you keep forgetting to latch the gate, and she'll be back down there tomorrow and the next day and the next, until the board of selectmen finally decides to shoot her themselves. And we'll be out five hundred pounds of beef this winter. Our freezer will be empty, Larry," I said through gritted teeth. "Don't you *get* it?"

He mumbled something that I took to be a concession and drove out to the road, turned left, and headed down the mile-long hill to the bottom, where we turned onto the narrow, unpaved lane that leads to the town cemetery. The moon had dropped behind the mountains now, and it was pitch dark. It was spooky, in a way, being in a cemetery at night like this. The headlights carved out some space in front of the car, but everything else was lost in blackness, until suddenly a leafy tree branch would drop in front of the windshield or a tombstone loomed up beside the car.

"We're never gonna find her here this late," Larry said. "I'm thinking we should wait for daylight." He was dead tired and still feeling the booze, I knew, and so was I, but no way was I going to let that cow wander around all night, I told him. Who knows where she'd be by morning? She could easily stroll from the cemetery onto Spruce Hill Road and get creamed by a semi hauling logs to Montreal. She could fall into the river and drown. Either way, she'd end up useless to us, I told him. A total loss cow.

Larry says, "Katie, is that her?" He stops the car, backs it up a few feet, and half-turns it off the road, so the headlights splash light uphill a distant ways into the graveyard. There's all kinds of gravestones up there casting these huge, long shadows against the grass and across the gravestones behind them. And here comes the cow, Protein, meandering her way between the granite stones and grave markers, munching on the fresh, dew-wet grass as she goes, swinging and swaying her big, bony hips, and totally ignoring us, like she's exactly where she belongs and we're not. She's nearly full grown but still a heifer, with big black and white splotches across her back and haunches and a mostly white head. I can see why she likes it here. The grass is thick and bright green and plentiful compared to the grass at our place. Also there's flowers that people have put on the graves, and she's eating them as well as the grass. It's peaceful here, unmolested and quiet, except for the occasional diesel moan of a truck climbing Spruce Hill on its way to the Northway and beyond. If I was a cow, and somebody'd left my gate unhitched, this is where I'd be, too.

Larry got out and told me to keep the lights on her. Then he opened the trunk and took out the bucket of grain. I slid into the driver's seat. The cow strolled slowly into the light, when, for the first time, she looked up at us. Holding the bucket like it was a peace offering, Larry walked tippy-toe toward her. "C'mon, girl, come an' get your supper," he sort of sang to her. "Supper, girl. Supper."

She ignored him and went back to munching on the abundant graveyard grass. Larry tried a few minutes longer to get her attention, but she wouldn't even raise her head. Finally he returned to the car, and I rolled down the window.

"What?" I said.

"I can't get her to eat from the bucket."

"Try setting it on the ground out there in front of the car a ways, and then step back into the shadows. Try that," I said.

He did as instructed, and after a while, ten minutes maybe—during which time I smoked a cigarette and Larry stood in the dark next to the car, watching silently—the cow at last edged up to the bucket and stuck her snout into it and began eating the grain.

"Get the gun!" I said to him.

"What?"

"Larry, get the fucking gun!"

He came over to the car, opened the rear door, and took out his twelve-gauge. "I don't need the damn gun," he said. Then he carried it into the glare of the headlights and stood next to the cow.

"Shoot her, Larry!"

He didn't say or do anything. Just stood there slump-shouldered with the gun in his right hand, watching the cow chomp away on the grain in the bucket. Finally, she pulled her head from the pail, slurped her lips with her thick gray tongue, and looked at Larry as if to thank him.

"Shoot her, for Christ's sake!"

"Why?"

"Because we don't have any more grain! Because I want you to! I don't know. Shoot the fucking cow, Larry. Just shoot her!"

He lifted the bucket, as if to check it for grain one last time, and the cow again stuck her muzzle into it. "All gone," Larry said to the cow. "Nothing left." Then he brought the barrel of the shotgun up and placed it next to the hard, flat forehead of the cow and fired. I jumped at the sound, as if I hadn't expected it. Yet I had expected it. I'd been calling for it. But it was as if I had been calling from a dream, not reality. Her eyes bulged in astonishment and rolled back, and blood spurted from her head. Her forelegs buckled at the knees, and she fell forward and flopped onto her side and was absolutely still. She seemed enormous then, bigger than the car. Blood poured from the large hole in her head onto the dewy grass. The light splashed over the body of the cow, the spreading puddle of blood, and the grass.

"What do we do now?" Larry said.

I didn't have a clue, but I said, "Your trouble is you just think one step at a time."

"You're the one wanted her dead." He got into the car on the passenger's side and lit a cigarette. "Shut the motor and lights off," he said. "We don't need 'em now."

I complied, and we sat there in the total dark for a while, smoking and not saying anything. It was almost like the cow wasn't there, like she was still up in the barn at our place, and Larry and I were sitting here in the car in the dark talking in low voices about the future.

"We need a front-loader," Larry said. "We can't leave her here. The dogs or a bear'll get into her."

He was right, so I started the car again, and while Larry stayed behind with the flashlight and his gun and guarded the cow, I drove into the village. By this time it was very late, two or three o'clock in the morning, not a car on the road, not a light. I knew whoever I called would be asleep, but at that moment it didn't seem like I had a choice. I pulled up beside the pay phone at Chick Lawrence's garage and got out and dialed Wade Whitney first, since he and Larry are old hunting buddies, but Wade said no, his front-loader was up on Adrian's Acres, where he was digging a cellar. Then I tried Randy LeClair, but all I got was an answering machine. "Hey, Randy," I said. "This is Katie Burks, and me and Larry was hoping you could give us a hand moving a dead cow. But I guess you're not around."

I was trying to remember who else in town owned a front-loader, when I looked beyond the gas pumps and saw in the shadows exactly what I was looking for. Chick Lawrence had a loader! Because he used it mainly for snow removal, not excavation, I'd forgotten it existed. His house was next door to his garage, so all I had to do was walk up to it and knock, which I did. Chick's a friendly guy and neighborly. He came to the door in his underwear, worried-looking, expecting an emergency, probably, a car wreck or something, as he's got the only tow truck in town. He seemed to relax when I explained our fix. "Well, okay," he said. "I'll meet you over to the cemetery in fifteen minutes or so," he said. "It sure is a nice night," he said, looking up at the starry sky.

Then he laughed, like he'd told a little joke. That's a mannerism of his.

I drove back to the cemetery and with the headlights of the car and a tap on the horn woke up Larry, who had fallen asleep against one of the tombstones. He stood and strolled over to the car snapping his flashlight. "Batteries're dead," he said, as if that explained everything. The cow was still there, a huge, black and white mound surrounded by a spreading puddle of blood.

"Watch where you walk," I said, just as he was about to step in the blood. Then I told him Chick Lawrence was coming right over, and he seemed visibly relieved and leaned against the fender and smoked a cigarette and studied the stars. I kept the motor running and the lights on and stared straight out over the hood at that damned cow. I don't know why, but at that moment I despised that poor animal. It was like she had done something unforgivable and had done it to me personally. It wasn't just the alcohol, which had pretty much worn off by then. There was lots about that night that I didn't understand. My telling Larry to bring the gun, for instance, and then hollering for him to shoot the cow. And I didn't understand how it had come to this, to sitting around in a graveyard in the middle of the night waiting for Chick Lawrence to show up with his front-loader so we can haul a dead cow back up the hill to our place. I wanted to blame Larry, but I couldn't. All he'd done was whatever I'd asked him to do. From the beginning, from when we first met in high school and started screwing in the backseat of his old Camaro right up to tonight, fourteen years later, Larry always did whatever I asked him to. The problem, I was beginning to see, lay in the asking.

"Larry," I said. "This is one of the lousiest nights of my life. And what's worse, it's typical."

"Typical." He paused. "That's what this is to you?"

"Yes."

"That's what I was afraid of," he said, and that was the end of it.

About twenty minutes later, here comes Chick and his big, yellow front-loader looking like some kind of prehistoric dinosaur with its head-high tires and great, wide-open mouth and its headlights like gigantic bug eyes flopping up and down as the vehicle made its slow, noisy way along the lane from the main road. He drew the loader up to the cow and cut the motor back to idle. He leaned out of the cab and called down, "How'd you come to shoot your cow here at the cemetery?"

Larry shrugged his shoulders. "I guess one thing just led to another."

"I guess to hell it did," Chick said and gave his little laugh. He backed the front-loader off a few feet and dropped the bucket to the ground, then came forward very slowly and with a surprising tenderness got the lower lip of the bucket underneath the cow. Gently he scooped the poor beast off the ground and lifted it, almost like a parent picking up a sleeping child. The body of the cow rolled heavily into the bucket and over onto its back so that it ended with all four of its legs sticking up in the air. It made a weird, almost comical sight, as Chick lifted the bucket into the air, backed around, and headed slowly away from the cemetery toward the main road.

Larry got in beside me, and I drove the Taurus behind Chick, turned left at the road, and followed him up the long stretch of Spruce Hill Road to our place. There were no other cars or trucks out at that hour, which is a good thing, because we were a peculiar, slow-moving, suspicious-looking procession. The loader was making about ten miles an hour at best, and from my position behind it I could see around the cab and catch glimpses of the cow's spindly legs and hoofs sticking out of the bucket, which Chick kept pretty high in the air, to keep the vehicle balanced and its rear wheels on the ground. Whenever the vehicle crossed a ripple or dip in the paving, the bucket bounced some, and the cow seemed almost to be alive then and struggling like it was prey to get loose of this monstrous mouth.

Finally we got to the top of the hill and turned off the road into our driveway. I glanced behind us and saw that the eastern sky was turning pink and pale blue. It was going to be a nice day. Chick stopped the loader and called down to us, "Where d'you want me to put 'er?"

Larry checked me, and I checked him back. We both wanted the other to answer Chick's question. Larry's eyes were sunk into his face and bloodshot, and his cheeks had gone all saggy, and he needed a shave. He looked more exhausted than I had ever seen him before. I must have looked the same to him. He exhaled through pursed lips, a silent whistle, and said, "Oh, Jesus, Katie. It's over, then. Isn't it?"

"We got to let it go, Larry."

"Do we have to? Can't we just do like before? Like we've always done?"

I leaned out the car window and hollered up to Chick, "Drop her on the dock in front of the barn, where the winch and chain are. We'll hang her up and butcher her there in a few minutes." He said fine, and I thanked him.

"Good night," he said to me. Then laughed, "Or good morning," and dropped the loader into gear and headed it in the direction of the barn.

I turned back to Larry. "We better cut up that cow," I said, "before it starts to spoil."

"I'll do it," he said, and he got out of the car. I got out, too, and we stood there, looking at each other over the roof of the old Taurus. "Katie, I'm really sorry. I'm sorry I couldn't do things a different way . . . and better. I'm sorry about the drinking, too."

"I know you are. I am, too."

"How come it happened tonight?"

"Larry, I don't know." We were silent for a moment. "It could've been any night," I said. "Could be it happened a long time ago, only we didn't know it then. Like one of those stars that flare up and die, and you don't see it happening until years later, because it's so far away."

"Maybe it's better we didn't see it when it happened," he said.

"Maybe it's more peaceful this way. I don't know. You go on inside, Katie, and get some sleep. I'll butcher the cow." He gave me a little wave and trudged down the driveway toward the barn. Dawn was coming on fast now, and I could see him in the pale gray light all the way to the barn. For a while I stood there by the front door of the house and continued to watch him. He hooked the chain onto the cow's hind legs just above the hoofs. Then he slowly hoisted the animal off the ground, and soon she was clear of the ground altogether and dangling heavily above the loading dock. He clipped the end of the chain into a ring bolted to the dock. When he disappeared into the barn, going to get his knives, I went into the house, to check the kids and to sleep. That same afternoon, he moved out.

With Ché in New Hampshire

So here I am, still wandering. All over the face of the earth. Mexico, Central America, South America. Then Africa. Working my way north to the Mediterranean, resting for a season in the Balearic Islands. Then Iberia, all of Gaul, the British Isles. Scandinavia. I show up in the Near East, disappearing as suddenly and unexpectedly as I appeared. Reappearing in Moscow. Before I can be interviewed, I have dropped out of sight again, showing up further east, photographed laughing with political prisoners outside Vladivostok, getting into a taxi in Kyoto, lying on a beach near Melbourne, drinking in a nightclub in Honolulu, a club known for its underworld clientele. Chatting amiably with Indians in Peru. When I drop out of sight altogether.

All this from the file they have on me in Washington. They know that somehow I am dangerous to them, but they are unable to determine in which way I am dangerous, for everything is rumor and suspicion, and I am never seen except when alone or in the cheerful company of harmless peasant-types. My finances are easily explained: I have none. I never own anything that I can't carry with me and can't leave out in the rain, and I am a hitchhiker wherever I go. I accept no money whatsoever from outside sources that might be considered suspicious. Occasionally, I find employment for a few weeks at some menial job—as a dockhand in Vera Cruz, a truck driver in North Africa, a construction worker in Turkey—and occasionally I accept lavish gifts from American women traveling to forget their wrecked lives at home.

Okay, so here I am again, wandering, and everything is different from the way it is now, except that I am alone. Everything else is different. And then one day late in spring, I turn up in Catamount, New Hampshire. Home. Alone, as usual. I'm about thirty-five, say. No older. A lot has happened to me in the interim: when I step down from the Boston-to-Montreal bus at McAllister's General Store, I am walking with an evident limp. My left leg, say, doesn't bend at the knee. Everything I own is in the duffle bag I carry, and I own nothing that cannot be left out in the rain.

Rerun my getting off the bus. The cumbersome Greyhound turns slowly off Route 28 just north of Pittsfield, where the small, hand-lettered sign points CATAMOUNT 1/2 MI., and then rumbles down into the heart of the valley, past the half dozen, century-old, decaying houses, past the Hawthorne House, past Conway's Shell station to McAllister's Gulf station and general store, where the bus driver applies the air brakes to his vehicle, which has been coasting since it turned off Route 28, and it hisses to a stop.

The door pops open in front of me, and I pitch my duffle down to the ground and ease my pain-racked body down the steps and out the door to where the duffle has landed.

A few old men and Bob McAllister, like turtles, sit in the late-morning sun on the roofless front porch that runs the width of the store building. Two of the men, one on each side of the screen door, are seated on straight-backed, soda-fountain chairs, which they lean back against the wall. One old man, squatting, scratches on the board floor with a penknife. The others (there should be more than three) are arrayed in various postures across the porch.

Even though the sun feels warm against my skin, the air is cool, reminding me of the winter that has just ended, the dirty remnants of snow in shady corners between buildings, snow that melted, finally, just last week, and the mushy dirt roads that are beginning to dry out at last. The old men seated on the stagelike platform stare down at me without embarrassment. They don't recognize me. Through the glass behind their heads I can see the semidarkness of the interior of the store and the shape of Alma McAllister's perpetually counting head. She is stationed at the checkout counter, which is actually a kitchen table. Beyond her, I can pick out the shapes of three or four parallel rows of canned foods, the meat locker, and the large refrigeration unit that holds all of McAllister's dairy products, his frozen foods, packaged bacon and sausage, eggs, cold drinks, and beer. And farther back in the store, I can make out the dim shapes of hoses, buckets, garden tools, work clothes, fishing rods, and the other items that finish out the store's inventory—Bob McAllister's guess at the material needs of his neighbors.

The old men staring at me wonder who the hell I might be. They don't recognize me at all, not yet anyway, although I was able to recognize them as soon as I saw their faces. It is I who have changed, not they, and I have thought of them many times in the last few years, whereas they probably have not once thought of me.

Bob McAllister, of course, is there. And old Henry Davis, he would have to be there, too. His sister died back in 1967, I recall as soon as I see his sun-browned, leathery face, remembering that I learned of the event from a letter my father wrote to me while I was in Florida waiting for instructions from Ché.

The others, now. There is John Alden, who claims he is a direct descendant of the original John and Priscilla Alden. He is. Gaunt, white-maned, and silent, except to speak of the time, and always dressed in a black suit, white shirt, and black necktie and drawing from his pocket the large gold watch that the Boston & Maine Railroad gave him when he retired back in 1962, drawing it out and checking its time against anybody else's—the radio's, the church's, Bob McAllister's, Timex's, anybody's who happens to walk into the store.

"What time you got, Henry?"

"I got ten-seventeen, John."

"Check it again, Henry, 'cause I got ten-twenty-one."

"Thanks, John, thanks a lot. Hell of a watch you got there. It ain't ever wrong, is it?"

"Not yet it ain't."

There are two or three others. There is Bob McAllister, who comes over to the bus as he has done every day for over twenty years and takes the bundle of Boston newspapers from the driver. There is Henry Davis, who plowed the few acres that my grandfather cultivated every year with corn and potatoes and the meadows that were hayed when I was a child—but that was before Henry and his horses got too old and Grandpa had to go to Concord and buy a John Deere tractor to replace Henry. And there is John Alden, who is a direct descendant of John and Priscilla. And there would be Dr. Wickshaw, too, because it's about ten years from now, and Dr. Wickshaw has retired, no doubt, has left his entire practice to that young Dr. Annis from Laconia, the new fellow from Laconia my father told me about in his letters.

That's four, which is enough. They don't recognize me. Although when Bob McAllister lifts himself off the porch and crosses between the Gulf gasoline pumps to the bus to receive the Boston papers, he stares at me quizzically, seeming to think that he knows me from some place and time, but he can't remember from where or when, so he merely nods, for courtesy's sake as well as safety's, and strolls by.

I bend down and pick up my duffle, heave it easily to my right shoulder—three years in the jungles of Guatemala have left me with one leg crippled and deep scars on my face and mind forever. But the years have also toughened me, and my arms and back are as hard as rock maple.

Close-up of the scar on my face. It starts, thin and white, like a scrap of white twine, high up on my left temple, and then runs jaggedly down to my cheekbone, where it broadens and jags suddenly back and down, eventually disappearing below my earlobe. I am reluctant to talk about how it happened, but anyone can see that it is the result of a machete blow.

The driver closes the door to his bus and releases the air brakes hurriedly, for he is no doubt relieved to be rid of a passenger whose silent intensity somehow unnerved him from the moment he left the Park Square Greyhound Bus Terminal in Boston until the moment when the man, without having said a word to anyone, finally rose from his seat immediately behind the driver and stepped down in Catamount. The driver closes the door to his bus, releases the air brakes hurriedly, and the big, slab-sided, silver vehicle pulls away, heads back to Route 28 for Alton Bay and Laconia, and then north to Montreal.

The cool, dry air feels wonderful against my face. It's been too long. I've been away from this air too long this time. I had forgotten its clarity, the way it handles the light—gently, but with crispness and efficiency. I had forgotten the way a man, if he gets himself up high enough, can see through the air that fills the valley between him and a single tree or chimney or gable miles away from him, making the man feel like a hawk floating thousands of feet above the surface of the earth, looping lazily in a cloudless sky, hour after hour, while tiny creatures huddle in warm, dark niches below and wait for him to grow weary of the hunt and drift away.

Leaving Mexico City. As I boarded the Miami-bound jet, I promised myself that, if I could make it all the way back home, I would not leave again. I renew this promise now while walking up the road, moving away from McAllister's store and the silent chorus on the porch, past the three or four houses that sit ponderously on either side of the road north of the bus stop and south of the white Congregational church and the dirt road just beyond the church on the left, the road that leads to the northern, narrow end of the valley. I am limping. Yes, right, I am limping, but while my disabled leg slows me somewhat, it doesn't tire me, and I think nothing of walking the three and one half miles from McAllister's in the village to my father's trailer in the park at the north end of the valley. With Ché in Guatemala I have walked from the Iza- bal Lake to San Agustín Acasaguastlán, crossing the highest peaks in Guatemala, walking, machete in hand, through clotted jungle for twenty days without stopping, walking from sunrise till sunset every day, eating only in the morning before leaving camp and at night just before falling into exhausted sleep. In three years we never set up a fixed camp, and that is why the Guatemalan Army, with their CIA and American Army advisers, never caught up with us. We kept on the move constantly, like tiny fish in an enormous, green sea.

I know that receding behind me, shrinking smaller and smaller in the distance, there are four old men who are trying to figure out who I am, where I've come from, and why I have come from there to Cata- mount. As soon as one of them, probably Dr. Wickshaw (he would be the youngest of the four, the one with the most reliable memory), fig- ures out who I am and that I have come home to Catamount again, maybe this time for good, as soon as they have discovered that much of my identity, they will try to discover the rest—where I have been and what I have been doing all these years.

"How long's it been since he last took off, Doc? Five, six years?"

"No, no, longer. Close to ten, actually. As I recall now, he took off for parts unknown right after he come up from Florida to see his dad, who was all laid up with a heart attack, y'know. Angina pectoris, if my mem- ory serves me correctly, was what it was. You remember when ol' Tom took sick, don't you? Paralyzed him almost completely. And the boy, he drove all the way up from Florida soon's he heard his dad was in trouble, even quit his fancy job with this big advertising company down there and everything. Just to make sure his dad was okay. Now that's a son for you. A damn sight better than most of the sons these days, let me tell you. The boy stayed around for a few weeks till his dad got back on his feet, and then he took off again. Nobody around here knew where he went to, though. Just dropped out of sight."

"How 'bout Boston, Doc? Used to live down in Boston, I heard. You think he went to Boston?"

"Naw, John, we'd a known it if he'd been in Boston all these years."

"Maybe this time the boy's come home for good. He sure looks like he's been through hell, don't he?"

"Smashed his patella, I'd say, Bob, though I couldn't offer as to how, or how he picked up that scar on his face. It sure does change his looks, though. I'd hardly recognized him if it wasn't for the fact that I was the one who brought him into the world in the first place."

No. *Erase that remark.* Wipe it out. Doc would never think such a thing, let alone say it, and Bob McAllister hates and distrusts me, I'm sure. Won't even give me a credit for a dollar's worth of gasoline. Be damned if I want to help those people out of their misery. If Doc Wickshaw ever saw me getting off a bus in Catamount, limping, scarred, back in town again after a mysterious three-year absence (five? ten?), he'd fear for my father's peace of mind, and, as soon as I was safely out of sight, he'd be on the phone, warning him to be careful, Buddy's back in town.

But that's okay, that's okay now, because everything is different. I'm about thirty-five, say. Maybe thirty-six, but no older. I'm wearing khaki trousers, a white shirt, open at the throat, and high, brown work shoes that have steel toes. My hair is cut fairly short, and my face and the backs of my hands are deeply tanned. I look like a construction worker, except for the limp and the scar, and when you are a tall, cold-looking man who looks like a construction worker, except that you limp badly and bear a cruel machete scar across your face, what do people think? They think they're looking at a veteran of guerrilla warfare, that's what they think.

Okay. So here's these four old turtles sitting in the sun on McAllister's porch, and the Boston-to-Montreal bus wheezes up, stopping ostensibly to let off the Boston papers as usual, but instead of just the wire-bound packet of *Boston Globes, Herald-Travelers,* and *Record-Americans* being pitched out the door, I get off, too, first chucking my duffle bag down the steps ahead of me. The bus driver, moving quickly to give me a hand, is sent back to his seat by my fierce, prideful glare, which silently says to him: I *can make it on my own.* "Okay . . . ," he says, almost calling me Soldier, but suddenly thinking better of it, sensing somehow that I have fought not for a nation, but for a *people,* and thus have worn no uniform, have worn only what the people themselves, the peasants, wear.

I like the idea of not having a car, of arriving by bus, carrying everything I own in a single duffle bag and owning nothing that can't be left out in the rain. No household goods are carried on *my* back, no, sir. Just a duffle, U.S. Army surplus, brought all the way home from the jungles of Guatemala. And inside it—two changes of clothing, a copy (in a waterproof plastic bag) of Régis Debray's *Révolution dans la Révolution?* which has been as a Bible to me. Also in a waterproof plastic bag: the notes for my book (Did I come back to Catamount for this, to write my own book, a book about my experiences with Ché in Guatemala, a book which in actuality would be a theoretical textbook thinly disguised as a memoir?). And the Ten Essentials: maps (of Belknap County, New Hampshire, obtainable from the U.S. Geological Survey, Washington, D.C.), a good compass, a flashlight, sunglasses, emergency rations (raisins, chick-peas, and powdered eggs), waterproofed matches, a candle for fire starting, a

U.S. Army surplus blanket, a pocketknife, and a small first-aid kit. That's it. Everything I own is there. The Ten Essentials. No, I need to have another: I need one of those one-man Boy Scout cooking kits. And maybe I should have a gun, a small handgun. A black, snub-nosed .38, maybe. I would've had trouble, though, with the customs officials in Mexico City—they would've been alerted that I might be coming through and would be carrying something important and dangerous, like secret instructions from Ché to supporters and sympathizers inside the U.S. Maybe I should leave Mexico from Mérida, after crossing overland from Guatemala through the low jungles of the Yucatán in hundred-degree heat, walking all the way, and then suddenly in the line of American tourists checking out of Mérida for Miami. It's when you arrive inside the United States that they check your baggage. They never bother you when you leave a place, only when you come back.

Say I picked up the gun *after* I arrived in Miami, picked it up in a pawnshop. Say I managed to lose the agent assigned to follow me, ducked into an obscure little pawnshop in the west end of the city, and purchased a .38 revolver for twenty-seven fifty. Later, at the airport coffee shop, I spot the agent. He's seated three tables from me, pretending to read his paper while waiting, like me, for his plane to Boston. He pretends to read, and he watches my every move. I get up from my chair, leaving a small tip, walk over to him, and say quietly: "I'm leaving now." Then smile. Probably they would arrest me at some point during my journey, but they would be unable to muster proof that I have been working in Bolivia with Ché for these three—no, five no, ten—years. They lost me in Mexico City, and so far as they can say for sure, that is, so far as they can legally prove, I've been in Mexico all that time. At least twice or three times a year, I slip back across the border to make my presence in Mexico known to the officials—I simply let myself be seen conspicuously drunk in a well-known restaurant—and then, taking off at night from a field near Cuernavaca in a small Beechcraft Bonanza piloted by a mercenary, a gunrunner from New Orleans, I return to the jungles of Bolivia. I am valuable to Ché for many reasons, one of which is my American citizenship, and so it is very important that I do not become persona non grata, at least not officially. "Conejo," Ché calls me, using my code name. "Conejo, you are valuable man to me y también a la revolución como soldad, pero también como norteamericano usted es muy borracho en los cafés. Comprendes, amigo?"

"Sí, Ché, yo comprendo." We embrace each other manfully, the way Latins will, and I leave with the pilot, slashing through the jungle to his plane, which he has cleverly camouflaged at the edge of a small clearing several miles down the valley from where we have camped.

Now, three thousand miles away. I have just disembarked, from a Greyhound bus in Catamount, New Hampshire. I stand next to the idling bus for a few moments, gazing passively at the scene before me, and upon receiving the blows of so much that is familiar and so much that subtly has grown strange to me, I become immobilized. I remember things that I didn't know I had forgotten. Everything comes into my sight as if somehow it were brand-new, virginally so, and yet also clearly, reassuringly, familiar. It would be the way my own face appeared to me when, after having grown a beard and worn it for almost two years, I went into a barbershop and asked to have it shaved off. And because I had to lie back in the chair and look up at the ceiling, while the barber first snipped my beard with scissors and then shaved me with a razor, I was unable to watch my beard gradually disappear and my face concurrently appear from behind it, and when I was swung back down into a seated position and peered at my face for the first time in several years, I was stunned by the familiarity of it, and also by its remarkable strangeness.

Dis Bwoy, Him Gwan

It was mid-October. The leaves were already off the trees and leathery brown on the frozen ground, and in the gray skies and early darkness you could feel winter coming on, when one afternoon around four-thirty a blue, late model Oldsmobile sedan with Massachusetts plates slowly entered the trailerpark. It was dark enough so that you couldn't see who was inside the car, but strange cars, especially out-of-state cars, were sufficiently unusual an event at the trailerpark that you wanted to see who was inside. Terry Constant had just left the manager's trailer with his week's pay for helping winterize the trailers, as he did every year at this time, when the car pulled alongside him on the lane, halfway to the trailer he shared with his sister, and Terry, who was tall, wearing an orange parka and Navy watch cap, leaned over and down to see who was inside and saw the face of a black man, which naturally surprised him, since Terry and his sister were the only black people he knew for miles around.

The car stopped, and the man inside rolled down the window, and Terry saw that there was a second man inside, a white man. Both looked to be in their late thirties and wore expensive wool sweaters and smoked cigars. The black man was very dark, darker than Terry, and not so much fat as thick, as if his flesh were packed in wads around him. The white man was gray-faced and unshaven and wore a sour expression, as if he had just picked a foul-tasting substance from behind a tooth.

"Hey, brudder," the black man said, and Terry knew the man was West Indian.

"What's happening," Terry said. He kept his hands in his jacket pockets and looked down from his full height.

"Me wan' t' find a particular youth-mon, him call himself Severance. You know dis mon, brudder?" The man smiled and showed Terry his gold.

"Bruce Severance?"

He grunted and said, "Dat de mon."

"He ain't here."

The man smiled steadily up at Terry for a few seconds. Finally he said, "But him live here."

"That trailer there," Terry said, pointing at a pale yellow Kenwood with a mansard roof. The trailer sat on cinder blocks next to a dirt driveway, and the yard was unkempt and bare, without shrubbery or lawn.

Terry stood and watched the car leave, then walked on, turning in at his sister's trailer, which was dark, for she wasn't home from work yet, and made to unlock the door, when he heard his name coming at him from the darkness.

"Terry!" A blond, long-haired kid in a faded Levi's jacket stepped around the back end of the trailer and came up to him.

"Yo, some dudes was just here looking for you."

"I know, I know, get the fuck inside," the kid said urgently, and he pushed at Terry's shoulder.

"Take it easy, man." He unlocked the door and stepped inside, and the skinny kid followed him like a shadow.

"Don't turn on the lights. No, go back to your room and turn on one light, then come here. If they know you were coming home and no lights go on, they'll figure something's up."

"What the hell you talking about, Severance? You high?"

"Just do it. I'll explain."

Terry did as he was told and came back to the darkened kitchen, where the white kid stood at the window and peeked out at the entrance to the trailerpark. Terry opened the refrigerator, throwing a wedge of yellow light into the room.

"Shut that fucking thing!" the kid cried.

"Take it easy, man. Jesus. Want a beer?"

"No. Yeah, okay, just shut the fucking door, will you?"

He took out two cans of Miller, quickly shut the refrigerator door, and dropped the room into darkness again. Handing one can to the kid, he slid onto a tall stool at the kitchen counter and snapped open his beer and took a long swallow. Across the room by the window, the kid opened his beer and started slurping it down.

"I thought you was down in Boston," Terry said.

"I was. But I came back up this morning."

"Where's your van? I didn't see it."

"I put it someplace."

"You put it someplace."

"Yeah. Listen, man, there's some heavy shit going down. When's your sister come home?"

"Around five-thirty," Terry said.

They sat in silence for a few seconds, and Terry said in a low voice, "Your deal came apart, huh? And that's your Jamaican dude out there, and his friend, right?"

"Right."

"They didn't want to buy your New Hampshire homegrown? Good old Granite State hemp grown wild in the bushes ain't smoke enough for the big boys. Funny." He paused and sipped his beer. "I'm not surprised."

"You're not, eh?"

"Not with those kinda guys. People get mad if you try to change the rules. But I guess you know that now."

The kid said nothing. A minute passed, and in a low voice, almost in a whisper, he said, "If you're not surprised, how come you never said anything?"

"You wouldn't have heard me."

"They just said they didn't want to buy, they wanted to sell."

"You let 'em try some smoke?"

"Yeah, sure. We met, just like usual. In the motel in Revere. And I gave them both a taste. Without telling them what it was, you know?"

"And first whack, they knew you had something they didn't sell you."

"Yeah. So they thought I was dealing boo for somebody else. They knew it wasn't red or gold or ganja or anything they'd smoked before, but they wouldn't believe this shit is growing wild all over the place up here. I told them all about the war, and the stuff about the Philippines and the government paying the farmers to grow hemp for rope and how the stuff went wild after the war, et cetera, et cetera. All of it! But they thought I was shitting them, man."

"I wouldn't have believed you, either."

"But it's true! You know that. You've seen it, you even helped me dry the damned stuff and brick and bale it. Jesus, Terry, you even smoke it yourself!"

"No more, man. The shit makes me irritable."

"It makes you high, too," the kid said quickly.

"You, maybe. But not me. So how come those dudes are up here now?"

"Yeah, well, I told them I have like five one-hundred-pound bales of the shit," the kid said in a low voice.

Terry sat in silence, took a sip of his beer, and said, "You're stupid, you know. Stupid. You oughta be selling insurance, not dope."

"I thought it would let them know I was like in business for myself and not dealing for some other supplier, if they knew I had five bales of my own. The Jamaican, Keppie, he just looked at me like I wasn't there anymore and said I should go to California, and I knew the whole thing had come apart. So I left them at the motel and drove back up. My van's parked on one of the lumber roads in the state park west of the lake. I walked in through the woods, and then I saw them, Keppie and Royce, his muscle guy. I was coming to get you," the kid added.

"Me! What the fuck do you want me for? I wouldn't touch this with a stick, man!"

"I need to get rid of the stuff."

"No shit. What are you going to do with it, throw it in the lake?"

"We can lug it into the woods, man. Just leave it. Nobody'll find it for months, and by then it'll be rotted out and nobody'll know what the hell it is anyhow." After a pause, the kid said, "I need you to help me, Terry."

"You're strong enough to carry one of those bales five times. You don't need me." Terry's voice was cold and angry. "You're an asshole. You know that?"

"Please. You can take your sister's car and we can do it in one trip. Alone on foot, it'll take me all night, maybe longer, and someone might see me." He talked rapidly, like a beggar explaining his poverty. He whined, and his voice almost broke with the fear and the shame. He was a nice enough kid, and most people liked him right away, because he enjoyed talking and usually talked about things that at first were interesting, organic gardening, solar energy, Transcendental Meditation, but he tended to lecture people on these subjects, which made him and the subjects soon boring. Terry hung out with him anyhow, smoked grass and drank in town with him at the Hawthorne House, mainly because the kid, Bruce, admired Terry for being black. Terry knew what that meant, but he was lonely and everyone else in town either feared or disliked him for being black. The kid usually had plenty of money, and he spent it generously on Terry, who usually had none, since, except for the occasional chores and repair work tossed his way by Marcelle Chagnon, the manager of the trailerpark, it was impossible for him to find a job here. Outside of his sister, who was his entire family and who, through happenstance, had located herself in this small mill town in New Hampshire working as a nurse for the only doctor in town, Terry had no one he could talk to, no one he could gossip with, no one he could think of as his friend. When you are a long way from where you think you belong, you will attach yourself to people you would otherwise ignore or even dislike. Terry had attached himself to Bruce Severance, the kid who sold grass to the local high school students and the dozen or so adults in town who smoked marijuana, the kid who drove around in the posh, black and purple van with the painting of a Rocky Mountain sunset on the sides and the bumper stickers attacking nuclear energy and urging people to heat their homes with wood, the kid who had furnished his trailer with a huge water bed and Day-Glo posters of Jimi Hendrix and the Grateful Dead, the kid who, to the amusement of his neighbors, practiced the one hundred twenty-eight postures of T'ai Chi outside his trailer every morning of the year, the kid who was now sitting across the darkened kitchen of the trailer owned by Terry's sister, his voice trembling as he begged Terry, four years older than he, a grown man despite his being penniless and dependent and alone, to please, please, please, help him.

Terry sighed. "All right," he said. "But not now."

"When?" The kid peered out the window again. "They probably went back to town, to drink or for something to eat. We should do it now. As soon as your sister gets home with the car."

"No. That's what I mean, I don't want my sister to know anything about this. This ain't her kind of scene. We can go over to your place and wait awhile, and I'll come home and ask her for the car for a few hours, and we'll load that bad shit of yours into the car and get it the hell out of here, and you can tell those dudes you were only kidding or some damned thing. I don't care what you tell them. Just don't tell them I helped you. Don't even tell them I *know* you, man." Terry got off the stool and headed for the door. "C'mon. I don't want to be here when my sister gets home."

"Terry," the kid said in a quick, light voice.

"What?"

"What *should* I tell them? I can't say I was only kidding. They know what that means."

"Tell them you were stoned. Tripping. Tell them you took some acid. I don't know. Beg."

"Yeah. Maybe that'll cool it with them," he said somberly, and he followed Terry out the door.

Keeping to the shadows behind the trailers, they walked to the far end of the park, crossed the short beach there, and came up along the lake, behind the other row of trailers, until they were behind the trailer where Bruce lived. "Go on in," Terry instructed him. "They couldn't see you now even if they were parked right at the gate."

The kid made a dash for the door, unlocked it, and slipped inside, with Terry right behind. When the kid had locked the door again, Terry suggested he prop a chair against the knob.

"Why? You think they'll break in?"

"A precaution. Who knows?"

"A dumb chair's not gonna stop guys like Keppie and Royce. Jesus, maybe we should've waited out in the woods till your sister got home!"

"No, man, forget it, will you?" Terry walked through the room, stumbling against a beanbag chair and giving it a kick. "You got any beer here? I shoulda grabbed a couple of beers from my sister."

"No. Nothing. Don't open the refrigerator, man. The light."

"Yeah," Terry said, his voice suddenly weary. He sat down heavily in the beanbag chair, and it hissed under his weight. "Jesus, it's cold in here. Can't you get some heat into this place?"

"I can't make a fire. They'll see the smoke."

"Forget the fucking woodstove, you goddamn freak. Turn up the damn thermostat. You got an oil heater, don't you?"

"Yeah, but no oil. I only use wood," the kid said with a touch of his old pride.

"Jesus." Terry wrapped his arms around himself and tried to settle deeper into the chair. He was wearing his orange parka and knit cap, but sitting still like this chilled him. Bruce had gone down the hall to a window where he could see the entrance to the trailerpark.

"Hey, man!" Terry called to him. "Your fucking pipes are gonna freeze, you know! You can't put a woodstove in a trailer and not have any oil heat and keep your pipes from freezing! It's a known fact!"

There was a knock on the door, softly, almost politely.

Terry stood up and faced the door.

When the second knock came, louder, Bruce was standing next to Terry. "Fuck, fuck, fuck," he said.

"Shut up!"

A clear voice spoke on the other side of the door. "Severance! Come now!"

There was the sound of a metal object working against the latch, and the lock was sprung, and the door swung open. The Jamaican stepped quickly inside, and the white man followed, showing the way with a flashlight.

"Much too dark in here, mon," the Jamaican said.

The man with the flashlight closed the door, found the wall switch, and flicked it on, and the four men faced each other.

"Ah! Severance! We got to have some more chat, mon," the Jamaican said. Then to Terry, "So, my brudder, my soul-bwoy. You gwan home now, we don't got no bidniss wit' you, mon." He flashed his gold teeth at Terry. Inside the small space of the trailer, both the Jamaican and his companion seemed much larger than they had in the car. They were taller and thicker than Terry, and in their presence Bruce looked like an adolescent boy.

"I was just telling him you were asking for him," Terry said slowly. Bruce was moving away, toward the kitchen area.

"Wait, mon! Stan' still!" the Jamaican ordered.

The other man switched off his flashlight and leaned his sweatered bulk against the door. "You," he said to Terry. "You live here?"

"No, man. Across the way, with my sister. She's a nurse in town."

"Why a black mon live up here wit' rednecks, mon?"

"My sister. She . . . she takes care of me."

"Gwan home now, mon," the Jamaican said, suddenly no longer smiling. The sour-faced man opened the door for Terry, and he took a step toward it.

"Wait, Terry!" the kid cried. "Don't leave me alone!"

"Shut your face, Severance. We got to have some more chat, me and you. Dis bwoy, him gwan."

Terry stepped out of the door, and the white man closed it behind him. It was cold outside. He stepped to the hard ground and walked quickly across the lane to his sister's trailer and went inside, locking the door carefully behind him. He crossed the room and took a position by the window where Bruce had stood earlier and in the darkness watched the trailer he had just fled. After a few moments, he saw the two men leave and walk down the lane, past the manager's trailer and through the gate. For a second, they were silhouetted by the headlights of a car coming from the other direction, and when the car passed the two men, Terry realized it was his sister's.

Swiftly, he left the window and ran from the trailer and crossed the lane. The lights were still on in the living room of Bruce's trailer, and the door was wide open, and as he came up the steps to the door, he looked into the living room and saw the kid slumped forward in the beanbag chair, the back of his head scarlet and wet where the bullets had entered, his lap and the floor below slick with blood still pouring from where they had exited, where his face had been.

Terry closed the door without entering, turned around, and walked away. His sister was pulling a heavy bag of groceries from the front seat of her car. He came up behind her and said, "You want help?"

"Yeah," she said. "Was that you just now, running over to Bruce's?" she asked over her shoulder and backed away from the bag of groceries.

"No," he said. "No. I was just getting my pay from Marcelle. I . . . I haven't seen Bruce. Not for a couple of days. Not since he went down to Boston."

"Good," she said. "I wish you'd stay away from that kid. He's nothing but trouble," she said.

The Fish

When Colonel Tung's first attempt to destroy the fish failed, everyone, even the Buddhists, was astonished. On the colonel's orders, a company of soldiers under the command of a young lieutenant named Han had marched out from the village early one morning as far as the bridge. Departing from the road there, the soldiers made their way in single file through the bamboo groves and shreds of golden mist to a clearing, where they stepped with care over spongy ground to the very edge of the pond, which was then the size of a soccer field. Aiming automatic weapons into the water, the troopers waited for the fish to arrive. A large crowd from the village gathered behind them and, since most of the people were Buddhists, fretted and scowled at the soldiers, saying, "Shame! Shame!" Even some Catholics from the village joined the scolding, though it had been their complaints that first had drawn the colonel's attention to the existence of the huge fish and had obliged him to attempt to destroy it, for pilgrimages to view the fish had come to seem like acts of opposition to his administration. In great numbers, the Buddhists from other districts were visiting the Buddhists in his district, sleeping in local homes, buying food from local vendors, and trading goods of various kinds, until it had begun to seem to Colonel Tung that there were many more Buddhists in his district than

Catholics, and this frightened him. Thus his opinion that the pilgrimages to view the fish were acts of political opposition, and thus his determination to destroy the fish.

Shortly after the soldiers lined up at the shore, the fish broke the surface of the water halfway across the pond. It was a silver swirl in the morning sun, a clean swash of movement, like a single brushstroke, for the fish was thought to be a reincarnation of Rad, the painter, an early disciple of Buddha. The soldiers readied their weapons. Lieutenant Han repeated his order: "Wait until I say to fire," he said, and there was a second swirl, a lovely arc of silver bubbles, closer to shore this time. The crowd had gone silent. Many were moving their lips in prayer; all were straining to see over and around the line of soldiers at the shore. Then there it was, a few feet out and hovering in the water like a cloud in the sky, one large dark eye watching the soldiers as if with curiosity, delicate fins fluttering gently in the dark water like translucent leaves. "Fire!" the lieutenant cried. The soldiers obeyed, and their weapons roared for what seemed a long time. The pond erupted and boiled in white fury, and when finally the water was still once again, everyone in the crowd rushed to the shore and searched for the remains of the fish. Even the lieutenant and his band of soldiers pushed to the mud at the edge of the water and looked for the fish, or what everyone thought would be chunks of the fish floating on the still surface of the pond. But they saw nothing, not a scrap of it, until they noticed halfway across the pond a swelling in the water, and the fish rolled and dove, sending a wave sweeping in to shore, where the crowd cried out joyfully and the soldiers and the young lieutenant cursed, for they knew that Colonel Tung was not going to like this, not at all.

Colonel Tung took off his sunglasses and glared at the lieutenant, then turned in his chair to face the electric fan for a moment. Finally, replacing his glasses, he said, "Let us assume that in that pond an enemy submarine is surfacing at night to send spies and saboteurs into our midst. Do you have the means to destroy it?" He tapped a cigarette into an ebony holder and lighted it. The lieutenant, like the colonel, a man trained at the academy but rapidly adapting his skills to life in the provinces, said yes, he could destroy such an enemy. He would mine the pond, he said, and detonate the mines from shore. "Indeed," the colonel said. "That sounds like a fine idea," and he went back to work.

From a rowboat, the soldiers placed in the pond ten pie-sized mines connected by insulated wires to one another and to a detonator and battery, and when everything was ready and the area had been cleared of civilians, Lieutenant Han set off the detonator from behind a mound of earth they had heaped up for this purpose. There was a deep, convulsive rumble, and the surface of the pond blew off, causing a wet wind that had the strength of a gale and tore leaves from the trees and bent the bamboo stalks to the ground. Immediately after the explosion, everyone from the village who was not already at the site rushed to the pond and joined the throng that encircled it. Everything that had ever lived in or near the pond seemed to be dead and floating on its surface—carp, crayfish, smelts, catfish, eels, tortoises, frogs, egrets, woodcocks, peccaries, snakes, feral dogs, lizards, doves, shellfish, and all the plants from the bottom, the long grasses, weeds, and reeds, and the banyans, mangroves, and other trees rooted in the water, and the flowering bushes and the lilies that had floated on the surface of the pond—everything that once had been alive now seemed dead. Many people wept openly, some prayed, burned incense, chanted, and others, more practical, rushed about with baskets, gathering up the unexpected harvest. The lieutenant and his soldiers walked intently around the pond, searching for the giant fish. When they could not find it, they rowed out to the middle of the pond and searched there. But still, amongst the hundreds of dead fish and plants, birds and animals floating in the water, they saw no huge silver fish, no carcass that could justify such carnage. As they began to row back toward shore, the lieutenant, who was standing at the bow, his hand shading his eyes from the milky glare of the water, saw once again the rolling, shiny side of the giant fish, its dorsal fin like a black knife slicing obliquely across their bow, when it disappeared, only to reappear off the stern a ways, swerving back and suddenly heading straight at the small, crowded boat. The men shouted in fear, and at the last possible second the fish looped back and dove into the dark waters below. The crowd at the shore had seen it, and a great cheer went up, and in seconds there were drums and cymbals and all kinds of song joining the cheers, as the soldiers rowed slowly, glumly, in to shore.

The reputation of the fish and its miraculous powers began to spread rapidly across the land, and great flocks of believers undertook pilgrimages to the pond, where they set up tents and booths on the shore. Soon the settlement surrounding the pond was as large as the village where the colonel's district headquarters was located. Naturally, this alarmed the colonel, for these pilgrims were Buddhists, and he, a Catholic, was no longer sure he could rule them. "We must destroy that fish," he said to the lieutenant, who suggested this time that he and his soldiers pretend to join the believers and scatter pieces of bread over the waters to feed the fish, as had become the custom. They would do this from the boat, he said, with specially sweetened chunks of bread, and when the fish had become accustomed to being fed this way and approached the boat carelessly close, they would lob hand grenades painted white as bread into the water, and the fish, deceived, would swallow one or two or more whole, as it did the bread, and that would be that. Colonel Tung admired the plan and sent his man off to implement it instantly. Lieutenant Han's inventiveness surprised the colonel and pleased him, although he foresaw problems, for if the plan worked, he would be obliged to promote the man, which would place Han in a position where he could begin to covet the colonel's position as district commander. This damned fish, the colonel said to himself, may be the worst thing to happen to me.

It soon appeared that Lieutenant Han's plan was working. The fish, which seemed recently to have grown to an even more gigantic size than before, was now almost twice the size of the boat. It approached the boat without fear and rubbed affectionately against it, or so it seemed, whenever the soldiers rowed out to the middle of the pond and scattered large chunks of bread, which they did twice a day. Each time, the fish gobbled the chunks, cleared the water all around, and swam rapidly away. The throng onshore cheered, for they, too, had taken the bait—they believed that the soldiers, under the colonel's orders, had come to appreciate the fish's value to the district as a whole, to Catholics as much as to Buddhists, for everyone, it seemed, was profiting from its presence—tentmakers, carpenters, farmers, storekeepers, clothiers, woodchoppers, scribes, entrepreneurs of all types, entertainers even, musicians and jugglers, and of course the manufacturers of altars and religious images and also of paintings and screens purported to have been made by the original Rad, the artist and early disciple of Buddha, now reincarnated as the giant fish.

When finally Lieutenant Han gave the order to float the specially prepared grenades out with the bread, several soldiers balked. They had no objections to blowing up the fish, but they were alarmed by the size of the crowd now more or less residing on the shore and, as usual, watching the soldiers in the boat in hopes of seeing the fish surface to feed. "If this time we succeed in destroying the fish," a soldier said, "the people may not let us get back to shore. There are now thousands of them, Catholics as well as Buddhists, and but ten of us." The lieutenant pointed out that the crowd had no weapons, and they had automatic rifles that could easily clear a path from the shore to the road and back to the village. "And once the fish is gone, the people will go away, and things will settle back into their normal patterns again." The soldiers took heart and proceeded to drop the grenades into the water with an equal number of chunks of bread. The fish, large as a house, had been lurking peacefully off the stern of the boat and now swept past, swooping up all the bread and the grenades in one huge swallow. It turned away and rolled, exposing its silver belly to the sun as if in gratitude, and the crowd cried out in pleasure. The music rose, with drums, cymbals, flutes joining happily and floating to the sky on swirling clouds of incense, while the soldiers rowed furiously for shore. The boat scraped gravel, and the troopers jumped out, dragged the boat up onto the mud, and made their way quickly through the throng toward the road. When they reached the road, they heard the first of the explosions, then the others in rapid succession, a tangled knot of bangs, as all the grenades went off, in the air, it seemed, out of the water and certainly not inside the fish's belly. It was as if the fish were spitting the grenades out just as they were about to explode, creating the effect of a fireworks display above the pond, which must have been what caused the people gathered at the shore to break into sustained, awestruck applause and then, long into the day and the following night, song.

Now the reputation of the miraculous fish grew tenfold, and busloads of pilgrims began to arrive from as far away as Saigon and Bangkok. People on bicycles, on donkeys, in trucks and in oxcarts made their way down the dusty road from the village to the pond, where as many of them as could find a spot got down to the shore and prayed to the fish for help, usually against disease and injury, for the fish was thought to be especially effective in this way. Some prayed for wealth or for success in love or for revenge against their enemies, but these requests were not thought likely to be answered, though it surely did no harm to try. Most of those who came now took away with them containers filled with water from the pond. They arrived bearing bowls, buckets, fruit tins, jars, gourds, and even paper cups, and they took the water with them back to their homes in the far corners of the country, where many of them were able to sell off small vials of the water for surprisingly high prices to those unfortunate neighbors and loved ones unable to make the long overland journey to the pond. Soldiers, too, whenever they passed through Colonel Tung's district, came to the pond and filled their canteens with the magical waters. More than once a helicopter landed on the shore, and a troop of soldiers jumped out, ran to the pond, filled their canteens, and returned to the helicopter and took off again. Thus, when Lieutenant Han proposed to Colonel Tung that this time they try to destroy the fish by poisoning the water in the pond, the colonel demurred. "I think that instead of trying to kill the fish, we learn how to profit from it ourselves. It's too dangerous now," he observed, "to risk offending the people by taking away what has become their main source of income. What I have in mind, my boy, is a levy, a tax on the water that is taken away from this district. A modest levy, not enough to discourage the pilgrims, but more than enough to warrant the efforts and costs of collection." The colonel smiled slyly and set his lieutenant to the task. There will be no promotions now, he said to himself, for there are no heroics in tax collecting.

A sort of calm and orderliness settled over the district, which pleased everyone, Colonel Tung most of all, but also Lieutenant Han, who managed to collect the tax on the water so effectively that he was able without detection to cut a small percentage out of it for himself, and the soldiers, who felt much safer collecting taxes than trying to destroy a miraculous and beloved fish, and the people themselves, who, because they now paid a fee for the privilege of taking away a container of pond water, no longer doubted the water's magical power to cure illness and injury, to let the blind see, the lame walk, the deaf hear, and the dumb talk. The summer turned into fall, the fall became winter, and there were no changes in the district, until the spring, when it became obvious to everyone that the pond was much smaller in diameter than it had been in previous springs. The summer rains that year were heavy, although not unusually so, and the colonel hoped that afterwards the pond would be as large as before, but it was not. In

September, when the dry season began, the colonel tried to restrict the quantity of water taken from the pool. This proved impossible, for by now too many people had too many reasons to keep on taking water away. A powerful black market operated in several cities, and at night tanker trucks edged down to the shore, where they sucked thousands of gallons of water out, and the next morning the surface of the pond would be yet another foot lower than before, and encircling it would be yet another mud aureole inside the old shoreline.

At last there came the morning when the pond was barely large enough to hold the fish. The colonel, wearing sunglasses, white scarf, and cigarette holder, and Lieutenant Han and the soldiers and many of the pilgrims walked across the drying mud to the edge of the water, where they lined up around the tiny pool, little more than a puddle now, and examined the fish. It lay on its side, half exposed to the sun. One gill, blood red inside, opened and closed, but no water ran through. One eye was above water, one below, and the eye above was clouded over and fading to white. A pilgrim who happened to be carrying a pail leaned down, filled his pail, and splashed the water over the side of the fish. Another pilgrim with a gourd joined him, and two soldiers went back to the encampment and returned with a dozen containers of various types and sizes, which they distributed to the others, even including the colonel. Soon everyone was dipping his container into the water and splashing it over the silvery side of the huge, still fish. By midday, however, the sun had evaporated most of the water, and the containers were filled with more mud than moisture, and by sunset they had buried the fish.

The Moor

It's about 10:00 P.M., and I'm one of three, face it, middle-aged guys crossing South Main Street in light snow, headed for a quick drink at the Greek's. We've just finished a thirty-second-degree induction ceremony at the Masonic Hall in the old Capitol Theater building and need a blow. I'm the tall figure in the middle, Warren Low, and I guess it's my story I'm telling, although you could say it was Gail Fortunata's story, since meeting her that night after half a lifetime is what got me started.

I'm wearing remnants of makeup from the ceremony, in which I portrayed an Arab prince—red lips, streaks of black on my face here and there, not quite washed off because of no cold cream at the Hall. The guys tease me about what a terrific nigger I make, that's the way they talk, and I try to deflect their teasing by ignoring it, because I'm not as prejudiced as they are, even though I'm pleased nonetheless. It's an acting job, the thirty-second, and not many guys are good at it. We are friends and businessmen, colleagues—I sell plumbing and heating supplies, my friend Sammy Gibson is in real estate, and the other, Rick Buckingham, is a Chevy dealer.

We enter the Greek's, a small restaurant and fern bar, pass through the dining room into the bar in back like regulars, because we are regulars and like making a point of it, greeting the Greek and his help. Small comforts. Sammy and Rick hit uselessly on one of the waitresses, the pretty little blond kid, and make a crack or two about the new gay waiter who's in the far corner by the kitchen door and can't hear them. Wise guys.

The Greek says to me, What's with the greasepaint? Theater group, I tell him. He's not a Mason, I think he's Orthodox Catholic or something, but he knows what we do. As we pass one table in particular, this elderly lady in the group looks me straight in the eyes, which gets my attention, because otherwise she's just some old lady. Then for a split second I think I know her, but decide not and keep going. She's a large, baggy, bright-eyed woman in her late seventies, possibly early eighties. Old.

Sammy, Rick, and I belly up to the bar, order drinks, the usuals, comment on the snow outside, and feel safe and contented in each other's company. We reflect on our wives and ex-wives and our grown kids, all elsewhere. We're out late and guilt-free.

I peek around the divider at her—thin, silver-blue hair, dewlaps at her throat, liver spots on her long flat cheeks. What the hell, an old lady. She's with family, some kind of celebration—two sons, they look like, in their forties, with their wives and a bored teenage girl, all five of them overweight, dull, dutiful, in contrast to the old woman, who despite her age looks smart, aware, all dressed up in a maroon knit wool suit. Clearly an attractive woman once.

I drift from Sammy and Rick, ask the Greek, "Who's the old lady, what's the occasion?"

The Greek knows her sons' name, Italian—Fortunata, he thinks. "Doesn't register," I say. "No comprendo."

"The old lady's eightieth," says the Greek. "We should live so long, right? You know her?"

"No, I guess not." The waitresses and the gay waiter sing "Happy Birthday," making a scene, but the place is almost empty anyhow, from the snow, and everybody seems to like it, and the old lady smiles serenely.

I say to Sammy and Rick, "I think I know the old gal from some-place, but can't remember where."

"Customer," says Sammy, munching peanuts.

Rick says the same, "Customer," and they go on as before.

"Probably an old girlfriend," Sammy adds.

"Ha-ha," I say back.

A Celtics-Knicks game on TV has their attention, double over-time. Finally the Knicks win, and it's time to go home, guys. Snow's piling up. We pull on our coats, pay the bartender, and, as we leave, the old lady's party is also getting ready to go, and when I pass their table, she catches my sleeve, says my name. Says it with a question mark. "Warren? Warren Low?"

I say, "Yeah, hi," and smile, but still I don't remember her.

Then she says, "I'm Gail Fortunata. Warren, I knew you years ago," she says, and she smiles fondly. And then everything comes back, or almost everything. "Do you remember me?" she asks.

"Sure, sure I do, of course I do. Gail. How've you been? Jeez, it's sure been a while."

She nods, still smiling. "What's that on your face? Makeup?"

"Yeah. Been doing a little theater. Didn't have any cold cream to get it all off," I say lamely.

She says, "I'm glad you're still acting." And then she introduces me to her family, like that, "This is my family."

"Howdy," I say, and start to introduce my friends Sammy and Rick, but they're already at the door.

Sammy says, "S'long, Warren, don't do anything I wouldn't do," and Rick gives a wave, and they're out.

"So, it's your birthday, Gail. Happy birthday."

She says, "Why, thank you." The others are all standing now, pulling on their coats, except for Gail, who still hasn't let go of my sleeve, which she tugs and then says to me, "Sit down a minute, Warren. I haven't seen you in what, thirty years. Imagine."

"Ma," the son says. "It's late. The snow."

I draw up a chair next to Gail, and, letting go of the dumb pretenses, I suddenly find myself struggling to see in her eyes the woman I knew for a few months when I was a kid, barely twenty-one, and she was almost fifty and married and these two fat guys were her skinny teenage sons. But I can't see through the old lady's face to the woman she was then. If that woman is gone, then so is the boy, this boy.

She looks up at one of her sons and says, "Dickie, you go without me. Warren will give me a ride, won't you, Warren?" she says, turning to me. "I'm staying at Dickie's house up on the Heights. That's not out of your way, is it?"

"Nope. I'm up on the Heights, too. Alton Woods. Just moved into a condo there."

Dickie says, "Fine," a little worried. He looks like he's used to losing arguments with his mother. They all give her a kiss on the cheek, wish her a happy birthday again, and file out into the snow. A plow scrapes past on the street. Otherwise, no traffic.

The Greek and his crew start cleaning up, while Gail and I talk a few minutes more. Although her eyes are wet and red-rimmed, she's not teary, she's smiling. It's as if there are translucent shells over her bright blue eyes. Even so, now when I look hard I can glimpse her the way she was, slipping around back there in the shadows. She had heavy, dark red hair, clear white skin smooth as porcelain, broad shoulders, and she was tall for a woman, almost as tall as I was, I remember exactly, from when she and her husband once took me along with them to a VFW party, and she and I danced while he played cards.

"You have turned into a handsome man, Warren," she says. Then she gives a little laugh. "Still a handsome man, I mean."

"Naw. Gone to seed. You're only young once, I guess."

"When we knew each other, Warren, I was the age you are now."

"Yeah. I guess that's so. Strange to think about, isn't it?"

"Are you divorced? You look like it."

"Yeah, divorced. Couple of years now. Kids, three girls, all grown up. I'm even a grandpa. It was not one of your happy marriages. Not by a long shot."

"I don't think I want to hear about all that."

"Okay. What do you want to hear about?"

"Let's have one drink and one short talk. For old times' sake. Then you may drive me to my son's home."

I say fine and ask the Greek, who's at the register tapping out, if it's too late for a nightcap. He shrugs why not, and Gail asks for a sherry and I order the usual, vodka and tonic. The Greek scoots back to the bar, pours the drinks himself because the bartender is wiping down the cooler, and returns and sets them down before us. "On the house," he says, and goes back to counting the night's take.

"It's odd, isn't it, that we never ran into each other before this," she says. "All these years. You came up here to Concord, and I stayed there in Portsmouth, even after the boys left. Frank's job was there."

"Yeah, well, I guess fifty miles is a long ways sometimes. How is Frank?" I ask, realizing as soon as I say it that he was at least ten years older than she.

"He died. Frank died in nineteen eighty-two."

"Oh, jeez. I'm sorry to hear that."

"I want to ask you something, Warren. I hope you won't mind if I speak personally with you."

"No. Shoot." I take a belt from my drink.

"I never dared to ask you then. It would have embarrassed you then, I thought, because you were so scared of what we were doing together, so unsure of yourself."

"Yeah, no kidding. I was what, twenty-one? And you were, well, not scary, but let's say impressive. Married with kids, a sophisticated woman of the world, you seemed to me. And I was this apprentice plumber working on my first job away from home, a kid."

"You were more than that, Warren. That's why I took to you so easily. You were very sensitive. I thought someday you'd become a famous actor. I wanted to encourage you."

"You did." I laugh nervously because I don't know where this conversation is going and take another pull from my drink and say, "I've done lots of acting over the years, you know, all local stuff, some of it pretty serious. No big deal. But I kept it up. I don't do much nowadays, of course. But you did encourage me, Gail, you did, and I'm truly grateful for that."

She sips her sherry with pursed lips, like a bird. "Good," she says. "Warren, were you a virgin then, when you met me?"

"Oh, jeez. Well, that's quite a question, isn't it?" I laugh. "Is that what you've been wondering all these years? Were you the first woman I ever made love with? Wow. That's . . . Hey, Gail, I don't think anybody's ever asked me that before. And here we are, thirty years later." I'm smiling at her, but the air is rushing out of me.

"I just want to know, dear. You never said it one way or the other. We shared a big secret, but we never really talked about our own secrets. We talked about the theater, and we had our little love affair, and then you went on, and I stayed with Frank and grew old. Older."

"You weren't old."

"As old as you are now, Warren."

"Yes. But I'm not old."

"Well, were you?"

"What? A virgin?"

"You don't have to answer, if it embarrasses you."

I hold off a few seconds. The waitress and the new kid and the bartender have all left, and only the Greek is here, perched on a stool in the bar watching *Nightline*. I could tell her the truth, or I could lie, or I could beg off the question altogether. It's hard to know what's right. Finally, I say, "Yes, I was. I was a virgin when I met you. It was the first time for me," I tell her, and she sits back in her chair and looks me full in the face and smiles as if I've just given her the perfect birthday gift, the one no one else thought she wanted, the gift she never dared to ask for. It's a beautiful smile, grateful and proud and seems to go all the way back to the day we first met.

She reaches over and places her small, crackled hand on mine. She says, "I never knew for sure. But whenever I think back on those days and remember how we used to meet in your room, I always pretend that for you it was the first time. I even pretended it back then, when it was happening. It meant something to me."

For a few moments neither of us speaks. Then I break the spell. "What do you say we shove off? They need to close this place up, and the snow's coming down hard." She agrees, and I help her slide into her coat. My car is parked only halfway down the block, but it's a slow walk to it, because the sidewalk is a little slippery and she's very careful.

When we're in the car and moving north on Main Street, we remain silent for a while, and finally I say to her, "You know, Gail, there's something I've wondered all these years myself."

"Is there?"

"Yeah. But you don't have to tell me, if it embarrasses you."

"Warren, dear, you reach a certain age, nothing embarrasses you."

"Yeah, well. I guess that's true."

"What is it?"

"Okay, I wondered if, except for me, you stayed faithful to Frank. And before me."

No hesitation. She says, "Yes. I was faithful to Frank, before you and after. Except for my husband, you were the only man I loved."

I don't believe her, but I know why she has lied to me. This time it's my turn to smile and reach over and place my hand on hers.

The rest of the way we don't talk, except for her giving me directions to her son's house, which is a plain brick ranch on a curving side street up by the old armory. The porch light is on, but the rest of the house is dark. "It's late," I say to her.

"So it is."

I get out and come around and help her from the car and then walk her up the path to the door. She gets her key from her purse and unlocks the door and turns around and looks up at me. She's not as tall as she used to be.

"I'm very happy that we saw each other tonight," she says. "We probably won't see each other again."

"Well, we can. If you want to."

"You're still a very sweet man, Warren. I'm glad of that. I wasn't wrong about you."

I don't know what to say. I want to kiss her, though, and I do, I lean down and put my arms around her and kiss her on the lips, very gently, then a little more, and she kisses me back, with just enough pressure against me to let me know that she is remembering everything, too. We hold each other like that for a long time.

Then I step away, and she turns, opens the door, and takes one last look back at me. She smiles. "You've still got makeup on," she says. "What's the play? I forgot to ask."

"Oh," I say, thinking fast, because I'm remembering that she's Catholic and probably doesn't think much of the Masons. "*Othello*," I say.

"That's nice, and you're the Moor?"

"Yes."

Still smiling, she gives me a slow pushing wave with her hand, as if dismissing me, and goes inside. When the door has closed behind her, I want to stand there alone on the steps all night with the snow falling around my head in clouds and watch it fill our tracks on the path. But it actually is late, and I have to work tomorrow, so I leave.

Driving home, it's all I can do to keep from crying. Time's come, time's gone, time's never returning, I say to myself. What's here in front of me is all I've got, I decide, and as I drive my car through the blowing snow it doesn't seem like much, except for the kindness that I've just exchanged with an old lady, so I concentrate on that.

Searching for Survivors

Poor Henry Hudson, I miss him. It's almost as if I had been aboard the leaking *Discovery* myself, a cabin boy or maybe an ordinary seaman, and had been forced to decide, Which will it be, slip into line behind the callow mutineers and get the hell out of this closing, ice-booming bay and home again to dear, wet England? Or say nay and climb over the side behind the good Commodore, the gentle, overthrown master of the *Discovery*, settling down next to him in the open shallop, the slate gray, ice-flecked water lurking barely six inches below the gunwales of the overloaded rowboat, as the ship puts on sail, catches a safe slice of wind rising out of the Arctic, and drives for open seas, east and south.

I would've had no choice—assuming I was given one. I would have stuck with the bigger boat and would have watched the smaller one, Hudson standing darkly iron-willed in the low bow, as it gradually became a black speck on the gray, white-rimmed sheet behind us, and then disappeared altogether.

It's so easy to forget him, to let my memory of him gradually disappear, the way his image, for one who stood at the stern of the *Discovery*, disappeared: 1611, after all, is a long ways back. Which is why I'm truly grateful whenever I happen to be reminded of him and his loss, and mine—when driving over the Hudson River, say, the

fiery red sun setting behind feculent New Jersey marshes, or when
driving the curly length of the Henry Hudson Parkway north of
Manhattan.

Oddly, reminded of Hudson, I'm always reminded in turn of other
things. Mainly automobiles. The automobiles of my adolescence, for
some reason. There must be deep associations. When I end a dark day
by suddenly, accidentally, conjuring bright images of Henry Hudson
lost in the encroaching white silence of his bay, I usually remember the
first car I ever owned. It was the unadorned frame of a 1929 Model A
Ford. I was fifteen, not old enough to take a car out on the road legally,
but that was all right because I intended to spend the next two years
building the frame of a thirty-year-old car into a hot rod. Hot rods were
very important to almost everyone, one way or another, in the late
fifties. My closest friend, Daryl, who was sixteen, was building his hot
rod out of a 1940 Ford coupe up on cinder blocks behind his father's
garage. He already had an engine for it, a '53 Chrysler overhead valve V-8,
which lay on the floor of the garage in front of his father's parked car.
That car was an impeccable 1949 Hudson Hornet, which Daryl, whenever his father felt reckless enough to grant it, was old enough to drive
and did. This happened rarely, however, because the Hudson was
Daryl's father's obsession. I remember him as a tense, thin man, short
and drawn in on himself like a hair-triggered crossbow, always rubbing
gently the sleek skin of that car with a clean, soft cloth in the speckled
orange, autumn sunlight of a Saturday afternoon, the slow circles of the
cloth seeming to tranquilize the grim man as he worked.

Almost a decade old, the Hudson was still in precisely the condition
as the day Daryl's father had purchased it, in 1949, March, at the Hudson
assembly plant in Michigan, after having followed it step by step down
the entire length of the assembly line, watching it magically becoming
itself, until it was emptied out the dark mouth of the factory into the
shattering sunlight of the test track. Then, with meticulously organized

pleasure, he had driven it all the way home to Wakefield, Massachusetts.

No other single experience with a machine compared to the exquisitely abstracted, yet purely sensual pleasure provided by riding in Daryl's father's Hudson. The car was deep green, the color of oak leaves in July, and the restrained stabs of chrome on the grille and bumpers and around the headlights and taillights merely deepened the sense of well-being that one took from the huge expanses of color. Shaped more or less like an Indian burial mound from the Upper Mississippi Valley, whether stilled or in motion, the vehicle expressed permanence and stability, blocky, arrogant pacts with eternity.

Later on, when I was nineteen, I was footloose and almost broke, and needing transportation from central Florida out to the West Coast, I bought a breaking-down 1947 Studebaker for fifteen dollars, and it got me as far as Amarillo, Texas, where it wheezingly expired. Then for a long time I didn't own a car. I hitchhiked or used public transportation or rode around passively in friends' cars—lost touch completely with the needs of an earlier aesthetic.

Then, a few years after the Studebaker and Texas, when I was about twenty-three, I happened to be living in Boston, working as a timekeeper on a construction job at the Charlestown Navy Yard, and one silver-frosted morning in February, I walked sleepily out of the MTA station and headed down the brick sidewalk toward the dry-docked USS *Constitution* and the derrick-cluttered Navy Yard beyond and nearly collided with my old friend Daryl. He was dressed in an expensive-looking, charcoal gray, pin-striped suit with a vest and black wool overcoat with a silver fur collar. He wore a derby, a black bowler, perched atop his narrow head, and he was clenching a black, tightly furled umbrella.

Daryl! I shouted. I hadn't seen him in five or six years at least. How the hell *are* you!

He responded politely, but with painful reserve, obviously eager to get away from me. He was working on State Street, he told me (when I asked), aiming to be a broker, taking night courses in business administration, living in a flat here in Charlestown in the interim. I asked him about his family, of course, as a matter of simple courtesy, but also because I really had liked and respected his father, that grimly organized sensualist. Daryl told me that his father, a foreman at the Wonder bread factory in Somerville, had retired two years ago and then had died six months later of a heart attack. His mother now lived alone in a condominium in Maryland.

We shook hands and exchanged addresses and promised to get in touch as soon as possible, so we could really sit down and have a talk. Then we rushed off in our opposite directions.

I strode quickly through the gate to the Yard and jogged past warehouses toward the new steam plant, and for a second I felt lonelier then I'd ever felt before. Nowadays loneliness was probably the last thing old Daryl was troubled by.

I pictured his small blue eyes darting past my own as they sought a spot in space over my shoulder and about twelve feet behind me, where they could rest easy while Daryl and I talked to each other. No way to deny it: I truly had expected him to become a successful racing driver. Or at least a well-known mechanic.

I live in the country now, in central New Hampshire, and two months ago I answered an ad in the local newspaper and bought a Norwegian elkhound puppy, a male, a gray puff of fur with a pointed black face and curl of a tail. I named him Hudson, giving him the second name of Frobisher, so I could be sure I was naming him, not for a car, but for the explorers of the Arctic seas—appropriate for a dog of that explicit a breeding.

It's occurred to me lately that in a few years, if I want to, I can put together a team of these rugged Arctic dogs, and I can race them in nearby Laconia, where the annual National Sled Dog Championship Races are held. The prize money isn't much, but it's said that great satisfaction derives from handling a team of dogs under such strenuous circumstances. There's a regular racecourse, and you're supposed to end up back where you started, on Main Street in Laconia, after a couple hours of following red triangular flags through the surrounding countryside. I know that I would pull off the course after a while, never finishing the race. I'd light out for the backcountry, where you can drive all day on top of ten feet of snow and ice. Imagine driving a dozen half-wild, Norwegian elkhound sled dogs into billowing sheets of snow, leaving the settlement and swiftly disappearing behind the dogs into timeless, silent whiteness.

When spring came, I'd be circling the muddied edge of Hudson Bay on foot, looking at the wet ground for pieces of old iron or charred wood, or maybe a yellowed, half-rotted journal—signs that Hudson had made it to shore. If he made it that far, the Cree or the Esquimaux would have helped him, and he would have survived there peacefully into old age, telling and retelling to the few of us who'd elected to leave the *Discovery* with him the amazing tales of earlier voyages.

There was the 1607 attempt for the Moscovy Company to cut across the Arctic, north from Norway all the way to 80 degrees latitude at Hakluyt's Headland on Spitsbergen, before fields of ice finally stopped him. There was the second voyage for the Muscovy, in 1608, eastward around the top of Russia, until he was blocked by ice, headlands, and headwinds.

There was the 1609 voyage, for the Dutch East India Company. This time, headed northeast around Russia again, mutiny stopped him, and he turned back.

Then there was the year, 1610, financed by a group of Englishmen, that Hudson and his entire crew in the *Discovery* lay icebound in his bay atop the North American continent.

After the second and final mutiny, there was the year it took for Hudson and his three loyal sailors to cross the bay to the western shore, dragging the shallop filled with their dwindling supplies all the way across the endless silent ice pack.

Black Man and White Woman in Dark Green Rowboat

It was the third day of an August heat wave. Within an hour of the sun's rising above the spruce and pine trees that grew along the eastern hills, a blue-gray haze had settled over the lake and trailerpark, so that from the short, sandy spit that served as a swimming place for the residents of the trailerpark you couldn't see the far shore of the lake. Around seven, a man in plaid bathing trunks and white bathing cap, in his sixties but still straight and apparently in good physical condition, left one of the trailers and walked along the paved lane to the beach. He draped his white towel over the bow of a flaking, bottle green rowboat that had been dragged onto the sand and walked directly into the water and when the water was up to his waist he began to swim, smoothly, slowly, straight out in the still water for two hundred yards or so, where he turned, treaded water for a few moments, and then started swimming back toward shore. When he reached the shore, he dried himself and walked back to his trailer and went inside. By the time he closed his door the water was smooth again, a dark green plain beneath the thick, gray-blue sky. No birds moved or sang; even the insects were silent.

In the next few hours, people left their trailers to go to their jobs in town, those who had jobs—the nurse, the bank teller, the carpenter, the

355

woman who worked in the office at the tannery, and her little girl, who would spend the day with a baby-sitter in town. They moved slowly, heavily, as if with regret, even the child.

Time passed, and the trailerpark was silent again, while the sun baked the metal roofs and sides of the trailers, heating them up inside, so that by midmorning it was cooler outside than in, and the people came out and tried to find a shady place to sit. First to appear was a middle-aged woman in large sunglasses and white shorts and halter, her head hidden by a floppy, wide-brimmed, cloth hat. She carried a book and sat on the shaded side of her trailer in an aluminum and plastic-webbing lawn chair and began to read her book. Then from his trailer came the man in the plaid bathing trunks, bareheaded now and shirtless and tanned to a chestnut color, his skin the texture of old leather. He wore rubber sandals and proceeded to hook up a garden hose and water the small, meticulously weeded vegetable garden on the slope behind his trailer. Every now and then he aimed the hose down and sprayed his bony feet. From the first trailer in from the road, where a sign that said MANAGER had been attached over the door, a tall, thick-bodied woman in her forties with cropped, graying hair, wearing faded jeans cut off at midthigh and a floppy T-shirt that had turned pink in the wash, walked slowly out to the main road, a half mile, to get her mail. When she returned she sat on her steps and read the letters and advertisements and the newspaper. About that time a blond boy in his late teens with shoulder-length hair, skinny, tanned, shirtless, and barefoot in jeans, emerged from his trailer, sighed, and sat down on the stoop and smoked a joint. At the last trailer in the park, the one next to the beach, an old man smoking a cob pipe and wearing a sleeveless undershirt and beltless khaki trousers slowly scraped paint from the bottom of an overturned rowboat. He ceased working and watched carefully as, walking slowly past him toward a dark green rowboat on the sand, there came a young black man with a fishing rod in one hand and a tackle box in the other. The man was tall and, though slender, muscular. He wore jeans and a pale blue, unbuttoned, short-sleeved shirt.

The old man said it was too hot for fishing, they wouldn't feed in this weather, and the young man said he didn't care, it had to be cooler on the lake than here on shore. The old man agreed with that, but why bother carrying your fishing rod and tackle box with you when you don't expect to catch any fish?

"Right," the young man said, smiling. "Good question." Placing his box and the rod into the rowboat, he turned to wait for the young woman who was stepping away from the trailer where, earlier, the middle-aged woman in shorts, halter, and floppy hat had come out and sat in the lawn chair to read. The young woman was a girl, actually, twenty or maybe twenty-one. She wore a lime green terry-cloth bikini and carried a large yellow towel in one hand and a fashion magazine and small brown bottle of tanning lotion in the other. Her long, honey blond hair swung from side to side across her tanned shoulders as she walked down the lane to the beach, where both the young man and the old man watched her approach them. She made a brief remark about the heat to the old man, said good morning to the young man, placed her towel, magazine, and tanning lotion into the dark green rowboat, and helped the young man shove the boat off the hot sand into the water. Then she jumped into the boat and sat herself in the stern, and the man, barefoot, with the bottoms of his jeans rolled to his knees, waded out, got into the boat, and began to row.

For a while, as the man rowed and the girl rubbed tanning lotion slowly over her arms and legs and across her shoulders and belly, they said nothing. The man pulled smoothly on the oars and watched the girl, and she examined her light brown skin and stroked it and rubbed the oily, sweet-smelling fluid onto it. After a few moments, holding to the gunwales with her hands so that her entire body got exposed to the powerful sun, she leaned back, closed her eyes, and stretched her legs toward the man, placing her small, white feet over his large, dark feet. The man studied the wedge of her crotch, then her navel, where a puddle of sweat was collecting, then the rise of her small breasts, and finally her long throat glistening in the sunlight. The man was sweating from the effort of rowing and he said he should have brought a hat. He stopped rowing, let the blades of the oars float in the water, and removed his shirt and wrapped it around his head like a turban. The girl, realizing that he had ceased rowing, looked up and smiled at him. "You look like an Arab. A sheik."

"A galley slave, more likely."

"No, really. Honestly." She lay her head back again and closed her eyes, and the man took up the oars and resumed rowing. They were a long ways out now, perhaps a half-mile from the trailerpark. The trailers looked like pastel-colored shoe boxes from here, six of them lined up on one side of the lane, six on the other, with a cleared bit of low ground and marsh off to one side and the outlet of the lake, the Catamount River it was called, on the other. The water was deep there, and below the surface and buried in the mud were blocks of stone and wooden lattices, the remains of fishing weirs the Indians constructed here and used for centuries, until the arrival of the Europeans. In the fall when the lake was low you could see the tops of the huge boulders the Indians placed into the stream to make channels for their nets and traps. There were weirs like this all over northern New England, most of them considerably more elaborate than this, so no one here paid much attention to these, except perhaps to mention the fact of their existence to a visitor from Massachusetts or New York. It gave the place a history and a certain significance when outsiders were present that it did not otherwise seem to have.

The girl lifted her feet away from the man's feet, drawing them back so that her knees pointed straight at his. She turned slightly to one side and stroked her cheekbone and lower jaw with the fingertips and thumb of one hand, leaning her weight on the other forearm and hand. "I'm already putting on weight," she said.

"It doesn't work that way. You're just eating too much."

"I told Mother."

The man stopped rowing and looked at her.

"I told Mother," she repeated. Her eyes were closed and her face was directed toward the sun and she continued to stroke her cheekbone and lower jaw.

"When?"

"Last night."

"And?"

"And nothing. I told her that I love you very much."

"That's all?"

"No. I told her everything."

He started rowing again, faster this time and not as smoothly as before. They were nearing a small, tree-covered island. Large, rounded rocks lay around the island, half-submerged in the shallow water, like the backs of huge, coal-colored hippos. The man peered over his shoulder and observed the distance to the island, then drew in the oars and lifted a broken chunk of cinder block tied to a length of clothesline rope and slid it into the water. The rope went out swiftly and cleanly as the anchor sank and then suddenly stopped. The man opened his tackle box and started poking through it, searching for a deepwater spinner.

The girl was sitting up now, studying the island with her head canted to one side, as if planning a photograph. "Actually, Mother was a lot better than I'd expected her to be. If Daddy were alive, it would be different," she said. "Daddy . . ."

"Hated niggers."

"Jesus Christ!"

"And Mother loves 'em." He located the spinner and attached it to the line.

"My mother likes you. She's a decent woman, and she's tired and lonely. And she's not your enemy, any more than I am."

"You're sure of that." He made a long cast and dropped the spinner between two large rocks and started winding it back in. "No, I know your mamma's okay. I'm sorry. Tell me what she said."

"She thought it was great. She likes you. I'm happy, and that's what is really important to her, and she likes you. She worries about me a lot, you know. She's afraid for me, she thinks I'm *fragile*. Especially now, because I've had some close calls. At least that's how she sees them."

"Sees what?"

"Oh, you know. Depression."

"Yeah." He cast again, slightly to the left of where he'd put the spinner the first time.

"Listen, I don't know how to tell you this, but I might as well come right out and say it. I'm going to do it. This afternoon. Mother's coming with me. She called and set it up this morning."

He kept reeling in the spinner, slowly, steadily, as if he hadn't heard her, until the spinner clunked against the side of the boat and he lifted it dripping from the water, and he said, "I hate this whole thing. H*ate*! Just know that much, will you?"

She reached out and placed a hand on his arm. "I know you do. So do I. But it'll be all right again afterwards. I promise. It'll be just like it was."

"You can't promise that. No one can. It won't be all right afterwards. It'll be lousy."

"I suppose you'd rather I just did nothing."

"Yes. That's right."

"Well. We've been through all this before. A hundred times." She sat up straight and peered back at the trailerpark in the distance. "How long do you plan to fish?"

"An hour or so. Why? If you want to swim, I'll row you around to the other side of the island and drop you and come back and get you later."

"No. No. That's all right. There are too many rocks anyhow. I'll go in when we get back to the beach. I have to be ready to go by three-thirty."

"Yeah. I'll make sure you get there on time," he said, and he made a long cast off to his right in deeper water.

"I love to sweat," she said, lying back and showing herself once again to the full sun. "I love to just lie back and sweat."

The man fished, and the girl sunbathed. The water was as slick as oil, the air thick and still. After a while, the man reeled in his line and removed the silvery spinner and went back to poking through his tackle box. "Where the hell is the damn plug?" he mumbled.

The girl sat up and watched him, his long, dark back twisted toward her, the vanilla bottoms of his feet, the fluttering muscles of his shoulders and arms, when suddenly he yelped and yanked his hand free of the box and put the meat of his hand directly into his mouth. He looked up at the girl in rage.

"What? Are you all right?" She slid back in her seat and drew her legs up close to her and wrapped her arms around her knees.

In silence, still sucking on his hand, he reached with the other hand into the tackle box and came back with a pale green and scarlet plug with six double hooks attached to the sides and tail. He held it as if by the head delicately with thumb and forefinger and showed it to her.

The girl grimaced. "Ow! You poor thing."

He took his hand from his mouth and clipped the plug to his line and cast it toward the island, dropping it about twenty feet from the rocky shore, a short ways to the right of a pair of dog-sized boulders. The girl picked up her magazine and began to leaf through the pages, stopping every now and then to examine an advertisement or photograph. Again and again, the man cast the flashing plug into the water and drew it back to the boat, twitching its path from side to side to imitate the motions of an injured, fleeing, pale-colored animal.

Finally, lifting the plug from the water next to the boat, the man said, "Let's go. Old Merle was right, no sense fishing when the fish ain't feeding. The whole point is catching fish, right?" he said, and he removed the plug from the line and tossed it into his open tackle box.

"I suppose so. I don't like fishing anyhow." Then after a few seconds, as if she were pondering the subject, "But I guess it's relaxing. Even if you don't catch anything."

The man drew up the anchor, pulling in the wet rope hand over hand, and finally he pulled the cinder block free of the water and set it dripping behind him in the bow of the boat. They had drifted closer to the island now and were in the cooling shade of the thicket of oaks and birches that crowded together over the island. The water turned suddenly shallow here, only a few feet deep, and they could see the rocky bottom clearly.

"Be careful," the girl said. "We'll run aground in a minute." She watched the bottom nervously. "Take care."

The man looked over her head and beyond, all the way to the shore and the trailerpark. The shapes of the trailers were blurred together in the distance so that you could not tell where one trailer left off and another began. "I wish I could just leave you here," the man said, still not looking at her.

"What?"

The boat drifted silently in the smooth water between a pair of large rocks, barely disturbing the surface. The man's dark face was somber and ancient beneath the turban that covered his head and the back of his neck. He leaned forward on his seat, his forearms resting wearily on his thighs, his large hands hanging limply between his knees. "I said, I wish I could just leave you here," he said in a soft voice, and he looked down at his hands.

She looked nervously around her, as if for an ally or a witness. "We have to go back."

"You mean, you have to go back."

"That's right," she said.

He slipped the oars into the oarlocks and started rowing, turning the boat and shoving it quickly away from the island. Facing the trailerpark, he rowed along the side of the island, then around behind it, out of sight of the trailerpark and the people who lived there, emerging again in a few moments on the far side of the island, rowing steadily, smoothly, powerfully. Now his back was to the trailerpark, and the girl was facing it, looking grimly past the man toward the shore.

He rowed, and they said nothing more. In a while they had returned to shore and life among the people who lived there. A few of them were in the water and on the beach when the dark green rowboat touched land and the black man stepped out and drew the boat onto the sand. The old man in the white bathing cap was standing in waist-deep water, and the woman who was the manager of the trailerpark stood near the edge of the water, cooling her feet and ankles. The old man with the cob pipe was still chipping at the bottom of his rowboat, and next to him, watching and idly chatting, stood the kid with the long blond hair. They all watched silently as the black man turned away from the dark green rowboat and carried his fishing rod and tackle box away, and then they watched the girl, carrying her yellow towel, magazine, and bottle of tanning lotion, step carefully out of the boat and walk to where she lived with her mother.

Xmas

He was a popular teacher of political science at the state university, was a man entering middle age in flight from the wreckage of two failed marriages. He refused to call them that, however—"failed," as if marriage were an experiment, a test of some giddy hypothesis he'd cooked up in his youth. Gregory was sensitive to value-laden language. Besides, in each case, his commitment to the marriage had been total, absolute, without hedges, without a control. Gregory had loved both women.

He preferred to think of his marriages as "ended"; to him they were distinct blocks in time that may as easily have been the best of times as the worst. Or why not simply the time of his life? For they had been that, too. Gregory Dodd was one of those men who in their mid-forties enjoy casting their past in a slightly elegiac light.

The important thing was that both marriages were ended now, that's all—the brief marriage of his adolescence and the fifteen-year marriage of his young manhood: over and done with, and sufficiently behind him that he was able to begin anew, as it were, and he had done that, he believed, with Susan. The elegiac view, even if somewhat premature, makes renewal possible. So that, by falling in love with Susan, Gregory felt that he had moved into a new block of time, one that was as endless-seeming as each of the others had been in the beginning, and he was thrilled again. And now, once more, it was Christmas Eve, and even though Gregory's own three nearly grown children were in the home of their mother, his second ex-wife, he was nonetheless playing Santa Claus again, loading his car with presents for Susan and her three children, much younger than his, driving down on a snowy night from his house in New Hampshire to Susan's shabby flat just beyond Boston in Jamaica Plain, Handel's *Messiah* roaring from the radio and, at the chorus, full-throated Santa at the wheel singing gladly along: *Hallelujah, hallelujah, hal-la-loo-loo-yah!*

In New Hampshire, the snow had been dry and blew at the car from the darkness ahead in long white strings, and driving on the Interstate was easy. He kept the Audi at seventy all the way into Charlestown. But here in the city, as he crossed the Fens from Kenmore Square to Huntington, taking the quicker back way across Boston's South End to Jamaica Plain, the snow was wet and fell in fat flakes that slickened and made driving difficult. It was the night before Christmas, and traffic was light; the nearly empty city streets and darkened brick buildings were beautiful to Gregory: they exuded a stoical melancholy that reminded him of an Edward Hopper painting, although he couldn't remember which one.

He had overspent, he knew, as usual, but what the hell, it would be worth it to see Susan's grateful delight when he brought into her living room and heaped under the tinsel-covered tree the dozens of carefully wrapped gifts he'd carted all the way down from New Hampshire for her children. And for her, too—a lovely, dark green, velour robe, Braudel's *Civilization and Capitalism, 15th–18th Century*, all three volumes, an espresso machine he'd ordered in October from the Williams-Sonoma catalog, and an antique cameo pin he had found in a boutique in Portsmouth. He would have to march up and down those narrow, sour-smelling stairs from the car three times to unload it all.

Susan was ten years younger than Gregory, a photographer whose harshly documentary style was out of favor, especially in Boston, and who lived close to the same line of poverty that most of her subjects, blacks and Hispanics in the projects and the worst sections of Roxbury, lived below. She viewed her poverty as the direct consequence and expression of her art; Gregory regarded it as a permanent form of bohemianism and a plight, which he tried to ameliorate with his bourgeois common sense and generosity. He balanced Susan's checkbook for her and for her birthday had bought her a dishwasher.

Near the Museum of Fine Arts, Gregory slowed and turned left off Huntington onto a potholed side street, following the taillights of the only other car in sight. The two vehicles moved past dark, high buildings—alternating rows of warehouses and public housing from the fifties and sixties—where here and there a short string of Christmas lights or a solitary electric candle blinked from a window as if with sarcasm. The car ahead had slowed; the driver seemed to be looking for a number on one of the graffiti-splashed doorways. This was not so much a neighborhood as a zone of half-destroyed buildings located between construction sites, a no-man's-land still being fought over by opposing armies; people lived here, but not by choice, and only temporarily.

In the seventies Susan and her ex-husband, the father of her three daughters, had been active in the Weather Underground. Her radical past and marriage she regarded as a chapter in her life that had ended, although the momentum of that chapter had carried over long enough for her to have been five months pregnant with her third child before finally obtaining a divorce. By then her husband had gone underground altogether, and separating her life from his, she felt, had been like granting him his last wish. It had certainly been the best thing for the children. A year later, with two white women and a black man, he tried to rob a Brink's truck in Framingham, and a guard had been shot

and killed. Susan's ex-husband and one of the women had been captured the following day in upstate New York, and the rest, as she said,
was history.

Gregory had tried to get Susan to tell him more about her life with
her ex-husband; he was fascinated by it, slightly aroused in a sexual way
that he did not understand, and he wanted either to chase his arousal
into desire and satisfy it or else to exorcise it altogether. There were no
pictures of the man in her apartment, and the children never spoke of
him. It was as if he had died before they were born and their only parent was their mother.

Though the girls were little more than a year apart in age, the way
Susan described it, she and their father had never actually cohabited:
"Oh, God, it goes back to college, really, to Brandeis. But he was married
to the Movement, from the start, like an organizer, sort of. He'd show up
for a few days, and then he'd be gone for a month, sometimes longer,"
she said in her vague and elliptical way, which frustrated and sometimes annoyed Gregory.

Usually, when they talked about her marriage it was late at night in
bed, after making love, over cigarettes and the last glass of wine from
the second bottle. He didn't want to press her on the subject, to insist
that she provide details, instances, dates and times and specific circumstances—although he surely did want to know them all—for fear that
she would think he was unnaturally fixated on this closed chapter of
her life. "It was like, every time we made love, I got pregnant. I couldn't
take the pill, it made me sick and fluttery and all, and nothing worked.
We didn't do it all that much," she said, and lightly laughed.

"Well, three times at least," Gregory said.

"At *least*," she said, and she punched him on the shoulder. "C'mon,
Gregory, it's history."

"I know, I know. I'm only kidding you."

The vehicle ahead suddenly stopped, and Gregory hit the brakes, and the Audi slid and came to a stop a few feet behind it. Gregory reached over and turned down the radio, puzzled. The car ahead of him was a battered, ten-year-old Chrysler with a huge, flat trunk; the number plate was wired loosely to the rear bumper, and Gregory imagined fixing it with a pair of twenty-cent stove bolts.

The rear window of the Chrysler was covered with snow, and Gregory couldn't see inside. He cut left and pulled out to pass by, and as he drew abreast of the other car, it moved out also, as if to make a U-turn in the middle of the street. Gregory jumped on his brakes and spun the wheel. The Chrysler drew quickly in front of him, the Audi swerved, and when its front bumper ticked the rear bumper of the other car, Gregory thought he heard the number plate clang.

Abruptly, the other car stopped, half-turned in the middle of the deserted street, blocking Gregory's passage. The driver stepped from the Chrysler and walked slowly toward Gregory. He was a black man, tall and wide, in a leather jacket and watch cap, scowling. A second black man got out of the Chrysler and came along behind. They were both middle-aged, his age, and seemed irritated, but not threatening. A mistake, Gregory thought. He must not have known I was so close to him. Gregory pressed the button and lowered his window, to explain and even apologize for nearly colliding with the man's car and ruining Christmas for all of them.

He said, "I thought you were stopped—" and the larger of the two men simply said, "Yeah," and slammed his fist through the open window straight into Gregory's face. Then they turned and walked back to their car and got in. Gregory spat a piece of tooth, touched his lip with fingertips, and came away with blood; he looked at the steering wheel and thought: I must have hit the wheel when I stopped; I must have broken my mouth by accident; something that I don't know about must be what just happened.

The Chrysler pulled back onto the street and moved slowly away, its taillights shrinking in the snowy distance, and Gregory began to tremble. Rage washed over him like a cold wave, and when he was covered, his entire body turned suddenly hot. He touched his lips again and found that they had swollen to nearly twice their normal size. His shirt was spattered with his blood, and when he groped through his mouth with his tongue, he realized that a tooth had been broken and several others loosened by the blow.

The Chrysler was gone now, and Gregory was alone on the street, sitting in his car with all his presents for Susan and her children. What was he to do now? Where could he go, his face all bloody and swollen, his chest heaving, his hands clenched to the steering wheel as if he were being yanked violently from the car? He was utterly ridiculous to himself. He was a fool, a man whose life was unknown to him and out of control, a man whose past was lost to him, and whose future was a deliberate, willed fantasy. He felt like an unattached speck of matter afloat in space, and all he wanted was to be in his own home with his own children and their mother, in his proper place, his life intact, all the parts connected and sequential.

He put the car into gear and drove slowly away, toward Susan's home, where she lived with her children. He knew that she would be alarmed when she saw him and then would comfort and take care of him. But they would not be the same together as they had been before and as he had planned, so that while he drove he had to fight against the new and terrible longing to turn back.

The Guinea Pig Lady

The story of Flora Pease, how she got to be the way she is now, isn't all that uncommon a story, except maybe in the particulars. You often hear in these small towns of a woman no one will deal with anymore, except to sell her something she wants or needs—food, clothing, or shelter. In other words, you don't have a social relationship with a woman like Flora, you have an economic one, and that's it. But that's important, because it's what keeps women like Flora alive, and, after all, no matter what you might think of her, you don't want to let her die, because, if you're not related to her somehow, you're likely to have a friend who is, or your friend will have a friend who is, which is almost the same thing in a small town. And not only in a small town, either—these things are true for any group of people that knows its limits and plans to keep them.

When Flora Pease first came to the trailerpark and rented number 11, which is the second trailer on your left as you come in from Old Road, no one in the park thought much about her one way or the other. She was about forty or forty-five, kind of flat-faced and plain, a red-colored person, with short red hair and a reddish tint to her skin. Even her eyes, which happened to be pale blue, looked red, as if she smoked too much and slept too little, which, as it later turned out, happened to be true. Her body was a little strange, however, and people remarked on that. It was blocky and square-shaped, not exactly feminine and not exactly masculine, so that while she could almost pass for either man or woman, she was generally regarded as neither. She wore mostly men's work shirts and ankle-high work boots, which, except for the overcoat, was not all that unusual among certain women who work outside a lot and don't do much socializing. But with Flora, because of the shape of her body, or rather, its shapelessness, her clothing only contributed to the vagueness of her sexual identity. Privately, there was probably no vagueness at all, but publicly there was. People elbowed one another and winked and made not quite kindly remarks about her when she passed by them on the streets of Catamount or when she passed along the trailerpark road on her way to or from town. The story, which came from Marcelle Chagnon, who rented her the trailer, was that Flora was retired military and lived off a small pension, and that made sense in one way, given people's prejudices about women in the military, and in another way, too, because at that time Captain Dewey Knox (U.S. Army, ret.) was already living at number 6, and people at the park had got used to the idea of someone living off a military pension instead of working for a living.

What didn't make sense was how someone who seemed slightly cracked, as Flora came quickly to seem, could have stayed in the military long enough to end up collecting a pension for it. Here's how she first came to seem cracked. She sang out loud, in public. She supposedly was raised here in Catamount, and though she had moved away when she was a girl, she still knew a lot of the old-timers in town, and she would walk into town every day or two for groceries and beer, singing in a loud voice all the way, as if she were the only person who could hear her. But by the time she had got out to Old Road, she naturally would have passed someone in the park who knew her, so she had to be aware that she wasn't the only person who could hear her. Regardless, she'd just go right on singing in a huge voice, singing songs from old Broadway musicals, mostly. She knew all the songs from *Oklahoma* and *West Side Story* and a few others as well, and she sang them, one after the other, all the way into town, then up and down the streets of town, as she stopped off at the A & P, Brown's Drug Store, maybe Hayward's Hardware, finally ending up at the Hawthorne House for a beer, before she headed back to the trailerpark. Everywhere she went, she sang those songs in a loud voice that was puffed up with feeling, if it was a happy song, or thick with melancholy, if it was sad. You don't mind a person whistling or humming or maybe even singing to herself under her breath while she does something else, sort of singing absentmind-edly. But you do have to wonder about someone who forces you to listen to her the way Flora Pease forced everyone within hearing range to listen to her Broadway songs. Her voice wasn't half-bad, actually, and if she had been singing for the annual talent show at the high school, say, and you were sitting in the audience, you might have been pleased to listen, but at midday in June on Main Street, when you're coming out of the bank and about to step into your car, it can be a slightly jarring expe-rience to see and hear a person who looks like Flora Pease come strid-ing down the sidewalk singing in full voice about how the corn is as high as an elephant's eye.

The second thing that made Flora seem cracked early on was the way she never greeted you the same way twice, or at least twice in a row, so you could never work out exactly how to act toward her. You'd see her stepping out of her trailer early on a summer day—it was summer when she first moved into the park, so everyone's remembered first impressions naturally put her into summertime scenes—and you'd give a friendly nod, the kind of nod you offer people you live among but aren't exactly friends with, just a quick, downward tip of the face, fol-lowed by a long, upsweeping lift of the whole head, with the eyes closed for a second as the head reaches its farthest point back. Afterwards, resuming your earlier expression and posture, you'd continue walking, wholly under the impression that, when your eyes were closed and your head tilted back, Flora had given you the appropriate answering nod. But no, or apparently no, because she'd call out, as you walked off, "Good *morn*-ing!" and she'd wave her hands at you as if brushing cobwebs away. "*Wonderful* morning for a walk!" she'd bellow (her voice was a loud one), and caught off guard like that, you'd agree and hurry away. The next time you saw her, however, the next morning, for instance, when once again you walked out to the row of mailboxes for your mail and passed her as, mail in hand, she headed back in from Old Road, you'd recall her greeting of the day before and how it had caught you off guard, and you'd say, "Morning," to her and maybe smile a bit and give her a friendly and more or less direct gaze. But what you'd get back would be a glare, a harsh, silent stare, as if you'd just made an improper advance on her. So you'd naturally say to yourself, "The hell with it," and that would be fine until the following morning, when you'd try to ignore her, and she wouldn't let you. She'd holler the second she saw you, "Hey! A scorcher! Right? Goin' to be a scorcher today, eh?" It was the sort of thing you had to answer, even if only with a word, "Yup," which you did, wondering as you said it what the hell was going on with that woman.

Everyone in the park that summer was scratching his or her head and asking what the hell was going on with the woman in number 11. Doreen Tiede, who lived with her five-year-old daughter, Maureen, in number 4, which was diagonally across the park road from Flora Pease's trailer, put Marcelle on the spot, so to speak, something Doreen could get away with more easily than most of the other residents of the park. Marcelle Chagnon intimidated most people. She was a large, hawk-faced woman, and that helped, and she was French Canadian, which also helped, because it meant that she could talk fast and loud without seeming to think about it first, and most people who were not French Canadians could not, so most people tended to remain silent and let Marcelle have her way. In a sense Marcelle was a little like Flora Pease—she was sudden and unpredictable and said what she wanted to, or so it seemed, regardless of what you might have said first. She didn't exactly ignore you, but she made it clear that it didn't matter to her what you thought of her or anything else. She always had business to take care of. She was the resident manager of the Granite State Trailerpark, which was owned by the Granite State Realty Development Corporation down in Nashua, and she had certain responsibilities toward the park and the people who lived there that no one else had. Beyond collecting everyone's monthly rent on time, she had to be sure no one in the park caused any trouble that would hurt the reputation of the park; she had to keep people from infringing on other people's rights, which wasn't all that simple, since in a trailerpark people live within ten or fifteen feet of each other and yet still feel they have their own private dwelling place and thus have control over their own destiny; and she also had to assert the rights of the people in the park whenever those rights got stepped on by outsiders, by Catamount police without a warrant, say, or by strangers who wanted to put their boats into the lake from the trailerpark dock, or by ex-husbands who might want to hassle ex-wives and make their kids cry. These things happened, and Marcelle was always able to handle them efficiently, with force and intelligence, and with no sentimentality, which, in the end, is probably the real reason she intimidated most people. She seemed to be without sentimentality.

Except when dealing with Doreen Tiede, that is. Which is why Doreen was able to put Marcelle on the spot and say to her late one afternoon in Marcelle's trailer at number 1, "What's with that woman, Flora Pease? Is she a fruitcake, or what? And if she is, how come you let her move in? And if she isn't a fruitcake, how come she looks the way she does and acts the way she does?" There were in the park, besides

Doreen, Marcelle, and Flora, three additional women, but none of them could make Marcelle look at herself and give a straight answer to a direct question. None of them could make her forget her work and stop, even for a second. Only Doreen could get away with embarrassing Marcelle, or at least with demanding a straight answer from her, and getting it, too, probably because both Doreen and Marcelle looked tired in the same way, and each woman understood the nature of the fatigue and respected it in the other. They didn't feel sorry for it in each other; they respected it. There were twenty or more years between them, and Marcelle's children had long ago gone off and left her—one was a computer programmer in Billerica, Massachusetts, another was in the Navy and making a career of it, a third was running a McDonald's in Seattle, Washington, and a fourth had died. Because she had raised them herself, while at the same time fending off the attacks of the man who had fathered them on her, she thought of her life as work and her work as feeding, housing, and clothing her three surviving children and teaching them to be kindly, strong people, despite the fact that their father happened to have been a cruel, weak person. A life like that, or rather, twenty-five years of it, can permanently mark your face and make it instantly recognizable to anyone who happens to be engaged in similar work. Magicians, wise men, and fools are supposed to be able to recognize each other instantly, but so, too, are poor women who raise children alone.

They were sitting in Marcelle's trailer, having a beer. It was five-thirty, Doreen was on her way home from her job at the tannery, where she was a bookkeeper in the office. Her daughter, Maureen, was with her, having spent the afternoon with a baby-sitter in town next door to the kindergarten she attended in the mornings, and was whining for supper. Doreen had stopped in to pay her June rent, a week late, and Marcelle had accepted her apology for the lateness and had offered her a beer. Because of the lateness of the payment and Marcelle's graciousness, Doreen felt obliged to accept it, even though she preferred to get home and start supper so Maureen would stop whining.

Flora's name had come up when Maureen had stopped whining and had suddenly said, "Look, Momma, at the funny lady!" and had pointed out the window at Flora, wearing a heavy, ankle-length coat in the heat, sweeping her yard with a broom. She was working her way across the packed dirt yard toward the road that ran through the center of the park, raising a cloud of dust as she swept, singing in a loud voice something from *Fiddler on the Roof*—"If I were a rich man . . ."—and the two women and the child watched her, amazed. That's when Doreen had demanded to know what Marcelle had been thinking when she agreed to rent a trailer to Flora Pease.

Marcelle sighed, sat heavily back down at the kitchen table, and said, "Naw, I knew she was a little crazy. But not like this." She lit a cigarette and took a quick drag. "I guess I felt sorry for her. And I needed the money. We got two vacancies now out of twelve trailers, and I get paid by how many trailers have tenants, you know. When Flora came by that day, we got three vacancies, and I'm broke and need the money, so I look the other way a little and I say, sure, you can have number eleven, which is always the hardest to rent anyhow, because it's on the backside away from the lake, and it's got number twelve and number ten right next to it and the swamp behind. Number five I'll rent easy, it's on the lake, and nine should be easy too, soon's people forget about Tom Smith's suicide. It's the end of the row and has a nice yard on one side, plus the toolshed in back. But eleven has always been a bitch to rent. So here's this lady, if you want to call her that, and she's got a regular income from the Air Force, and she seems friendly enough, lives alone, she says, has relations around here, she says, so what the hell, even though I can already see she's a little off. I figure it was because of her being maybe not interested in men, one of those women. And I figure, what the hell, that's her business, not mine, I don't give a damn what she does or who she does it with, so long as she keeps to herself. So I say, sure, take number eleven, thinking maybe she won't. But she did."

Marcelle sipped at her can of beer, and Doreen went for hers. The radio was tuned quietly in the background to the country-and-western station from Dover. Doreen reached across the counter to the radio and turned up the volume, saying to no one in particular, "I like this song."

"That's 'cause you're not thirty yet, honey. You'll get to be thirty, and then you'll like a different kind of song. Wait."

Doreen smiled from somewhere behind the fatigue that covered her face. It was a veil she had taken several years ago, and she'd probably wear it until she died or lost her memory, whichever came first. She looked at her red-painted fingernails. "What happens when you're forty, and then fifty? You like a different kind of song then too?"

"Can't say for fifty yet, but, yes, for forty. Thirty, then forty, and probably fifty, too. Sixty, now, that's the question. That's when you decide you don't like any of the songs they play, and so you go and sit in front of the TV and watch game shows," she laughed.

"Well, I'll tell you," Doreen said, finishing her beer off and standing to leave, "that Flora Pease over there, she's going to be trouble, Marcelle. You made a big mistake letting her in the park. Mark my words."

"Naw. She's harmless. A little fruity, that's all. We're all a little fruity, if you want to think about it," she said. "Some are just more able to cover it up than others, that's all."

Doreen shook her head and hurried her daughter out the screened door and along the road to number 4. When she had left, Marcelle stood up and from the window over the sink watched Flora, who swept and sang her way back from the road across her dirt yard to the door, then stepped daintily up the cinder blocks and entered her home.

Then, in August that summer, a quarrel between Terry Constant and his older sister, Carol, who lived in number 10 next door to Flora, caused young Terry to fly out the door one night around midnight and bang fiercely against the metal wall of their trailer. It was the outer wall of the bedroom where his sister slept, and he was doubtless pounding that particular wall to impress his sister with his anger. No one in the park knew what the quarrel was about, and at that hour no one much cared, but when Terry commenced his banging on the wall of the trailer, several people were obliged to involve themselves with the fight. Lights went on across the road at number 6, where Captain Knox lived alone, and 7, where Noni Hubner and her mother, Nancy, lived. It wasn't unusual for Terry to be making a lot of noise at night, but it was unusual for him to be making it this late and outside the privacy of his own home.

It was easy to be frightened of Terry if you didn't know him—he was about twenty-five, tall and muscular and very dark, and he had an expressive face and a loud voice—but if you knew him, he was, at worst, irritating. To his sister Carol, though, he must often have been a pure burden, and that was why they quarreled. She had come up from Boston a few years ago to work as a nurse for a dying real estate man who had died shortly after, leaving her sort of stuck in this white world, insofar as she was immediately offered a good job in town as Doctor Wickshaw's nurse and had no other job to go to anywhere else and no money to live on while she looked. So she took it. Then her mother down in Boston died, and Terry moved in with his sister for a spell and stayed on, working here and there and now and then for what he called monkey money as a carpenter's helper or stacking hides in the tannery. Sometimes he and Carol would have an argument, caused, everyone was sure, by Terry, since he was so loud and insecure and she was so quiet and sure of herself, and then Terry would be gone for a month or so, only to return one night all smiles and compliments. He was skillful with tools and usually free to fix broken appliances or plumbing in the trailerpark, so Marcelle never objected to Carol's taking him back in—not that Marcelle actually had a right to object, but if she had fussed about it, Carol would have sent Terry packing. People liked Carol Constant, and because she put up with Terry, they put up with him, too. Besides, he was good-humored and often full of compliments and, when he wasn't angry, good to look at.

Captain Knox was the first to leave his trailer and try to quiet Terry. In his fatherly way, embellished somewhat by his white hair and plaid bathrobe and bedroom slippers, he informed Terry that he was waking up working people. He stood across the road in the light from his window, tall and straight, arms crossed over his chest, one bushy black eyebrow raised in disapproval, and said, "Not everybody in this place can sleep till noon, young man."

Terry stopped banging for a second, peered over his shoulder at the man, and said, "Fuck you, Knox!" and went back to banging on the tin wall, as if he were hammering nails with his bare fists. Captain Knox turned and marched back inside his trailer, and, after a few seconds, his lights went out.

Then the girl, Noni Hubner, in her nightgown, appeared at the open door of number 7. Her long, silky blond hair hung loosely over her shoulders, circling her like a halo lit from behind. A woman's voice, her mother's, called from inside the trailer, "Noni, don't! Don't go out there!"

The girl waved the voice away and stepped out to the landing, barefoot, delicately exposing the silhouette of her body against the light of the living room behind her.

Now the mother shrieked, "Noni! Come back! He may be on drugs!"

Terry ceased hammering and turned to stare at the girl across the road. He was wearing a T-shirt and khaki work pants and blue tennis shoes, and his arms hung loosely at his sides, his chest heaving from the exertion of his noisemaking and his anger, and he smiled over at the girl and said, "Hey, honey, you want to come beat on my drum?"

"You're waking everyone up," she said politely.

"Please come back inside, Noni! *Please!*"

The black man took a step toward the girl, and she whirled and disappeared inside, slamming the door and locking it, switching off the lights and dumping the trailer back into darkness.

Terry stood by the side of the road looking after her. "Fuck," he said. Then he noticed Flora Pease standing next to him, a blocky figure in a long overcoat, barefoot, and carrying in her arms, as if it were a baby, a small, furry animal.

"What you got there?" Terry demanded.

"Elbourne." Flora smiled down at the chocolate-colored animal and made a quiet, clucking noise with her mouth.

"What the hell's an Elbourne?"

"Guinea pig. Elbourne's his name."

"Why'd you name him Elbourne?"

"After my grandfather. How come you're making such a racket out here?"

Terry took a step closer, trying to see the guinea pig more clearly, and Flora wrapped the animal in her coat sleeve, as if to protect it from his gaze.

"I won't hurt ol' Elbourne. I just want to see him. I never seen a guinea pig before."

"He's a lot quieter than you are, mister, I'll tell you that much. Now, how come you're making such a racket out here banging on the side of your house?"

"That ain't my house. That's my *sister's* house!"

"Oh," Flora said, as if she now understood everything, and she extended the animal toward Terry so he could see it entirely. It was long-haired, shaped like a football, with circular, dark eyes on the sides of its head and small ears and tiny legs tucked beneath its body. It seemed terrified and trembled in Flora's outstretched hands.

Terry took the animal and held it up to examine its paws and involuted tail, then brought it close to his chest and, holding it in one large hand, tickled it under the chin with his forefinger. The animal made a tiny cluttering noise that gradually subsided to a light *drr-r-r*, and Terry chuckled. "Nice little thing," he said. "How many you got, or is this the only one?"

"Lots."

"Lots? You got a bunch of these guinea pigs in there?"

"I said so, didn't I?"

"I suppose you did."

"Give him back," she said and brusquely reached out for the animal.

Terry placed Elbourne into Flora's hands, and she turned and walked swiftly on her short legs around the front of her trailer. After a few seconds, her door slammed shut, and the lights went out, and Terry was once again standing alone in darkness in the middle of the trailerpark. Tiptoeing across the narrow belt of knee-high weeds and grass that ran between the trailers, he came up close to Flora's bedroom window. "No pets allowed in the trailerpark, honey!" he called out, and he turned and strolled off to get some sleep, so he could leave this place behind him early in the morning.

Either Terry didn't find the opportunity to tell anyone about Flora Pease having "lots" of guinea pigs in her trailer or he simply chose not to mention it, because it wasn't until after he returned to the trailerpark, two months later, in early October, that anyone other than he had a clue to the fact that, indeed, there were living in number 11, besides Flora, a total of seventeen guinea pigs, five of which were male. Of the twelve females, eight were pregnant, and since guinea pigs produce an average of 2.5 piglets per litter, in a matter of days there would be an additional twenty guinea pigs in Flora's trailer, making a total of thirty-seven. About two months after birth, these newcomers would be sexually mature, with a two-month gestation period, so that if half the new-borns were females, and if the other mothers continued to be fertile, along with the four original females, then sometime late in December there would be approximately one hundred fifteen guinea pigs resid-ing in Flora's trailer, of which fifty-four would be male and sixty-one female. These calculations were made by Leon LaRoche, who lived at number 2, the second trailer on your right as you entered the park. Leon worked as a teller for the Catamount Savings and Loan, so calcu-lations of this sort came more or less naturally to him.

"That's a *minimum!*" he told Marcelle. "One hundred fifteen guinea pigs, fifty-four males and sixty-one females. Minimum. And you don't have to be a genius to calculate how many of those filthy little animals will be living in her trailer with her by March. Want me to compute it for you?" he asked, drawing his calculator from his jacket pocket again.

"No, I get the picture." Marcelle scowled. It was a bright, sunny Sun-day morning in early October, and the two were standing in Marcelle's kitchen, Marcelle, in flannel shirt and jeans, taller by half a hand than Leon, who, in sport coat, slacks, shirt and tie, was dressed for mass, which he regularly attended at St. Joseph's Catholic Church in Cata-mount. It was a conversation last night with Captain Knox that had led young Leon to bring his figures to the attention of the manager, for it was he, the Captain, who had made the discovery that there were pre-cisely seventeen guinea pigs in Flora's trailer, rather than merely "lots," as Terry had discovered, and the Captain was alarmed.

It hadn't taken much imagination for the Captain to conclude that something funny was going on in number 11. When you are one of the three or four people who happen to be around the park all day because you are either retired or unemployed, and when you live across the road from a woman who announces her comings and goings with loud singing, which in turn draws your attention to her numerous expeditions to town for more food than one person can possibly consume, and when you notice her carting into her trailer an entire bale of hay and daily emptying buckets of what appears to be animal feces, tiny pellets rapidly becoming a conical heap behind the trailer, then before long you can conclude that the woman is doing something that requires an explanation. And when you are a retired captain of the United States Army, you feel entitled to require that explanation, which is precisely what Captain Dewey Knox did.

He waited by his window until he saw Flora one morning carrying out the daily bucket of droppings, and he strode out his door, crossed the road, and passed her trailer to the back, where he stood silently behind her, hands clasped behind his back, briar pipe stuck between healthy teeth, one dark, bushy eyebrow raised, so that when the woman turned with her empty bucket, she met him face to face.

Switching the bucket from her right hand to her left, she saluted smartly. "Captain," she said. "Good morning, sir."

The Captain casually returned the salute, as befitted his rank. "What was your rank at retirement, Pease?"

"Airman Third Class, sir." She stood not exactly at attention, but not exactly at ease, either. It's difficult when retired military personnel meet each other as civilians: their bodies have enormous resistance to accepting the new modes of acknowledging each other, with the result that they don't quite operate as either military or civilian bodies, but as something uncomfortably neither.

"Airman Third, eh?" The Captain scratched his cleanly shaved chin. "I would have thought after twenty years you'd have risen a little higher."

"No reason to, sir. I was a steward in the officers' clubs, sir, mostly in Lackland, and for a while, because of my name, I guess," she said, smiling broadly, "at Pease down in Portsmouth. Pease Air Force Base," she added.

"I know that. You were happy being a steward, then?"

"Yes, sir. Very happy. That's good duty, sir. People treat you right, especially officers. I once kept house for General Curtis LeMay, a very fine man who could have been vice president of the United States. Once I was watching a quiz show on TV and that question came up, 'Who was George Wallace's running mate?' and I knew the answer. But that was after General LeMay had retired—"

"Yes, yes, I know," the Captain interrupted. "I thought the Air Force used male stewards in the officers' clubs."

"Not always, sir. Some of us like that duty, and some don't, so if you like it, you have an advantage, if you know what I mean, and most of the men don't much like it, especially when it comes to the housekeeping, though the men don't mind being waiters and so forth . . ."

The Captain turned aside to let Flora pass and walked along beside her toward the door of her trailer. At the door they paused, unsure of how to depart from one another, and the Captain glanced back at the pyramid of pellets and straw. "I've been meaning to ask you about that, Pease," he said, pointing with his pipe stem.

"Sir?"

"What is it?"

"Shit, sir."

"I surmised that. I mean, what kind of shit?"

"Guinea pig shit, sir."

"And that implies you are keeping guinea pigs."

Flora smiled tolerantly. "Yes, sir, it does."

"You know the rule about pets in the trailerpark, don't you, Pease?"

"Oh, sure I do."

"Well, then," he said, "what do you call guinea pigs?"

"I don't call them pets, sir. Dogs and cats I call pets. But not guinea pigs. I just call them guinea pigs. They're sort of like plants, sir," she explained patiently. "You don't call plants pets, do you?"

"But guinea pigs are alive, for heaven's sake!"

"There's some would say plants are alive, too, if you don't mind my saying so, sir."

"That's different! These are animals!" The Captain sucked on his cold pipe, drew ash and spit into his mouth, and coughed.

"Animals, vegetables, minerals, all that matters is that they're not like dogs and cats, which are pets, because they can cause trouble for people. They're more like babies. That's why they have rules against pets in places like this, sir," she explained. "But not babies."

"How many guinea pigs have you?" the Captain coldly inquired.

"Seventeen."

"Males and females alike, I suppose."

"Yes, sir," she said, smiling broadly. "Twelve females, and eight of them is pregnant at this very moment. If you take good care of them, they thrive," she said with pride. "Like plants," she added, suddenly serious.

"But they're not plants! They're animals, and they produce . . . waste materials," he said, again pointing with the stem of his pipe at the pile behind the trailer. "And they're dirty."

Flora stepped onto her cinder-block stairs, bringing herself to the same height as the Captain. "Sir, guinea pigs are not dirty. They're cleaner than most people I know, and I know how most people can be. Don't forget, I was a steward for twenty years almost. And as for producing 'waste materials,' even plants produce waste materials. It's called oxygen, sir, which we human people find pretty useful, if you don't mind my saying so, sir. And, as a matter of fact, come next spring you might want me to let you take some of that pile of waste material I got going over to your place." She shoved her chin in the direction of Captain Knox's trailer, where there was a now-dormant ten-foot-by-ten-foot garden plot on the slope facing the lake. Then she turned and abruptly entered her home.

That same evening, the Captain, in number 6, telephoned Leon LaRoche, in number 2, to explain the situation. "I'd take it to her myself," he said, meaning to Marcelle Chagnon, "but she's got it into her head that I'm trying to take over her job of running this place, so every time I ask her to do something, she does the opposite."

LaRoche understood. "I'll put a little data together first," he said. "Guinea pigs are like rats, aren't they?"

"Very much."

LaRoche was eager to please the older man, as he admired and even envied him a little. He had once confessed to Doreen, after her ex-husband had made one of his brutal, unexpected visits and had been hauled away by the Catamount Police Department, that he was open-minded about the idea of marriage, assuming he met the right person and all, but if it turned out that he remained a bachelor all his life, he hoped he would be able to achieve the dignity and force, by the time he reached sixty or sixty-five, of a Captain Dewey Knox, say.

That night LaRoche researched guinea pigs in volume 7 of his complete *Cooper's World Encyclopedia*, which he had obtained, volume by volume, by shopping every week at the A & P, and learned that guinea pigs, or cavies (*Rodentia caviidae*), a descendant of the Peruvian *Cavia aperea porcellus*, which were kept by the Indians for food and even today are sold as a delicacy in many South American marketplaces, have a life expectancy of eight years maximum, an average litter size of 2.5, a gestation period of sixty-three days, and reach reproductive maturity in five to six weeks. He further learned that the female goes through estrus every sixteen days for fifty hours, during which time the female will accept the male continuously, but only between the hours of 5:00 P.M. and 5:00 A.M. He also discovered that 8 percent of all guinea pig pregnancies end in abortion, a variable that made his calculations somewhat complicated but also somewhat more interesting to perform. He learned many other things about guinea pigs that night, but it was the numbers that he decided to present to Marcelle. He thought of telling her that guinea pigs are coprophagists, eaters of feces, a habit necessitated by their innate difficulty in digesting cellulose tissue, creating thereby a need for bacteria as an aid to digestion, but thought better of it. The numbers, he decided, would be sufficient to make her aware of the gravity of the situation.

The next morning, a crisp, early fall day, with the birches near the lake already gone to gold and shimmering in the clear air, LaRoche walked next door to Marcelle's trailer fifteen minutes before his usual departure time for Sunday mass and presented her with the evidence and the mathematical implications of the evidence. Captain Dewey Knox's testimony was unimpeachable, and Leon LaRoche's logic and calculations were irrefutable. Marcelle's course of action, therefore, was inescapable. The guinea pigs would have to go, or Flora Pease would have to go.

"I need this like I need a hole in the head," Marcelle griped, when LaRoche had left her alone with her cup of coffee and cigarette. Winter was coming on fast, and she had to be sure all the trailers were winterized, storm windows repaired and in place, exposed water pipes insulated, heating units all cleaned and operating at maximum efficiency to avoid unnecessary breakdowns and expensive service calls, contracts for fuel oil and snowplowing made with local contractors and approved by the Granite State Realty Development Corporation, leaky roofs patched, picnic tables and waterfront equipment and docks stored away until spring, and on and on—a long list of things to do before the first snowfall in November. Not only that, she had to collect rents, not always a simple job, and sometime this month she had to testify in court in the case involving Doreen's ex-husband, since Marcelle had been the one to control him with her shotgun when Doreen called the police, and Terry Constant had taken off again for parts unknown, so she had no one to help her, no one (since Terry had a deal with his sister whereby his work for Marcelle helped pay her rent) she could afford. And now in the middle of all this she had to cope with a fruitcake who had a passion for raising guinea pigs and didn't seem to realize that they were going to breed her out of her own home right into the street. No sense treating the woman like a child. Rules were rules, and it wasn't up to Flora Pease to say whether her guinea pigs were pets, it was up to management, and Marcelle was management. The pigs would have to go, or else the woman would have to go.

Days went by, however, and, for one reason or another, Marcelle left Flora alone, let her come and go as usual without bothering to stop her and inform her that guinea pigs were pets and pets were not allowed in the trailerpark. Terry came back, evidently from New York City, where he'd gone to hear some music, he said, and she put him to work winterizing the trailers, which, for another week, as she laid out Terry's work and checked after him to be sure he actually did it, allowed Marcelle to continue to ignore the problem. Leon LaRoche thought better of the idea of bringing up the topic again and generally avoided her, although he did get together several times with Captain Knox to discuss Marcelle's obvious unwillingness to deal forthrightly with what would very soon turn into a sanitation problem. Something for the health department, Captain Knox pointed out.

Finally, one morning late in the month, Marcelle went looking for Terry. It was a Saturday, and ordinarily she didn't hire him on Saturdays, because it brought forward speeches about exploitation of the minorities and complaints about not getting paid time and a half, which is what anyone else would have to pay a man to work on Saturdays, unless, of course, that man happens to be a black man in a white world. Marcelle more or less accepted the truth of Terry's argument, but that didn't make it any easier for her to hire him on Saturdays, since she couldn't afford to pay him the six dollars an hour it would have required. On this day, however, she had no choice in the matter—the weather prediction was for a heavy freeze that night and Sunday, and half the trailers had water pipes that would surely burst if Terry didn't spend the day nailing homosote skirting to the undersides.

He wasn't home, and his sister, Carol, didn't know where he'd gone, unless it was next door to visit that woman, Flora Pease, where he seemed to spend a considerable amount of his time lately, Carol observed cautiously. Yes, well, Marcelle didn't know anything about that, nor did she much care where Terry spent his spare time, so long as he stayed out of her hair (Carol said she could certainly understand that), but right now she needed him to help her finish winterizing the trailerpark by nightfall or they would have to spend the next two weeks finding and fixing water pipe leaks. Carol excused herself, as she had to get dressed for work, and Marcelle left in a hurry for Flora's trailer.

At first when she knocked on the door there was no answer. A single crow called from the sedgy swamp out back, a leafless and desolate-looking place, with a skin of ice over the reedy water. The skeletal, low trees and bushes clattered lightly in the breeze, and Marcelle pulled the collar of her denim jacket tightly against her face. The swamp, which was more of a muskeg than an actual swamp, lay at the southern end of about three thousand acres of state forest—most of the land between the northwest shore of Skitter Lake and the Turnpike, Route 28, which ran from the White Mountains, fifty miles to the north, to Boston, ninety miles to the south. The trailerpark had been placed there as a temporary measure (before local zoning restrictions could be voted into action) to hold and initiate development on the only large plot of land available between the town of Catamount and the Skitter Lake State Forest. That was right after the Korean War, when the Granite State Realty Development Corporation, anticipating a coming statewide need for low-income housing, had gone all over the state purchasing large tracts of land that also happened to lie close to cities and towns where low-income people were employed, usually mill towns like Catamount, whose tannery kept between seventy and eighty families marginally poor. As it turned out, the trailerpark was all the Granite State Realty Development Corporation could finance in Catamount, for it soon became apparent that no one in the area would be able to purchase houses, if the Corporation built single-family dwellings, or pay high enough rents to justify the expense of constructing a town house apartment complex. Soon it became clear that the best use the Corporation could make of the land and trailers was as collateral for financing projects elsewhere in the state, in the larger towns and cities where there were people who could afford to buy single-family dwellings or rent duplex apartments. In the meantime, the Corporation maintained the twelve trailers just adequately, paid the relatively low taxes, and came close to breaking even on its investment. Marcelle had been the first tenant in the trailerpark, moving out of a shabby, wood-frame tenement building in town because of her kids, who, she believed, needed more space, and she had immediately become the manager—when the company representative recognized her tough-mindedness, made evident, as soon as there were no more vacancies, by her ability to organize a rent strike to protest the open sewage and contaminated water. They had installed septic tanks and leach fields, and she had continued as resident manager ever since.

Flora's door opened a dark inch, and Marcelle saw a bit of cheek, blond hair, and an eye looking through the inch. She shoved against the door with the flat of one hand, pushing it back against the face behind it, and stepped up the cinder blocks and in, where she discovered the owner of the cheek, blond hair, and eye—Bruce Severance, the college kid who lived in number 3, between LaRoche and Doreen.

"Hold it a minute, man," he said uselessly, rubbing his nose from the blow it had received from the door and stepping back into the room to make space for the large, gray-haired woman. The room, though dark from the venetian blinds being drawn, was filled with at least two other people than Bruce and Marcelle, batches of oddly arranged furniture, and what looked like merchandise counters from a department store.

"Don't you have any lights in here, for Christ's sake?" Marcelle

demanded. She stood inside the room in front of the open door, blinking as she tried to accustom herself to the gloom and see who else was
there. "Why are all the blinds drawn? What the hell are you doing here,
Severance?" Then she smelled it. "Grass! You smoking your goddamned
hippie pot in here with Flora?"

"Hey, man, it's cool."

"Don't 'man' me. And it isn't cool. I don't let nothing illegal go on
here. Something illegal goes on, and I happen to find out about it, I call
in the goddamned cops. Let them sort out the problems. I don't need
problems, I got enough of them already to keep me busy."

"That's right, baby, you don't want no more problems," came a soft
voice from a particularly dark corner.

"Terry! What the hell are you doing here?" She could make out a
lumpy shape next to him on what appeared to be a mattress on the
floor. "Is that Flora over there?" Marcelle asked, her voice suddenly a bit
shaky. Things were changing a little too fast for her to keep track of.
You don't mind the long-haired hippie kid smoking a little grass and
maybe yakking stupidly, the way they do when they're stoned, with
probably the only person in the trailerpark who didn't need to get
stoned herself in order to understand him. You don't really mind that.
A kid like Bruce Severance, you knew he smoked marijuana, but it was
harmless, because he did it for ideological reasons, the same reasons
behind his vegetarian diet and his T'ai Chi exercises and his way of getting a little rest, Transcendental Meditation—he did all these things, not
because they were fun, but because he believed they were good for him,
and good for you, too, if only you were able to come up with the wisdom, self-discipline, and money so that you, too, could smoke marijuana instead of drink beer and rye whiskey, eat organic vegetables
instead of supermarket junk, study and practice exotic, ancient Oriental forms of exercise instead of sitting around at night watching TV.
You, too, could learn how to spend a half hour in the morning and a half

hour in the evening meditating, instead of sleeping to the last minute before getting up and making breakfast for yourself and the kid and rushing off to work and in the evening dragging yourself home just in time to make supper for the kid. And if you could accomplish these things, you would be like Bruce Severance, a much improved person. That was one of Bruce's favorite phrases, "much improved person," and he believed that it ought to be a universal goal and that only ignorance (fostered by the military-industrial complex), sheer laziness, and/or purely malicious ideological opposition (that is to say, a "fascist mentality") kept the people he lived among from participating with him in his several rites. So, unless you happened to share his ideology, you could easily view his several rites as harmless, mainly because you could also trust the good sense of the poor people he lived among, and also their self-discipline and the day-to-day realities they were forced to struggle against. A fool surrounded by sensible poor people remains a fool and is, therefore, seldom troublesome. But when it starts to occur to you that some of the poor people are not sensible—which is what occurred to Marcelle when she peered into the dingy, dim clutter of the trailer and saw Terry sprawled out on a mattress on the floor with Flora Pease clumped next to him, both with marijuana cigarettes dangling from their lips—that's when you start to view the fool as troublesome.

"Listen, Bruce," she said, wagging a finger at the boy, "I don't give a good goddamn about you wearing all them signs about legalizing pot and plastering bumper stickers against nuclear energy and so on all over your trailer, just so long as you take 'em down and clean the place up the way you found it when you leave here. And I don't mind you putting that kind of stuff on your clothes," she said, pointing with her forefinger at the image of a cannabis plant on the chest of Bruce's tie-dyed T-shirt. "Because what you do behind your own closed door and how you decorate your trailer or your van or your clothes is all your own private business. But when you start mixing all this stuff up together like this," she said, waving a hand contemptuously in the direction of Terry and Flora, "well, that's a little different."

"Like what, man?" Bruce asked. "C'mon, will you? And hey, calm down a little, man. No big thing. We're just having us a little morning toke, then I'm headin' out of here. No big thing."

"Yeah, it's cool," Terry said lightly from the corner.

Marcelle shot a scowl in his direction. "I don't want no dope dens in this park. I got my job to look out for. You do anything to make my job risky, I'll come down on you," she said to Terry. "And you, too," she said to Bruce. "And you, too, sister," she said to Flora. "Like a goddamned ton of bricks!"

"No big thing, man," Bruce said, closing the door behind her, wrapping them all in the gray light of the room. Now Marcelle noticed the sharp, acidic smell of animal life, not human animals, but small, furred animals—urine and fecal matter and straw and warm fur. It was the smell of a nest. It was both irritating and at the same time comforting, that smell, because she was both unused to the smell and immediately familiar with it. Then she heard it, a chattering, sometimes clucking noise that rose and ran off to a purr, then rose again like a shudder, diminishing after a few seconds to a quiet, sustained hum. She looked closely at what she had thought at first were counters and saw that they were cages, large waist-high cages, a half dozen of them, placed in no clear order around the shabby furniture of the room, a mattress on the floor, a rocker, a pole lamp, a Formica-topped kitchen table, and, without the easy chair, a hassock. Beyond the living room, she could make out the kitchen area, where she could see two more of the large cages.

"You want a hit, man?" Terry asked, holding his breath as he talked, so that his words came out in high-pitched, breathless clicks. He extended the joint toward her, a relaxed smile on his lips. Next to him, Flora, who lay slumped against his muscular frame like a sack of grain dropped from several feet above, seemed to be dozing.

"That's what *she* looks like, like she got hit."

"Ah, no, Flora's happy. Ain't you, Flora honey?" Terry asked, chucking her under the chin.

She rolled her head and came gradually to attention, saw Marcelle, and grinned. "Hi, Mrs. Chagnon!" she cried, just this side of panic. "Have you ever smoked marijuana?"

"No."

"Well, I have. I love to smoke marijuana!"

"That right?"

"Yep. I can't drink, it makes me crazy, and I start to cry and hit people and everything..."

"Right on," Bruce said.

"... so I drink marijuana, I mean, I smoke marijuana, and then I feel real fine and everything's a joke, just the way it's s'posed to be. The trouble is, I can't get the knack of rolling these little cigarettes, so I need to have someone roll them for me, which is why I asked these boys here to come in and help me out this morning. You want a seat? Why don't you sit down, Mrs. Chagnon? I been meaning to ask you over to visit sometime, but I been so busy, you know?" She waved toward the hassock for Marcelle to sit down.

"You sure you don't want a hit, Marcelle baby?" Terry offered again. "This's some dynamite shit. Flora's got herself some dynamite grass, right, man?" he said to Bruce.

"Oh, wow, man. Dynamite shit. Really dynamite shit."

"No, thanks." Marcelle sat gingerly on the hassock in the middle of the room. Bruce strolled loosely over and dropped himself on the mattress, plucked the joint from Terry's hand, and sucked noisily on it. "So *you're* the one who smokes the marijuana," Marcelle said to Flora. "I mean, these boys didn't..."

"Corrupt her?" Bruce interrupted. "Oh, wow, man, no way! She corrupted us!" he said, laughing and rolling back on the mattress. "Dynamite shit, man! What fucking dynamite grass!"

"He's just being silly," Flora explained. "It makes you a little silly sometimes, Mrs. Chagnon. Nothing to worry about."

"But it's illegal."

"These days, Mrs. Chagnon, what isn't? I mean, honestly."

"Yeah, well, I suppose it's okay, so long as you do it in the privacy of your own home, I mean."

"Really, Mrs. Chagnon! I would never be so foolish as to risk being arrested by the police!" Flora was now sitting pertly, her legs crossed at the ankles, gesturing limp-wristedly as she talked.

Marcelle sighed heavily. "I came over here looking for Terry to help me finish winterizing, because we got a cold snap coming. But I can see he won't be any good today, all doped up like he is . . ."

"Hey, man!" Terry said and sat up straight, his feelings hurt. "You paying time and a half, you got yourself a man. In fact, you pay time and a half, you might getcha self two men," he said, waving toward Bruce. "You need a few bucks, man?"

"No, no, not today. I gotta study for a quiz on Monday, and I haven't even looked at the stuff . . ."

"Right, right," Terry said. "College boys gotta study for quizzes and stuff. But that's okay. More for me, as I always say." His voice was crisp and loud again, which to Marcelle was cheering, for she had been made anxious by his slurred, quiet, speech as if his voice had an edge she couldn't see—if he was going to say things that cut, she wanted to be able to see them coming, and usually, with Terry, she could do that, so she was relieved to hear him yammering away again, snapping and slashing with his sarcasm and bravado.

"Hey, Flora," Terry suddenly said, "now that you got the boss lady here, whyn't you show her all your little furry friends! C'mon, baby, show the boss lady all your furry little friends!" He jumped up and urged Marcelle to follow. "C'mere and take a peek at these beasties. She's got a whole heap of 'em."

"Not so many," Flora said shyly from the mattress.

"I gotta go," Bruce said. "I gotta study," he added and quickly let himself out the door.

Marcelle said not now and told Terry that he could start work by putting the winter skirting around Merle Ring's trailer, which was the most exposed in the park, located as it was out there on the point facing the lake. She reminded him where the sheets of homosote were stored, and he took off, not before, as usual, synchronizing watches with her, so that, as he put it, she wouldn't be able later on to say he didn't work as long as he did. "I've been screwed that way too many times," he reminded her.

Then he was gone, and Marcelle was alone in the trailer with Flora—alone with Flora and her animals, which to Marcelle seemed to number in the hundreds. Their scurrying and rustling in the cages and the chittering noises they made filled the silence, and the smell of the animals thickened the air. Flora moved about the room with a grace and lightness that Marcelle had never seen in her before. She seemed almost to be dancing, and Marcelle wondered if it was the effect of the marijuana, an effect caused by inhaling the smoke-filled air, because, after all, Flora was a heavy, awkward woman who moved slowly and deliberately, not in this floating, delicate, improvisational way, as if she were underwater.

"Flora! You can't keep these animals in here anymore!"

Flora ignored the words and waved for Marcelle to follow her into the kitchen area, where the babies were. "The babies and the new mommies, actually," she went on with obvious pride. As soon as they were weaned, she would place the mommies back with the daddies in the living room. Soon, she pointed out, she was going to have to build some more cages, because these babies would need to be moved to make room for more. She repeated what she had told Captain Knox: "When you take care of them, they thrive. Just like plants."

Marcelle Chagnon said it again, this time almost pleading. "You can't keep these animals in here anymore!"

Flora stopped fluttering. "It's getting colder, winter's coming in. I must keep them inside, or they'll freeze to death. Just like plants."

Marcelle Chagnon crossed her arms over her chest and for the third time informed Flora that she would not be able to keep her guinea pigs insider the trailer.

Finally, the words seemed to have been understood. Flora stood still, hands extended as if for alms, and cried, "What will I do with them, then? I can't put them outside. They're weak little animals, not made for this climate. You want me to *kill* them? Is that what you're telling me? That I have to *kill* my babies?"

"I don't know what the hell you're going to do with them!" Marcelle was angry now. Her head had cleared somewhat, and she knew again that this was Flora's problem, not hers. "It's your problem, not mine. I'm not God. What you do with the damned things is your business . . ."

"But I'm not God, either!" Flora cried. "All I can do is take care of them and try to keep them from dying unnaturally," she explained. That was all anyone could do and, therefore, it was what one had to do. "You do what you can. When you can take care of things, you do it. Because when you take care of things, they thrive." She said it as if were a motto.

"Then I'll have to call the health board and have them take the guinea pigs out. I don't want the scandal, it'll make it hard to rent, and it's hard enough already, but if I can't get you to take care of these animals by getting rid of them, I'll have someone else do it."

"You wouldn't do that!" Flora said, shocked.

"Yes."

"Then you'll have to get rid of me first," she said. "You'll have to toss *me* into the cold first, let me freeze or starve to death first, before I'll let you do that to my babies." She pushed her square chin defiantly out and glared at Marcelle.

"Oh, Jesus, what did I do to deserve this?"

Quickly, as if she knew she had won, Flora started reassuring

Marcelle, telling her not to worry, no one would be bothered by the animals, their shit was almost odorless and would make fertilizer for the several vegetable and flower gardens in the park, and she, Flora, took good care of them and kept their cages clean, so there was no possible health hazard, and except for their relatively quiet chitchat, the animals made no noise that would bother anyone. "People just don't like the *idea* of my having guinea pigs, that's all," she explained. "The *reality* of it don't bother anyone, not even Captain Knox. If people were willing to change their ideas, then everyone could be happy together," she said brightly.

In a final attempt to convince her to give up the guinea pigs, Marcelle tried using some of Leon LaRoche's calculations. She couldn't remember the specific numbers, but she understood the principle behind them. "You realize you're going to have twice as many of these things by spring. And how many have you got now, seventy-five or a hundred, right?"

Flora told her not to worry herself over it, she already had plenty to worry about with the trailerpark and winter coming and all. She should forget all about the guinea pigs, Flora told her with sympathy, and look after the people in the trailerpark, just as she always had. "Life is hard enough, Mrs. Chagnon, without us going around worrying about things we can't do anything about. You let me worry about taking care of the guinea pigs. That's something I can do something about, and you can't, so therefore it's something I *should* do something about, and you shouldn't even try." Her voice had a consoling, almost motherly tone, and for a second Marcelle wanted to thank her.

"All right," Marcelle said brusquely, gathering herself up to her full height. "Just make sure these bastards don't cause any trouble around here, and make sure there isn't any health hazard from . . . whatever, bugs, garbage, I don't know, anything . . . and you can keep them here. Till the weather gets warm, though. Only till spring."

Marcelle moved toward the door, and Flora smiled broadly. She modestly thanked Marcelle, who answered that, if Flora was going to smoke pot here, she'd better do it alone and not with those two big-mouthed jerks, Terry and Bruce. "Those jerks, one or the other of 'em, will get you in trouble. Smoke it alone, if you have to smoke it."

"But I don't know how to make those little cigarettes. My fingers are too fat, and I spill it all over."

"Buy yourself a corncob pipe," Marcelle advised. "Where do you buy the stuff from, anyway?" she suddenly asked, as she opened the door to leave and felt the raw chill from outside.

"Oh, I don't *buy* it!" Flora exclaimed. "It grows wild all over the place, especially along the Old Road where there used to be a farm, between the river and the state forest." There were, as part of the land owned by the Corporation, ten or fifteen acres of old, unused farmland now grown over with brush and weeds. "They used to grow hemp all over this area when I was a little girl," Flora told her. "During the War, for rope. But after the War, when they had to compete with the Fil-ipinos and all, they couldn't make any money at it anymore, so it just kind of went wild."

"That sure is interesting," Marcelle said, shaking her head. "And I don't believe you. But it's okay, I don't need to know who you buy your pot from. I don't *want* to know. I already know too much," she said, and she stepped out and closed the door behind her.

The trailerpark was located three and a half miles northwest of the center of the town of Catamount, a mill town of about five thousand people situated and more or less organized around a dam and millpond first established on the Catamount River some two hundred years ago. The mill had originally been set up as a gristmill, then a lum-ber mill, then a shoe factory, and, in modern times, a tannery that processed hides from New Zealand cattle and sent the leather to Colombia for the manufacture of shoes.

To get to the trailerpark from the town, you drove north out of town past the Hawthorne House (named for the author Nathaniel Hawthorne, who stopped there overnight in May of 1864 with the then ex-president Franklin Pierce on the way to the White Mountains for a holiday; the author died the following night in a rooming house and tavern not unlike the present Hawthorne House, located in Plymouth, New Hampshire, but the legend had grown up in the region that he had died in his bed in Catamount), then along Main Street, past the half dozen or so blocks of local businesses and the large white Victorian houses that once were the residences of the gentry and the owners of the mill or shoe factory or tannery, whichever it happened to be at the time, and that were now the residences and offices of the local physician (for whom Terry's sister, Carol Constant, worked), dentist, lawyer, certified public accountant, and mortician. A ways beyond the town, you came to an intersection. To your right, Mountain Road sloped crookedly toward the hill that gave the town its name, Catamount Mountain, so named by the dark presence in colonial times of mountain lions and the rocky top of the hill. Turning left, however, you drove along Old Road, called that only recently and for the purpose of distinguishing between it and New Road, or the Turnpike, that ran north and south between the White Mountains and Boston. When, three and a half miles from town, you crossed the Catamount River, you turned right at the tipped, flaking sign, GRANITE STATE TRAILERPARK, posted off the road behind a bank of mailboxes standing like sentries at the intersection. Passing through some old, brush-filled fields and a pinewoods that grew on both sides of the narrow, paved lane, you emerged into a clearing, with a sedge-thickened swamp on your left, the Catamount River on your right, and, beyond, a cluster of somewhat battered and aging house trailers. Some were in better repair than others, and some, situated in obviously more attractive locations than others, were alongside the lake, where they exhibited small lawns and flower gardens and other signs of domestic tidiness and care. The lake itself stretched beyond the trailerpark, four and a half miles long and in the approximate shape of a turkey. For that reason, for over a hundred years it had been called Turkey Pond until Ephraim Skitter, who owned the shoe factory, left the town a large endowment for its library and bandstand, and in gratitude the town fathers changed the name of the lake. That, in turn, gave the name Skitter to the large parcel of land that bordered the north and west sides of the lake, becoming by 1950, when the Turnpike was built, the Skitter Lake State Forest. All in all, it was a pretty piece of land and water. If you stood out on the point of land where the trailerpark was situated, with the swamp and pinewoods behind you, you could see, out beyond the deep blue water of the lake, spruce-covered hills that lumped their way northward all the way to the mauve-colored wedges at the horizon, the world-famous White Mountains.

In the trailerpark itself were an even dozen trailers, pastel-colored blocks, some with slightly canted roofs, some with low eaves, but most of them simply rectangular cubes sitting on cinder blocks, with dirt or gravel driveways beside them, usually an old car or pickup truck parked there, with some pathetic, feeble attempt at a lawn or garden evident, but evident mainly in a failure to succeed as such. Some of the trailers, Leon LaRoche's, for example, looked to be in better repair than others, and a few even indicated that the tenants were practically affluent and could afford embellishments such as glassed-in porches, wrought-iron railings at the doorstep, toolsheds, picnic tables and lawn furniture by the shore, and a new or nearly new car in the driveway. The trailer rented to Noni Hubner's mother, Nancy, was one of these—Nancy Hubner was a widow whose late husband had owned the Catamount Insurance Company and was rumored to have had a small interest in the tannery—and Captain Dewey Knox's was another. Captain Knox, like Nancy Hubner, was from an old and relatively well off family in town, as suggested by the name of Knox Island, located out at the northern end of Skitter Lake, where the turkey's eye was. Captain Knox enjoyed recalling childhood summer picnics on "the family island" with his mother and his father, a man who had been one of the successful hemp growers before and during the war, or "War Two," as Captain Knox called it. Prior to that, his father had been a dairy farmer, but after the War decided to sell his land and moved to Maryland, where he died within six months and where Captain Knox's mother, a woman in her eighties, still lived. Captain Knox's return to Catamount after his retirement, he said, had been an act of love. "For this region, this climate, this people, and the principles and values that have prospered here." He talked that way sometimes.

Two of the twelve trailers, numbers 5 and 9, were vacant at this time, number 9 having been vacated only last February as the result of the suicide of a man who had lived in the park as long as Marcelle Chagnon and who had been extremely popular among his neighbors. Tom Smith was his name, and he had raised his son alone in the park, and when his son, at the age of twenty-one or so, had gone away, Tom had withdrawn into himself, and one gray afternoon in February he shot himself in the mouth. He had been a nice man, everyone insisted, though no one had known him very well. In fact, people seemed to think he was a nice man mainly because his son Buddy was so troublesome, always drunk and fighting at the Hawthorne House and, according to the people in the park, guilty of stealing and selling in Boston their TV sets, stereos, radios, jewelry, and so forth. Tom Smith's trailer, number 9, wasn't a particularly fancy one, but it was well located at the end of the land side of the park, right next to Terry and Carol Constant and with a view of the lake. But even so, Marcelle hadn't yet been able to rent it, possibly because of the association with Tom's suicide, but also possibly because of there being black people living next door, which irritated Marcelle whenever it came up, bringing her to announce right to the prospective tenant's face, "Good, I'm glad you don't want to rent that trailer, because we don't want people like you living around here." That would be the end of the tour, and even though Marcelle felt just fine about losing that particular kind of tenant, her attitude certainly did not help her fill number 9, which cost her money. But you had to admire Marcelle Chagnon—she was like an old Indian chief, the way she came forward to protect her people, even if with nothing but her pride, and even at her own expense.

Number 5, the other vacancy, was located between Doreen Tiede, the divorcée who lived with her little girl, and Captain Knox, and was on the lake side of the park, facing the stones and sticks where the lake flowed into the Catamount River and where the Abenaki Indians, back before the whites came north from Massachusetts and drove the Indians away to Canada, had built their fishing weirs. Number 5 was a sleek, sixty-eight-foot-long Marlette with a mansard roof, very fancy, a replacement for the one that burned to the ground a few years ago. A young, newly married couple, Ginnie and Claudel Bing, had moved in, and only three months later, returning home from a weekend down on the Maine coast, found it leveled and still smoldering in the ground, the result of Ginnie's having left the kitchen stove on. They had bought the trailer, financed through the Granite State Realty Development Corporation, and were renting only the lot and services, and their insurance on the place hadn't covered half of what they owed (as newlyweds, they were counting on a long and increasingly rewarding future, so they had purchased a new car and five rooms of new furniture, all on time). Afterwards, they broke up, Claudel lost his job, became something of a drunk, and ended up living alone in a room at the Hawthorne House and working down at the tannery. It was a sad story, and most people in the park knew it and remembered it whenever they passed the shining new trailer that the Corporation moved in to replace the one the Bings had burned down. Because the new trailer was expensive, the rent was high, which made it difficult for Marcelle to find a tenant for it, but the Corporation didn't mind, since it was being paid for anyhow by Claudel Bing's monthly checks. Corporations have a way of making things come out even in the end.

There was in the park one trailer, an old Skyline, that was situated more favorably than any other in the park, number 8, and it was out at the end of the shoreline side, where the road became a cul-de-sac and the shore curved back around toward the swamp and state forest. It was a plain, dark gray trailer, with the grass untended, uncut, growing naturally all around, as if no one lived there. A rowboat lay tilted on one side where someone had drawn it up from the lake behind the trailer, and there was an ice-fishing shanty on a sledge waiting by the shore for winter, but there were no other signs of life around the yard, no automobile, none of the usual junk and tools lying around, no piles of gravel, crushed stone, or loam to indicate projects under way and forsaken for lack of funds, no old and broken toys or tricycles or wagons, nothing out back but a single clothesline stretching from one corner of the trailer back to a pole that looked like a small chokecherry tree cut from the swamp. This was where Merle Ring lived.

Merle Ring was a retired carpenter, retired by virtue of his arthritis, though he could still do a bit of finish work in warm weather, cabinetmaking and such, to supplement his monthly social security check. He lived alone and modestly and in that way managed to get by all right. He had outlived and divorced numerous wives, the number varied from three to seven, depending on who Merle happened to be talking to, and he had fathered on these three to seven women at least a dozen children, most of whom lived within twenty miles of him, but none of them wanted Merle to live with him or her because Merle would only live with him or her if, as he put it, he could be the boss of the house. No grown child would accept a condition like that, naturally, and so Merle lived alone, where he was in fact and indisputably the boss of the house.

Merle, in certain respects, was controversial in the park, though he did have the respect of Marcelle Chagnon, which helped keep the controversy from coming to a head. He was mouthy, much given to offering his opinions on subjects that involved him not at all, which would not have been so bad, however irritating it might have been, had he not been so perverse and contradictory with his opinions. He never seemed to mean what he said, but he said it so cleverly that you felt compelled to take him seriously. Then, later, when you brought his opinion back to him and tried to make him own up to it and take responsibility for its consequences, he would laugh at you for ever having taken him seriously in the first place. He caused no little friction in the lives of many of the people in the park. When one night Doreen Tiede's ex-husband arrived at the park drunk and threatening violence, Merle, just coming in from a long night of hornpout fishing on the lake, stopped and watched with obvious amusement, as if he were watching a movie and not a real man cockeyed drunk and shouting through a locked door at a terrorized woman and child that he was going to kill them both. Buck Tiede caught sight of old Merle standing there at the edge of the road, where the light just reached him, his string of hornpout dangling next to the ground.

"You old fart!" Buck, a large and disheveled man, roared at Merle. "What the hell you lookin' at! G'wan, get the hell outa here!" He made a swiping gesture at Merle, as if chasing a dog.

Then, according to Marcelle, who had come up in the darkness carrying her shotgun, Merle said to the man, "Once you kill her, Buck, it's done. Dead is dead. If I was you and wanted that woman dead as you seem to, I'd just get me some dynamite and blow the place all to hell. Or better yet, just catch her someday coming out of work down to the tannery, and snipe her with a high-powered rifle from a window on the third floor of the Hawthorne House. Then she'd be dead, and you could stop all this hollering and banging on doors and stuff."

Buck stared at him in amazement. "What the hell are you saying?"

"I'm saying you ought to get yourself a window up in the Hawthorne House that looks down the hill to the tannery, and when she comes out the door after work, plug her. Get her in the head, to be sure. Just bang, and that'd be that. You could do your daughter the same way. Dead is dead, and you wouldn't have to go around like this all the time. If you was cute about it, you'd get away with it all right. I could help you arrange it. Give you an alibi, even." He held up the string of whiskered fish. "I'd tell 'em you was out hornpouting with me."

"What are you telling me to do?" Buck took a step away from the door toward Merle. "You're crazy."

"Step aside, Merle, I'll take care of this," Marcelle ordered, shouldering the tiny man out of the way and bringing her shotgun to bear on Buck Tiede. "Doreen!" she called out. "You hear me?"

Buck made a move toward Marcelle.

"Stay right where you are, mister, or I'll splash you all over the wall. You know what a mess a twelve-gauge can make?"

Buck stood still.

A thin, frightened voice came from inside. "Marcelle, I'm all right! Oh God, I'm sorry for all this! I'm so sorry!" Then there was weeping, a woman's and a child's.

"Forget sorry. Just call the cops. I'll hold Mister Bigshot here until they come."

And she did hold him, frozen and silent at the top of the steps, while Doreen called the police, who came in less than five minutes and hauled Buck off to spend the night in jail. Merle, once Marcelle and her shotgun had taken charge of the situation, had strolled on with his fish.

The cops came and went, blue lights flashing, and later Marcelle returned home, her shotgun slung over her thick arm, and when she entered her kitchen, she found Merle sitting at the kitchen table over a can of Budweiser, reading her copy of *People* magazine.

"You're crazy, dealing with Buck Tiede that way," she said angrily.

"What way?"

"Telling him to shoot Doreen from a room in the Hawthorne House! He's just liable to do that, he's a madman when he's drinking!" She cracked open a can of beer and sat down across from the old man.

He closed the magazine. "I never told him to kill her. I just said how he might do it, if he wanted to kill her. The way he was going about it seemed all wrong to me." He smiled and showed his brown teeth through his beard.

"What if he actually went and did it, shot her from the Hawthorne House some afternoon as she came out of work? How would you feel then?"

"Good."

"Good! Why, in the name of Jesus, Mary, and Joseph, would you feel good?"

"Because we'd know who did it."

"But you said you'd give him an alibi!"

"That was just a trick. I wouldn't, and that way he'd be trapped. He'd say he was with me all afternoon fishing, and then I'd come out and say no, he wasn't. I'd fix it so there'd be no way he could prove he was with me, because I'd make sure someone else saw me fishing alone, and that way he'd be trapped, and they'd take him over to Concord and hang him by the neck until dead."

"Why do you fool around like that with people?" she asked, genuinely curious. "I don't understand you, old man."

He got up, smiled, and flipped the copy of *People* magazine across the table. "It's more interesting than reading this kind of stuff," he said and started for the door. "I put an even dozen hornpouts in your freezer."

"Thanks. Thanks a lot," she said absently, and he went out.

Merle heard about Flora's guinea pigs from Nancy Hubner, the widow in number 7, who heard about them from her daughter, Noni, who was having a love affair with the college boy, Bruce Severance. He told her one night in his trailer, after they had made love and were lying in darkness on the huge water bed he'd built, smoking a joint while the stereo played the songs of the humpback whale quietly around them. Noni had been a college girl in Northern California before her nervous breakdown, so she understood and appreciated Bruce more than anyone else in the park could. Most everyone tolerated Bruce goodhumoredly—he believed in knowledge and seemed to be earnest in his quest for it, and what little knowledge he had already acquired, or believed he had acquired, he dispensed liberally to anyone who would listen. He was somberly trying to explain to Noni how yogic birth control worked, and how "basically feminist" it was, because the responsibility was the man's, not the woman's.

"I wondered how come you never asked me if I was protected," she said.

"No need to, man. It's all in the breathing and certain motions with the belly, so the sperm gets separated from the ejaculatory fluid prior to emission. It's really quite simple."

"Amazing."

"Yeah."

"Overpopulation is an incredible problem."

"Yeah. It is."

"I believe that if we could just solve the overpopulation problem, all the rest of the world's problems would be solved, too. Like wars."

"Ecological balance, man. The destruction of the earth."

"The energy crisis. Everything."

"Yeah, man. It's like those guinea pigs of Flora Pease's. Flora, she's got these guinea pigs, hundreds of them by now. And they just keep on making new guinea pigs, doubling their numbers every couple of months. It's incredible, man."

Noni rolled over on her belly and stretched out her legs and wiggled her toes. "Do you have the record of Dylan's, the one where he sings all those country-and-western songs, way before anyone even *heard* of country and western? What's it called?"

"*Nashville Skyline?*"

"Yeah, that's it. Isn't it incredible, how he was singing country and western way before anyone even heard of it?"

"Yeah, he's really incredible, Dylan. Anyhow . . ."

"Do you have it, the record?" she interrupted.

"No, man. Listen, I was telling you something."

"Sorry."

"That's okay, man. Anyhow, Flora's guinea pigs, it's like they're a *metaphor.* I mean, it's like Flora is some kind of god, and the first two guinea pigs, the ones she bought from the five-and-dime in town, were Adam and Eve, and that trailer of hers is the world. Be fruitful and multiply, Flora told them, and, fine, they go out and do what they're programmed to do, and pretty soon they're like taking over the world, which is the trailer, so that Flora, who's like God, can't take care of them anymore. No matter how hard she works, they eat too much, they shit too much, they take up too much room. So what happens?"

Silence.

"What happens?" Bruce repeated.

"A flood, maybe?"

"No, man, it's not that literal, it's a metaphor. What happens is, Flora moves out. She leaves the trailer to the guinea pigs. Twilight of the gods, man. God is dead!"

"That's really incredible."

"Yeah," Bruce said, drifting into still deeper pools of thought.

After a few moments, Noni got up from the bed and drew on her clothes. "I better get home, my mother'll kill me. She thinks I'm at the movies with you."

"Naw, man, she knows where you are. All she's got to do is walk three doors down and see my van's still here. C'mon, she *knows* we're making it together. She's not that out of it."

Noni shrugged. "She believes what she wants to believe. Sometimes I think she still doesn't believe Daddy's dead, and it's been over four years now. There's no point in forcing things on people. You know what I mean?"

Bruce understood, but he didn't agree. People needed to face reality, it was good for them and good for humanity as a whole, he felt. He was about to tell her why it was good for them, but Noni was already dressed and heading for the door, so he said good night instead and waved from the bed as she slipped out the door.

When later that same evening she told her mother that Flora Pease was raising hundreds of guinea pigs in her trailer, it was not so much because Noni was interested in Flora or the guinea pigs, as because her mother, Nancy, was quizzing her about the movie she was supposed to have seen with Bruce.

"That's not true," the woman said.

"What's not?" Noni switched on the TV set and sat down cross-legged on the floor.

"About the guinea pigs. Where'd you hear such a thing?"

"Bruce. Do you think I could study yoga somewhere around here?"

"Of course not. Don't be silly." Nancy lit a cigarette and sat down on the sofa, where she'd been reading this month's Book-of-the-Month Club selection, a novel that gently satirized the morals and mores of

Westchester County's smart set. "Bruce. I don't know about that boy. How can he be a college student when the nearest college is the state university in Durham, which is over forty miles from here?"

"I don't know." Noni was sliding into the plot intricacies of a situation comedy about two young women who worked on an assembly line in Milwaukee and made comically stupid errors of judgment and perception. "It's a correspondence school or something, in Vermont. He has to go there and see his teachers for a couple of weeks twice a year or something. It's the new thing in education."

Nancy didn't know how it could be much of an education, and it certainly didn't explain why Bruce lived where he did and not at his college or even at his parents' home, as Noni did.

"I don't know," Noni said.

"Don't you ever ask, for heaven's sake?"

"No."

That was their conversation for the night. At eleven, Nancy yawned and went to bed in her room at the far end of the trailer, the rooms of which were carpeted and furnished lavishly and resembled the rooms of a fine apartment. Around midnight, Noni rolled a joint and went to her room, next to her mother's, and smoked it, and fell asleep with her light on. She bought her marijuana from Bruce. So did Terry. Also Leon LaRoche, who had never tried smoking grass before, but certainly did not reveal that to Bruce, who knew it anyhow and charged him twice the going rate. Doreen Tiede bought grass from Bruce, too. Not often, however; about once every two or three months. She liked to smoke it in her trailer with men she went out with and came home with, so she called herself a social smoker, but Bruce knew what that meant. Over the years, Bruce had bought his grass from several people, most recently from a Jamaican named Keppie who lived in the West Roxbury area of Boston, but who did business from a motel room in Revere. Next year, Bruce had decided, he would harvest the hemp crop Flora Pease had discovered, and he could sell the grass back, running it the other direction, to Keppie and his Boston friends. He figured there must be five hundred pounds of the stuff growing wild out there, just waiting for a smart guy like him to cut, dry, chop, and pack. He might have to cut Terry Constant in, but that would be fine, because in this business you often needed a partner who happened to be black.

The next morning, on her way to town to have her hair cut and curled, Nancy Hubner picked up Merle Ring. Merle was walking out from the trailerpark and had almost reached Old Road, when he heard the high-pitched whirr of Nancy's powerful Japanese sedan and without turning around stepped off the road into the light, leafless brush. There had been an early snow in late October that winter, and then no snow throughout November and well into December, which had made it an excellent year for ice fishing. After the first October snow, there was a brief melt and then a cold snap that lasted for five weeks now, so that the ice had thickened daily, swiftly becoming iron-hard and black and smooth. All over the lake, fishing shanties had appeared, and all day and long into the night men and sometimes women sat inside the shanties, keeping warm from tiny kerosene or coal-burning heaters, sipping from bottles of whiskey, watching their lines, and yakking slowly to friends or meditating alone and outside of time and space, until the flag went up and the line got yanked and the fisherman would come crashing back into that reality from the other. The ice had hardened sufficiently to bear even the weight of motor vehicles, and now and then you could look out from the shore and see a car or pickup truck creeping across the slick ice and stopping at one of the shanties, bringing society and a fresh six-pack or pint of rye. No one visited Merle's shanty, though he certainly had plenty of friends of various ages and sexes. He had made it known that, when he went ice fishing, it was as if he were going into religious withdrawal and meditation, a journey into the wilderness, as it were, and if you were foolish or ignorant enough to visit him out there on the ice in his tiny, windowless shack with the stovepipe chimney sticking up and puffing smoke, you would be greeted by a man who seemed determined to be left alone. He would be cold, detached, abstracted, unable or unwilling to connect to the person standing self-consciously before him, and after a few moments you would leave, your good-bye hanging unanswered in the air, and Merle would take a sip from his fifth of Canadian Club and drift back into his trance.

Nancy braked her car to a quick stop next to Merle, lowered the window and asked if he wanted a lift into town. She liked the old man, or perhaps it would be more accurate to say that the old man intrigued her, as if she believed he knew something about the world they lived in together that she did not know and that would profit her greatly if she did know. So she courted him, fussed over him, seemed to be looking after his comfort and welfare, behaving the way, as she once said to Noni, his daughters ought to behave.

Merle apparently knew all this, and more, though you could never be sure with him. He got inside the low, sleek car, slammed the door shut, and surrounded himself with the smell of leather and the pressure of fan-driven heat. "Morning, Mrs. Hubner. A fine, crispy morning, isn't it?"

She agreed and asked him where she could drop him. A fast, urgent driver, she was already flying past the intersection of Old Road and Main Street and was approaching the center of town. She drove so as to endanger, but didn't seem to know it. It was as if her relation to the physical act of driving was the same as her relation to poverty—abstract, wholly theoretical, and sentimental—which, from Merle's perspective, made her as dangerous a driver as she was a citizen.

Merle and Nancy exchanged brief remarks, mostly solicitous on her part as to the present condition of Merle's arthritis and mostly whining on his part as to the same thing. Merle knew that by whining he could put Nancy at her ease, and in encounters as brief as this he, like most people, enjoyed being able to put people at their ease. It made things more interesting for him later on. Stopping in front of Hayward's Hardware and Sporting Goods Store, where Merle was headed for traps, she suddenly asked him a direct question (since she was now sufficiently at her ease to trust that he would answer directly and honestly and in that way might be brought to reveal more than he wished to): "Tell me, Mr. Ring, is it true that that woman, Flora in number eleven, you know the one, is raising hundreds of guinea pigs in her trailer?"

"Yes," he said, lying, for he had heard nothing of it. "Though I'm not sure of the numbers. It's hard to count 'em after a certain point, sixty, say."

"Don't you think that's a little . . . disgusting? I mean, the *filth*! I think the woman ought to be put away, don't you?" she asked, still trying to get information.

"What would you do with all those guinea pigs then?"

"Let the SPCA take them, I suppose. They know how to handle these things, when things like this get out of hand. Imagine, all those tiny animals crowded into a trailer, and remember, number eleven is not one of the larger trailers in the park, you know."

"I guess you're right, the SPCA could kill 'em for us, once we'd got Flora locked up someplace. The whole thing would probably drive her right over the edge, anyhow, taking away her animals and killing 'em like that, tossing 'em into that incinerator they got. That'd push ol' Flora right over the edge. She'd be booby-hatch material for sure then, whether she is now or not."

"You're making fun of me, Mr. Ring. Aren't you?"

"No, no, no, I'm not making fun of you, Mrs. Hubner," he said, opening the door and stepping out, not without difficulty, because of the shape of the car and his stiff back. "I'll check into it for you, ma'am. Get the facts of the situation, so to speak. Because you're probably right. I mean, something will have to be done, eventually, by someone. Because those kinds of animals, rodents and such, they breed fast, and before you know it, one hundred is two hundred, two hundred is four, four is eight, and so on."

"Thank you so much, Mr. Ring," she said with clear relief. He was such a nice man. She wondered if there was some way she could make his life a little easier. At his age, to be alone like that, it was simply awful.

Merle closed the door, waved, and walked into Hayward's and Nancy drove on to Ginnie's Beauty Nook on Green Street across from Knight's Paint Store, where Ginnie and her husband, Claudel, had rented the upstairs apartment after their trailer burned down. That was over three years ago, or maybe four. Nancy couldn't remember, until it came back to her that it had happened the summer Noni turned fifteen and started having migraines and saying she hated her, and then Nancy remembered that was the summer her husband died. So it must be over four years now since Ginnie and Claudel moved into town and rented that apartment over Knight's Paint Store. Isn't it amazing how time flies when you're not paying attention, she reflected.

A week later, Merle woke late, after having spent most of the night out on the lake in his ice house, and because the sun was shining, casting a raw light that somehow pleased him, he decided to visit Flora Pease and determine if all this fuss over her guinea pigs was justified. Since talking with Nancy Hubner, he had spoken only to Marcelle Chagnon about the guinea pigs, and her response had been to look heavenward, as if for help or possibly mere solace, and to say, "Just don't talk to me about that crazy woman, Merle, don't start in about her. As long as she doesn't cause any troubles for me, I won't cause any troubles for her. But if *you* start in on this, there'll be troubles. For me. And that means for her, too, remember that."

"Makes sense," Merle said, and for several days he went strictly about his business—ice fishing, eating, cleaning, reading the Manchester *Union Leader*, puttering with his tools and equipment—slow, solitary activities that he seemed to savor. He was the kind of person who, by the slowness of his pace and the hard quality of his attention, appeared to take sensual pleasure from the most ordinary activity. He was a small, lightly framed man and wore a short, white beard, which he kept neatly trimmed. His clothing was simple and functional, flannel shirts, khaki pants, steel-toed work shoes—the same style of clothing he had worn since his youth, when he first became a carpenter's apprentice and determined what sort of clothing was appropriate for that kind of life. His teeth were brown, stained from a lifetime of smoking a cob pipe, and his weathered skin was still taut, indicating that he had always been a small, trim man. There was something effeminate about him that, at least in old age, made him physically attractive, especially to women, but to men as well. Generally, his manner with people was odd and somewhat disconcerting, for he was both involved with their lives and not involved, both serious and not serious, both present and absent. For example, a compliment from Merle somehow had the effect of reminding the recipient of his or her vanity, while an uninvited criticism came out sounding like praise for having possessed qualities that got you singled out in the first place.

Though seasonably cold (fifteen degrees below freezing), the day was pleasant and dry, the light falling on the rock ground directly, so that the edges of objects took on an unusual sharpness and clarity. Merle knocked briskly on Flora's door, and after a moment, she swung it open. She was wrapped in a wool bathrobe that must have been several decades old and belonged originally to a very large man, for it flowed around her blocky body like a carpet. Her short hair stuck out in a corolla of dark red spikes, and her eyes were red-rimmed and watery-looking, as, grumpily, she asked Merle what he wanted from her.

"A look," he chirped, smiling.

"A look. At what?"

"At your animals. The guinea pigs I been hearing about."

"You heard about them? What did you hear?" She stood before the door, obstructing his view into the darkened room beyond. An odor of fur and straw, however, seeped past and merged warmly with the cold, almost sterile air outdoors.

Merle sniffed with interest at the odor, apparently relishing it. "Heard you got a passel of 'em. I never seen one of these guinea pigs before and was wondering what in hell they look like. Pigs?"

"No. More like fat, furry chipmunks," Flora said, easing away from the door. She still had not smiled, however, and was not ready to invite Merle inside. "Mrs. Chagnon send you over here?" she demanded. "That woman is putting me on the spot. I can't have any friends anymore to visit or to talk to me here, or else I'll get into trouble with that woman."

"No, Marcelle didn't send me, she didn't even want to talk about your guinea pigs with me. She just said as long as they don't cause her any trouble, she won't cause you any trouble."

"That's what I mean," Flora said, defiantly crossing her short, thick arms over her chest. "People come around here and see my guinea pigs, and then I get into trouble. If they don't come around here and don't see nothing, then it's like the guinea pigs, for them, don't exist. That kid, Terry, the black one, he started it, when all I was doing was trying to be friendly, and then he went and dragged the other kid, the white one, in here, and they got to smoking my hemp, and then pretty soon here comes Mrs. Chagnon, and I get in trouble. All I want is to be left alone," she said with great clarity, as if she said it to herself many times a day.

Merle nodded sympathetically. "I understand how you feel. It's like when I won the lottery, that was back a ways before you come here, and everybody thought I had a whole heap more money than I had, so everyone was after me for some."

That interested Flora. She had never met anyone who had won the lottery. In fact, she was starting to believe that it was all faked, that no one ever won, that those people jumping up and down hysterically in the TV ads were just actors. Now, because of Merle's having won, her faith in the basic goodness of the world was magically restored. "This means they probably went to the moon, too!" she said with clear relief.

"Who?"

"The astronauts."

"You didn't believe that, the rocket to the moon? I thought you used to be in the Air Force."

"That's why I had so much trouble believing it," she said and stood aside and waved him in.

Inside, when his eyes had grown accustomed to the dim light of the room, this is what Merle saw: large, waist-high, wood-framed, chicken-wire pens that were divided into cubicles about two feet square. The pens were placed throughout the room in no apparent order or pattern, which gave the room, despite the absence of furniture, the effect of being incredibly cluttered, as if someone were either just moving in or all packed to move out. As far as Merle could see, the rooms adjacent to this one were similarly jammed with pens, and he surmised that the rooms he couldn't see, the bedroom at the back and the bathroom, were also filled with pens like these. In each cubicle there was a pair of grown or nearly grown guinea pigs or else one grown (presumably female) pig and a litter of two or three piglets. Merle could see and hear the animals in the nearby cubicles scurrying nervously in their cages, but the animals closest to him were crouched and still, their large round eyes rolling frantically and their noses twitching as, somehow, Merle's own odor penetrated the heavy odor of the room.

Flora reached down and plucked a black and white spotted pig from the cage it shared with a tan, long-haired mate. Cradling it in her arm and stroking its nose with her free hand, she walked cooing and clucking over to Merle and showed him the animal. "This here's Ferdinand," she said. "After the bull."

"Ah. May I?" he said, reaching out to take Ferdinand.

Merle held the animal as Flora had and studied its trembling, limp body. It seemed to offer no defense and showed no response except stark terror. When Merle placed it back into its cubicle, it remained exactly where he had placed it, as if waiting for a sudden, wholly deserved execution.

"How come you like these animals, Flora?"

"Don't *you* like them?" she bristled.

"I don't feel one way or the other about them. I was wondering about you."

She was silent for a moment and moved nervously around the cages, checking into the cubicles as she moved. "Well, somebody's got to take care of them. Especially in this climate. They're really not built for the ice and snow."

"So you don't do it because you like them?"

"No. I mean, I like looking at them and all, the colors are pretty, and their little faces are cute and all. But I'm just taking care of them so they won't die, that's all."

There was a silence, and Merle said, "I hate to ask it, but how come you let them breed together? You know where that'll lead?"

"Do you know where it'll lead if I *don't* let them breed together?" she asked, facing him with her hands fisted on her hips.

"Yup."

"Where?"

"They'll die out."

"Right. That answer your question?"

"Yup."

Merle stayed with her for the next half hour, as she showed him her elaborate watering system—a series of interconnected hoses that ran from the cold water spigot in the kitchen sink around and through all the cages, ending back in the bathroom sink—and her cleverly designed system of trays beneath the cages for removing from the cages the feces and spilled food, and her gravity-fed system of grain troughs, so that all she had to do was dump a quart a day into each cage and the small trough in each individual cubicle would be automatically filled. She designed and built the cages herself, she explained, and, because she was no carpenter, they weren't very fancy or pretty to look at. But the basic idea was a good one, she insisted, so that, despite her lack of skill, the system worked, and consequently every one of her animals was clean, well-fed, and watered at all times. "You can't ask for much more in this life, can you?" she said proudly as she led Merle to the door.

He guessed no, you couldn't. "But I still think you're headed for troubles," he told her, and he opened the door to leave.

"What do you mean? What's going on?" Suddenly she was suspicious of him and frightened of Marcelle Chagnon again, with her suspicion of the one and fear of the other swiftly merging and becoming anger at everyone.

"No, no, no. Not troubles with Marcelle or any of the rest of the folks in the park. Just with the breeding and all. In time, there will be too many of them. They breed new ones faster than the old ones die off. It's simple. There will come a day when you won't have any more room left in there. What will you do then?"

"Move out."

"What about the animals?"

"I'll take care of them. They can have the whole trailer. They'll have lots of room if I move out."

"But you don't understand," Merle said calmly. "It goes on forever. It's numbers, and it doesn't change or level off or get better. It gets worse and worse, faster and faster."

"*You* don't understand," she said to him. "Everything depends on how you look at it. And what looks worse and worse to you might look better and better to me."

Merle smiled, and his blue eyes gleamed. He stepped down to the ground and waved pleasantly at the grim woman. "You are right, Flora Pease. Absolutely right. And I thank you for straightening me out this fine morning!" he exclaimed, and, whistling softly, he walked off for Marcelle's trailer, where he would sit down at her table and drink a cup of coffee with her and recommend to her that, in the matter of Flora and her guinea pigs, the best policy was no policy, because Flora was more than capable of handling any problem that the proliferation of the guinea pigs might create.

Marcelle was not happy with Merle's advice. She was a woman of action and it pained her to sit still and let things happen. But, she told Merle, she had no choice in this matter of the guinea pigs. If she tried to evict Flora and the animals, there would be a ruckus and possibly a scandal; if she brought in the health department, there was bound to be a scandal; if she evicted Flora and not the guinea pigs, then she'd have the problem of disposing of the damn things herself. "It's just gone too far," she said, scowling.

"But everything's fine right now, at this very moment, isn't it?" Merle asked, stirring his coffee.

"I suppose you could say that."

"Then it hasn't gone too far. It's gone just far enough."

At this stage, just before Christmas, everyone had an opinion as to what ought to be done with regard to the question of the guinea pigs.

FLORA PEASE: Keep the animals warm, well-fed, clean, and breeding. Naturally, as their numbers increase, their universe will expand. (Flora didn't express herself that way, for she would have been speaking to people who would have been confused by language like that coming from her. She said it this way: "When you take

care of things, they thrive. Animals, vegetables, minerals, same
with all of them. And that makes you a better person, since it's the
taking care that makes *people* thrive. Feeling good is good, and feeling better is better. No two ways about it. All people ever argue
about anyhow is how to go about feeling good and then better.")

DOREEN TIEDE: Evict Flora (she could always rent a room at the
Hawthorne House, Claudel Bing had and, God knows, he was
barely able to tie his own shoes for a while, he was so drunk, though
of course he's much better now and may actually move out of the
Hawthorne House one of these days, and in fact the man was starting to look like his old self again, which was not half bad), and then
call in the SPCA to find homes for the animals (the ones that
couldn't be placed in foster homes would have to be destroyed—
but, really, all they are is animals, rodents, rats, almost).

TERRY CONSTANT: Sneak into her trailer one day when she's in town
buying grain, and, one by one, liberate the animals. Maybe you
ought to wait till spring and then just set them free to live in the
swamp and the piney woods and fields between Old Road and the
trailerpark. By the time winter came rolling around again, they'd
have figured out how to tunnel into the ground and hibernate like
the rest of the warm-blooded animals. The ones that didn't learn
how to survive, well, too bad for them. Survival of the fittest.

BRUCE SEVERANCE: The profit motive, man. That's what needs to be
invoked here. Explain to Flora that laboratories pay well for clean,
well-fed guinea pigs, especially those bred and housed under such
controlled conditions as Flora has established. Explain this, pointing out how it'll enable her to breed guinea pigs for both fun and
profit for an indefinite period of time, for as long as she wants,
when you get right down to it. Show her that this is not only
socially useful but it'll provide her with enough money to take
even better care of her animals than now.

NONI HUBNER: Bruce's idea is a good one, and so is Leon LaRoche's, and Captain Knox has a good idea too. Maybe we ought to try one first, Captain Knox's, say, since he's the oldest and has the most experience of the world, and if that doesn't work, we could try Leon LaRoche's, and then if that fails, we can try Bruce's. That would be the democratic way.

LEON LAROCHE: Captain Knox's idea, of course, is the logical one, but it runs certain risks and depends on his being able to keep Flora, by the sheer force of his will, from reacting hysterically or somehow "causing a scene" that would embarrass the trailerpark and we who live in it. If the *Suncook Valley Sun* learned that we had this sort of thing going on here, that we had a village eccentric living here among us at the trailerpark, we would all suffer deep embarrassment. I agree, therefore, with Doreen Tiede's plan. But my admiration, of course, is for Captain Knox's plan.

CAROL CONSTANT: I don't care what you do with the damned things, just do something. The world's got enough problems, real problems, without people going out and inventing new ones. The main thing is to keep the poor woman happy, and if having a lot of little rodents around is what makes her happy, and they aren't bothering anyone else yet, then, for God's sake, leave her alone. She'll end up taking care of them herself, getting rid of them or whatever, if and when they start to bother her—and they'll bother her a lot sooner than they bother us, once we stop thinking about them all the time. Her ideas will change as soon as the guinea pigs get to the point where they're causing more trouble than they're giving pleasure. Everybody's that way, and Flora Pease is no different. You have to trust the fact that we're all human beings.

NANCY HUBNER: Obviously, the guinea pigs are Flora's substitutes for a family and friends. She's trying to tell us something, and we're not listening. If we, and I mean all of us, associated more with Flora on a social level, if we befriended her, then her need for these filthy animals would diminish and probably disappear. It would be something that in the future we could all laugh about, Flora laughing right along with us. We should drop by for coffee, invite her over for drinks, offer to help redecorate her trailer, and so on. We should be more charitable. It's as simple as that. Christian charity. I know it won't be easy—Flora's not exactly socially "flexible," if you know what I mean, but we are, at least most of us are, and therefore it's *our* responsibility to initiate contact, not hers, poor thing.

CAPTAIN DEWEY KNOX: It's her choice, no one else's. Either she goes, or the animals go. She decides which it's to be, we don't. If she decides to go, fine, she can take the animals with her or leave them behind, in which case I'm sure some more or less humane way can be found to dispose of them. If she stays, also fine, but she stays without the animals. Those are the rules—no pets. They're the same rules for all of us, no exceptions. All one has to do is apply the rules, and that forces onto the woman a decision that, however painful it may be for her, she must make. No one can make that decision for her.

MARCELLE CHAGNON: If she'd stop the damned things from breeding, the whole problem would be solved. At least it would not bother me anymore, which is important. The only way to get her to stop breeding them, without bringing the Corporation or the health board or the SPCA or any other outsiders into it, is to go in there and separate the males from the females ourselves, and when she comes back from town, say to her, Okay, Flora, this is a compromise. Sometimes people don't understand what a compromise is until you force it on them. It's either that or we sit around waiting for this thing to explode, and then it'll be too late to compromise, because the outsiders will be in charge.

MERLE RING: Let Flora continue to keep the animals warm, well-fed, clean, and breeding. Naturally, as their numbers increase, their universe will expand. And as a result, all the people in the trailerpark, insofar as they observe this phenomenon, will find their universe expanding also. (It's understood that Merle did not express himself this way, for he would have been expressing himself to people who would have been offended by language like that. Here's how he put it: "It'll be interesting to see what the woman does with her problem—if it ever actually becomes a problem. And if it never becomes a problem, that should be interesting, too.")

Flora's life up to now ought to have prepared her for what eventually happened with the guinea pigs. It had been a hard life, beginning with the death of her mother when Flora was barely a year old. Flora's father was what in these parts is often called a rough carpenter, meaning that he could use a hammer and saw well enough to work as a helper to a bona fide carpenter. Usually he was the one who nailed together the plywood forms for making cellar walls and then, when the cement had set, tore the forms apart. During the fall and winter months, when it was too cold for cement to pour, the bona fide carpenters moved to interior work, which required a certain skill and a basic fluency with numbers, and Flora's father was always among the first in the fall unemployment line.

There were three older children, older by one, two, and three years, and after the mother died, the children more or less took care of themselves. They lived out beyond Shackford Corners in a dilapidated house that appeared to be falling into its own cellar hole, an unpainted, leaky, abandoned house heated in winter by a kerosene stove, with no running water and only rudimentary wiring. The father's way of raising his children was to stay drunk when he was not working, to beat them if they cried or intruded on his particular misery, and, when he

was working, to leave them to their own devices, which were not especially healthful devices. When Flora's older brother was six, he set off
one of the blasting caps that he found near the lumber camp a half mile
behind the house in the woods and blew one of his arms off and almost
died. When Flora's only sister was eleven, she was raped by an uncle visiting from Saskatchewan and after that could only gaze blankly past
your head when you tried to talk to her or get her to talk to you. Flora's
older brother, when he was fourteen and she thirteen, sickened and
died of what was determined by the local health authorities to have
been malnutrition, at which point the remaining three children were
taken away from the father and placed into the care of the state, which
meant, at that time, the New Hampshire State Hospital over in Concord, where they had a wing for juveniles who could not be placed in
foster homes or who were drug addicts or had committed crimes of
violence but were too young to be tried as adults. Four years later, Flora
was allowed to leave the mental hospital (for that is what it was) on the
condition that she join the United States Air Force, where she spent
the next twenty years working in the main as a maid, or steward, in officers' clubs and quarters at various bases around the country. She was
not badly treated by the Air Force itself, but numerous individual ser-
vicemen, enlisted men as well as officers, treated her unspeakably.

Despite her life, Flora remained good-naturedly ambitious for her
spirit. She believed in self-improvement, believed that it was possible,
and that not to seek it was reprehensible, was, in fact, a sin. And sinners
she viewed the way most people view the stupid or the poor—as if their
stupidity or poverty were their own fault, the direct result of sheer laziness and a calculated desire to exploit the rest of humankind, who, of
course, are intelligent or well-off as a direct result of their willingness
to work and not ask for help from others. This might not seem a particularly enlightened way to view sinners, and it certainly was not a
Christian way to view sinners, but it did preserve a kind of chastity for

Flora. It also, of course, made it difficult for her to learn much, in moral terms, from the behavior of others. There was probably a wisdom in that, however, a trade-off that made it possible for her to survive into something like middle age without falling into madness and despair.

Within a week of having moved into the trailerpark, Flora had purchased her first pair of guinea pigs. She went into the Catamount five-and-dime looking for goldfish, but when she saw the pair of scrawny, matted animals in their tiny, filthy cages at the back of the store, she forgot the goldfish, which by comparison looked relatively healthy, despite the cloudiness of the water in their tank. She built her cages herself, mostly from cast-off boards and chicken wire she found at the town dump and carried home. The skills required were not great, were, in fact, about the same as had been required of her father in the construction of cement forms. At the dump she also found pieces of garden hose she needed to make her watering system and the old gutters she hooked up as grain troughs.

Day and night, she worked for her guinea pigs, walking to town and hauling back fifty-pound bags of grain, dragging back from the dump more old boards, sheets of tin, gutters, and so on. As the guinea pigs multiplied and more cages became necessary, Flora soon found herself working long hours into the night alone in her trailer, feeding, watering, and cleaning the animals, while out behind the trailer the pyramid of mixed straw, feces, urine, and grain gradually rose to waist height, then to shoulder height, finally reaching to head height, when she had to start a second pyramid, and then, a few months later, a third. And as the space requirements of the guinea pigs increased, her own living space decreased, until finally she was sleeping on a cot in a corner of the back bedroom, eating standing up at the kitchen sink, stashing her clothing and personal belongings under her cot, so that all the remaining space could be devoted to the care, housing, and feeding of the guinea pigs.

By the start of her third summer at the trailerpark, she had begun to lose weight noticeably, and her usually pinkish skin had taken on a gray pallor. Never particularly fastidious anyhow, her personal hygiene now could be said not to exist at all, and the odor she bore with her was the same odor given off by the guinea pigs, so that, in time, to call Flora Pease the Guinea Pig Lady was not to misrepresent her. Her eyes grew dull, as if the light behind them were slowly going out, and her hair was tangled and stiff with dirt, and her clothing seemed increasingly to be hidden behind stains, smears, spills, drips, and dust.

"Here comes the Guinea Pig Lady!" You'd hear the call from the loafers outside McCallister's News & Variety leaning against the glass front, and a tall, angular teenager with shoulder-length hair and acne, wearing torn jeans and a Mothers of Invention T-shirt, would stick his long head inside and call your name, "C'mere, take a look at this, man!"

You'd be picking up your paper, maybe, or because McCallister's was the only place that sold it, the racing form with yesterday's Rockingham results and today's odds. The kid might irritate you slightly—his gawky, witless pleasure, his slightly pornographic acne, the affectation of his T-shirt and long hair—but still, your curiosity up, you'd pay for your paper and stroll to the door to see what had got the kid so excited.

In a low, conspiratorial voice, the kid would say, "The Guinea Pig Lady."

She'd be on the other side of the street, shuffling rapidly along the sidewalk in the direction of Merrimack Farmers' Exchange, wearing her blue, U.S. Air Force, wool, ankle-length coat, even though this was May and an unusually warm day even for May, and her boot lacings were undone and trailing behind her, her arms chopping away at the air as if she were a boxer working out with the heavy bag, and she was singing in a voice moderately loud, loud enough to be heard easily across the street, "My Boy Bill" from Carousel.

"Hey, honey!" the kid wailed, and the Guinea Pig Lady, though she

ignored his call, stopped singing at once. "Hey, honey, how about a little nookie, sweets!" The Guinea Pig Lady sped up a bit, her arms churning faster against the air. "Got something for ya, honey! Got me a lick-
ing stick, sweet lips!"

If you already knew who the woman was, Flora Pease, of the Granite State Trailerpark out at Skitter Lake, and knew about the guinea pigs
and, thereby, could guess why she was headed for the grain store, you'd
ease past the kid and away. But if you didn't know who she was, you
might ask the kid, and he'd say, "The Guinea Pig Lady, man. She lives
with these hundreds of guinea pigs in the trailerpark out at Skitter
Lake. Just her and all these animals. Everybody in town knows about it,
but she won't let anyone inside her trailer to see 'em, man. She's got
these huge piles of shit out behind her trailer, and she comes into town
all the time to buy feed for 'em. She's a fuckin' freak, man! A freak! And
nobody in town can do anything about 'em, the guinea pigs, I mean,
because so far nobody out at the trailerpark will make a formal complaint about 'em. You can bet your ass if I lived out there I'd sure as shit
make a complaint. I'd burn the fucking trailer to the ground, man. I
mean, that's disgusting, all them animals. Somebody ought to go out
there some night and pull her outa there and burn the place down. It's a
health hazard, man! You can get a disease from them things!"

One September morning, after about a week of not having seen Flora
leave her trailer once, even to empty the trays of feces out back, Marcelle decided to make sure the woman was all right, so she stepped
across the roadway and knocked on Flora's door. The lake, below a
cloudless sky, was deep blue, and the leaves of the birches along the
shore were yellowing. There had already been a hard frost, and the
grass and weeds and low scrub shone dully gold in the sunlight.

There was no answer. Marcelle knocked again, firmly this time, and
called Flora's name.

A moment later she heard a low, muffled voice from inside. "Go away." Then silence, except for the breeze off the lake.

"Are you all right? It's me, Marcelle!"

Silence.

Marcelle tried the door. Locked. She called again, "Flora, let me in!" and stood with her fists jammed against her hips. She breathed in and out rapidly, her large brow pulled down in alarm. A few seconds passed, and she called out, "Flora, I'm coming inside!"

Moving quickly to the top step, she pitched her shoulder against the door just above the latch, which immediately gave way and let the door blow open, causing Marcelle to stagger inside, off-balance, blinking in the darkness and floundering in the odor of the animals as if she'd fallen in a huge tub of warm water. "Flora!" she yelled. "Flora, where are you?" Bumping against the cages, she made her way around them and into the kitchen area, shouting Flora's name and peering in vain into the darkness. In several minutes, she had made her way to the bedroom in back, and there in a corner she found Flora on her cot, wrapped in a blanket, looking almost unconscious, limp, bulky, gray. Her hands were near her throat, clutching the top of the blanket like the hands of a frightened, beaten child, and she had her head turned toward the wall, with her eyes closed. She looked like a sick child to Marcelle, like her own child, Joel, who had died when he was twelve— the fever had risen, and the hallucinations had come until he was out of his head with them, and then, suddenly, while she was mopping his body with damp washcloths, the wildness had gone out of him, and he had turned on his side, drawn his skinny legs up to his belly, and died.

Flora was feverish, though not with as high a fever as the boy, Joel, had endured, and she had drawn her legs up to her, bulking her body into a lumpy heap beneath the filthy blanket. "You're sick," Marcelle announced to the woman, who seemed not to hear her. Marcelle straightened the blanket, brushed the woman's matted hair away from her face, and looked around the room to see if there wasn't some way she could make her more comfortable. The room was jammed with the large, odd-shaped cages, and Marcelle could hear the animals rustling back and forth on the wire flooring, now and then chittering in what she supposed was protest against hunger and thirst.

Taking a backward step, Marcelle yanked the cord and opened the venetian blind, and sunlight tumbled into the room. Suddenly Flora was shouting, "Shut it! Shut it! Don't let them see! No one can see me!"

Marcelle closed the blind, and the room once again filled with the gloom and shadow that Flora believed hid the shape of the life being lived here. "I got to get you to a doctor," Marcelle said quietly. "Doctor Wickshaw's got office hours today. You know Carol Constant, his nurse, that nice colored lady who lives next door? You got to see a doctor, missy."

"No. I'll be all right soon," she said in a weak voice. "Just the flu, that's all." She pulled the blanket up higher, covering most of her face, but exposing her dirty bare feet.

Marcelle persisted, and soon Flora began to curse the woman, her voice rising in fear and anger, the force of it pushing Marcelle away from the cot, "You leave me alone, you bitch! I know your tricks, I know what you're trying to do! You just want to get me out of here so you can take my babies away from me! I'm fine, I can take care of my babies fine, just fine! Now you get out of my house! Go on, get!"

Marcelle backed slowly away, then turned and walked to the open door and outside to the sunshine and the clean fall air.

Doctor Wickshaw, Carol told her, doesn't make house calls. Marcelle sat at her kitchen table, looked out the window, and talked on the telephone. She was watching Flora's trailer, number 11, as if watching a bomb about to explode.

"I know that," Marcelle said, holding the receiver between her shoulder and cheek so both hands could be free to light a cigarette. "Listen, Carol, this is Flora Pease we're talking about, and there's no way I'm going to be able to get her into that office. But she's real sick, and it could be just the flu, but it could be meningitis, for all I know. My boy died of that, you know, and you have to do tests and everything before you can tell if it's meningitis." There was silence for a few seconds. "Maybe I should call the ambulance and get her over to the Concord Hospital. I need somebody who knows something to come here and look at her," she said, her voice rising.

"Maybe on my lunch hour I'll be able to come by and take a look," Carol said. "At least I should be capable of saying if she should be got to a hospital or not."

Marcelle thanked her and hung up the phone. Nervously tapping her fingers against the table, she thought to call in Merle Ring or maybe Captain Knox, to get their opinions of Flora's condition, and then decided against it. That damned Dewey Knox, he'd just take over, one way or the other, and after reducing the situation to a choice between two courses, probably between leaving her alone in the trailer and calling the ambulance, he'd insist that someone other than he do the choosing, probably Flora herself, who, of course, would choose to be left alone. Then he'd walk off believing he'd done the right thing, the *only* right thing. Merle would be just as bad, she figured, with all his smart-ass comments about illness and death and leaving things alone until they have something to say to you that's completely clear. Some illnesses lead to death, he'd say, and some lead to health, and we'll know before long which it is, and when we do, we'll know how to act. Men. Either they take responsibility for everything, or they take responsibility for nothing.

Around one, Carol Constant arrived in her little blue sedan, dressed in a white nurse's uniform and looking, to Marcelle, very much like a medical authority. Marcelle led her into Flora's trailer, after warning her about the clutter and the smell—"It's like some kinda burrow in there," she said as they stepped through the door—and Carol, placing a plastic tape against Flora's forehead, determined that Flora was indeed quite ill, her temperature was 105 degrees. She turned to Marcelle and told her to call the ambulance.

Immediately, Flora went wild, bellowing and moaning about her babies and how she couldn't leave them, they needed her. She thrashed against Carol's strong grip for a moment and then gave up and fell weakly back into the cot.

"Go ahead and call," Carol told Marcelle. "I'll hold on to things here until they come." When Marcelle had gone, Carol commenced talking to the ill woman in a low, soothing voice, stroking her forehead with one hand and holding her by the shoulder with the other, until, after a few moments, Flora began to whimper and then to weep, and finally, as if her heart were broken, to sob. Marcelle had returned from calling the ambulance and stood in the background almost out of sight, while Carol soothed the woman and crooned, "Poor thing, you poor thing."

"My babies, who'll take care of my babies?" she wailed.

"I'll get my brother Terry to take care of them," Carol promised, and for a second that seemed to placate the woman.

Then she began to wail again, because she knew it was a lie and when she came back her babies would be gone.

No, no, no, no, both Carol and Marcelle insisted. When she got back, the guinea pigs would be here, all of them, every last one. Terry would water and feed them, and he'd clean out the cages every day, just as she did.

"I'll make sure he does," Marcelle promised, "or he'll have his ass in a sling."

That calmed the woman, but just then two young men dressed in white, the ambulance attendants, stepped into the room, and when Flora saw them, their large, grim faces and, from her vantage point, their enormous, uniformed bodies, her eyes rolled back, and she began to wail, "No, no, no! I'm not going! I'm not going!"

The force of her thrashing movements tossed Carol off the cot onto the floor. Moving swiftly, the two young men reached down and pinned Flora against her cot. One of them, the larger one, told the other to bring his bag, and the smaller man rushed out of the trailer to the ambulance parked outside.

"I'm just going to give you something to calm yourself, ma'am," the big man said in a mechanical way. The other man was back, and Carol and Marcelle, regarding one another with slight regret and apprehension, stepped out of his way.

In seconds, Flora had been injected with a tranquilizer, and while the two hard-faced men in white strapped her body into a four-wheeled, chromium and canvas stretcher, she descended swiftly into slumber. They wheeled her efficiently out of the trailer as if she were a piece of furniture and slid her into the back of the ambulance and were gone, with Marcelle following in her car.

Alone by the roadway outside Flora's trailer, Carol watched the ambulance and Marcelle's battered old Ford head out toward Old Road and away. After a moment or two, drifting from their trailers one by one, came Nancy Hubner, her face stricken with concern, and Captain Dewey Knox, his face firmed to hear the grim news, and Merle Ring, his face smiling benignly.

"Where's my brother Terry?" Carol asked the three as they drew near.

It was near midnight that same night. Most of the trailers were dark, except for Bruce Severance's, where Terry, after having fed, watered, and cleaned the ravenous, thirsty, and dirty guinea pigs, was considering a business proposition from Bruce that would not demand humiliating labor for mere monkey-money, and Doreen Tiede's trailer, where Claudel Bing's naked, muscular arm was reaching over Doreen's head to snap off the lamp next to the bed—when, out by Old Road, the Guinea Pig Lady came shuffling along the lane between the pinewoods. She moved quickly and purposefully, just as she always moved, but silently now. She wore the clothes she'd worn in the morning when the men had taken her from her cot and strapped her onto the stretcher—old bib overalls and a faded, stained, plaid flannel shirt. Her face was ablaze with fever. Her red hair ringed her head in a stiff, wet halo that made her look like an especially blessed peasant figure in a medieval fresco, a shepherd or stonemason rushing to see the Divine Child.

When she neared the trailerpark, sufficiently close to glimpse the few remaining lights and the dully shining, geometric shapes of the trailers through the trees and, here and there, a dark strip of the lake beyond, she cut to her left and departed from the road and made for the swamp. Without hesitation, she darted into the swamp, locating even in darkness the pathways and patches of dry ground, moving slowly through the mushy, brush-covered muskeg, emerging from the deep shadows of the swamp after a while at the edge of the clearing directly behind her own trailer. Soundlessly, she crossed her backyard, passed the head-high pyramids standing like dolmens in the dim light, and stepped through the broken door of the trailer.

The trailer was in pitch darkness, and the only sound was that of the animals as they chirped, bred, and scuffled in their cages through the nighttime. With the same familiarity she had shown cutting across the swamp, Flora moved in darkness to the kitchen area, where she opened a cupboard and drew from a clutter of cans and bottles a red one-gallon can of kerosene. Then, starting at the farthest corner of the trailer, she dribbled the kerosene through every room, looping through and around every one of the cages, until she arrived at the door. She placed the can on the floor next to the broken door, then stepped nimbly outside, where she took a single step toward the ground, lit a wooden match against her thumbnail, tossed it into the trailer, and ran.

Instantly, the trailer was a box of flame, roaring and snapping and sending a dark cloud and poisonous fumes into the night sky as the paneling and walls ignited and burst into flame. Next door, wakened by the first explosion and terrified by the sight of the flames and the roar of the fire, Carol Constant rushed from her bed to the road, where everyone else in the park was gathering, wide-eyed, confused, struck with wonder and fear.

Marcelle hollered at Terry and Bruce, ordering them to hook up garden hoses and wash down the trailers next to Flora's. Then she yelled to Doreen. Dressed in a filmy nightgown, with the naked Claudel Bing standing in darkness behind her, the woman peered through her half-open door at the long, flame-filled coffin across the lane. "Call the fire department, for Christ's sake! And tell Bing to get his clothes on and get out here and help us!" Captain Knox gave orders to people who were already doing what he ordered them to do, and Nancy Hubner, in nightgown, dressing gown, and slippers, hauled her garden hose from under the trailer and dragged it toward the front, screeching as she passed each window along the way for Noni to wake up, wake up and get out here and help, while inside, Noni slid along a stoned slope of sleep—dreamless, and genuinely happy. Leon LaRoche appeared fully dressed in clean and pressed khaki work clothes with gloves and silver-colored hard hat, looking like an ad agency's version of a construction worker. He asked the Captain what he should do, and the Captain pointed him toward Bruce and Terry, who were hosing down the steaming sides of the trailers next to the fire. At the far end of the row of trailers, in darkness at the edge of the glow cast by the flames, stood Merle Ring, uniquely somber, his arms limply at his sides, in one hand a fishing rod, in the other a string of hornpout.

A few moments later, the fire engines arrived, but it was already too late to save Flora's trailer or anything that had been inside it. All they could accomplish, they realized immediately, was to attempt to save the rest of the trailers, which they instantly set about doing, washing down the metal sides and sending huge, billowing columns of steam into the air. Gradually, as the flames subsided, the firemen turned their hoses and doused the dying fire completely. An hour before daylight, they left, and behind them, where Flora's trailer had been, was a cold, charred, shapeless mass of indistinguishable materials—melted plastic, crumbled wood and ash, blackened, bent sheet metal, and charred flesh and fur.

By the pink light of dawn, Flora emerged from the swamp and came to stand before the remains of the pyre. She was alone, for the others, as soon as the fire engines left, had trudged heavily and exhausted to bed. Around nine, Marcelle Chagnon was stirred from her sleep by the telephone—it was the Concord Hospital, informing her that the woman she had signed in the day before, Flora Pease, had left sometime during the night without permission, and they did not know her whereabouts.

Marcelle wearily peered out the window next to the bed and saw Flora standing before the long, black heap across the lane. She told the woman from the hospital that Flora was here. She must have heard last night that her trailer burned down, over the radio, maybe, and hitch-hiked back to Catamount. She assured the woman that she would look after her, but the woman said not to bother, she only had the flu and probably would be fine in a few days, unless, of course, she caught pneumonia hitchhiking last night without a hat or coat on.

Marcelle hung up the phone and continued to watch Flora, who stood as if before a grave. The others in the park, as they rose from their beds, looked out at the wreckage, and, seeing Flora there, stayed inside, and left her alone. Eventually, around midday, she slowly turned and walked back to the swamp.

Marcelle saw her leaving and ran out to stop her. "Flora!" she cried, and the woman turned back and waited in the middle of the clearing. Marcelle trotted heavily across the open space, and when she came up to her, said to Flora, "I'm sorry."

Flora stared at her blankly, as if she didn't understand.

"Flora, I'm sorry ... about your babies." Marcelle put one arm around the woman's shoulders, and they stood side by side, facing away from the trailerpark.

Flora said nothing for a few moments. "They wasn't my babies. Babies make me nervous," she said, shrugging the arm away. Then, when she looked up into Marcelle's big face, she must have seen that she had hurt her, for her tone softened. "I'm sorry, Mrs. Chagnon. But they wasn't my babies. I know the difference, and babies make me nervous."

That was in September. The fire was determined to have been "of suspicious origin," and everyone concluded that some drunken kids from town had set it. The several young men suspected of the crime, however, came up with alibis, and no further investigation seemed reasonable.

By the middle of October, Flora Pease had built an awkwardly pitched shanty on the land where the swamp behind the trailerpark rose slightly and met the pinewoods, land that might have belonged to the Corporation and might have been New Hampshire state property. But it was going to take a judge, a battery of lawyers, and a pair of surveyors before anyone could say for sure. As long as neither the Corporation nor the state fussed about it, no one was willing to make Flora tear down her shanty and move.

She built it herself from stuff she dragged from the town dump down the road and into the woods to the swamp—old boards, galvanized sheet metal, strips of tar paper, cast-off shingles—and furnished it the same way, with a discolored, torn mattress, a three-legged card table, an easy chair with the stuffing blossoming at the seams, and a moldy rug that had been in a children's playhouse. It was a single room, with a tin woodstove for cooking and heat, a privy out back, and a kerosene lantern for light.

For a while, a few people from the trailerpark went on occasion to the edge of the swamp and visited with her. You could see her shack easily from the park, as she had situated it on a low rise where she had the clearest view of the charred wreckage of old number 11. Bruce Severance, the college kid, dropped by fairly often, especially in early summer, when he was busily locating the feral hemp plants in the area and needed her expert help, and Terry Constant went out there, "just for laughs," he said. He used to sit peacefully on a stump in the sun and get stoned on hemp and rap with her about his childhood and dead mother. Whether Flora talked about her childhood and her dead mother Terry never said. It got hard to talk about Flora. She was just there, the Guinea Pig Lady, even though she didn't have any guinea pigs, and there wasn't much anyone could say about it anymore, since everyone more or less knew how she had got to be who she was, and everyone more or less knew who she was going to be from here on out.

Merle used to walk out there in warm weather, and he continued to visit Flora long after everyone else had ceased doing it. The reason he went out, he said, was because you got a different perspective on the trailerpark from out there, practically the same perspective he said he got in winter from the lake when he was in his ice house. And though Marcelle never visited Flora's shack herself, every time she passed it with her gaze, she stopped her gaze and for a long time looked at the place and Flora sitting outside on an old metal folding chair, smoking her cob pipe and staring back at the trailerpark. She gazed at Flora mournfully and with an anger longing for a shape, for Marcelle believed that she alone knew the woman's secret.

Queen for a Day

The elder of the two boys, Earl, turns from the dimly lit worktable, a door on sawhorses, where he is writing. He pauses a second and says to his brother, "Cut that out, willya? Getcha feet off the walls."

The other boy says, "You're not the boss of this family, you know." He is dark-haired with large brown eyes, a moody ten-year-old lying bored on his cot with sneakered feet slapped against the faded green, floral print wallpaper.

Earl crosses his arms over his narrow chest and stares down at his brother from a considerable height. The room is cluttered with model airplanes, schoolbooks, papers, clothing, hockey sticks and skates, a set of barbells. Earl says, "We're supposed to be doing homework, you know. If she hears you tramping your feet on the walls, she'll come screaming in here."

"She can't hear me. Besides, you're not doing homework. And I'm reading," he says, waving a geography book at him.

The older boy sucks his breath through his front teeth and glares. "You really piss me off, George. With you doing that, rubbing your feet all over the wallpaper like you're doing, it makes me all distracted." He turns back to his writing, scribbling with a ballpoint pen on lined paper in a schoolboy's three-ring binder. Earl has sandy blond hair and pale blue eyes that turn downward at the corners and a full red mouth. He's more scrawny than skinny, hard and flat-muscled, and suddenly tall for his age, making him a head taller than his brother, taller even than his mother now, and able to pat their sister's head as if he were a full-grown adult already.

He turned twelve eight months ago, in March, and in May their father left. Their father is a union carpenter who works on projects in distant corners of the state—schools, hospitals, post offices—and for a whole year the man came home only on weekends. Then, for a while, every other weekend. Finally, he was gone for a month, and when he came home the last time, it was to say good-bye to Earl, George, and their sister, Louise, and to their mother, too, of course, she who had been saying (for what seemed to the children years) that she never wanted to see the man again anyhow, ever, under any circumstances, because he just causes trouble when he's home and more trouble when he doesn't come home, so he might as well stay away for good. They can all get along better without him, she insisted, which was true, Earl was sure, but that was before the man left for good and stopped sending them money, so that now, six months later, Earl is not so sure anymore that they can get along better without their father than with him.

It happened on a Saturday morning, a day washed with new sunshine and dry air, with the whole family standing somberly in the kitchen, summoned there from their rooms by their mother's taut, high-pitched voice, a voice that had an awful point to prove. "Come out here! Your father has something important to say to you!"

They obeyed, one by one, and gathered in a line before their father, who, dressed in pressed khakis and shined work shoes and cap, sat at the kitchen table, a pair of suitcases beside him, and in front of him a cup of coffee, which he stirred slowly with a spoon. His eyes were filled with dense water, the way they almost always were on Sunday mornings, from his drinking the night before, the children knew, and he had trouble looking them in the face, because of the sorts of things he and their mother were heard saying to one another when they were at home together late Saturday nights. This Sunday morning it was only a little worse than usual—his hands shook some, and he could barely hold his cigarette; he let it smolder in the ashtray and kept on stirring his coffee while he talked. "Your mother and me," he said in his low, roughened voice, "we've decided on some things you kids should know about." He cleared his throat. "Your mother, she thinks you oughta hear it from me, though I don't quite know so much about that as she does, seeing as how it's not completely my idea alone." He studied his coffee cup for a few seconds.

"They should hear it from you because it's what you *want!*" their mother finally said. She stood by the sink, her hands wringing each other dry, and stared at the man. Her face was swollen from crying, which, for the children, was not an unusual thing on a Sunday morning when their father was home. They still did not know what was coming.

"Adele, it's *not* what I want," he said. "It's what's got to be, that's all. Kids," he said, "I got to leave you folks, for a while. A long while. And I won't be comin' back, I guess." He grabbed his cigarette with thumb and forefinger and inhaled the smoke fiercely, then placed the butt back into the ashtray and went on talking, as if to the table: "I don't want to do this, I hate it, but I got to. It's too hard to explain, and I'm hoping that someday you'll under-stand it all, but I just . . . I just got to live someplace else now."

Louise, the girl, barely six years old, was the only one of the three children who could speak. She said, "Where are you going, Daddy?"

"Upstate," he said. "Back up to Holderness. I got me an apartment up there, small place."

"That's not all he's got up there!" their mother said.

"Adele, I can walk outa here right this second," he said smoothly. "I don't have to explain a goddamned thing, if you keep that kinda stuff up. We had an agreement."

"Yup, yup. Sorry," she said, pursing her lips, locking them with an invisible key, throwing the key away.

Finally, Earl could speak. "Will . . . will you come and see us? Or can we maybe come visit you, on weekends and like that?"

"Sure, son, you can visit me, anytime you want. It'll take a while for me to get the place set up right, but soon's I get it all set up for kids, I'll call you, and we'll work out some nice visits. I shouldn't come here, though, not for a while. You understand."

Earl shook his head somberly up and down, as if his one anxiety concerning the event had been put satisfactorily to rest.

George, however, had turned his back on his father, and now he was taking tiny, mincing half-steps across the linoleum-covered kitchen floor toward the outside door. He stopped a second, opened the door, and stood on the landing at the top of the stairs, and no one tried to stop him, because he was doing what they wanted to do themselves, and then they heard him running pell-mell, as if falling, down the darkened stairs, two flights, to the front door of the building, heard it slam behind him, and knew he was gone, up Perley Street, between parked cars, down alleys, to a hiding place where they knew he'd stop, sit, and bawl, knew it because it was what they wanted to do themselves, especially Earl, who was too old, too scared, too confused, and too angry. Earl said, "I hope everyone can be more happy now."

His father smiled and looked at him for the first time and clapped him on the shoulder. "Right, son," he said. "You, you're the man of the house now. I know you can do it. You're a good kid, and, listen, I'm proud of you. Your mother, your brother and sister, they're all going to need you a hell of a lot more than they have before, but I know you're up to it, son. I'm countin' on you," he said, and he stood up and rubbed out his cigarette. Then he reached beyond Earl with both hands and hugged Earl's sister, lifted her off her feet and squeezed her tight, and when the man set her down, he wiped tears away from his eyes. "Tell

Georgie . . . well, maybe I'll see him downstairs or something. He's upset, I guess. . . ." He shook Earl's hand, drew him close, quickly hugged him, and let go and stepped away. Grabbing up his suitcases in silence, without looking once at his wife or back at his children, he left the apartment.

For good. "And good riddance, too," as their mother immediately started saying to anyone who would listen. Louise said she missed her daddy, but she seemed to be quickly forgetting that, since for most of her life he had worked away from home, and George, who stayed mad, went deep inside himself and said nothing about it at all, and Earl—who did not know how he felt about their father's abandoning them, for he knew that in many ways it was the best their father could do for them and in many other ways it was the worst—spoke of the man as if he had died in an accident, as if their mother were a widow and they half orphaned. This freed him, though he did not know it then, to concentrate on survival, survival for them all, which he now understood to be his personal responsibility, for his mother seemed utterly incapable of guaranteeing it, and his brother and sister were still practically babies. Often, late at night, lying in his squeaky, narrow cot next to his brother's, Earl would say to himself, "I'm the man of the house now," and somehow just saying it, over and over, "I'm the man of the house now," like a prayer, made his terror ease back from his face, and he could finally slip into sleep.

Now, with his father gone six months and their mother still fragile, still denouncing the man to everyone who listens, and even to those who don't listen but merely show her their faces for a moment or two, it's as if the man were still coming home weekends drunk and raging against her and the world, were still betraying her, were telling all her secrets to another woman in a motel room in the northern part of the state. It's as if he were daily abandoning her and their three children over and over again, agreeing to send money, and then sending nothing, promising to call and write letters, and then going silent on them, planning visits and trips together on weekends and holidays, and then leaving them with not even a forwarding address, forbidding them, almost, from adjusting to a new life, a life in which the man who is their father and her husband does not betray them anymore.

Earl decides to solve their problems himself. He hatches and implements, as best he can, plans, schemes, designs, all intended to find a substitute for the lost father. He introduces his mother to his hockey coach, who turns out to be married and a new father; and he invites in for breakfast and to meet his ma the cigar-smoking vet with the metal plate in his skull who drops off the newspapers at dawn for Earl to deliver before school. But the man turns out to dislike women actively enough to tell Earl, right to his face: "No offense, kid, I'm sure your ma's a nice lady, but I got no use for 'em is why I'm single, not 'cause I ain't met the right one yet or something." And to the guy who comes to read the electric meter one afternoon when Earl's home from school with the flu and his mother's at work down at the tannery, where they've taken her on as an assistant bookkeeper, Earl says that he can't let the man into the basement because it's locked, he'll have to come back later when his mom's home, so she can let him in herself. The man says, "Hey, no problem, I can use last month's reading and make the correction next month," and waves cheerfully good-bye, leaving Earl suddenly, utterly, shockingly aware of his foolishness, his pathetic, helpless longing for a man of the house.

For a moment, he blames his mother for his longing and hates her for his fantasies. But then quickly he forgives her and blames himself and commences to concoct what he thinks of as more realistic, more dignified plans, schemes, designs: sweepstakes tickets; lotteries; raffles—Earl buys tickets on the sly with his paper route money. And he enters contests: essay contests for junior high school students that provide the winner with a weeklong trip for him and a parent to Washington, D.C.; and the National Spelling Bee, which takes Earl only to the county level before he fails to spell *alligator* correctly. A prize, any kind of award from the world outside their tiny, besieged family, Earl believes, will make their mother happy at last. He believes that a prize will validate their new life somehow and will thus separate it, once and for all, from their father. It will be as if their father never existed.

"So what are you writing?" George demands from the bed. He walks his feet up the wall as high as he can reach, then retreats. "I know it ain't homework, you don't write that fast when you're doing homework. What is it, a *love* letter?"

"No, asshole. Just take your damned feet off the wall, will you? Ma's gonna be in here in a minute screaming at both of us." Earl closes the notebook and pushes it away from him carefully, as if it is the Bible and he has just finished reading aloud from it.

"I want to see what you wrote," George says, flipping around and setting his feet, at last, onto the floor. He reaches toward the notebook. "Lemme see it."

"C'mon, willya? Cut the shit."

"Naw, lemme see it." He stands up and swipes the notebook from the table as Earl moves to protect it.

"You little sonofabitch!" Earl says, and he clamps onto the notebook with both hands and yanks, pulling George off his feet and forward onto Earl's lap, and they both tumble to the floor, where they begin to fight, swing fists and knees, roll and grab, bumping against furniture in the tiny, crowded room, until a lamp falls over, books tumble to the floor, model airplanes crash. In seconds, George is getting the worst of it and scrambles across the floor to the door, with Earl crawling along behind, yanking his brother's shirt with one hand and pounding at his head and back with the other, when suddenly the bedroom door swings open, and their mother stands over them. She grabs both boys by their collars and shrieks, "What's the matter with you! What're you doing! What're you doing!" They stop and collapse into a bundle of legs and arms, but she goes on shrieking at them. "I can't *stand* it when you fight! Don't you know that? I can't *stand* it!"

George cries, "I didn't do anything! I just wanted to see his homework!"

"Yeah, sure," Earl says. "Innocent as a baby."

"Shut up! Both of you!" their mother screams. She is wild-eyed, glaring at them, and, as he has done so many times, Earl looks at her face as if he's outside his body, and he sees that she's not angry at them at all, she's frightened and in pain, as if her sons are little animals, rats or ferrets, with tiny, razor-sharp teeth biting at her ankles and feet.

Quickly, he gets to his feet and says, "I'm sorry, Ma. I guess I'm just a little tired or something lately." He pats his mother on her shoulder and offers a small smile. George crawls on hands and knees to his bed and lies on it, while Earl gently turns their mother around and steers her out the door to the living room, where the television set drones on, Les Paul and Mary Ford, playing their guitars and singing bland harmonies. "We'll be out in a few minutes for *Dobie Gillis*, Ma. Don't worry," Earl says.

"Jeez," George says. "How can she stand that Les Paul and Mary Ford stuff? Even Louise goes to bed when it comes on, and it's only what, six-thirty?"

"Shut up."

"Up yours."

Earl leans down and scoops up the fallen dictionary, pens, airplanes, and lamps and places them back on the worktable. The black binder he opens squarely in front of him, and he says to his brother, "You want to see what I was writing? Go ahead and read it. I don't care."

"I don't care, either. Unless it's a *love* letter."

"No, it's not a *love* letter."

"What is it, then?"

"Nothing," Earl says, closing the notebook. "Homework."

"Oh," George says, and he marches his feet up the wall and back again.

Nov. 7, 1953

Dear Jack Bailey,

I think my mother should be queen for a day because she has suffered
a lot more than most mothers in this life and she has come out of it very
cheerful and loving. The most important fact is that my father left her
alone with three children, myself (age 12 $^1/_2$), my brother George (age 10),
and my sister Louise (age 6). He left her for another woman though that's
not the important thing, because my mother has risen above all that. But
he refuses to send her any child support money. He's been gone over six
months and we still haven't seen one red cent. My mother went to a
lawyer but the lawyer wants $50 in advance to help her take my father
to court. She has a job as assistant bookkeeper down at Belvedere's
Tannery downtown and the pay is bad, barely enough for our rent and
food costs in fact, so where is she going to get $50 for a lawyer?

Also my father was a very cruel man who drinks too much and
many times when he was living with us when he came home from work
he was drunk and he would yell at her and even hit her. This has caused
her and us kids a lot of nervous suffering and now she sometimes has
spells which the doctor says are serious, though he doesn't know exactly
what they are.

We used to have a car and my father left it with us when he left (a
big favor) because he had a pickup truck. But he owed over $450 on the
car to the bank so the bank came and repossessed the car. Now my mother
has to walk everywhere she goes which is hard and causes her varicose
veins and takes a lot of valuable time from her day.

My sister Louise needs glasses the school nurse said but "Who can pay
for them?" my mother says. My paper route gets a little money but it's
barely enough for school lunches for the three of us kids which is what we
use it for.

My mother's two sisters and her brother haven't been too helpful

because they are Catholic, as she is and the rest of us, and they don't
believe in divorce and think that she should not have let my father leave
her anyhow. She needs to get a divorce but no one except me and my
brother George think it is a good idea. Therefore my mother cries a lot at
night because she feels so abandoned in this time of her greatest need.

The rest of the time though she is cheerful and loving in spite of her
troubles and nervousness. That is why I believe that this courageous long-
suffering woman, my mother, should be Queen for a Day.

Sincerely yours,

Earl Painter

Several weeks slide by, November gets cold and gray, and a New Hampshire winter starts to feel inevitable again, and Earl does not receive the
letter he expects. He has told no one, especially his mother, that he has
written to Jack Bailey, the smiling, mustachioed host of the Queen for a
Day television show, which Earl happened to see that time he was
home for several days with the flu, bored and watching television all
afternoon. Afterwards, delivering papers in the predawn gloom, in
school all day, at the hockey rink, doing homework at night, he could
not forget the television show, the sad stories told by the contestants
about their illness, poverty, neglect, victimization, and, always, their
bad luck, luck so bad that you felt it was somehow deserved. The studio audience seemed genuinely saddened, moved to tears, even, by
Jack Bailey's recitation of these narratives, and then elated afterwards,
when the winning victims, all of them middle-aged women, were
rewarded with refrigerators, living room suites, vacation trips, washing
machines, china, fur coats, and, if they needed them, wheelchairs, pros-
thetic limbs, twenty-four-hour nursing care. As these women wept for
joy, the audience applauded, and Earl almost applauded, too, alone
there in the dim living room of the small, cold, and threadbare apartment in a mill town in central New Hampshire.

Earl knows that those women's lives surely aren't much different than his mother's life, and in fact, if he has told it right, if somehow he has got into the letter what he has intuited is basically wrong with his mother's life, it will be obvious to everyone in the audience that his mother's life is actually much worse than those of many or perhaps even most of the women who win the prizes. Earl knows that, although his mother enjoys good health (except for "spells") and holds down a job and is able to feed, house, and clothe her children, there is still a deep, essential sadness in her life that, in his eyes, none of the contestants on *Queen for a Day* has. He believes that if he can just get his description of her life right, other people—Jack Bailey, the studio audience, millions of people all over America watching it on television—*everyone* will share in her sadness, so that when she is rewarded with appliances, furniture, and clothing, maybe even a trip to Las Vegas, then everyone will share in her elation, too. Even he will share in it.

Earl knows that it is not easy to become a contestant on *Queen for a Day*. Somehow, your letter describing the candidate has first to move Jack Bailey, and then your candidate has to be able to communicate her sufferings over television in a clear and dramatic way. Earl noticed that some of the contestants, to their own apparent disadvantage, downplayed the effect on them of certain tragedies—a child with a birth defect, say, or an embarrassing kind of operation or a humiliating dismissal by an employer—while playing up other, seemingly less disastrous events, such as being cheated out of a small inheritance by a phony siding contractor or having to drop out of hairdressing school because of a parent's illness, and when the studio audience was asked to show the extent and depth of its compassion by having its applause measured on a meter, it was always the woman who managed to present the most convincing mixture of courage and complaint who won.

Earl supposes that Jack Bailey telephones the writer of the letter nominating a particular woman for *Queen for a Day* and offers him and his nominee the opportunity to come to New York City's Radio City Music Hall to tell her story in person, and then, based on how she does in the audition, Jack Bailey chooses her and two other nominees for a particular show, maybe next week, when they all come back to New York City to tell their stories live on television. Thus, daily, when Earl arrives home, he asks Louise and George, who normally get home from school an hour or so earlier than he, if there's been any calls for him. You're sure? No mail, either, no letters?

"Who're you expectin' to hear from, lover boy, your *girlfriend*?" George grins, teeth spotted with peanut butter and gobs of white bread.

"Up yours," Earl says, and heads into his bedroom, where he dumps his coat, books, hockey gear. It's becoming clear to him that, if there's such a thing as a success, he's evidently a failure. If there's such a thing as a winner, he's a loser. I oughta go on that goddamned show myself, he thinks. Flopping onto his bed face-first, he wishes he could keep on falling, as if down a bottomless well or mine shaft, into darkness and warmth, lost, and finally blameless, gone, gone, gone. And soon he is asleep, dreaming of a hockey game, and he's carrying the puck, dragging it all the way up along the right, digging in close to the boards, skate blades flashing as he cuts around behind the net, ice chips spraying in white fantails, and when he comes out on the other side, he looks down in front of him and can't find the puck, it's gone, dropped off behind him, lost in his sweeping turn, the spray, the slash of the skates, and the long sweeping arc of the stick in front of him. He brakes, turns, and heads back, searching for the small black disc.

At the sound of the front door closing, a quiet click, as if someone is deliberately trying to enter the apartment silently, Earl wakes from his dream, and he hears voices from the kitchen, George and Louise and his mother:

"Hi, Mom. We're just makin' a snack, peanut butter sandwiches."

"Mommy, George won't give me—"

"Don't eat it directly off the knife like that!"

"Sorry, I was jus'—"

"You heard me, mister, don't answer back!"

"Jeez, I was jus'—"

"I don't *care* what you were doing!" Her voice is trembling and quickly rising in pitch and timbre, and Earl moves off his bed and comes into the kitchen, smiling, drawing everyone's attention to him, the largest person in the room, the only one with a smile on his face, a relaxed, easy, sociable face and manner, normalcy itself, as he gives his brother's shoulder a fraternal squeeze, tousles his sister's brown hair, nods hello to his mother, and says, "Hey, you're home early, Ma. What happened, they give you guys the rest of the day off?"

Then he sees her face, white, tight, drawn back in a cadaverous grimace, her pale blue eyes wild, unfocused, rolling back, and he says, "Jeez, Ma, what's the matter, you okay?"

Her face breaks into pieces, goes from dry to wet, white to red, and she is weeping loudly, blubbering, wringing her hands in front of her like a maddened knitter. "Aw-w-w-w!" she wails, and Louise and George, too, start to cry. They run to her and wrap her in their arms, crying and begging her not to cry, as Earl, aghast, sits back in his chair and watches the three of them wind around each other like snakes moving in and out of one another's coils.

"Stop!" he screams at last. "Stop it! All of you!" He pounds his fist on the table. "Stop crying, all of you!"

They obey him. George first, then their mother, then Louise, who goes on staring into her mother's face. George looks at his feet, ashamed, and their mother looks pleadingly into Earl's face, expectant, hopeful, knowing that he will organize everything.

In a calm voice, Earl says, "Ma, tell me what happened. Just say it slowly, and it'll come out okay, and then we can all talk about it, okay?"

She nods, and George unravels his arms from around her neck and steps away from her, moving to the far wall of the room, where he stands and looks out the window and down to the bare yard below. Louise snuggles her face in close to her mother and sniffles.

"I . . . I lost my job. I got fired today," their mother says. "And it wasn't my fault." She starts to weep again, and Louise joins her, bawling now, and George at the window starts to sob, his small shoulders heaving.

Earl shouts, "Wait! Wait a minute, Ma, just *tell* me about it. Don't cry!" he commands her, and she shudders, draws herself together again, and continues.

"I . . . I had some problems this morning, a bunch of files I was supposed to put away last week got lost. And everybody was running around like crazy looking for them, because they had all these figures from last year's sales in them or something, I don't know. Anyhow, they were important, and I was the one who was accused of losing them. Which I didn't. But no one could find them, until finally they turned up on Robbie's desk, down in shipping, which I couldn't've done, since I never *go* to shipping anyhow. But Rose blamed me, because she's the head bookkeeper, and she was the last person to use the files, and she was getting it because they needed them upstairs, and . . . well, you know, I was just getting yelled at and yelled at, and it went on after lunch . . . and, I don't know, I just started feeling dizzy and all, like I was going to black out again. And I guess I got scared and started talking real fast, so Rose took me down to the nurse, and I did black out then. Only for a few seconds, though, and when I felt a little better, Rose said maybe I should go home for the rest of the day, which is what I wanted to do, anyhow. But when I went back upstairs to get my pocketbook and coat and my lunch, because I hadn't been able to eat my sandwich, I was so nervous and all, and then Mr. Shandy called me into his office. . . ." She makes a twisted, little smile, helpless and confused, and quickly continues. "Mr. Shandy said I should maybe take a lot of time off. Two weeks sick leave with pay, he said, even though I was only working there six months. He said that would give me time to look for another job, one that wouldn't cause me so much worry, he said. So I asked him, 'Are you firing me?' and he said, 'Yes, I am,' just like that. 'But it would be better for you all around,' he said, 'if you left for medical reasons or something.'"

Earl slowly exhales. He's been holding his breath throughout, though from her very first sentence he has known what the outcome would be. Reaching forward, he takes his mother's hands in his, stroking them as if they were an injured bird. He doesn't know what will happen now, but he is not afraid. Not really. Yet he knows that he should be terrified, and when he says this to himself, *I should be terrified,* he answers by observing simply that this is not the worst thing. The worst thing that can happen to them is that one or all of them will die. And because he is still a child, or at least enough of a child not to believe in death, he knows that no one in his family is going to die. He cannot share this secret comfort with anyone in the family, however. His brother and sister, children completely, cannot yet know that death is the worst thing that can happen to them; they think this is, that their mother has been fired from her job, which is why they are crying. And his mother, no longer a child at all, cannot believe with Earl that the worst thing will *not* happen, for this is too much like death and may somehow lead directly to it, which is why she is crying. Only Earl can refuse to cry. Which he does.

Later, in the room she shares with her daughter, their mother lies fully clothed on the double bed and sleeps, and it grows dark, and while George and Louise watch television in the gloom of the living room, Earl writes:

Nov. 21, 1953

Dear Jack Bailey,

Maybe my first letter to you about why my mother should be queen for a day did not reach you or else I just didn't write it good enough for you to want her on your show. But I thought I would write again anyhow, if that's okay, and mention to you a few things that I left out of that first letter and also mention again some of the things in that letter, in case you did not get it at all for some reason (you know the Post Office). I also want to mention a few new developments that have made things even worse for my poor mother than they already were.

First, even though it's only a few days until Thanksgiving my father who left us last May, as you know, has not contacted us about the holidays or offered to help in any way. This makes us mad though we don't talk about it much since the little kids tend to cry about it a lot when they think about it, and me and my mother think it's best not to think about it. We don't even know how to write a letter to my father, though we know the name of the company that he works for up in Holderness (a town pretty far from here) and his sisters could tell us his address if we asked, but we won't. A person has to have some pride, as my mother says. Which she has a lot of.

We will get through Thanksgiving all right because of St. Joseph's Church, which is where we go sometimes and where I was confirmed and my brother George (age 10) took his first communion last year and where my sister Louise (age 6) goes to catechism class. St. Joe's (as we call it) has turkeys and other kinds of food for people who can't afford to buy one so we'll do okay if my mother goes down there and says she can't afford to buy a turkey for her family on Thanksgiving. This brings me to the new developments.

My mother just got fired from her job as assistant bookkeeper at the tannery. It wasn't her fault or anything she did. They just fired her because she has these nervous spells sometimes when there's a lot of pressure on her, which is something that happens a lot these days because of my father and all and us kids and the rest of it. She got two weeks pay but that's the only money we have until she gets another job. Tomorrow she plans to go downtown to all the stores and try to get a job as a

saleslady now that Christmas is coming and the stores hire a lot of extras.
But right now we don't have any money for anything like Thanksgiving
turkey or pies, and we can't go down to Massachusetts to my mother's
family, Aunt Dot's and Aunt Leona's and Uncle Jerry's house, like we used
to because (as you know) the bank repossessed the car. And my father's
sisters and all, who used to have Thanksgiving with us, sometimes, have
taken our father's side in this because of his lies about us and now they
won't talk to us anymore.

I know that lots and lots of people are poor as us and many of
them are sick too, or crippled from polio and other bad diseases. But I
still think that my mother should be Queen for a Day because of other
things.

Because even though she's poor and got fired and has dizzy spells and
sometimes blacks out, she's a proud woman. And even though my father
walked off and left all his responsibilities behind, she stayed here with us.
And in spite of all her troubles and worries, she really does take good care
of his children. One look in her eyes and you know it.

Thank you very much for listening to me and considering my
mother for the Queen for a Day television show.

Sincerely,

Earl Painter

The day before Thanksgiving their mother is hired to start work the
day after Thanksgiving in gift wrapping at Grover Cronin's on Moody
Street, and consequently she does not feel ashamed for accepting a
turkey and a bag of groceries from St. Joe's. "Since I'm working, I don't
think of it as charity. I think of it as a kind of loan," she explains to Earl
as they walk the four blocks to the church.

It's dark, though still late afternoon, and cold, almost cold enough to
snow, Earl thinks, which makes him think of Christmas, which in turn
makes him cringe and tremble inside and turn quickly back to now, to

this very moment, to walking with his tiny, brittle-bodied mother down the quiet street, past houses like their own—triple-decker wood-frame tenements, each with a wide front porch like a bosom facing the narrow street below, lights on in kitchens in back, where mothers make boiled supper for kids cross-legged on the living room floor watching *Kukla, Fran & Ollie*, while dads trudge up from the mills by the river or drive in from one of the plants on the Heights or maybe walk home from one of the stores downtown, the A&P, J.C. Penney's, Sears: the homes of ordinary families, people just like them. But with one crucial difference, for a piece is missing from the Painter family, a keystone, making all other families, in Earl's eyes, wholly different from his, and for an anxious moment he envies them. He wants to turn up a walkway to a strange house, step up to the door, open it, and walk down the long, dark, sweet-smelling hallway to the kitchen in back, say hi and toss his coat over a chair and sit down for supper, have his father growl at him to hang his coat up and wash his hands first, have his mother ask about school today, how did hockey practice go, have his sister interrupt to show her broken dolly to their father, beg him to fix it, which he does at the table next to his son, waiting for supper to be put on the table, all of them relaxed, happy, relieved that tomorrow is a holiday, a day at home with the family, no work, no school, no hockey practice. Tomorrow, he and his father and brother will go to the high school football game at noon and will be home by two to help set the table.

Earl's mother says, "That job down at Grover Cronin's? It's only . . . it's a temporary job, you know." She says it as if uttering a slightly shameful secret. "After Christmas I get let go."

Earl jams his hands deeper into his jacket pockets and draws his chin down inside his collar. "Yeah, I figured."

"And the money, well, the money's not much. It's almost nothing. I added it up, for a week and for a month, and it comes out to quite a lot less than what you and me figured out in that budget, for the rent and food and all. What we need. It's less than what we need. Never mind Christmas, even. Just regular."

Earl and his mother stop a second at a curb, wait for a car to pass, then cross the street and turn right. Elm trees loom in black columns overhead; leafless branches spread in high arcs and cast intricate shadows on the sidewalk below. Earl can hear footsteps click against the pavement, his own off-beat, long stride and her short, quick one combining in a stuttered rhythm. He says, "You gotta take the job, though, don't you? I mean, there isn't anything else, is there? Not now, anyhow. Maybe soon, though, Ma, in a few days, maybe, if something at the store opens up in one of the other departments, dresses or something. Bookkeeping, maybe. You never know, Ma."

"No, you're right. Things surprise you. Still. . . ." She sighs, pushing a cloud of breath out in front of her. "But I am glad for the turkey and the groceries. We'll have a nice Thanksgiving, anyhow," she chirps.

"Yeah."

They are silent for a few seconds, still walking, and then she says, "I've been talking to Father LaCoy, Earl. You know, about . . . about our problems. I've been asking his advice. He's a nice man, not just a priest, you know, but a kind man, too. He knows your father, he knew him years and years ago, when they were in high school together. He said he was a terrible drinker even then. And he said . . . other things. He said some other things the other morning, that I've been thinking about since."

"What morning?"

"Day before yesterday. Early. When you were delivering your papers. I felt I just had to talk to someone, I was all nervous and worried, and I needed to talk to someone here at St. Joe's anyhow, because I wanted to know about how to get the turkey and all, so I came over, and he was saying the early mass, so I stayed and talked with him awhile afterwards. He's a nice priest, I like him. I always liked Father LaCoy."

"Yeah. What'd he say?" Earl knows already what the priest said, and he pulls himself further down inside his jacket, where his insides have hardened like an ingot, cold and dense, at the exact center of his body.

Up ahead, at the end of the block, is St. Joseph's, a large, squat parish church with a short, broad steeple, built late in the last century of pale yellow stone cut from a quarry up on the Heights and hauled across the river in winter on sledges. "Father LaCoy says that your father and me, we should try to get back together. That we should start over, so to speak."

"And you think he's right," Earl adds.

"Well, not exactly. Not just like that. I mean, he knows what happened. He knows all about your father and all, I told him, but he knew anyhow. I told him how it was, but he told me that it's not right for us to be going on like this, without a father and all. So he said, he told me, he'd like to arrange to have a meeting in his office at the church, a meeting between me and your father, so we could maybe talk some of our problems out. And make some compromises, he said."

Earl is nearly a full head taller than his mother, but suddenly, for the first time since before his father left, he feels small, a child again, helpless, dependent, pulled this way or that by the obscure needs and desires of adults. "Yeah, but how come . . . how come Father LaCoy thinks Daddy'll even listen? He doesn't *want* us!"

"I know, I know," his mother murmurs. "But what can I do? What else can I do?"

Earl has stopped walking, and he shouts at his mother, like a dog barking at the end of a leash: "He can't even get in touch with Daddy! He doesn't even know where Daddy is!"

She stops and speaks in a steady voice. "Yes, he can find him all right. I told him where Daddy was working and gave him the name of McGrath and Company, and also Aunt Ellie's number. So he can get in touch with him, if he wants to. He's a priest."

"A priest can get in touch with him, but his own wife and kids can't?"

His mother has pulled up now, and she looks at her son with a hardness in her face that he can't remember having seen before. She tells him, "You don't understand. I know how tough it's been for you, Earl, all this year, from way back, even, with all the fighting, and then when your father went away. But you have got to understand a little bit how it's been for me, too. I can't . . . do this all alone like this."

"Do you love Daddy?" he demands. "*Do you*? After . . . after everything he's done? After hitting you like he did those times, and the yelling and all, and the drinking, and then, then the worst, after leaving us like he did! Leaving us and running off with that *girl*friend or whatever of his! And not sending any money! Making you have to go to work, with us kids coming home after school and nobody at home. Ma, he *left* us! Don't you know that? He *left* us!" Earl is weeping now. His skinny arms wrapped around his own chest, tears streaming over his cheeks, the boy stands straight-legged and stiff on the sidewalk in the golden glow of the streetlight, his wet face crossed with shadows from the elm trees, and he shouts, "I *hate* him! I hate him, and I never want him to come back again! If you let him come back, I swear it, I'm gonna run away! I'll leave!"

His mother says, "Oh, no, Earl, you don't mean that," and she reaches forward to hold him, but he backs fiercely away.

"No! I do mean it! If you let him back into our house, I'm leaving."

"Earl. Where will you go? You're just a boy."

"So help me, Ma, don't treat me like this. I can go lots of places, don't worry. I can go to Boston, I can go to Florida, I can go to lots of places. All I got to do is hitchhike. I'm not a little kid anymore," he says, and he draws himself up and looks down at her.

"You *don't* hate your father."

"Yes, Ma. Yes, I do. And you should hate him, too. After all he did to you."

They are silent for a moment, facing each other, looking into each other's pale blue eyes. He is her son, his face is her face, not his father's.

Earl and his mother have the same sad, downward-turning eyes, like teardrops, the same full red mouth, the same clear voice, and now, at this moment, they share the same agony, a life-bleeding pain that can be stanched only with a lie, a denial.

She says, "All right, then. I'll tell Father LaCoy. I'll tell him that I don't want to talk to your father, it's gone too far now. I'll tell him that I'm going to get a divorce." She opens her arms, and her son steps into them. Above her head, his eyes jammed shut, he holds on to his tiny mother and sobs, as if he's learned that his father has died.

His mother says, "I don't know when I'll get the divorce, Earl. But I'll do it. Things'll work out. They have to. Right?" she asks, as if asking a baby who can't understand her words.

He nods. "Yeah . . . things'll work out," he says.

They let go of one another and walk slowly on toward the church.

Dec. 12, 1953

Dear Jack Bailey,

Yes, it's me again and this is my third letter asking you to make my mother Adele Painter into queen for a day. Things are much worse now than last time I wrote to you. I had to quit the hockey team so I could take an extra paper route in the afternoons because my mother's job at Grover Cronin's is minimum wage and can't pay our bills. But that's okay, it's only junior high so it doesn't matter like it would if I was in high school. So I don't really mind.

My mother hasn't had any of her spells lately, but she's still really nervous and cries a lot and yells a lot at the kids over little things because she's so worried about money and everything. We had to get winter coats and boots this year from the church, St. Joe's, and my mom cried a lot about that. Now that Christmas is so close everything reminds her of how poor we are now, even her job which is wrapping gifts. She has to stand on her feet six days and three nights a week so her varicose veins are a lot worse than before, so when she comes home she usually has to go right to bed.

My brother George comes home now after school and takes care of Louise until I get through delivering papers and can come home and make supper for us, because my mother's usually at work then. We don't feel too sad because we've got each other and we all love each other but it is hard to feel happy a lot of the time, especially at Christmas.

My mother paid out over half of one week's pay as a down payment to get a lawyer to help her get a divorce from my father and get the court to make him pay her some child support, but the lawyer said it might take two months for any money to come and the divorce can't be done until next June. The lawyer also wrote a letter to my father to try and scare him into paying us some money but so far it hasn't worked. So it seems like she spent that money on the lawyer for nothing.

Everything just seems to be getting worse. If my father came back the money problems would be over.

Well, I should close now. This being the third time I wrote in to nominate my mother for Queen for a Day and so far not getting any answer, I guess it's safe to say you don't think her story is sad enough to let her go on your show. That's okay because there are hundreds of women in America whose stories are much sadder than my mom's and they deserve the chance to win some prizes on your show and be named queen for a day. But my mom deserves that chance too, just as much as that lady with the amputated legs I saw and the lady whose daughter had that rare blood disease and her husband died last year. My mom needs recognition just as much as those other ladies need what they need. That's why I keep writing to you like this. I think this will be my last letter though. I get the picture, as they say.

Sincerely,

Earl Painter

The Friday before Christmas, Earl, George, Louise, and their mother are sitting in the darkened living room, George sprawled on the floor, the others on the sofa, all of them eating popcorn from a bowl held in Louise's lap and watching The Jackie Gleason Show, when the phone rings.

"You get it, George," Earl says.

Reggie Van Gleason III swirls his cape and cane across the tiny screen in front of them, and the phone goes on ringing. "Get it yourself," says George. "I always get it, and it's never for me."

"Answer the phone, Louise," their mother says, and she suddenly laughs at one of Gleason's moves, a characteristic high-pitched peal that cuts off abruptly, half a cackle that causes her sons, as usual, to look at each other and roll their eyes in shared embarrassment. She's wearing her flannel bathrobe and slippers, smoking a cigarette, and drinking from a glass of beer poured from a quart bottle on the floor beside her.

Crossing in front of them, Louise cuts to the corner table by the window and picks up the phone. Her face, serious most of the time anyhow, suddenly goes dark, then brightens, wide-eyed. Earl watches her, and he knows who she is listening to. She nods, as if the person on the other end can see her, and then she says, "Yes, yes," but no one, except Earl, pays any attention to her.

After a moment, the child puts the receiver down gently and returns to the sofa. "It's Daddy," she announces. "He says he wants to talk to the boys."

"I don't want to talk to him," George blurts, and stares straight ahead at the television.

Their mother blinks her eyes, opens and closes her mouth, looks from George to Louise to Earl and back to Louise again. "It's Daddy?" she says. "On the telephone?"

"He says he wants to talk to the boys."

Earl crosses his arms over his chest and shoves his body back into the sofa. Jackie Gleason dances delicately across the stage, a graceful fat man with a grin.

"Earl?" his mother asks, eyebrows raised.

"Nope."

The woman stands up slowly and walks to the phone. She speaks to their father; all three children watch carefully. She nods, listening, now and then opening her mouth to say something, closing it when she's interrupted. "Yes, yes," she says. And, "Yes, they're both here." She listens again, then says, "Yes, I know, but I should tell you, Nelson, the children . . . the boys, they feel funny about talking to you. Maybe . . . maybe you could write a letter first or something. It's sort of . . . hard for them. They feel very upset, you see, especially now, with the holidays and all. We're all very upset, and worried. And with me losing my job and having to work down at Grover Cronin's and all . . ." She nods, listens, her face expressionless. "Well, Lord knows, that would be very nice. It would have been very nice a long time ago, but no matter. We surely need it, Nelson." She listens again, longer this time, her face gaining energy and focus as she listens. "Well, I'll see, I'll ask them again. Wait a minute," she says, and puts her hand over the receiver and says, "Earl, your father wants to talk to you." She smiles wanly.

Earl squirms in his seat, crosses and uncrosses his legs, looks away from his mother to the wall opposite. "I got nothin' to say to him."

"Yes, but . . . I think he wants to say some things to you, though. Can't hurt to let him say them."

Silently, the boy gets up from the couch and crosses the room to the phone. As she hands him the receiver, his mother smiles with a satisfaction that bewilders and instantly angers him.

"H'lo," he says.

"H'lo, son. How're ya doin', boy?"

"Okay."

"Attaboy. Been a while, eh?"

"Yeah. A while."

"Well, I sure am sorry for that. You know, that it's been such a while and all. But I been going through some hard times myself. Got laid off, didn't work for most of the summer because of that damned strike. You read about that in the papers?"

"No."

"How's the paper route?"

"Okay."

"Hey, son, look, I know it's been tough, believe me, I know. It's been tough for everyone. So I know what you've been going through. No kidding. But it's gonna get better, things're gonna get better now. And I want to try and make it up to you guys a little, what you had to go through this last six months or so. I want to make it up to you guys a little, you and Georgie and Louise. Your ma, too. If you'll let me. Whaddaya say?"

"What?"

"Whaddaya say you let me try to make it up a little to you?"

"Sure. Why not? Try."

"Hey. Listen, Earl, that's quite an attitude you got there. We got to do something about that, eh? Some kind of attitude, son. I guess things've done a little changing around there since the old man left, eh? Eh?"

"What'd you expect? That everything'd stay the same?" Earl hears his voice rising and breaking into a yodel, and his eyes fill with tears.

"No, of course not. I understand, son. I understand. I know I've made some big mistakes this year, lately. Especially with you kids, in dealing with you kids. I didn't do it right, the leaving and all. It's hard, Earl, to do things like that right. I've learned a lot. But, hey, listen, everybody deserves a second chance. Right? Even your old man?"

"I guess so. Yeah."

"Sure. Damn right," he says, and then he adds that he'd like to come by tomorrow afternoon and see them, all of them, and leave off some Christmas presents. "You guys got your tree yet?"

Earl can manage only a tiny, cracked voice: "No, not yet."

"Well, that's good, real good. 'Cause I already got one in the back of the truck, a eight-footer I cut this afternoon myself. There's lots of trees out in the woods here in Holderness. Not many people and lots of trees. Anyhow, I got me a eight-footer, Scotch pine. The best. Whaddaya think?"

"Yeah. Sounds good."

His father rattles on, while Earl feels his chest tighten into a knot and tears spill over his cheeks. The man repeats several times that he's really sorry about the way he's handled things these last few months. But it's been hard for him, too, and it's hard for him even to say this, he's never been much of a talker, but he knows he's not been much of a father lately, either. That's all over now, though, over and done with, he assures Earl; it's all a part of the past. He's going to be a different man now, a new man. He's turned over a new leaf, he says. And Christmas seems like the perfect time for a new beginning, which is why he called them tonight and why he wants to come by tomorrow afternoon with presents and a tree and help set up and decorate the tree with them, just like in the old days. "Would you go for that? How'd that be, son?"

"Daddy?"

"Yeah, sure, son. What?"

"Daddy, are you gonna try to get back together with Mom?" Earl looks straight at his mother as he says this, and though she pretends to be watching Jackie Gleason, she is listening to his every word. As is George, and probably even Louise.

"Am I gonna try to get back together with your mom, eh?"

"Yeah."

"Well . . . that's a hard one, boy. You asked me a hard one." He is silent for a few seconds, and Earl can hear him sipping from a glass and then taking a deep draw from his cigarette. "I'll tell you, boy. The truth is, she doesn't want me back. You oughta know that by now. I left because *she* wanted me to leave, son. I did some wrong things, sure, lots of 'em, but I did not want to leave you guys. No, right from the beginning, this thing's been your mom's show. Not mine."

"Daddy, that's a lie."

"No, son. No. We fought a lot, your mom and me, like married people always do. But I didn't want to leave her and you kids. She told me to. And now, look at this—*she's* the one bringing these divorce charges and all, not me. You oughta see the things she's charging me with."

"What about . . . what about her having to protect herself? You know what I mean. I don't want to go into any details, but you know what I mean. And what about your *girl*friend?" he sneers.

His father is silent for a moment. Then he says, "You sure have got yourself an attitude since I been gone. Listen, kid, there's lots you don't know anything about, that nobody knows anything about, and there's lots more that you *shouldn't* know anything about. You might not believe this, Earl, but you're still a kid. You're a long ways from being a man. So don't go butting into where you're not wanted and getting into things between your mom and me that you can't understand anyhow. Just butt out. You hear me?"

"Yeah, I hear you."

"Lemme speak to your brother."

"He doesn't want to talk to you," Earl says, and he looks away from George's face and down at his own feet.

"Put your mother on, Earl."

"None of us wants to talk to you."

"Earl!" his mother cries. "Let me have the phone," she says, and she rises from the couch, her hand reaching toward him.

Earl places the receiver in its cradle. Then he stands there, looking into his mother's blue eyes, and she looks into his.

She says, "He won't call back."

Earl says, "I know."

The Visit

In late April of a recent year, I drove from my home in New York City across New Jersey to deliver a lecture at East Stroudsburg University, which is located in Pennsylvania at the southern end of the Pocono Mountains, not far from the Delaware Water Gap. I arrived a few hours earlier than my hosts expected me, so that, once there, I was free to drive twenty miles farther north to the small town of Tobyhanna, where my mother and father lived with me and my brother and sister for a single year, 1952, when I was twelve, my brother ten, my sister six.

For the five of us, the year we lived in Tobyhanna was the most crucial year of our shared life. It defined us: we were that family; we have remained that family. The following summer, my mother and father got divorced, and from then on, although we were the same, everything else was different. Not better, just different.

Looking back, I see that both my parents were careening out of control with rage, frustration, and fear. For years, my father had been plotting ways to leave my mother, whose dependency and hysteria had imprisoned him then, as later they would me. For her part, my mother had been just as busy trying to keep him from leaving, which only made him feel more trapped today than yesterday. He was thirty-eight; his life was skidding past. And he thought that he was somehow better than she, a more important person in the overall scheme of things than she, and he acted accordingly. This made my mother wild.

My father was a plumber, and he had been hired by a New England contractor as superintendent of all the plumbing, heating, and air-conditioning installation in an enormous Army shipping and storage depot being built in Tobyhanna. It was one of the first big postwar military bases commissioned by the Eisenhower administration. My father was the company's man sent down from Hartford to run its largest out-of-state job, an extraordinary position for a young journeyman pipe fitter with no more than a high school education, a man whose biggest job up to then had been adding a wing to the Veterans' Hospital in Manchester, New Hampshire. But he was bright, and he worked hard, and he was very good-looking, and lucky. People liked him, especially men, and women flirted with him.

He was a heavy drinker, though, starting at it earlier every day. And with each additional long night's stay at the bar in Tobyhanna, he turned increasingly nasty and sometimes violent. The job he held was, in fact, way over his head, and he was terrified—not of being fired, but of being found out, and not so much by other people, as by himself.

I drove my car into Tobyhanna, a poor, bedraggled batch of houses and garages and trailers strung along a winding two-lane road abandoned long ago for the Stroudsburg-Scranton highway, and saw at once the bar where my father used to spend his evenings after work and as much of his weekends as he could steal from the house in the woods where he had established his nervous wife and three children. It was a small, depressing, impoverished town, despite the presence of the Army depot—or perhaps because of it.

I drew my car up to the bar on the main street, shut off the motor, and went inside. It was dark, dirty, and damp, smelled of old beer, sweat, and pickled, hard-boiled eggs, with a jukebox in the back, a U-shaped linoleum-covered bar that ran the length of the room, and several dim, flickering neon beer signs in the window.

I ordered a beer from the middle-aged woman behind the bar, whose exact, round, dun-colored double—her twin, I thought, or surely her sister—sat on a stool on the other side of the bar. She sat next to a man with a tracheotomy who was talking to her in a harsh, electronic moan.

A second man was perched on a stool a ways down from me—a scrawny fellow in his mid-fifties whose arms were covered with badly drawn tattoos. His head was wobbling on his neck above a bottle of beer, and he seemed not to notice when I sat down.

The place had not changed a bit in the thirty-four years since I last entered it. The doubling image of the round woman behind the bar and the woman sitting by the man with the hole in his throat acted like a drug or a mathematical formula or a vision, instantly doubling the place itself with my memory of it, matching my arrival in Tobyhanna today with my memory of a Saturday in winter, when my father drove me and my younger brother into town with him—ostensibly to pick up a few groceries or some such errand. It's no longer clear to me why we three males left the house and hearth for town that day, just as it was not clear to me why I decided to drive north from Stroudsburg, when I more easily and pleasantly could have strolled around the college campus for a few hours, killing time. There was a powerful need to go there, but no remembered reason.

I remember my father bringing my brother and me straight into the bar with him, and I remember his cronies—soldiers and construction workers—buying my brother and me Cokes and potato chips. They teased us, because we were miniaturized imitations of men, and praised us for our manliness, because they were men, while down along the bar my father leaned over a friend's shoulder and talked intently into his ear, then smiled at a fat woman (or so she looked to me) with bright red lipstick who sat next to him and patted her forearm affectionately, and soon he switched his attention completely over to her, leaving his male friend to drink alone for a while. I watched this take place.

The bartender waddled over to me, picked up my nearly empty bottle, and studied it and set it back down. "Want another?"

I shook my head no.

She lit a cigarette, inhaled furiously, a large, red-faced woman smoking like a steamship, and she studied my face the way she had examined my beer bottle. "You're not from around here," she stated.

"Last time I was in here was thirty-four years ago," I said.

She laughed, once, more a bark than a laugh. "It hasn't changed."

"Nope," I said. "It's the same."

The man next to me at the bar, his head wobbling like a heavy flower on a stem, was alert, more or less, and watching me now. "You ain't old enough to've been in here thirty-four years ago," he growled.

"I was only a kid then. With my father. My father brought me in here."

The man sat up straight and swept his arms around and pointed at each of the four corners of the dingy room. "This place, it hasn't changed," he said. "Where you from?"

"New York City."

"Hah!" he laughed. "This," he said, waving his arms again, indicating the three other people in the bar as if they were a place, "this is the way to live! You never lock your doors here. It's safe," he proclaimed. "Not like, not like your goddamned New York City."

I nodded in agreement, got off my stool, and made for the door.

He called after me, "Hey, buddy! You're welcome!" He grinned through loose red lips and broken teeth and started to cackle at his joke on me and then cough and finally wheeze and whoop with joy, while I hurried out the front door to my car.

On our way home from the bar, me in front in the passenger's seat, my brother in back, my father said, "Listen, boys, let's just say we spent the time at the depot. In the office. I should've gone over some draw-ings there, anyhow, so we might's well say that's what we did, right?" He looked over at me intently. "Right?"

"Sure," I said. "I don't care."

I peered out the window at the pale curtains of snow falling, the houses that occasionally flashed past, the dark shadows of trees, and of the Poconos closing off the sky. I didn't care.

My brother didn't say anything, but my father never asked him to. I was the one he worried about; I was the one my mother would interrogate.

The house itself had not changed. Except for a coat of blue-gray paint, it was still the same two-story farmhouse with the long shed attached at the rear and the weather-beaten, unpainted barn across the circular drive. The two stone chimneys at the ends of the house were matched by the pair of huge maple trees next to the road. Hanging from one of the trees was a small wooden sign. RETTSTADT'S RESTAURANT, it said. SERVING DINNERS FRI. TO SAT. 5 P.M. TO 9 P.M. I could not imagine who would drive all the way out from Tobyhanna—five miles through the woods on a narrow, winding, hilly road, passing barely a dozen other houses on the way, broken-down and half-finished bungalows and trailers set on cinder blocks among car chassis and old refrigerators and tires—for dinner at Rettstadt's.

I looked at my watch, 4:45, and drew my car off the road, pulled into the driveway, and parked by the back porch, facing the door that, when we lived there, opened into the kitchen. By now, my limbs felt weak and awash with blood, and my heart was pounding furiously, as if I were at the entrance to a cave.

By the time my father and brother and I arrived home, the snow was coming down heavily, and my father told my mother that the snow had slowed him up, he had got stuck twice, and, besides, he had to spend quite a while at the office at the depot working on some drawings for

Monday. That was why we were so late getting home from town.

My mother looked at him wearily. It was the same old story, the same old challenge tossed down, the dare for her to take him on one more time: either believe the liar or enrage him by forcing him to tell the truth.

I know from photographs that my mother was a pretty woman—small, blond, precisely featured, with lively hazel eyes and a sensitive mouth. "Petite," she liked to say of herself. People said she looked like beautiful women—Claudette Colbert, Ann Blyth, Bette Davis—and she did. Not like any one of them, but she belonged to that particular caste of beauty. I remember her that afternoon standing before the stove, a ladle in hand, a steaming pot before her—but that, too, is a generic image, like her beauty. It was a Saturday afternoon; it was snowing.

My brother dodged around her and disappeared like a mouse through the living room toward the stairs and the unused bedroom on the second floor, a kind of attic in the back where we had set up our electric trains. My sister—I have no idea where she was, possibly in the kitchen, possibly with a friend for the afternoon: country children often visited each other on weekends; it made the driving back and forth easier for the parents. I hung around by the kitchen door, as if waiting for orders from one or the other of my parents. They were looking angrily at one another, however, and did not seem to know that I existed.

My mother said, "I know where you've been. I can smell it on you. I can smell her, too."

My father's face reddened, and he glowered down at her from his full height, which, because my mother was small and I was only twelve years old, seemed a considerable height, though he was never any taller than six feet, which turned out to be my height as well. He began to shout at her. It was at first a welling-up and then an overflow of anger, wordless—or no words that I can recall—a kind of sustained roar, which she answered by letting loose with shrieks, cries, calls, wails—again, with no words that I can recall now and surely could not hear then, for the tone was all one needed in order to understand the sad rage this man and woman felt toward one another, like a pair of beasts caught side by side, each with a limb in the jaws of the same cruel trap, and then they begin to gnaw on the flesh and bone of their own trapped limbs.

What in 1952 had been the kitchen was now a restaurant dining room, the floor covered with bright green, indoor-outdoor carpeting, the walls paneled over in imitation pine with five-and-dime framed pictures of a trout stream with a deer bending its head to drink, a barn and silo and amber waves of grain, a covered bridge with throngs of fall foliage behind it. I smelled food cooking and walked through the door that had once led to the woodshed behind the kitchen and discovered that it led now to a large, open room filled with stainless steel counters, dishwashers, sinks, and stoves. I saw in the far corner of the room a small man in white pants and T-shirt scrubbing utensils in a sink. He saw me and waved, as if he'd been expecting me. He was in his late fifties, I guessed, square-faced, short, thick-bodied.

I said, "I'm not here to eat, don't worry."

He smiled and nodded. "We're not set up yet, anyhow. Too early, friend."

"Yes, well, I'm not here to eat," I repeated. "I used to live here."

He squinted across the room at me. Then he pursed his lips and pronounced my last name. My very name!

"Yes!" I said, astonished. "That's right!" I did not know this man, I had never seen him before. I felt my father loom up beside me, huge and red and full of heat, and I looked automatically to my left, where I felt his presence most, and leaned away from him, then recovered, and stood straight and regarded the small man in white before me.

He put down the spoon he'd been scrubbing and took a step

closer. He said my father's first name and his last. "The plumber. Right? The plumbing guy?"

"Well, yes. My father. I'm not him, though. I'm his son."

He examined my face for a few seconds, as if he did not believe me. He was looking at a gray-haired man in his late forties, a man nearly a decade older than my father had been in 1952. I was, however, more likely my father than my father's son.

I told him that my father had died over five years ago.

He was sad to hear that and asked what he died of.

I said, "He pretty much drank himself to death."

He nodded. "Yeah, well, those construction guys. They all hit the booze pretty hard. I ran the food concession for that job your dad was on, down there at the depot," he said. "I was a kid then, just out of the service. I knew your dad. What a guy he was! Memorable. He had what you call real personality, your dad." He wiped his hands with a towel and stuck one out to shake. "George Rettstadt," he said. "I bought this place a few years after your dad lived here. He rented it, right? Brought your mom and the kids out from someplace in New England for a while, right? C'mon and look around, if you want. I've made loads of changes, as you can see," he said, waving his arms at the four corners of the room, like the drunk at the bar.

I agreed. There had been a lot of changes. But even so, it was the same house, and it smelled the same to me, the light fell at familiar angles through the maple trees and tall, narrow windows, rooms opened into rooms where they always had. Rettstadt had turned woodshed into kitchen and kitchen into dining room, he had covered walls and floors, and he had lowered ceilings, hung brass lamps and tacky pictures. He had altered the whole function of the house—though he still lived in it, he assured me, upstairs. The living room was now a large second dining room that was for private parties, which he said was most of his business. "You know, Lions Club, Boy Scouts, stuff like that. Reunions, weddings, like that."

Rettstadt walked ahead of me, pointing out the changes, while I saw only the house that lay hidden beneath this one, the white house under the blue one, the drab, decaying farmhouse in the woods where a young man had stuck his unhappy wife and bewildered children while he drove into town to work every day and to drink every night and tried to invent a man he could never become.

On that snowy Saturday long ago, while my mother shrieked at my father and he barked back like an angry dog at her small, spitting face, I finally darted past them and fled the kitchen for the bedroom upstairs that I shared with my brother. It was a corner room with a pair of long windows on one side and our twin beds on the other. I remember lying on my bed, the one nearer the windows, reading a comic book, probably, with my wet feet on the clean bedspread, my arm crooked back to support my head, when suddenly the door flew open, and my mother was hovering above me like a great bird, clutching my shirt, and yanking me up beside her on the bed.

"Tell me!" she cried. "Tell me where you went! Don't *you* lie to me, too!" She raised her hand and held it, palm out, a few inches from my face, as if she wanted me to read it, and she said, "Don't you lie to me, or I swear, I'll go crazy. Tell me where you went all afternoon! I know he took you to the bar, and he didn't go to the depot. He just went to the bar. And a woman was there, I know it. Tell me the truth."

I did not protest, I did not hesitate. I nodded my head up and down, and said, "We went to the bar in town. Nowhere else. A woman was there."

She smiled, wiped the tears from her cheeks, and stood. "Good boy," she said. "Good boy." She turned and left the room. I lay back down trembling, and in a few seconds the buzz of the electric trains from the attic room in back replaced the buzz in my head, and I believe I fell asleep.

When George Rettstadt asked me if I wanted to see how he'd changed the rooms upstairs, where he said he had fixed up a large apartment for himself and his wife, I felt my chest tighten. "No," I said very quickly, as if he had invited me to look steadily at a gruesome object. "No, that's okay, I'm in kind of a hurry, anyhow," I said, easing toward the door. "I wanted to walk around the yard a minute. I wanted to see where my brother and sister and I used to play. You know."

Rettstadt said, "Sure, take all the time you want. Look at whatever you want to look at, everything's unlocked. We never lock our doors out here, you know." He opened the door, we shook hands, and I stepped out, breathing rapidly.

I did poke into the barn, but there was nothing about it that spoke to me. I stood inside the dark, cluttered building, and it was as if I were resting, idling, conserving energy for a more strenuous exertion to come.

A moment later, I had walked around the back of the house, crossed through the tangled brush and crumbling stone walls in the gathering dusk, and had come to stand next to the house on the far side, just below my old bedroom window.

My father's heavy footsteps on the stairs had wakened me. He swung open the bedroom door, and I knew instantly, as if I had been standing downstairs in the kitchen between my mother and father, what had happened between them when she returned from my room armed with my betrayal, and with utter clarity and an almost welcoming acceptance, I knew what would happen now between him and me.

Violence produces white light and heat inside the head, and it happens both to the person who administers the beating and to the person who is beaten. It is never dark and cold. It happens at the instant of violent contact, before pain is felt, or fear, even, or guilt, so that pain, fear, and guilt come to be seen as merely the price one pays after the fact for this extraordinary immolation. It's as if violence were a gift worth any price. Beyond the light and the heat, it's a gift that engenders gorgeous dreams of retribution, and they last for tens of generations of fathers and children, husbands and wives—it's a gift that shapes and drives fantasies of becoming huge as a glacier and hard as iron, fast as light, and sudden, like a volcano.

When you are hit in the head or slammed in the ribs and thrown to the floor by a powerful man, you find instantly that you are already halfway into a narrative that portrays your return to that moment, a narrative whose primary function is to provide reversal: to make the child into the man, the weak into the strong, the bad into the good. *Listen to me*: you are locked into that narrative, and no other terms, except those present at its inception, at the very opening of the drama, are available for the reversal—and, *oh!* when that happens, I have risen up from my narrow bed in the upstairs corner room I shared with my brother in Tobyhanna in 1952, and I overwhelm my dead father's rage with an awful, endless rage of my own.

I eventually moved away from that spot beneath the window of the bedroom and got into my car and drove back to Tobyhanna and then on down to East Stroudsburg University, where that evening I gave my lecture to a small gathering of students and teachers, who seemed appreciative and expressed it with good-natured, gentle applause. Afterwards, we ate and drank a little wine in a local restaurant, and I drove home to New York City.

I will not go back to the house in Tobyhanna or to the bar in town, just as—after having been there once—I have not returned to any of the other houses we lived in when I was growing up, or to the apartments and barrooms in Florida and Boston and New Hampshire, where I first learned the need to protect other people from myself, people who loved me, male and female, and utter strangers, male and female. I go back to each, one time only, and I stand silently outside a window or a door, and I deliberately play back the horrible events that took place there. Then I move on.

I have traveled a lot in recent years, and consequently have completed almost all my journeys now. And when I have returned to every place where someone beat me or I beat someone, when there is no place left to go back to, then for the rest of my life I will have only my memories, these stories, to go to—for the heat, for the light, for the awful, endlessly recurring end of it.

Lobster Night

Stacy didn't mean to tell Noonan that when she was seventeen she was struck by lightning. She rarely told anyone and never a man she was attracted to or hoped soon to be sleeping with. Always, at the last second, an alarm in the center of her brain went off, and she changed the subject, asked a question, like, "How's your wife?" or, "You ready for another?" She was a summertime bartender at Noonan's, a sprawling log building with the main entrance and kitchen door facing the road and three large, plate-glass, dining-room windows in back and a wide, redwood deck cantilevered above the yard for taking in the great sunset views of the Adirondack Mountains. The sign said NOONAN'S FAMILY RESTAURANT, but in fact it was a roadhouse, a bar that—except in ski season and on summer weekends when drive-by tourists with kids mistakenly pulled in for lunch or supper—catered mostly to heavy drinkers from the several nearby hamlets.

The night that Stacy told Noonan about the lightning was also the night she shot and killed him. She had rented an A-frame at off-season rates in one of the hamlets and was working for Noonan only till the winter snows blew in from Quebec and Ontario. From May to November, she usually waited tables or tended bar in one or another of the area restaurants and the rest of the year taught alpine skiing at Whiteface

481

Mountain. That was her real job, her profession, and she had the healthy, ash blond good looks of a poster girl for women's Nordic sports: tall, broad-shouldered, flat-muscled, with square jaw and high cheekbones. Despite appearances, however, she viewed herself as a plain-faced, twenty-eight-year-old ex-athlete, with the emphasis on *ex-*. Eight years ago, she was captain of the nationally ranked St. Regis University downhill ski team, only a sophomore and already a star. Then in the Eastern Regionals she pushed her luck, took a spectacular, cartwheeling spill in the giant slalom, and shattered her left thigh. The video of the last ten seconds of her fall was still being shown at the front of the sports segment on the evening news from Plattsburgh.

A year of physical therapy, and she returned to college and the slopes, but she'd lost her fearlessness and, with it, her interest in college, and dropped out before fall break. Her parents had long since swapped their house for an RV and retired to a semipermanent campground outside Phoenix; her three older brothers had drifted downstate to Albany for work in construction; but Stacy came back anyhow to where she'd grown up. She had friends from high school there, mostly women, who still thought of her as a star: "Stace was headed for the Olympics, y'know," they told strangers. Over time, she lived briefly and serially with three local men in their early thirties, men she called losers even when she was living with them—slow-talking guys with beards and ponytails, rusted-out pickup trucks, and large dogs with bandannas tied around their necks. Otherwise and most of the time, she lived alone.

Stacy had never tended bar for Noonan before this, and the place was a little rougher than she was used to. But she was experienced and had cultivated a set of open-faced, wise-guy ways and a laid-back manner that protected her from her male customers' presumptions. Which, in spite of her ways and manner, she needed: she was a shy, northcountry girl who, when it came to personal matters, volunteered very little about herself, not because she had secrets, but because there was so much about herself that she did not yet understand. She did understand, however, that the last thing she wanted or needed was a love affair with a man like Noonan—married, twenty years older than she, and her boss. She was seriously attracted to him, though. And not just sexually. Which was why she got caught off guard.

It was late August, a Thursday, the afternoon of Lobster Night. The place was empty, and she and Noonan were standing hip to hip behind the bar, studying the lobster tank. Back in June, Noonan, who did all the cooking himself, had decided that he could attract a better class of clientele and simplify the menu at the same time if during the week he offered nightly specials, which he advertised on a chalkboard hung from the Family Restaurant sign outside. Monday became Mexican Night, with dollar margaritas and all the rice and refried beans you can eat. Tuesday was Liver 'n' Onions Night. Wednesday was Fresh Local Corn Night, although, until mid-August, the corn came, not from Adirondack gardens, but from southern New Jersey and Pennsylvania by way of the Grand Union supermarket in Lake Placid. And Thursday—when local folks rarely ate out and therefore needed something more than merely special—was designated Lobster Night. Weekends, he figured, took care of themselves.

Noonan had set his teenage son's unused tropical fish tank at the end of the bar, filled it with water, and arranged with the Albany wholesaler to stock the tank on his Monday runs to Lake Placid with a dozen live lobsters. All week, the lobsters rose and sank in the cloudy tank like dark thoughts. Usually, by Tuesday afternoon, the regulars at the bar had given the lobsters names like Marsh and Redeye and Honest Abe, local drinking, hunting, and bar-brawling legends, and had handicapped the order of their execution. In the villages around, Thursday quickly became everyone's favorite night for eating out, and soon Noonan was doubling his weekly order, jamming the fish tank, and making Lobster Night an almost merciful event for the poor crowded creatures.

"You ought to either get a bigger tank or else just don't buy so many of them," Stacy said.

Noonan laughed. "Stace," he said. "Compared to the cardboard boxes these guys've been in, the fish tank is lobster heaven. Four days of swimmin' in this, they're free range, practically." He draped a heavy hand across her shoulder and drummed her collarbone with a fingertip. "They don't know the difference, anyhow. They're dumber than fish, y'know."

"You don't know what they feel or don't feel. Maybe they spend the last few days before they die flipping out from being so confined. I sure would."

"Yeah, well, I don't go there, Stace. Trying to figure what lobsters feel, that's the road to vegetarianism. The road to vegans-ville."

She smiled at that. Like most of the Adirondack men she knew, Noonan was a dedicated, lifelong hunter—mainly of deer, but also of game birds and rabbits, which he fed to his family and sometimes put on the restaurant menu as well. He shot and trapped animals he didn't eat, too—foxes, coyotes, lynxes, even bear—and sold their pelts. Normally, this would disgust Stacy or at least seriously test her acceptance of Noonan's character. She wasn't noticeably softhearted when it came to animals or sentimental, but shooting and trapping creatures you didn't intend to eat made no sense to her. She was sure it was cruel and was almost ready to say it was sadistic.

In Noonan, though, it oddly attracted her, this cruelty. He was a tall, good-looking man in an awkward, rough-hewn way, large in the shoulders and arms, with a clean-shaven face and buzz-cut head one or two sizes too small for his body. It made him look boyish to her, and whenever he showed signs of cruelty—his relentless, not quite good-natured teasing of Gail, his regular waitress, and the LaPierre brothers, two high-school kids he hired in summers to wash dishes and bus tables—to her he seemed even more boyish than usual. It was all somehow innocent, she thought. It had the same strange, otherworldly innocence of the animals that he liked to kill. A man that manly, that *different* from a woman, can actually make you feel more womanly—as if you were of a different species. It freed you from having to compare yourself to him.

"You ever try that? Vegetarianism?" Noonan asked. He tapped the glass of the tank with a knuckle, as if signaling one of the lobsters to come on over.

"Once. When I was seventeen. I kept it up for a while, two years, as a matter of fact. Till I busted up my leg and had to quit college." He knew the story of her accident; everyone knew it. She'd been a local hero before the break and had become a celebrity afterwards. "It's hard to keep being a vegetarian in the hospital, though. That's what got me off it."

"No shit. What got you *on* it?"

That's when she told him. "I was struck by lightning."

He looked at her. "Lightning! Jesus! Are you kidding me? How the hell did *that* happen?"

"The way it always happens, I guess. I was doing something else at the time. Going up the stairs to bed, actually, in my parents' house. It was in a thunderstorm, and I reached for the light switch on the wall, and, Bam! Just like they say, a bolt out of the blue."

"But it didn't kill you," Noonan tenderly observed.

"No. But it sure could've. You could say it *almost* killed me, though."

"But it didn't."

"Right. But it *almost* killed me. That's not the same as 'it didn't kill me.' If you know what I mean."

"Yeah, but you're okay now, right? No lingering aftereffects, I mean. Except, of course, for your brief flirtation with the veg-world." He squeezed the meat of her shoulder and smiled warmly.

She sighed. Then smiled back—she liked his touch—and tried again: "No, it really changed me. It did. A bolt of lightning went through my body and my brain, and I almost died from it, even though it only lasted a fraction of a second and then was over."

"But you're okay now, right?"

"Sure."

"So what was it like, getting hit by lightning?"

She hesitated a moment before answering. "Well, I thought I was shot. With a gun. Seriously. There was this loud noise, like an explosion, and when I woke up, I was lying at the bottom of the stairs, and Daddy and Mom were standing over me like I was dead, and I said, 'Who shot me, Daddy?' It really messed with my mind for a long time. I tried to find out if anybody else I knew had been struck by lightning, but nobody had. Although a few people said they knew someone or heard of someone who'd been hit and survived it. But nobody I ever met myself had been through it. I was the only person I knew who'd had this particular experience. Still am. It's strange, but when you're the only person you know who's gone through something that's changed you into a completely different person, for a while it's like you're on your own planet, like if you're a Vietnam vet and don't know anyone else who was in Vietnam, too."

"I can dig it," Noonan said somberly, although he himself had not been in Vietnam.

"You get used to it, though. And then it turns out to be like life. I mean, there's you, and there's everybody else. Only, unlike the way it is for everybody else, this happened to me in a flash, not over years and so slow you don't even realize how true it is. Know what I mean?"

"How true what is?"

"Well, just that there's you, and there's everybody else. And that's life."

"Sure, I can understand that." He turned away from the tank and looked into Stacy's blue eyes. "It's the same for me. Only with me it was on account of this goddamned bear. Did I ever tell you about the bear that tore my camp down?"

She said, "No, Noonan. You didn't."

"It's the same thing, like getting struck by lightning and afterwards feeling like you're a changed man." It was years ago, he said, when he was between marriages and drinking way too much and living in his hunting camp up on Baxter Mountain because his first wife had got the house in the divorce. He got drunk every night in town at the Spread Eagle or the Elm Tree or the old Dew Drop Inn, and afterwards, when he drove back to Baxter Mountain, he'd park his truck at the side of the road, because the trail was too rough even for a four-by-four, and walk the two miles through the woods to his camp. It was a windblown, one-room cabin with a sleeping loft and a woodstove, and one night, when he stumbled back from the village, the place had been trashed by a bear. "An adolescent male, I figured, it being springtime, who'd been kicked out of his own house and home. Not unlike myself. I had a certain sympathy for him, therefore. But he'd wrecked my cabin looking for food and had busted a window going out, and I knew he'd come back, so I had to take him down."

The next evening, Noonan blew out his kerosene lantern, climbed into the sleeping loft with a bottle of Jim Beam, his Winchester 30.06, and his flashlight, and waited. Around midnight, as if brushing away a cobweb, the bear tore off the sheet of polyurethane that Noonan had tacked over the broken window, crawled into the cabin, and made for the same cupboard he'd emptied the night before. Noonan, half-drunk by now, clicked on his flashlight, caught the startled bear in its beam, and fired, but only wounded him. Maddened with pain, the bear roared and stood on his hind legs, flinging his forelegs in the air right and left, and before Noonan could fire again, the animal had grabbed onto a timber that held up the loft and ripped it from its place, tearing out several other supporting timbers with it, until the entire cabin was collapsing around Noonan and the wounded bear. The structure was feeble any-how, made of old cast-off boards tacked together in a hurry twenty years ago, never rebuilt, never renovated, and it came down upon Noo-nan's head with ease. The bear escaped into the night, but Noonan lay trapped under the fallen roof of the cabin, unable to move, his right arm broken, he assumed, and possibly several ribs. "That's when it hap-pened," he said.

"What?" Stacy dipped a dozen beer mugs two at a time into cold water, pulled them out, and stuck them into the freezer to frost for later on.

"Just like you said. It changed my life, Stace."

"No kidding. How?" She refilled the salt shakers on the bar.

"Well, I stopped drinking, for one thing. That was a few years later, though. But I lay there all that night and most of the next day. Until this beautiful young woman out looking for her lost dog came wandering by. And, Stace," he said, his voice suddenly lowered, "I married her."

She put her fists on her hips and checked him out. "Seriously?"

He smiled. "Well, yeah, sort of. I'd actually known her a long time beforehand, and she'd visited me a few times at my camp, let us say. But, yeah, I did marry her . . . eventually. And we were very happy. For a while."

"Uh-huh. For a while."

Noonan nodded, smiled, winked. Then bumped her hip with his and said, "I gotta get the kitchen set up. We can pursue this later, Stace. If you want."

She didn't answer. She started slinging bottles of beer into the dark-ness of the cooler, and when she next looked up, he was gone, and a pair of road workers were coming through the door, hot and sunburned and thirsty.

The day had been clear with wispy fantails of clouds in the east, promis-ing a soft, late-summer sunset over the mountains for the folks dining out at Noonan's Family Restaurant. It was unusually busy that evening, even for Lobster Night. Depressed by a quarrel earlier with her pregnant daughter over money, Gail fell quickly behind in her orders and, after being yelled at, first by her hungry customers in the dining room and then by Noonan in the kitchen, where seven or eight bright red lobsters on their platters awaited pickup, she broke down and ran sobbing into the ladies' room. She came out, but only after Stacy went after her and promised to help in the dining room, where fifteen kids from three unrelated French Canadian families were banging their silverware rhythmically against their glasses. Back in the kitchen, halfway into the supper hour, Donny LaPierre threw down his dish towel and told Noonan to take his job and shove it, he didn't graduate high school just to get treated like an idiot for minimum wage. His younger brother Timmy, who would graduate the following year, high-fived Donny and said, "Whoa! Way cool, DL," and the two walked out together.

Noonan stood at the door and bellowed, "Don't even *think* about gettin' paid for this week!" and the boys gave him the finger from the parking lot and laughed and started hitching to Lake Placid.

Eventually, Gail and Stacy, between them, got everyone satisfactorily served, and the diners and their children quieted down, and order was restored, even in the kitchen—where Noonan, almost grateful for the chance to do it right, took over the dishwasher's job himself. At the bar, four bored, lonely regulars, men of habit, were drinking and smoking cigarettes and watching Montreal lose to the Mets on television. Stacy gave them a round on the house for their patience, and all four smiled and thanked her and resumed watching the game.

In the fish tank, the one last lobster bumped lazily against the glass. Stacy wiped down the bar and came to a slow stop by the tank. She leaned down and gazed into what she believed was one of the lobster's eyes—more of a greenish knob than an eyeball, anatomically absurd to her—and tried to imagine what the world of Noonan's Family Restaurant looked like through that knob and the thirty-gallon cell of cloudy water surrounding it and beyond that the lens of the algae-stained glass wall. It probably looks like an alien planet out here, she thought. Or incomprehensibly foreign, like some old-time Chinese movie, so you don't even know what the story's about, who's the good guy and who's the bad guy. Or maybe, instead of an actual place or thing, to a lobster it looks like only an idea out here. That scared her.

There must be some kind of trade-off among the senses, she reasoned, like with blind and deaf people. If one sense is weak, another must be strong, and vice versa. Lobsters, she figured, probably couldn't see very well, living as they did way at the dark bottom of the sea. To distinguish food from friend and friend from foe, they would need powerful senses of smell and hearing. She brought her face up close to the glass and almost touched it with her nose. The lobster bobbled and jiggled just beyond, as if struggling to use its weak eyes and tank-impaired hearing and olfactory senses to determine if Stacy was a thing that could eat it or breed with it or be eaten by it. So much in the life of any creature depends upon being able to identify the other creatures accurately, Stacy thought. In the tank, and out of it, too. And this poor beast, with only its ridiculous eyes to depend upon, was lost; was wholly, utterly, lost. She reached toward the lobster, as if to pat it, to comfort and reassure it that she would not eat it, and she could not breed with it, and would not make a decent meal for it, either.

Noonan's large hand dropped unseen from above, as if through dark water, and came to rest upon hers. She turned, startled, and there was his face a bare few inches away, his large, blood-shot, brown eyes and his porous, peach-colored skin with black whiskers popping through like lopped-off stalks, soft caves of nostrils, red lips, tobacco-stained teeth, wet tongue. She yanked her hand away and stepped back, bringing him into a more appropriate and safe focus, with the bar between them like a fence, keeping him out or her in, she wasn't sure, but it didn't matter, as long as they were on opposite sides of it.

"You scared me!" she said.

He leaned across the bar and smiled indulgently. Behind her, the men drank beer and watched baseball. She heard the crowd at the ballpark chitter in anticipation of the pitch. From the dining room came the low rumble of families distributing food among themselves and their hushed commentaries as they evaluated its quality and the size of their portions, praise and disappointment voiced equally low, as if both were gossip, and the clink of their forks and knives, gulps, chomps, an old man's sudden laugh, the snap of lobster claws and legs breaking.

"Stace, soon's you get the chance, c'mon out to the kitchen. There's something I want to tell you." He turned and abruptly strode to the dining room, spoke a moment to Gail, sympathetically offering to let her go home early, Stacy guessed, getting rid of witnesses, and gathered up a tub of dirty dishes left behind by Timmy LaPierre. As Noonan disappeared into the kitchen, he glanced over at Stacy, and though a stranger would have thought him expressionless, she saw him practically speaking with his face, saw him using it to say in a low, cold voice, "Stace, as soon as we're alone here tonight, I'm going to take you down."

She decided to force the issue, to go back to the kitchen right now, before Gail left, while there was still a fairly large number of people in the dining room and the four guys at the bar, and if Noonan said what she expected him to say and did what she expected him to do, then she would walk out the door just like the LaPierre boys had, take off in her car, the doors locked and windows up, the wheels spinning, kicking gravel, and squealing rubber as she left the parking lot and hit the road to Lake Placid.

Who the hell did he think he was, anyhow, coming on to her like that, him a married man, middle-aged, practically? Sure, she had been attracted to him from the first time she saw him, when he interviewed her for the job and had made her turn and turn again, while he sat there on the barstool and looked her over with genuine interest, almost with innocence, as if she were a bouquet of wildflowers he'd ordered for his wife. "Turn around, Stace. Let me see the other side." She had actually liked his suddenness, his fearless, impersonal way of telling her exactly what he wanted from her, instructing her to wear a tight, white T-shirt and black jeans or shorts to work in and to be friendly with the customers, especially the males, because he wanted return business, not one-night stands, and men will come back and stay late again and again, if they think the pretty girl behind the bar likes them personally. She had smiled like a coconspirator when he told her that and said, "No problema, Mr. Noonan."

"Hey, you can call me Charlie, or you can call me Noonan. Just don't call me at home, and never call me Mister. You're hired, Stace. Go change the dress and be back here by six."

But all that was before she told him about having been struck by lightning. Until then, she had thought it was safe to flirt with him, he was married, after all; and he was so unlike the losers she usually hooked up with that she had decided it was harmless as well as interesting to be attracted to him, nothing could come of it, anyhow; and wasn't it intelligent, after all, for a young woman to want a successful older man's attention and approval? Wasn't that how you learned about life and who you were?

Somehow, this afternoon everything had changed. She couldn't have said how it had changed or why, but everything was different now, especially between her and Noonan. It wasn't what he had done or not done or even anything he had said. It was what she had said.

A woman who has been struck by lightning is not like other people. Most of the time Stacy could forget that fact, could even forget what that horrible night had felt like, when she was only seventeen and thought that she had been shot in the head. But all she had to do was say the words, reestablish the fact, and the whole thing came back in full force—her astonishment, the physical and mental pain, and the long-lasting fear, even to today, that it would happen to her again. The only people who say lightning never strikes twice in the same place have never been struck once. Which was why she was so reluctant to speak of it.

But Noonan had charmed her into speaking of it, and all at once, there it was again, as if a glass wall had appeared between her and other people, Noonan especially. The man had no idea who she was. But that wasn't his fault. It was hers. She had misled him. She had misled herself. She checked the drinks of the customers at the bar. Then, to show Gail where she was headed, she pointedly flipped a wave across the dining room and walked back to the kitchen.

When she entered, Noonan was leaning against the edge of the sink, his large, bare arms folded across his chest, his head lowered: a man absorbing a sobering thought.

Stacy said, "What'd you want to tell me?" She stayed by the door, propping it open with her foot.

He shook his head as if waking from a nap. "What? Oh, Stace! Sorry, I was thinking. Actually, Stace, I was thinking about you."

"Me?"

"Yeah. Close the door. Come on in." He peered around her into the dining room. "Is Gail okay? She's not crying or anything anymore, is she?"

"No." Stacy let the door slide shut behind her. The exhaust fan chugged above the stove, and the dishwasher sloshed quietly next to the sink, tinkling the glasses and silverware inside and jiggling the plates. On a shelf by the rear door, a portable radio played country-and-western music at low volume—sweetly melancholic background music. There was a calming order and peacefulness to the kitchen, a low-key domesticity about it that, even though the room was as familiar to her as the kitchen of her rented A-frame, surprised Stacy. She felt guilty for having been so suspicious of Noonan and so quick to judge and condemn him. He was an ordinary man, that's all, a basically harmless and well-intended man; she had no reason to fear him. She liked his boyish good looks, didn't she? and enjoyed his smoky, baritone voice and unapologetic northcountry accent, and she was pleased and flattered by his sudden flashes of intimacy. "What did you want to tell me, Noonan?" she repeated, softly this time, invitingly.

He leaned forward, eyes twinkling, mischief on his mind, and looked right and left, as if not wishing to be overheard. "What do you say we cook that last lobster and split it between ourselves?" He gave her a broad smile and rubbed his hands together. "Don't tell Gail. I'll boil and chill the sucker and break out the meat and squeeze a little lime juice over it, and we'll eat it later, after we close up, just the two of us. Maybe open a bottle of wine. Whaddaya say?" He came up to her and put his arm around her shoulder and steered her toward the door. "You go liberate the animal from its tank, and I'll bring the kettle to a roiling boil, as they say."

"No." She shrugged out from under his arm.

"Huh? What d'you mean, 'No'?"

"Just that. No. I don't want a quiet little tête-à-tête out here with you after we close. I don't want to make it with you, Noonan! You're married, and I resent the way you act like it doesn't matter to you. Or worse, me! You act like your being married doesn't matter to *me*!"

Noonan was confused. "What the fuck? Who said anything about making it? Jesus!"

She exhaled heavily. "I'm sorry," she said. "You're right. I don't know what you've got in mind, Noonan. Really. I don't know why I said all that. I'm just . . . I'm scared, I guess."

"You? Scared? Hah!" She was young and beautiful and healthy, she was an athlete, a woman who could pick and choose among men much younger, more available, better-looking, and richer than he. What did she have to be scared of? Not him, that's for sure. "Man, you are one screwed up broad, let me tell you." He shook his head slowly in frustration and disgust. "Look, I don't give a shit you don't want to join me in a whaddayacallit, a tête-à-tête. Suit yourself. But I am gonna eat me some lobster anyhow. Alone!" he said, and he sailed through the door into the dining room.

Stacy slowly crossed the kitchen to the back door, last used by the LaPierre brothers on their way to the parking lot and road beyond. It was a screened door, and moths and mosquitoes batted against it and swarmed around the yellow bulb on the wall outside. On this side of the restaurant, it was already dark. Out back, where the building faced west and the mountains, the sky was pale orange, with long, silver-gray clouds tinged with purple floating up high and blood red strips of cloud near the horizon. She decided she'd better return to the bar. There would be a few diners, she knew, who would want to take an after-dinner drink onto the deck and watch the sunset.

Before she could get out the door, Noonan, his face dark with confused anger, strode back into the kitchen, carrying the last lobster in his dripping wet hand. The lobster feebly waved its claws in the air, and its thick, armored tail curled in on itself and snapped back in a weak, hopeless attempt to push Noonan away. "Here, you do the honors!" Noonan said to Stacy and held the lobster up to her face. With his free hand, he flipped the gas jet below the slow-boiling lobster pot to high. "Have you ever boiled a live lobster, Stacy? Oh, it's a real turn-on." He leered, but it was an angry leer. "You're gonna love it, Stacy, especially the way it turns bright red as soon as you drop it into the boiling water. It won't sink right away, of course, because it's still alive and will struggle to climb out of the pot, just like you would. But even while it's trying to get out of the boiling water, it'll be turning red, and then it'll slow in its struggle, and you'll see it give up, and when that happens, it's dead and cooked and ready to be eaten. Yumm!"

He pushed the lobster at her, and it flailed its claws in her face, as if it were her hand clamped onto its back, not Noonan's. She didn't flinch or back away. She held her ground and looked into what passed for the animal's face, searching for an expression, some indicator of feeling or thought that would guide her own feelings and thoughts. But there was none, and when she realized there could be none, this pleased her, and she smiled.

"It's getting to you, right?" Noonan said. "I can tell, it's a turn-on for you, right?" He smiled back, almost forgiving her for having judged him so unfairly, and held the lobster over the pot of boiling water. Steam billowed around the creature's twisting body, and Stacy stared, transfixed, when from the dining room she heard the rising voices of the diners, their loud exclamations and calls to one another to come and see, hurry up, come and see the bear!

Stacy and Noonan looked at each other, she in puzzlement, he with irritated resignation. "Shit," he said. "This has got to be the worst god-damn night of my life!" He dropped the lobster into the empty sink and disappeared into the pantry, returning to the kitchen a few seconds later with a rifle cradled in his arm. "Sonofabitch, this's the last time that bastard gets into my trash!" he declared and made for the dining room, with Stacy following close behind.

She had never seen a black bear close-up, although it was not uncommon to come upon one in the neighborhood, especially in mid-summer, when the mountain streams ran dry and sent the normally shy creatures to the lower slopes and valleys, where the humans lived. Once, when driving back to college after summer vacation, she thought she spotted a large bear crossing the road a hundred yards ahead of her, and at first had assumed it couldn't be a bear, it must be a huge dog, a Newfoundland, maybe, moving slowly, until it heard her car coming and broke into a swift, forward-tilted lope and disappeared into the brush as she passed. She wasn't sure she hadn't imagined it. She stopped the car and backed up to where the animal had entered the brush, but there was no sign of its ever having been there, no broken weeds or freshly fallen leaves, even.

This time, however, she intended to see the bear up close, if possible, and to know for sure that she did not imagine it. When she got to the dining room, everyone, Gail and the regulars from the bar included, was standing at the windows, gazing down at the yard in back where the land sloped away from the building, pointing and murmuring small noises of appreciation, except for the children, who were stilled by the sight, not so much frightened by the bear as in awe of it. The adults seemed to be mainly pleased by their good luck, for now they would have something novel to report to their friends and family when they returned home. This would become the night they saw the bear at Noonan's.

Then Stacy saw Noonan and several other diners, all of them men, out on the deck. They, too, stared down into the yard below the dining room and in the direction of the basement door, where Noonan stashed his garbage and trash barrels in a locked, wooden, latticework cage. The men were somber and intent, taut and almost trembling, like hunting dogs on point.

Stacy edged up to the window. Behind the distant mountains, the sun was gloriously setting. Its last golden rays splashed across the neatly mowed yard behind the restaurant and shone like a soft spotlight upon the thick, black-pelted body of the bear. It was a large, adult male, over six feet tall on his hind legs, methodically, calmly, ripping away the sides and top of the lattice cage, sending torn boards into the air like kindling sticks, working efficiently, but at the bear's own placid pace, as if he were utterly alone and there were no audience of men, women, and children staring down at him from the dining-room windows overhead, no small gang of men out on the deck watching him like a hunting party gathered on a cliff above a watering hole, and as if

Noonan were not lifting his rifle to his shoulder, aiming it, and firing.

He shot once, and he missed the bear altogether. He fired a second time.

The bear was struck high in the back, and a tuft of black hair flew away from his chest where the bullet emerged, and the crowd in the dining room groaned and cried out, "He's shooting it! Oh, God, he's shooting it!" A woman screeched, "Tell him to stop!" and children began to bawl. A man yelled, "For God's sake, is he nuts?" Gail looked beseechingly at Stacy, who simply shook her head slowly from side to side, for she could do nothing to stop him now. No one could. People shouted and cried, a few sobbed, and children wailed, and Noonan fired a third time. He hit the bear in the shoulder, and the animal spun around, still standing, searching for the source of this terrible pain, not understanding that he should look up, that the man with the rifle, barely fifty yards away, was positioned out of sight above him and, because of his extreme anger, because of his refusal to be impersonal in this grisly business, was unable to kill him, and so he wounded the poor creature again and again, in the chest, in a paw, and shot him through the muzzle, until finally the bear dropped to all fours and, unsure in which direction to flee, tumbled first away from the restaurant downhill toward the woods, when, hit in the back, he turned and came lumbering, bleeding and in pain, straight toward the deck, where Noonan fired one last shot, hitting the bear this time in the center of his forehead, and the bear rolled forward, as if he had tripped, and died.

Rifle in hand, Noonan stomped in silence past the departing crowd, his gaze fixed rigidly on something inside, a target in his mind of a silhouetted bear. No one spoke to him or caught his eye as he passed; no one looked at his back, even, when he strode into the kitchen and the door swung shut behind him. The men who had stood with him on the deck outside were ashamed now to have been there. Making as little of it as possible, they joined their wives and friends, all of whom were lined up at the cash register, paying Gail, leaving cash on the table, or paying Stacy at the bar, and quickly heading for the parking lot and their cars. There were a few stunned, silent exceptions, older kids too shocked to cry or too proud, but most of the children were weeping, and some wailed, while the parents tried vainly to comfort them, to assure them that bears don't feel pain the same way humans do, and the man who shot the bear had to shoot it, because it was damaging his property, and not to worry, we will never come to this restaurant again, no matter what.

When everyone had left, Gail walked slowly from the dining room to the bar, where she took off her apron, folded it carefully, and set it on a barstool. "That's it for me," she said to Stacy. With trembling hands, she knocked a cigarette loose from the pack and lighted it and inhaled deeply. "Tell him he can mail me my pay," she said. "The fucker." She started for the door and then abruptly stopped. Without turning around, she said, "Stacy? Why the hell are you staying?"

"I'm not."

In a voice so low she seemed to be talking to herself, Gail said, "Yes, girl, you are." Then she was gone.

Stacy flipped off the lights in the bar and dining room one by one, unplugged the roadside sign, and locked the front entrance. When she pushed open the door to the kitchen, Noonan, standing at the far end of the long, stainless steel counter, looked up and scowled at her. He had cooked the last lobster and was eating it, eating it off the counter and with his hands: broken shells and the remains of its shattered carcass lay scattered in front him. He poked a forefinger into the thick, muscular tail and shoved a chunk of white meat out the other end, snatched it up, and popped it into his mouth.

"Eight fucking shots it took me!" he said, chewing. "That's what I get for stashing that goddamn pissant .22 here instead of laying in a real gun!" He waved contemptuously with the back of his hand at the rifle propped against the counter, and with his other hand pushed more lobster meat into his mouth. His face was red, and he was breathing rapidly and heavily. "I missed the first shot, y'know, only because I was so pissed off I didn't concentrate. But if I'd had a real gun, that second shot would've done the job fine. By God, tomorrow I'm bringing in my 30.06!" he declared.

Stacy picked up the .22 rifle and looked it over. She slid it into shooting position against her right shoulder and aimed along the barrel through the screened door and the fluttering cluster of moths to the outside lamp.

"Is it still loaded?" she asked.

"There's four rounds left, so don't fuck with it." He yanked the spindly legs off the underbelly of the lobster and sucked the meat from each and dropped the emptied tubes, one by one, onto the counter in front of him.

Slowly, Stacy brought the rifle around and aimed it at Noonan's skull. "Noonan," she said, and he turned.

"Yeah, sure."

She closed her eyes and pulled the trigger and heard the explosion, and when she opened her eyes, she saw in the middle of Noonan's broad, white forehead a dark hole the size of a dime, which instantly expanded to a quarter, and his large body jerked once as if electrocuted and flipped backwards, his astonished face gone from her sight altogether now, and she saw instead, the back of his head and a hole in it the size of a silver dollar. His body, like a large, rubberized sack of water, fell to the floor, spinning away from her as it descended and ending flat on its back, with Noonan's wide open eyes staring at the pot rack above the counter. Blood pumped from the hole in the rear of his skull onto the pale green linoleum and spread in a thickening, dark red puddle slowly toward her feet.

She lay the rifle on the counter beside the broken remains of the lobster and crossed to the stove, where the pot of water was still boiling, and shut off the gas flame. Slowly, as if unsure of where she was, she looked around the room, then seemed to make a decision, and perched herself on a stool next to the walk-in refrigerator. She leaned her head back against the cool, stainless steel door and closed her eyes. Never in her life, never, had Stacy known the relief she felt at that moment. And not since the moment before she was struck by lightning had she known the freedom.

A rattling Ford pickup truck stopped beside the darkened roadside sign, and the LaPierre brothers, Donny and Timmy, leaped from the truck bed to the side of the road. "Hey, good luck with ol' Noonan, you little assholes!" the driver said, and he and a male passenger in the cab cackled with laughter. Two beery, expansive carpenters, they were cousins of the LaPierres, heading home to their wives and kids late from the bars of Lake Placid. They waved cheerfully to the boys and pulled away.

Donny and Timmy crunched across the gravel parking lot. The kitchen light and the lamp outside were still on, and when the boys were halfway across the lot, they saw Stacy through the screened door seated on the stool by the big walk-in fridge. She was asleep, it looked like, or maybe just bored out of her mind listening to one of Noonan's dumb hunting stories.

"You think he's screwing Stacy?" Timmy asked.

"C'mon, man. Stacy's a babe. And he's ancient, man," Donny said. "It's cool she's still here, though," he added. "She likes us, and he'll hire us back just to look good."

"I wouldn't mind a little of that myself."

"A little of what?"

"Stacy, man!"

Donny punched his younger brother on the shoulder. "Yeah, well, you'll hafta wait your turn, little fella!" He laughed. He waved away the swarming cloud of moths and pulled the screened door open. Timmy entered first, and Donny, hiding his fading grin behind his hand, followed.

Author's Note

When I began writing, I wanted to be a poet, but had not the gift and fell in love instead with the short story, the form in prose closest to lyric poetry. In the intervening years, I've written a dozen or so novels, but the story form thrills me still. It invites me today, as it did back then, to behave on the page in a way that is more reckless, more sharply painful, and more broadly comic than is allowed by the steady, slow, bourgeois respectability of the novel, which, like a good marriage, demands long-term commitment, tolerance, and compromise. The novel, in order to exist at all, accrues, accretes, and accumulates itself in small increments, like a coral reef, and through that process invites from its creator leisurely, circumambulatory exploration. By contrast, stories are like perfect waves, if one is a surfer. Stories forgive one's mercurial nature, reward one's longing for ecstasy, and make of one's short memory a virtue.

As this book is published, I am turning sixty, and these stories represent the best work I have done in the form over the thirty-seven years since I began trying to write in prose—at least that's my hope. Rereading them has been like visiting my past and all-but-forgotten selves, the man I was (and was not) in my twenties, thirties, forties, and so on. To my surprise, the youth who wrote "Searching for Survivors," one of the earliest of the stories included here, although a somewhat melancholy and self-dramatizing fellow, turns out to be not significantly different than the quickly aging man who wrote the most recent, "Lobster Night." I suppose that should comfort me, but in fact it does not. It is, however, why I have arranged these stories thematically and dramatically, rather than in chronological order or by the titles of the collections in which they originally appeared. Because I was, when young, in many crucial ways the same writer I am today, I have felt free to take the old stories and set them beside the new, to recontextualize them. This has let me see them freshly and has allowed me to put them to a different use than when they were first written and published. In that way, in the making of this book, I've been able, despite my similarities to the younger person who has been using my name for these many years, to become a different writer than I was without it.

Twenty-two of the thirty-one stories selected for this volume were published in four earlier collections and have been revised for this edition. Nine are recent and uncollected. Among the early stories, I chose to include only those that did not on rereading make me cringe with embarrassment (several were written, after all, when I was in college) and that did not seem to require more than light revision. Most of the stories that I left out—and there were many more excluded than included—were failed experiments which were necessary for me to have attempted, for I would not have learned my craft if I had not written them; and while I now wish that I had not submitted them for publication, I nonetheless must admit that, if I had not published them, first in magazines and later in books, I doubt that I'd be able today to recognize them as failures. If I had tossed them out while they were still in manuscript form, strangled my darlings in their beds, as it were, I would not have learned from them as much as I have: in cold print, those stories taught me what I have no talent for or no abiding interest in.

From the beginning, my desire to write stories has been aided and abetted by editors who themselves love the form, and I would like to thank them here for that. Foremost among them is Ted Solotaroff, who published my stories early and often in *American Review* and *New American Review* and later edited the collections *Trailerpark* and *Success Stories* for HarperCollins. Then there is Daniel Halpern at *Antaeus*, Andy Ward and Rust Hills at *Esquire*, Mark Mirsky at *Fiction*, Joe David Bellamy at *Fiction International*, Rick Barthelme at *Mississippi Review*, William Phillips at *Partisan Review*, and the late James Boatwright at *Shenandoah*. I'm also grateful to Robert Jones, my present editor at HarperCollins, who escorted this volume into print with all his usual intelligence, tact, and energy. And finally, I especially want to thank my agent, Ellen Levine, who has been my faithful sidekick right from the start.

For those who care about such matters, I have listed here the previously collected stories under the titles of the collections in which they originally appeared.

From *Searching for Survivors* (1975):
"Searching for Survivors"
"With Ché in New Hampshire"
"Theory of Flight" (originally "With Ché at Kitty Hawk")
"The Neighbor"
"The Lie"
"Defenseman"
From *The New World* (1978):
"The Rise of the Middle Class"
"Indisposed"
"The Caul"
From *Trailerpark* (1981):
"The Guinea Pig Lady"
"Black Man and White Woman in Dark Green Rowboat"
"Dis Bwoy, Him Gwan"
"Comfort"

"The Burden"
"The Child Screams and Looks Back at You"
"The Fisherman"
From *Success Stories* (1986):
    "Queen for a Day"
    "The Fish"
    "Success Story"
    "Mistake"
    "Sarah Cole: A Type of Love Story"
    "Firewood"